T0029213

"*The Last Songbird* is rock noir at its best. It sneaks up on you like a hook line, and when it's over, you can't get it out of your head. Hapless hero/songwriter Addy Zantz is witty, gritty, and determined to solve the murder of his idol and muse, the legendary rock star Annie Linden. Daniel Weizmann's LA is half Warren Zevon and half Raymond Chandler. Bravo."

—T. JEFFERSON PARKER, Edgar Award-winning author of *CALIFORNIA GIRL*

"Weizmann's fiction is informed by his past as a highly influential and precocious young veteran of the punk scene, as well as by his lifelong passion for music, his career in journalism, and his love of noir and Los Angeles. This book is funny, poetic, gripping, and beautifully tackles themes of creativity, fame, and family."

—FRANCESCA LIA BLOCK, author of *DANGEROUS ANGELS: THE WEETZIE BAT BOOKS*

"Daniel Weizmann's *The Last Songbird* is a gripping, fast-paced, neo-noir mystery whose intriguing characters populate the streets of Los Angeles. When a seventies music icon suddenly disappears, her driver and friend begins a frantic search that leads him in pursuit of the truth. In turn, he will discover just as much about himself. Weizmann has written a smart, unforgettable page-turner of the best kind."

—GAIL TSUKIYAMA, author of *THE SAMURAI'S GARDEN*

"Propulsive and pitch perfect, *The Last Songbird* is a smart, fast-paced read about the costs of fame to both the spectacularly gifted and those left dazzled and dazed in their wake. In crackling prose, Daniel Weizmann masterfully takes the reader through the midnight precincts of LA to tell a gripping story of human fallibility—of triumph and failure, generosity and greed, love and disappointment—and the drive, against all odds, to set things right. A stunning debut."

—JOAN LEEGANT, author of *AN HOUR IN PARADISE*

"A terrific ride through the troubled, tangled lives surrounding a murdered LA music legend, told with the energy of the Germs and the urgency of X, with a captivating narrator who drives headlong in crime-fueled pursuit."

—GREGORY GALLOWAY, author of *JUST THIEVES*

"Weizmann skillfully crafts a gritty, unstoppable detective thriller rife with sleaze, sea foam, and broken dreams set against a crumbling LA backdrop. It's *Sunset Boulevard* meets *Once Upon A Time in Hollywood*."

—KATIE TALLO, author of *DARK AUGUST*

"*The Last Songbird* is my favorite kind of neo-noir—blending the bright lights of celebrity and fame with the primal urges and darkness that come with any good noir novel. Weizmann is a confident, polished storyteller who honors his influences while weaving his amateur detective through a complex mystery that will keep you turning the pages until you've reached the haunting finale. A sharp, memorable debut."

—ALEX SEGURA, author of *SECRET IDENTITY*

THE LAST SONGBIRD

A PACIFIC COAST HIGHWAY MYSTERY

THE
LAST
SONGBIRD

DANIEL WEIZMANN

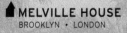

MELVILLE HOUSE
BROOKLYN · LONDON

The Last Songbird

First published in 2023 by Melville House
Copyright © Daniel Weizmann, 2022
All rights reserved
First Melville House Printing: March 2023

Melville House Publishing
46 John Street
Brooklyn, NY 11201
and
Melville House UK
Suite 2000
16/18 Woodford Road
London E7 0HA

mhpbooks.com
@melvillehouse

ISBN: 978-1-68589-030-8
ISBN: 978-1-68589-031-5 (eBook)

Library of Congress Control Number 2022949590

Designed by Patrice Sheridan

Printed in the United States of America
1 3 5 7 9 10 8 6 4 2
A catalog record for this book is available from the Library of Congress

1

HERE IT COMES HERE COMES THE NIGHT

The night Annie Linden disappeared, my world spun out with double-time speed.

I was thirty-seven, she was seventy-three. I was a Lyft driver and she was a pop icon—once. She was my pickup and I was running late.

I had already failed as a songwriter.

As a song plugger, a pop critic, a recording engineer.

No way could I afford to flop out as a Lyft driver.

Pacific Coast Highway opened up and I shot through the gap, gunned it for the last stretch of Zuma trying to make up for lost minutes. One lone cop car idled about a hundred yards from Annie's estate—I thought nothing of it. Then I pulled the silver '16 Jetta with the rear dent onto the gravel loop and saw the whirling red-and-blue lights. The gate was wide open— two more cop cars idled. Potted purple catmint wavered in their hot white beams.

A policeman got out of one of the black-and-whites, approaching with the look of a man ready for violence. Big guy but short, built like a brick oven.

"Name?"

"Adam Zantz."

"Who you here to see, Mr. Zantz."

I pointed at my light-up Lyft Amp. "Ms. Linden—she's my regular. She just called for an eight o'clock pickup."

"Called?"

"About an hour ago—we're . . . off-app."

"How's that work?"

"I—she has my number, she wouldn't use the app after our first ride."

He grumbled. "You don't look like a Lyft driver." I wasn't sure what a Lyft driver was supposed to look like. Me, I was a five-foot-eight skinny Jew with a big schnoz and eyes that telegraphed every damn thing I was feeling—present worry included. I zipped up my black hoodie as his Motorola rang. He turned his back to me. "I'm here at beachfront—the Linden residence. . . . Yeah, her. There's a 187 on the premises—beach adjacent, maybe more." My heart thumped, gooseflesh. The cop went on. "I got two guys inside, so send another two units. . . . Huh? . . . No, surveillance went down forty minutes ago." He signed off, then gave me the glare. "You know the place?"

"Pretty well, yeah. There's a security man named Troy by the main gate." Troy's booth was a Tudor octagon of one-way mirrors that made it look like one of those zoetrope whirligigs. Too small for anyone—way too small for Troy.

"This where you planned to pick up Ms. Linden, right here?"

"No. She stays down in the beach house. There's actually four properties here. Pool house, guest house, beach house. And the main house she doesn't visit too much."

"Whyzat?" He seemed jumpy.

"She likes the beach house?" I said. "It's small, manageable, *conducive to the creative process*? Listen, you going to tell me what the heck is going on here?"

"Why don't you get creative and call her. Now, on your phone."

I tried—no answer. I didn't leave a message. I looked up at the cop, held back worst-case scenarios. I had gotten her text at 7:24—*AZ beach house 8pm come to my arms.* Classic Annie corniness—she sent lyrics in texts: *"let's chase the moonlight," "we sell seashells," "when the jungle shadows fall."* But tonight was different. Only days before, she had said, "I'm almost ready for that thing we talked about." I thought *come to my arms* was maybe code for *let's go look into those people I wanted you to find.* Then again it just as easily could've been *get over here, let's cruise, I'm restless.* Vaguery, typical Annie—but my pulse was racing.

"Let me try her PA—*he* mostly stays in the main house." I left out that Bix Gelden had been recently fired since he'd been fired and rehired so many times. For all I knew, he *was* in the main house. But his line just rang and rang too. This time, I left a message. "Bix, it's Adam—can you let Annie know I'm out in the loop?" I shot the cop a questioning look and he nodded, so I went on. "Also, there are some police out front here—looks like there's been some trouble, so . . . get back to me A-SAP, alright?" I hung up, shrugged.

"How come you're so sure the PA's on the premises?"

"He pretty much lives here."

Two more police cars screeched into the loop. Now we were a fleet, five vehicles strong.

"Take a ride down the hill," the cop said. "Show us where you planned to pick up Ms. Linden."

"You got it." For his compadres, he waved a finger to the

sky and moved back to his car. I put the Jetta in drive. We caravanned down the long, sloping private road to the beach house gate, also already open. The ocean roared and crashed its looping rhythm—white sand and gray-black Pacific horizon came into view. The lights were out in her place, no candles. That was not unusual though, since she wrote songs in the pitch dark. Outside, the lonely hemp hammock hung between sloping palms, empty and jiggling in the cool night breeze.

I stopped the car. A different cop came out and said, "Hang back," and they entered, hands on gun belts. From my vantage point, I could see their shadows casing the place in the dark. My mind was trying to outrace my pulse: *No Annie, no Gelden, 187, what the—*. The deck chairs were moist from fog, the heat lamps off. Annie's estate was one of about two dozen mansions along the point that lined up in front of the mighty Pacific like giant beasts stopped in their tracks. Other homes had long, jutting staircases down to the beach. That wouldn't do for a seventy-three-year-old chain smoker. I was about one minute from panic with my hand on the inside door handle when I heard and then saw an ambulance coming down the hill behind us. Two people in some kind of red uniforms I didn't recognize got out—a guy and a girl, with a stretcher.

"Oh fuck," I whispered to the ocean, in full dread now. Anyone who worked for a senior had the kind of thoughts I was having—I didn't burst into tears. But I did say: *Be prepared to mourn—later.* I dialed Troy, the security man—my third no answer. In one hectic move, I got out of the car, slammed the car door, and made for the beach house and its searching cops. The automatic lights didn't go on—that was odd but not supernatural, since they were faulty when there were too many headlights nearby. A strong salt breeze held me in place. I cursed myself a second time for being late.

Now I stood in the dizzying red-blue crosshatch of police lights coming through the hedges that flanked Annie's beach bungalow driveway. The cop blocking the door made a flat hand gesture—as in, get back into your car, but I didn't. My heart was not yet completely pounding. I stood alongside the Jetta for about three minutes, which felt like ten. A new cop exited the beach house, a tall African American with a boyish, handsome face.

I approached and said, "Excuse me, sir? I'm Ms. Linden's driver. She was expecting me about fifteen minutes ago."

He went incredulous. "Annie Linden uses Lyft?"

"Is she—"

"Sir, I'm going to need you to stay by your car until we're ready to question you."

Two more cops came out of the beach house, expressionless. One asked a question I didn't hear. The other said, "No, she's missing."

"And *he* was found where?"

"On the periphery, they've got some storage units up there on the highway side."

The units were garages. Annie had a six-car garage and one beat-up Cortina she never drove. And who was "he"? *He* could be Baxter "Bix" Gelden. Bix could have OD'd. Bix could have I-don't-know-what. Bix was an accidental fatality waiting to happen. But then one of the cops said, "Now who is it I'm supposed to call?" and soon the crew in red came down the path with a stretcher carrying a body wrapped in a white sheet and I knew it was Troy because nobody was that long and lean. His black and yellow steel-toe Skechers poked out at the edge like two big orioles standing at attention. I got off the hood and stepped to the battalion.

"Can somebody tell me what the hell is going on here? Ms. Linden is a client of mine, I'm basically staff here—"

With a single, solemn nod, he broke out a notepad. "So you were planning on taking Ms. Linden where exactly?"

"I'm not sure, she usually tells me when I get here. If that. Sometimes she just wants to drive the coast. She intimated she might just want to ride. Who is that in the sheet?" I was hoping against hope.

"Intimated how?"

"I don't know. She said to get her at eight, but that's it."

A fifth cop car screeched up and an older man in a Patagonia windrunner got out of the passenger seat with the administrative stride of a non-listener.

"Can we rope this off already?" he announced. "You got a slowdown on PCH, eyeballs everywhere."

"Chief, this guy's from Uber. He says Annie Linden called him for a ride."

"This is *the* Annie Linden, I take it?" the Chief asked, still acting like I wasn't there.

The young cop said, "Annie who?"

"You kiddin' me?" the Chief said. "Only the greatest songbird of our time."

"*Your* time, Chief," the young cop said, and his partners tittered.

The Chief ignored them, turned to me like he trusted me more than his underlings, even though I was closer to their age than his.

"You ever meet staff here?"

"Yes, sir."

His tone went grave. "Would you be willing to identify a body?"

I nodded and we hoofed it back up the hill to the idling ambulance. They opened the back door and pulled the sheet off Troy's young and shocked face. A wave of anguish crashed down upon me.

"His name is Troy," I said—the muscles of my jaw pulled into a deep scowl. "Troy Banks. He's grounds security." *Was.*

The Chief said, "You have a way of contacting Ms. Linden at this time?"

"I can try her private line again." I listened to two rings in the bracing sea-salt air and smarted when it went straight to voicemail. I shook my head.

The Chief gestured to the beach house. "Let's go inside." He made it sound like I was invited.

Raised off the sand by a smooth wooden deck, the bungalow lay still, as placid as the ocean wasn't. By instinct, my hands reached to flip the indoor lights. The simple living room stared back at us, looking empty and dumbfounded. Just an innocent little studio apartment that had no idea it was attached to a chateau on the beach. Some disarray, toppled cassettes, half a bottle of red and one empty glass. Little blue kitchen, bathroom, bedroom, empty. The Chief rummaged around and I kept my mouth shut.

I'd left one thing out of our little conversation, a favor Annie had asked of me, only days earlier. She'd been anxious, halting. "I've got an idea. You told me you did some investigation work once, right?"

"Well, yeah, I worked for an investigator a long time ago," I said, "but I was just a lackey . . . you know, doing repos, serving papers, lame stuff."

But she was adamant. "I need to find out about someone, some people from my past. *Something isn't what I thought*, I—"

"Are you being harassed?"

"No no, nothing like that." But she sounded distracted, keyed up, almost confused. "I'm just—look, I'm getting *older*. And I want to, I need to . . . close some circles, look into some people."

"Whatever it is," I'd said with a shrug, "Say when, I'm your man."

"Now that's what I like to hear."

And then she took my hand, and hers was cool, bony, trembling a little as she reeled off her list and—

"Adam—no joking. You're more than a driver to me. I value our conversations. And I would never ask you to do this if I didn't trust you."

The haunted look in her eyes was dogging me now.

The Chief picked up a stray cassette and shook his head to no one in particular. The ocean mocked us with its rolling, crashing rumble song.

They cut me loose at midnight. Sleep was out of the question. I headed back down PCH, radio off, a new melody looping, distant, driving me on, driving me mad.

The jukebox id was at it again.

The jukebox id was telling me *she's not there.*

The jukebox id was saying Annie had secrets, secrets that bring tears.

Not everybody had the jukebox id, but if you had it, you knew it. Song fragments spun in your head, nonstop. You didn't solicit, they sprang from nowhere, little 45s collapsing onto the turntable of your soul—then the needle drops. *Please don't bother trying to find her—*

2

I'D GLADLY
LOSE ME TO FIND YOU

From PCH shooting south, I rang Annie again, then Bix again, then Annie twice more. Nothing. Deep night rose around me, the fog bank swirling in like a nightmare loop. In a panic, I dialed Double Fry, my buddy Ephraim Freiberger. He picked up on half a ring, his voice low and taut.

"Adam, I heard."

"You *heard*?"

"About Annie Linden, missing, yeah."

"How is that even possible?"

"I picked the APB up on Coast Guard radio. I was all like, holy shit, Adam's muse."

"That's nutball," I said. "The cops made me swear to keep my mouth shut."

"Yeah well, then do that."

Boat bum Fry was usually studying Torah or out on a job at this hour—he shot paparazzi-style for TMZ and the *Reporter*—but tonight I could hear his twin nieces chirping in the background. They were up late for a pair of eleven year olds.

"You in the Marina?"

"Naw, I'm babysitting at my sister's, big funsville with Uncle Fry. So . . . what the hell?"

"I don't know, man, I'm still trying to piece it together. She was a no-show . . . or . . . she's missing. Her security guard—" My voice cracked. "I'm not on speaker, am I?"

"You're good."

"He was *murdered*, dude. Her gate guard."

"Jesus."

"Shot."

"And . . . she didn't call you or—?"

"*Nope*. They made me ID his body."

My jitters cooled him into a cupped whisper. "Brutal."

"Dude—where is she?"

"Don't . . . don't panic. She's flaked before, legends are known to flake. *Keep it down, you two, I'm on the damn phone!* Hopefully she was—"

I cut him off. "Fry—can you keep a secret?"

"You know I can."

"A few days back, she . . . "

"What?"

"She asked me to do something, to track down some people from her past."

"You think that's connected to this?"

"I have no fucking idea." I forced one deep breath. "Okay—I'm cruising."

"Where?"

"Her haunts?"

"It's getting late, Addy, maybe you should go home and call it a night. *Hey, I said quiet!*" The girls broke into peals of slumber party laughter. "I'd join you but I gotta deal with these two cuckoo-heads."

"Understood."

"If you're bad trippin' why don't you come over here?"

"Talk later."

"Serious, Adam, there's a couch."

"Uhhhh no. Thanks though."

"*Adam*. I know you care about this old lady, you've done a big mitzvah befriending her, but—"

"It's not charity, dude. We have these great talks, she's helping me get my songwriting bug back. Least I can do is look for her. What the *fuck*."

"I know, I know. But the guard got *shot*? Please be careful, okay? A person like Annie Linden, who knows what kind of a jam she's in."

I signed off distracted, driving nowhere, driving in circles, and it was getting late. I thought about tapping on her ex-husband's door but he was not the kind of guy you wake up at 2:00 a.m. At Venice I pulled a frantic three-point turn and cut back up Santa Monica to scope out a few hotels. Annie was like Carole King—you knew her songs, her voice, but you *might* not spot her on the street, and it was her sometimes habit to sit in these hotel lobbies in a floppy hat and people-watch. "Anonymity is ecstasy." But I was afraid to be too obvious about asking after her and the two valet guys I knew didn't flag me down, they would have said something.

Now I forced hope like the last toothpaste in a crinkled tube. She'd probably call in the morning, all apologetic, but a text would have been nice, with or without the poetry—*I'm ok goodnight*. I dialed her again, dialed Bix. Nada. I was way too jumpy to head home, so I headed for Hollywood. Maybe I could pick up a customer or two before dawn.

As I navigated the blinking city streets, the terms of our side hustle came back to me in hasty collage. There was something or someone Annie was after, I wasn't even sure *she* knew what, but she wanted my help. She'd reeled off a short list of random things to look into—a dead phone line, financial records, a Xerox of an old lease contract, some classifieds in some old newspapers.

"I may have you talk to Eva, too," she said. "And I need to find this . . . this cassette."

"Who has it—the cassette?"

"That's what I want to know."

"But . . . what's on it?"

"Just stuff," she said. "Silly songs. I'll explain later."

But later was now and she was missing.

And I had to ask: Was it really any of my business? I was her Lyft driver, not her legal guardian, and we had no official agreement of any kind. It was like we had an "unspoken bargain"—I'd help her track down whatever the hell she was looking for, and maybe, just maybe she'd find me a real way into the biz. I couldn't even say Annie and I were *that* close but then again, who could? I'd only been hacking for a few months when I met her and soon we were off-app, she had my direct line. Of course, back then, I didn't think driving was going to become a way of life. I had a demo—more than a demo, eleven songs—and I knew better than to play it for my riders, but when they'd step out of the car, I'd Bluetooth it on endless repeat, scanning for flaws, praying it was better than it was, electrified by the pandemonium of words surfing melody. I'd pretend they were on the radio, these songs, *my* songs.

Driving for a living
Till the break of dawn
Driving for a living
'cause I'm overdrawn
Leaning on the horn in the pouring rain

Driving you around is driving me insane
But you're arriving
And I'm surviving
Driving for a living

I loved and hated them, these meshugenah ditties. They'd sprung from my head like Zeus's daughters. Even on the job, at the wheel, with complete strangers in the back, new lyrics seized me like a kidnapper, and I could still picture myself hunched over the upright piano in some half-lit room, sipping wine from a plastic cup and comping chords in a trance, trying this note then that one, pushing the melody, stretching and bending it, reaching for the element of surprise. Grind or no grind, I was a song machine in the blood.

And then—late one eve, about three years ago, my life turned on a dime.

I was pinged in Malibu by a Ms. A. M. Linden to take her from her seaside estate to the airport. I pulled up and there she was: *the* Annie Linden.

She was thin in person, fair, a wisp of a woman, waiting for me at the big doors in a black trench coat and white Converse, a little old-school teal Samsonite at her feet. Her long gray hair was up in a chaotic bundle. When I got out of the car to get her stuff, she said, "Don't give me any shit—I'm going to be smoking cigarettes in your vehicle. I'll tip you for your future emphysema."

"The tip won't be necessary, Ms. Linden." I opened the back door for her. "Long flight?"

"Twelve hours to London." She groaned, I shook my head. On some instant invisible terrain, we understood each other. She was more frail in person than you would guess, but at the same time she vibrated with a crazy life force that defied years. On that first ride, she must have been in her late sixties already, but before I'd even pulled out of the loop of her mansion on the sea, I felt weakened, enthralled as we drove into the dark night and shot down PCH, the ocean song thundering alongside us.

Checking her in the rearview one too many times, I had to remind myself that she was A) a famous person that didn't want to be bothered, and B) an elderly woman traveling alone in the wee hours. Hence the get-up, superannuated incognito. But I couldn't help stealing glances—her beauty was so peculiar, that elfin face, her wisdom right there in her wide-awake skeptical moon eyes, her calm/uncalm gaze at the ocean hinting at some feminine form of wonder I could only guess about.

"You always work these hours?" she asked.

"Any hours," I said. "I'm an insomniac. Figure I might as well get paid for it."

"Yeah? What keeps you up?"

No pause: "A broken heart—what else."

She smiled. "I'm an insomniac with a broken heart too. Nice to meet a fellow traveler."

The first of countless rides—the very next day I got a call. She must've looked up the Lost and Found page for riders on the Lyft website, because she meandered through some story about having left an antique barrette in my car before asking for my direct number, just in case she needed a ride someday. I got the funny feeling the barrette was just an excuse. I gave her my digits and said, "Call anytime, twenty-four-seven," and she said, "Done deal"—it came to me vivid as yesterday now as I checked my phone and turned onto Sunset, all lit up at 3:37 a.m. A city of disconnection, the ultimate madness. The cellphone sat shotgun like an unforgiving passenger—no texts, no calls. I didn't have the heart to clamp it to the dash, turn on the app, and start catching late night riders. My worry was twisting in on itself, going desperate. And it was crazed how I got hooked on Annie so fast, ride after ride, because, as canaries go, she had never been my personal favorite, not by a longshot. She was so iconic to the generation or two before mine that I almost considered her a joke. All that stuff about captivity of the spirit, and her glassy voice on those records—she sang a little too pure, too crystalline for human ears. Plus, some of her peers—Carole King, Stevie Nicks, Joni Mitchell—had better songs, catchier hooks.

But Annie Linden had what they didn't, a certain brittle intensity. She was a songwriter's songwriter, a taker of lyrical chances, and after that first drive together it wasn't long before I started downloading her albums one by one—they became my soundtrack while making the rounds. Some of the later records were so bad, it was like she was daring herself to flop. Also, the *sound* of her last albums really sucked—that crappy eighties plasticky thing, all compressed drum machines and Casios. She had switched producers and stuck with the new guy in defiance of all logic—later I learned she had married him for a while. Then, when the general public stopped looking, she faded into obscurity, barely writing and only for herself. But I didn't care, because to me she was always more than a rider, more than a star.

She said, "I thought your generation didn't believe in romance, didn't need it. But there's something mutant about you, kiddo—don't lose that."

After a few more trips, I had opened up to her. Told her about my mother, how I tried, and failed, to keep her out of the loony bin. It wasn't lost on me that Annie was like her in some way, my insane mother, only a little bolder. She even wore the same perfume, Rain or Rain Water or Rainy something. It set off a powerful feeling, beyond nostalgia—a black hole in the chest.

She said, "I'm with you—and I get it."

She said, "You're like a son to me."

She said, "I *should* jump your bones."

"I wouldn't stop you," I'd said with a wink.

"Don't worry," she cackled. "That would get in the way of me being your guardian angel. Just don't be late."

Now I was looping back to the beach for no good reason, redialing Annie, redialing Gelden, one last time, then another last time. The city never sleeps but it does shut its eyes in free-floating 5:00 a.m. anxiety. I caromed Sunset through the Palisades, all the way back to PCH and up past Topanga, her mansion. The same lone cop car idled at a distance down the street, lights out now. Across the gate, a single long strip of yellow tape had been pulled taut like a guitar string. If you weren't looking for it, you might not have noticed, if you happened to be driving the coast at this hour, probably up to no good.

It was time to go home.

Maybe, just maybe, I could zonk out.

I picked up Gatorade and a bear claw at 7-Eleven and headed for no-man's-land. Home wasn't that inviting, but at least it wasn't a tent under the freeway. I was living in the storage space of a recording studio near Mar Vista that was slowly going out of business—Santiago Sonic Lab Rehearsal & Tracking, also advertising Electronic Musical Instrument Repair, but they didn't even light up the sign anymore. Almost dawn—Sonic came into view, a baby blue two-story stucco box with a little makeshift plastic furniture patio and three parking spaces. When I pulled up, Old Man Santiago was already out there, pacing in his wife-beater and Bermuda shorts, black socks, and flip-flops, holding off his first smoke of the morning. He was short and bald but he carried a boxer's toughness. He'd played horn with Santana and Malo and backed up a bunch of doo-wop groups in the late fifties. That's when he'd gotten the tattoo—a sleepy-eyed hula girl.

"Zantz, you prowling around all night like a cat in heat again?"

"Just working, Mr. Santiago."

He fingered the unlit cigarette with great care. "*Riiiight,* some hard work." He almost lit it, then raised a dark, quizzical eyebrow. "By the way, guy called Bix came by here."

"Oh yeah?" My eyes throbbed, blinked. "When?"

"About 9:30, 10:00 last night. Nervous kind of dude. We were in session, right? I told him I could call you on the cell but he said not to disturb you no matter what."

"Yeah?"

"Then I says, 'So give me *your* number' and he refused. Said to tell you he was going to . . . some kind of *living home.* In Valley Village." Mr. Santiago shot me a knowing look, all subtext: *Zantz, you run with some nefarious losers, and I know from nefarious losers.*

I thanked him and turned right around, headed back to the silver wonder.

"Where you going now?" Mr. S. said.

"Valley Village."

"You sure do like to drive."

"Not as much as you'd think."

When I got into the car, he finally lit the cigarette. His day had begun.

3

TO DRINK ROTTING
WINE FROM YOUR HANDS

The Valley was a faraway place for a beach bum like Bix Gelden to be hiding out but there he was, at the only Valley Village sober living house Google coughed up, seated on the outdoor steps of a salmon stucco called the Laurel Arms, a dingy fourplex that did not exactly scream recovery. I waved him over. Looking agitated, he hoisted himself up and came toward me. His curly mop was thinning and his green Flying Burrito Brothers T-shirt was fading but those eyes had the same boyish hurt I remembered from our run-ins at Annie's.

I said, "What the fuck, dude," as he got in the ride and slammed the car door. "I've been calling you all night."

"I figured it's better if we stay off the phone." His voice was breathy, defensive.

"And why is that? What is happening here exactly? *Where is Annie?*"

"I have no idea."

"Then why are you hiding?"

"Can you drive please?" he said. "Take residential streets—

and don't park." His wide stubbly face and gray eyes were lit up, wild, as we prowled the morning suburbs.

I said, "Talk. Now."

"*I don't know, man.* I heard shots. I was in the main house. I called Troy. He didn't pick up so I went to his booth and nobody was there. The little TV screens were all off. I freaked. I ran halfway to the beach house and the door was open but the lights were out. I mean, I'm like—*in a nightmare.* I just, I panicked."

"Yeah, I got that. You ran."

"I drove. Fast."

"And you didn't think to call the cops?"

"I *did* call the cops. On a burner. I made up a name. Then I tried Troy like ten times."

I shook my head. "Troy is *gone*, man. He's dead."

Bix let out a shivering whimper, a dog's cry. "Why?"

"He was shot."

"And Annie?" His voice ratcheted up an octave.

"She's missing."

He whimpered again.

"*Bix*," I said, "why do you have a burner? And why didn't you tell the cops who you were? What were you thinking, man? This is completely insane."

He slammed his big body deep into the seat, as if he could throw off frustration.

"Because look at me, I'm all fucked up. I was high off my ass on speedballs. I can't believe I made it over Topanga."

"You could've called me direct."

"I didn't want your number on the burner. For your sake."

"Yeah? Then what am I doing here now? Aiding and abetting a fucking psycho? This is so not good, dude. You better call the cops. They *will* come looking for you. They're already looking. They told me to report any—"

"No way, *dude*. I was in Valley Village the whole time. That's all you need to know. End of story."

"Yeah?" I cut to a whisper, made a left—endless one-story homes, green grass, Pleasant Valley Sabbath morning. "*Where is she*, Bix?"

His face twisted in panic. "I was hoping you would know."

"Well, where are we going?"

"I need to score."

"Yeah, no, I'm not doing that, dude."

We circled the flat suburban blocks, two ragged losers without a destination—or a boss. Bix, staring out the window at this ranchy gentility, went wide-eyed like a fish out of water. We weren't close exactly, but he had been kind to me when I got dumped, this chubby defeatist, and I'd leaned on him, I was a wreck. Still, even then Bix scared me like a cautionary tale—*one less layer of defense and this could be you.*

"Bix, man," I said, "I didn't mean to bark at you. I just . . . "

He closed his eyes and shook his head. Soon the tears were cutting his face. I tried to say a comforting word but he turned away and we drove on in agonized silence. As usual during these moments of acute pathos and social discomfort at the wheel, involuntary lyric fragments started assembling in my head.

Beach boy
On the run
High and dry and under the gun
Tell me where you gonna go
When they
Blot out the sunlight, blot out the—

He'd worked for Annie a long time, fired, rehired, fired again. It was a neurotic trip. His late father had been her money manager or some such when they all lived at Topanga Beach a zillion years ago. The oceanfront town used to be a hippie hideaway in the sixties, but the place had been mowed down to make way for a state park that never happened. Massive evictions cut loose a whole settlement of free lovers, but former locals like Bix still surfed there because the point break made for a longer, gentler ride. Topanga Beach was all about the peaceful cradle.

And maybe that was the problem, it all came too easy too early—what did Bix Gelden know of civilian life? Annie said, "Nothing to brag about, but I practically raised that guy." She told me he tried to go to UCLA, but swiftly had a nervous breakdown. Among the landlubbers, his essence, his shyness, swelled like a seven-foot superwave and crashed down upon him. And so he retreated. Back to the water. Back to Annie who he had known since childhood. And from some maternal sense, she took him in, gave him PA work.

"I understand Bix," she had told me. "'Cause I don't get high anymore even when I get high. High isn't high."

People who fantasize about living on the beach—this was what they never figured. After a while, the ocean view, the salt air, even the thunderous ocean song disappears, and you are left with yourself, your place in the scheme of things. All that you reach for and all you can't hold runs up before you like the tide and reaches for *you*. It takes a very strong soul to keep from getting swept away.

Bix was calming now, but the secret melody in my head kept coming.

Beach boy
All at sea
In the halfway house you're halfway free
Now where you gonna go when they—

Like us, the song didn't know where it was headed. When his tears stopped, I said, "Bix, is there somewhere else I can take you?"

He shrugged.

I said, "I can't leave you like this. You going to be okay?"

"I just . . . keep thinking about Troy."

I tried to blot out the image. "Will you call the cops?"

He didn't answer but his eyes peered into dread dreamland—I had the unruly desire to make him feel safe.

"*Bix*, no matter what, you can turn to me. You've been decent to me and I don't forget that shit. Far as I'm concerned, I owe you."

He stared right through me.

I said, "Will I be able to reach you somehow? When Annie turns up?"

Another no answer—he wiped his stubbly, wet face with his wrist. Finally, he said, "Drop me off at 7-Eleven."

I pulled a U and let him out in the parking lot, down the street from Serenity House. I tore off, eager to go home and shower the night off, sleep away the spread of panicky double-vision. Halfway over Laurel Canyon, my cell rang. Fry—hard whisper:

"Addy."

Without another word I knew she was gone.

4

I COVER THE WATERFRONT
I'M WATCHING THE SEA

The next hours disappeared like a runaway car slipping into traffic, revving death with metallic force. On the 405 south— KNX 1070 spit out the report. "Singer-songwriter Annie Linden, two-time Grammy nominee and author of seven top 20 songs, has died. Her body was discovered this morning by an unnamed Hermosa Beach jogger just before dawn. At this time, authorities believe the singer likely drowned. The iconic folksinger was 73."

I weaved, somebody honked, road rage flared and I slammed the horn, tensed at the wheel, switched to KCRW. "—coroner's office has identified the woman as celebrated songwriter and Malibu resident Annie Linden, whose album *A Free Heart* was nominated for a Grammy in 1974. Sergeant Robert Higgins reports that police are investigating this as a homicide as Ms. Linden's death appears to be a drowning caused by force. Higgins adds that there were no indications that Ms. Linden intended to go for a swim and was not dressed in a bathing suit. He also adds that conditions in the water were dangerous due to the recent rainstorm. This is NPR.”

Then, her singing voice—too soon. I tapped for KPCC: “We spoke this morning with Chief Bottrell of Malibu–Lost Hills Division. ‘Investigations like this, you want to use as many resources as you can, get a fresh set of eyes.’” End of sound-bite, then the DJ gave a phone number for anonymous tips. I shook my head, repelling the onslaught of reality.

I pulled off at Rosecrans, turned into Oceanview Liquor, bought a $3.48 pint of some nasty-ass Banker's Club and drove to the Hermosa Pier. I parked, leaned back, slugged it, stupefied. The liquor sunk into me like a warning—I wasn't ready to walk. Grief came on like a slow fade-in, louder and louder. A life of disappearing acts: First my mother went batshit. Then my girlfriend and songwriting partner dumped me for someone with looks, money, talent, drive, and connections—that old Hollywood classic. I was still staggering from that puncture when I started working for Annie.

And now she was gone too?

I drank, stared at the ocean, reached for the cracked Samsung. Annie's forum spit out a frenzy of conspiratainment: She wasn't really dead, she OD'd, was in a coma, had been sleeping with the guard, he killed her, she him, it was cancer, it was AIDS, she changed her name and moved to Crested Butte, leapt off Point Dume. One talk-backer wrote: annie why? about a hundred times in a row. I had to agree.

One more drink before the walk.

I could admit that she was dead, but not that she was not alive. Maybe her health was worse than I suspected. You didn't get those extra ten years on a life like Annie's. Also—who did she have, really? Her ex, Kronski, was a serial womanizer. Her mentor, Eva—did they even still speak? Her sister, Barbara, was banned. Other than that, Annie had no real family, no close friends, just employees and fans—legions of useless fans, foaming over with electro-stim at her demise, confirming to each other that the unusually talented or beautiful were always to be punished, always, always.

I downed another slug, hit Wiki—they'd already added date of death.

Early life: . . . born in Wisconsin . . . grandfather tap-danced in vaudeville . . .

Career start: 1965–1969 . . . by age nineteen Linden had performed at the Gashouse, the Blue Grotto, . . . signed to RCA . . . revitalized the town's squarest label so that . . .

Critical reception: . . . "at every turn, she rode against the" . . . "when peace was in, she was all about the war of the heart" . . .

Period of transition: 1977–1982 . . . married producer Haywood Kronski . . . quit touring . . . elected herself to the margins . . . "By 1989 Annie Linden was totally off the grid" . . .

Et cetera, et cetera, blah blah blah.

But those were just the facts, and the facts are never even half the story. I flipped the phone in disgust, grabbed my flask and drank. Annie Linden never went off any grid at all, she just stopped selling her soul, but they don't write about that in Wikipedia. A person like her with those almond-shaped green falcon eyes, always observing, always seeming to restrain some child's shock at human cruelty, where could a person like Annie escape to? She certainly never escaped herself. The last of the stormy romantics, the oracle of love songs, who was *about* romantic love in a time when everyone seemed to be about everything else—no, Annie Linden, *my* Annie Linden never had any place to hide. Because she *believed* in love, like a religious devotee. She said as much to me on the road when I asked her where her songs came from.

"I think I write 'em," she said, "to try to understand how to survive my broken heart."

"Who broke it?" I was forward for a Lyft driver, but she just looked down and shook her head.

"But," I asked, "why'd you stop? I mean, were you afraid the record company would take the guts out of your music?"

"I was afraid they'd take the guts out of my body."

And she wanted me to find someone, she wanted—

Head going feverish, one last swig, I shoved the bottle in my coat pocket, got out and slammed the door, made my way down to the base of the pier. I was almost shaking as I approached, dirty sneakers treading the littered beach.

She wanted me to find something, to save her, she wanted—

But there was nothing to see.

A small crowd of gawkers lingered. Tilting thick wet pillars sheltered a floor of foam and glistening black sand. No crime scene tape, no cops. I turned away, clutching my belly. A few yards down the beach, the sight of a seagull walking nowhere, walking away, set me off and I started to weep to the too-big ocean, wet eyes making a bright haze of the sun rays.

ocean rider
crosswind glider
disappearer

Weeks before, on the clock, I had played her the first three tracks of my demo, watched her listen in the rearview. Her expression was maddeningly internal, concentrated, chin pointed forty-five degrees north and eyes elsewhere, intermittently closed. The first song was a strummy ukulele thing, almost a fake Music Hall number. Then a calypso with a fat reggae bassline, more upbeat. And then the slambang dance tune with all the bells and whistles, samples, scratches, backup vocals, the works. While she listened I tried to interject an apology—for the low sound quality, the poor musicianship, the general suckiness—but she raised a pointing finger to her lips and shushed. When the music stopped, she looked across the open car to the rearview, drew my eyes to hers.

Then she burst into a cackle.

"Jesus!" she said.

"What about him?"

"My Lyft driver is a real songwriter."

"No, I—"

"No *nothing*. A real fucking songwriter—did you . . . ? Is that why you asked to drive me or—?"

"No—no. Honest, I had no idea you'd be my—"

"Whatever. Those are incredible tunes, real songs."

"It's just a demo."

"It's just a little bag of diamonds in the rough is what it is. The last one is hooky as hell." She started humming the chorus. "I could sing the hell out of that one."

And then she did sing the chorus with insane superstar confidence and I started blushing like a teenybopper at the wheel. With every word, every note, she brought a jet propulsion, a dizzying weightlessness that lifted the song and sent it sky high—turned it into falling moon dust. In my 2016 VW Jetta.

"Annie, I *really* appreciate you taking the time to—"

"Can I keep it?"

"Keep what?"

"The disc, asshole."

"Yeah, of course. I mean, there is no disc, I can email you the tracks. But you don't have to. To like it, I mean. Just that you listened is way more than—"

"Oh no, send 'em, I want it. I'll try to hustle it for you. I mean—I don't know what my old fogy connections are worth, I can't promise miracles. But we'll find a home for it. *Gimme.*"

First my heart vibrated a little, like a tuning fork. Then, it was like honey rushed through my veins. The future, which had been choked off for so long, had suddenly reopened. "Thanks, boss."

"Watch the road, schmuck."

Later, when she got out at the loop, she was still humming the chorus—

The woman who was strangled, choked, tossed into these violent riptides—

By God knows who.

"How do I manage to survive with a broken heart?"

The ocean gave me the facts: The last person on earth to believe in me, the one person on earth who could have helped me, was gone.

5

YOU KNOW THAT
I TRIED TO BE WITH YOU

Troy's widow, Lauren Yvette Banks, lived at the bottom of a steep foothill in Leimart Park. I brought an arrangement of purple hyacinth, then almost balked when I arrived. The bungalow they lived in was purple.

A family of well-dressed mourners was leaving just as I arrived at the door. They didn't exactly give me dirty looks, but I felt the funny bristle of white intrusion. Lauren Yvette scrutinized me without surprise. She was stout, close-cropped, not too nice to look at, which was a little odd because Troy was a leading man type, young Denzel with muscle. She had seen my name on the police report.

"This is still raw for me," she said at the screen door, not opening it. "I may not be up for a pow-wow."

"I understand. Mostly I just wanted to let you know I loved Troy. We all did. He was the kindest, the absolute nicest gateman in my rounds."

"What do you want?"

I held up the flowers and she opened the screen door

with continued caution. When I handed her the bouquet, she waved me in with purse-lipped obligation. The small living room was shrouded, heavy cream curtains drawn. At the dining room table, a seven- or eight-year-old girl in Sunday best did homework. Calla lilies and carnations flanked a framed photo of Troy and a brochure from Evergreen Cemetery. Lauren said, "Mattilynn, please make Mama's guest some tea. The hot water's on."

"Green, herbal, or English Breakfast?" The girl didn't lift her head from the page.

I said, "English Breakfast."

The kid got up and half-sleepwalked into the kitchen, out of eyesight. Her mother turned her chin to me. "So—speak your piece, and then let us be."

I looked to the photo of Troy for support. "I think you know Annie very much loved Troy," I said. "Not that it helps. But she adored him."

"Yeah, well. Maybe I wish she didn't adore him so damn much. I told him to take a job in Brentwood or Holmby Hills or Cheviot Hills. Not be so adored."

"I understand."

"There's that word again. Maybe you *think* you understand more than you actually do."

"Help me understand better."

"Are you working with the police or something? Because the LAPD already got what they need from me."

I shook my head. "Not at all. I just, I really liked Troy. I always wondered how Annie found him."

"He found her. He knew her hairdresser Catelo. A decadent, unpleasant man. When Troy got tired of working at the salon, he called on Ms. Linden, much to my chagrin."

We were interrupted by Mattilynn balancing a tray with

tea, cups, cookies, sugar, Sweet'N Low, spoons, and sliced lemons. She shrugged nonplussed when I thanked her and Lauren Yvette cut her loose with a nod. The kid grabbed her homework off the table, disappearing down the hall. Only then did the full force of this fatherless room wash over me.

"Have that homework finished and let me know when you're done," her mother called after her, then turned back to me. "Mr. Zantz, when a rich, glamorous white woman puts her love on somebody of Troy's nature, he won't have a way to say no. Do you understand *that*? An old lady, a famous old white lady?"

"Troy's nature?"

She dropped to a hard whisper. "That's right. He wants to *be* her so bad, he'll do anything for her. Work overtime, go out of his way to do extras. And put himself in harm's way. It ain't love or respect. It's something else. And it's not healthy."

I was starting to get it. "I'm not sure it was so intense like that with Annie."

"Oh yes, it very much was." She put down her tea in one aggravated gesture. "I met the woman. She was a powerful little thing."

"True, but she just enjoyed Troy's company." I scrambled to change the subject.

"Look at *you*, you were her driver? You were probably hooked too. Probably still are."

It was a challenge—I held my tongue.

"Now," she went on, "imagine a man who has little education, who did prison time before tenth grade—a man who, you know, *loves princess movies* and . . . and maybe secretly saw himself as a little girl all along—imagine him falling into some kind of employment with a woman like Annie Linden. He thinks he met the real Cinderella or whatever."

"I see your point."

Lauren Yvette leaned back in the couch, as if she had finally accepted the fact that I was there. I looked back at the photo of Troy—a whole new guy appeared before my eyes. And too late.

She said, "You seem like a good guy and it was thoughtful of you to come here, but I gotta tell you—I don't understand any of this. I don't understand why he wasn't in his booth. And I don't understand a world where people attack old ladies. I'm *totally* at a loss."

"I am too."

"They say Troy made it as far as the far end of the property."

I said, "Do you know the house?"

"Not really. One time he drove me by."

"Troy made it all the way to where the hedges meet PCH. You sure you want to hear all this?"

"No. But I have to. My Troy could *run and climb*. He served in Iraq. Whoever got Troy surprised him." She scowled—she wanted to be in battle with me but she knew she was mostly in battle with herself.

I said, "He may have been chasing someone. Or maybe—"

"Don't they have cameras?"

"The police told me the surveillance was turned off that afternoon."

"Surveillance was *off*? Why?"

"I don't know. Nobody does yet. But Troy was heroic, Ms. Banks. He knew something wasn't right. And he took matters into his own hands."

Her head dropped. "Oh Troy. You foolish child of a man.

A cry from the room down the hall: "Mom, I'm finished."

6

THE WIND THE SUN
OR THE RAIN WE CAN BE
LIKE THEY ARE

Limos snaked up into Forest Lawn like they were pulling into an awards ceremony. Annie Linden's funeral was SRO. Above the green, sloping fields, the TMZ helicopter whirred like a big black bird staring down its prey. *Annie Linden, the final personal appearance*—true fans had to be there. I had to be there and wasn't invited, but I remembered that, long ago, Annie had passed along my info to an older couple who called me every so often for a ride. This time, I called them, to commiserate and to ask if they planned on going to the funeral— they had the juice to get in. Ray and Yuko had met on the set of *Star Trek*, the original series. They were married method actors of the Strasberg variety who'd both suffered the indignities of playing token Asians in dozens of sixties and seventies TV shows. They knew they were my Trojan Horse and they were cool with it.

"Oh, Adam." Svelte salt-and-pepper Yuko peered out

the window at the stream of cars ahead of us. "I'm glad you reached out. We *are* Annie's people, after all."

"That we are." Her husband was wide faced, intimidating in a Samoan ponytail, but his weary reserve was all gentility.

"This traffic." Yuko craned her neck. "Adam, we're at a dead stop."

"It won't be long," I said.

She fished a cellphone out of her purse.

"So many Tweets. So loved. Here, *New York Times*—'End of an Era.'"

"Yeah. Our era." Ray smiled his wry smile. "We're toast."

I was grateful for the sneak-in—I donned the black suit from my days at Bel Air Limo Livery to blend in. But as the cars inched, something miserable, unmanageable bubbled up inside. *Holy hell, get me through this day.* I dropped Ray and Yuko off at the chapel and parked up the hill, got out of the car and faced the blue sky, the rolling fields covered in rows of flat plaques like trapdoors to nowhere. *Is it real? Is she really gone?* I walked down the hill alone and got lost in the crowd.

Into the big doors, I scanned for familiar faces. No Bix. Also no Meghan, Annie's fan club prez. Ex-husband Kronski was there in a long leather trench coat, a shady Oscar statue in the seventy-degree sun. He said, *"My man"* and pointed at me when he saw me, like we were lifelong buds—pure Hollywood bullshit. A few other cronies I recognized from drop-offs walked past as if I was invisible. From out of the crowd stepped Catelo, Annie's hairdresser, in double-breasted crushed black velvet, with his crazy slanted 'fro and plastic green nerd glasses. He gave me a blank look. I pointed at myself. "The driver."

He nodded, solemn.

"So sorry about the bad news."

"We're *all* sorry," he said. But as soon as I was going to ask him about Troy, two guys he knew better showed up. They huddled—too haute for words—and spoke in hushes.

A security guard was eyeballing me with suspicion when a modern-sounding organ started up as the last of the pews filled. Could anybody in this somber hall be the someone or the people she was looking for? Who here knew about her long-lost tape, her dead phone line? I scurried and took a tight space in the back next to strangers, feeling guilty, but for all I knew, they could've snuck in too. Most of us in the room probably recognized the melody, "Windiest Day," from the *Long Distance Tunnel Digger* album. And most of us probably wondered what Annie would have had to say about that choice of selection. Then: the open casket. Her eyelids seemed to reverberate in the day glare. Even at rest— no peace.

A youngish priest, ruddy and redheaded, took the microphone and greeted the crowd with the glossy serenity of someone on really strong anti-anxiety meds. "All of us are born . . . with a special gift. But only some of us ever find it. And even fewer get a chance . . . to share it with the world. Annie Linden . . . found her gift very early. And she was able to share it . . . really and truly share it . . . with the *whole* world."

Books were opened and group prayers were recited with childlike compliance. On cue, the crowd fumbled into a heavy mainline Protestant jam—"God Be with You Till We Meet Again." I just sort of hummed along. The cross behind the priest was bare and wooden and I was surprised to find that I missed Jesus, his face, the zing of Catholic drama. A bare cross was too inviting—somebody could get nailed to it. As we were asked to be seated again, the blushing priest announced that several close friends and family had prepared a few words.

This made me uptight, because anyone who really knew Annie was going to have to talk around certain things. She wasn't made for officious tribute, least of all from family.

A composed, graying frizzy-haired brunette took the stand with her pages. "I'm Anne Marie's sister Barb," she said in a tightly wound way. The room practically gasped— *Annie had a sister?* But I had heard of her. Barbara cleared her throat. "Annie and I were different in almost every way. She was the rebel and I was the obedient one. For as long as I can remember, she was wild." This got titters, the crowd relaxed and so did Barbara. "But even though she was older, she was my baby sister, because I always wanted to protect her." Tears came, she let the script drop to her side. "And I will always love you, Annie. Underneath it all I . . . loved her. We loved each other very much." She reached for her eyes and wept to a silent room. And I was moved, maybe even more so because Annie hated Barbara's guts. *"That tight-ass is the perfect shrink—she could shrink the joy out of life itself!"* Those were Annie's words the single time I drove her to Barbara's house in Encino. *"Keep your cell phone on—I may have you come in with an excuse, get me out early. Let's just hope I don't strangle her."*

Next to take the pulpit were two aging black-jeaned musicians I didn't recognize, they'd played on this or that album. They fumbled through the reading of some Linden lyrics, which either they hadn't rehearsed or hadn't ever paid too much attention to, or maybe they were just much better at plucking instruments but they gave it their wobbly best.

She's the riptide
She won't let you by
Won't let you slide

But someday, someday when you find dry land
You'll understand
the secret beat in your heart.

Despite their foggy non-interpretation, the crazy power of Annie's words held up. How could she take something as beyond cliché as a heartbeat and make drama out of it, unleashing the mystical thing, the *feeling*? How could a space cadet like Annie have such a grip on what it's like to be alive?

Her manager was next, Mitzi Philomene, a *ballaboosta*, voracious and obese, with a wild blonde Jew-fro and dark round glasses, dressed in black-and-gray spiderweb muumuu, confident, imposing, a little nuts. Her Brooklynese rocked the room.

"Annie's friendship, Annie's music, Annie's very *being* was the light of my life. We were never together . . . I mean *together* together, her choice." At this the crowd of two hundred or so exclusive mourners burst into laughter. "But we had a kind of fifty-year love affair from the moment we met. And nobody will believe this. But we met at Ohrbach's Department Store, where Annie—" More laughs. "Let me finish! Where Annie was a *salesgirl*, in the perfume department. She was seventeen, practically a runaway. And she told me 'This perfume thing is just an act. Really, I'm a folksinger.' And I said, 'Well, I just happen to run a folk night at the Bido Lito.'" Mitzi started crying, but not in a contained way like the sister, she was really bawling, sniffling, and heaving—it almost sounded like a laugh. Some bald man in the front row leaned up and handed her a handkerchief. After a snort, Mitzi said, "I'm sorry, forgive me. I made bigger stars than Annie . . . but not to me. To me Annie was, she will always be, *the* star."

Big applause. To my left, three pews ahead, I saw a young

couple, really young, practically teens, that looked familiar, but I couldn't place them. The guy had a Brilliantine pomp combed tight, his skinny girlfriend had stringy bright purple hair falling over her eyes. They were solemn, not clapping too much or crying or playing along. They looked even more out of sorts than me in formal wear. Maybe they were in a band or something.

The whole room rose for a final prayer—a passage that could have been Old or New Testament, I couldn't tell. The mourners were given the opportunity to approach the body and say goodbye, but it was damn crowded so I waited in the vestibule door still searching for Bix and caught the large photo of Annie mounted on an easel, one of her last headshots blown up, black and white, fair and serene. She was beautiful alive and a new wave of loss crashed over me, almost blinding. For all her music and lyrics and wit and catty laughter, this old lady made me hear the silence within. It was the silence, the gaps that were her real gift. Annie Linden, once a person, now a spirit. She traveled through life and made it to the other side.

Or, I should say, *almost* made it. Someone rushed her trip.

"Can I see your invite?" A cop broke my reverie.

He was tall and wide—a wall of black uniform.

"I'm driving, I'm a driver. She was my friend, I brought a—"

"Yes, I remember you. From the crime scene." He raised eyebrows. "If you're here as *transportation*, I need you to get back in your vehicle."

I scurried back to the car, confused about how life, this fleeting thing, could contain such humiliations.

By the time Ray and Yuko emerged from the chapel and got in my car, it was already late afternoon.

On the way, Yuko said, "Oh God—they made an arrest."

Ray, looking at his own phone, said, "That they did."

My knuckles went white on the steering wheel while she read: "Former assistant Bix Gelden is being held without bail for the murders of Annie Linden and her security guard Troy Banks. Bix Gelden—Adam, do you know him?"

7

KEEP ME SANE IN THIS BURNING OVEN

The Visitor's Center at Wayside Pitchess Detention was soft, a carpeted interview room of unscratched yellow plastic chairs and white countertop tables, almost like a daycare. Cuffed to the table, Bix waited for the guard to step back. He was more alert than at our last encounter, hypervigilant. The drugs had worn off.

"They get you a lawyer?"

"Who's they? I picked one. A friend of the family."

"A good one I hope?"

His eyes flared. "Adam—*this is bullshit*."

I dropped to a whisper and a pasted-on smile of maximum agitation. "*Bixie*. Did you have anything to do with this?"

"No, man, And I have *no* fucking idea who did."

"What do they have? The DA, I mean. They couldn't drag you in on nothing."

His clownish, freshly shaven face was high in color, gray eyes on red alert. "I don't *know*. I ran. *Not smart*."

"Where'd they find you?"

"At Café Piccolo, down the street from Serenity House. First, they pull me in to ask questions about Troy. This fuckwad made me look at photos." Bix shook out the ugly memory, his red eyes welled. "Troy must have been running. I just can't figure out . . . was he running to help her, to escape someone, or—?"

"We can't know that." I had already worked through these confusions. "But why didn't he just take the golf cart? It's a long fucking way down to the beach cottage."

"Not for Troy. Troy was a *pro sprinter.*"

"I didn't know that."

Bix cracked a quiet whimper. "I ditched him. And he didn't make it."

"What do you mean ditched?"

"I ran like a chicken."

"Dude. Most people that hear gunshots . . ." But I could see that he was unassuageable. "I met the widow. And the kid."

Bix groaned. "*Mattilynn—*"

"Okay, man—but it's too late for all that. *You* have got to get out from under this. I'd like to meet your lawyer."

"Have you been back to Annie's place?"

"Of course not. It's completely roped off."

"There's some stuff there, stupid stuff. Some angry letters."

"Letters? Who writes letters?"

"I did. But—nothing, they were nothing. Bullshit."

"You were writing your boss angry letters? Like handwritten?"

"Well, yeah, but don't make it sound so crazy. I valued our relationship. Because she trusted me. And then she didn't. She fired me, I got pissed, what can I say? I didn't take it well."

I stared him down.

"I didn't kill her, Adam."

"I believe you."

And I did. Bix was weak but way too conscience-ridden, too nonconfrontational to murder anything but his hope and chances.

"The letters . . . were not nice. You have to help me get rid of them."

"I can't break in there, dude, you nuts?"

"You know the potted succulents alongside the main house? By her little fairy garden."

"Yeah, what about 'em?"

"There's a little empty pot with, like, a little toy wind-up dinosaur or dragon or some shit. Made of tin."

"Bix—"

"No, listen. Under the wind-up toy there's a master key."

"So what?"

"In the main house, in the office, she has all her letters filed, alphabetical. I did it myself."

"No way."

"I could give you the code, for the alarm."

"No. Way."

"Six. Seven. Three. Seven. Six."

"Fuck off."

"I'm grabbing at straws here, Zantz. *You* said you owe me. *You* said I could count on you."

"I am not going to trespass—"

"*In the office, the black filing cabinet.* Under my name. If they find those letters? I'm a dead man."

I said nothing.

He leaned in. "And if they pin this on me? We will never know who *actually*—"

I shot out of my seat and out the door, walked out the building in unshakable midday gloom. I was too keyed up to work—would probably scare the bejeezus out of my rides. I maneuvered my way out of downtown gridlock and looped onto the 10 heading west. Memory scattered with the freeway gravel sweeping under my wheels.

"Let's go down to the pier." Annie, white-haired, in black.

"You're all dressed up."

"I have a dinner date with the Salzmans of Brentwood. *Ugh.* I may flake but let's pretend I'm going."

"At your service." I opened the back door, she got in.

"I'm a mess. I had to fire Bix again."

"Oh no."

"Yeah, no—he just, he's *fixated*, I can't handle it. The guy seems to think that if he can win me over, he'll be someone else. In a way, he's just like the Salzmans. They have a . . . "

"Vicarious thing?"

"Right. And it's a delusion, infantile. *If I point at it, it's mine. It's me.*"

"Poor Bix," I said.

"Poor Bix, my ass. To live for someone else is sinful, it's super-crazy, and you just *might* end up with nothing."

Which was exactly what Bix *had* ended up with. He looked guilty, smelled guilty, on some cosmic level he *was* guilty, cornered by his own placidity. There was just one problem: I didn't believe he was actually guilty of murder, or even capable of it. This puffy-eyed guilt-monger vagabond swell, this frog of a man, surfer-frog-loser-motherfucker—I punched the steering wheel in dead-stop traffic. No way was I breaking into Annie's house to retrieve his goddamn letters. Who the hell was he to put me in danger? *And who the fuck could have done this?*

I was *not* breaking into Annie's house.

Not a chance.

But I could drive by—why not?

The yellow tape was gone. Onlookers came and went—fans dropped flowers, bizarre homemade paintings of Annie, cheapo computer printouts of her most famous snapshots, even a framed gold record of *Long Distance Tunnel Digger*, which would surely deteriorate out there in the sun and the rain. I pulled up into the drive.

Even if I'd been tempted to break in, which I wasn't, I had company. A couple of aging surfers were chilling on the hood of their vintage meadow mist green '58 Ford F100. The taller one was saturnine, his arms folded like a shield over a faded Ocean Pacific T-shirt. The shorter, skinnier man was his gray-ponytailed mascot. I was afraid they might be burglars casing the place. Something protective kicked in and I got out of the car.

I said, "You got a tough set of wheels."

The taller spoke. "Thanks, amigo. Just passing through and wanted to pay our respects. We loved this crazy old coot."

"You knew her?"

"Not exactly—we were booked to install a Jacuzzi here."

The skinnier bro in the KCRW T-shirt sighed with sorrow. "Ah, well. I guess that's that. No jacuzzi for Ms. Linden."

They hopped into the Ford and I breathed relief in the ocean breeze—any crazy ideas I might have had about breaking in had been foiled. I bid them adieu and their cool lowrider pickup fired up and went rambling down PCH into the horizon.

8

NO ONE ELEVATES YOU
ELEVATES YOU NOW

Back to work, the Lyft grind: a college girl and her dad, an old man and his groceries, a Pilates instructor late for her own class. Then, two monkey suits staring into their phones, a doe-eyed seven-year-old shlepping a blue backpack half his size, a slick British babe in a miniskirt headed for the Four Seasons—she claimed she was going to interview some sitcom star I'd never heard of. Then, the airport run—the arrivers, stunned to find themselves back in the LA web. Every person was a song in disguise, if only you could listen. I couldn't—my heart had tightened up to squeeze out the sorrow. I needed to see Ephraim Freiberger aka Double Fry. He would know how to let go of this mess. By the time I got to the marina, the afternoon sky was the color of the inside of a blood orange and the blues were coming down faster than night. I parked and got lost strolling the wet planks, looking for his boat.

Pelicans squawked at me low and hoarse from out on the buoys, giving directions I couldn't make out. Fry lived on a dirty white and navy blue forty-seven-foot Grand Banks his family had abandoned—he'd rechristened her *The Shechinah* in swirling blue cursive and swore to his Higher Power he'd never again be a landlubber. Like Bix, Fry was mostly unemployable, allergic to responsibility. Unlike Bix, Fry was cool with it. I found the good-looking bastard on the bow, stretched across a green-and-white plastic lawn chair. Upon his orange Hawaiian shirt rested a black hardbound gold-embossed volume of *Coastal Litigation Between World Wars*—light reading for Double Fry. A cracked-open red-and-green can of V-8 dangled from one hand, and five or six black camera lenses were lined up on a beach towel at his feet. Were it not for the yarn-knit Grateful Dead yarmulke almost sliding off his curly-haired head, you might mistake him for any Parrothead at the marina.

Usually, Fry cracked wise when he saw me. This time, he scoped my approach with unusual care, his fiery brow full of subdued dread. He put the big book and the drink down, straightened out his beanie. "Man—I don't know what to say."

"There's nothing *to* say." I clambered aboard and took a seat on some pillows, tarps flapping around us in the open breeze. "She's gone."

"You look beat down, Addy. Stay awhile."

I came to Fry for some cheer and common sense, but I could see in his reticence that he felt challenged here, searching for the compassionate word. He said, "I tried to pick up the Coast Guard reports on VHF—a lot of conjecture and bullshit. Truth is she could have floated in from anywhere."

"Really? You're saying Annie Linden could have been killed in Malibu, tossed into the water, and floated all the way to the South Bay?"

"Plausible," he said. "Not probable."

"I went to Wayside yesterday."

"You visited the PA?" Fry said.

I nodded.

"You know him, right?"

"Not well—I know him," I said. "He helped me out of a jam once."

"And?"

"And he's an idiot. But he's not a killer."

"Wow. Sounds like they're looking for a quick closer to shut everybody up."

"He fled the scene, he flipped out. And he wants *me* to help him," I said. "He's got some really bad ideas about how I should go about it, too."

"Do you *want* to help him?"

Stone gravity—I couldn't answer.

"Let's order dinner, Addy, I've got a shoot tonight."

He called in burritos from Takosher on Pico. Fry offered me some kind of gadget, which I turned down—he was toking THC oil on a black electronic pipe that lit up green when you dragged, communing with the collective digital unconscious. He whistled out a clear white vapor and avoided my eyes. "I only smoke on nights when I shoot. It increases my focus."

"Someday you'll explain to me how all this works—being a religious nut and a stoned-out paparazzi."

"It's simple. I don't shoot on Shabbat or holidays. I don't photograph nudity. And I don't sell any pictures that could potentially embarrass anyone."

"Which rules out, like, ninety-eight percent of the work."

"So be it."

"And embarrassing someone is strictly forbidden?"

"By the Torah, it's like murder." Observant Fry knew his rules and laws.

The burritos arrived, we ate them on the bow of *The Shechinah* in uncomfortable silence as the horizon faded into the blue night. As I dug for hot sauce packets in the bag, Fry broke the quiet. "Tell me about this assignment—she wanted you to find something for her."

I ran down the list—the classifieds, the bank records, the cassette—all the stuff Annie had mentioned.

Fry said, "I don't know, man. Sounds random. She could have been trying to track down anything—an old flame, some old jam session. Hard to believe things like that could get two people killed."

"I just don't see who would want to—" My voice croaked like a frightened child. Our eyes met. "Fry. Why did this happen?"

He shook his head.

"Addy, look me in the eye." He exhaled. "You're too good for your own good, you know that, right?"

"What the hell's that supposed to mean?"

"It means you're a good egg, you're a dope, but you're a gallant dope—and that's no small thing. There aren't too many left. But . . . "

"What."

"I don't want to bad trip you, but you're naive about these things. That's the dreamer, the songwriter in you. This happened because . . . these things happen. First of all, she had money. But also . . . Annie Linden had enemies. All famous people have 'em. And Linden left a serious impression." He raised a comic eyebrow. "She *was* unusually attractive for an old broad."

"You think every broad is hot, especially the over-seventy set."

"No, seriously, I saw her once, shopping for groceries at the Country Mart. She was so regal-looking, standing there, squeezing the green tomatoes, I didn't have the heart to take a snap."

"Look, enemies are one thing, but who the hell guns down a security guard so he can kidnap a seventy-three-year-old? And—and then tosses her into the ocean."

"I don't know. Not a mere fan. Not a thief." Fry considered our scrunched-up wrappers. "Maybe someone who really knew her. Someone pissed, *very* resentful."

I said, "Ugh."

"I'm *guessing*," Fry said, "somebody who wanted to do it for a long time? What about the ex-husband. You ever meet him?"

"Briefly—when he showed up she asked me to leave."

"Does she have a new spouse?"

"Nope—she was bizarrely faithful to the ex, and the guy just has babes dripping off him. And he isn't a pimp exactly but he's the least possessive guy I ever heard of. Bix told me he tried to pawn off some dancer chick he brought around—at his ex-wife's house no less. Apparently, he said to Bix, '*You like her? I'll tell her to make it with you.*' Just like that."

"What does Bix want you to do exactly?"

"Get some papers out of her house. Letters. I mean, why should I stick my neck out for this lunatic? Am I my brother's keeper?"

My heat was clipped by a wealthy couple ascending a sparkling yacht next-door without enthusiasm. Fry took this as a cue to toss the wrappers and start arranging his lenses in a silver suitcase. He was never a serious photographer, but Fry just had that ability to stand there and not quite be noticed—no small feat for a tall, bearded guy in a purple yarmulke. He'd graduated Cordoza Law back east, top of his class, and tried to hold down a Miracle Mile desk job for a few years at his mother's firm, but that didn't play. When he showed up to work stoned, his mom fired him, and Fry slipped through the cracks, drifted into bartending and waitering, and from there you've only got so many places to go.

Fry checked the charge on his Nikon D810 and fiddled with some knobs. He buttoned his Hawaiian shirt, inspected clean fingernails, latched a strap onto his camera. He was ready for paparazzi action. I myself was a camera with a too-wide aperture, taking in too much too fast. This was the invisible shape of grief—a blast of white light in the belly. But it was written all over my face. While I helped Fry zip the boat, he said, "Seriously, bubba, you want to wing me tonight? I'll pay you to drive me."

"I got an airport run in the morn but I'll sport you till then. I'm not sleeping these days anyway."

"I can tell."

"You know, man, it's weird, Annie and I weren't so so close, but those rides were one of the few things I looked forward to. I mean, she seemed to *actually* think my songwriting didn't suck. And she wanted to help me."

"That's not weird at all."

"And, *fuck*. I don't see how a guy like Bix will survive trial. He's guilt-ridden about merely existing."

"Well—" Fry shot me the gentle coaxer look, straight out of his lawyer playbook. "You're as close to this as anyone— you need to decide."

"Decide what?"

"If you're gonna dig in. And dig him out."

"*Me?* I'm a driver. What about the cops?"

He shrugged. "*Cops are cops.* Cops are civic employees. When you go into Office Depot, do you ask the employees for help? Of course not. Play detective, poke around."

"Yeah, I dig, but I wouldn't know where to start. I'm about as hardboiled as scrambled eggs."

"Didn't you used to do some investigation work or something?"

"Barely—my sister was trying to help me go straight, she got me a job with this square john downtown. A lot of Google searches and filing, waiting in line at the DMV for records. Three weeks in I got bored and walked off the job."

"Nevertheless, this is a real case. The code of the detective is to solve a case once it has begun."

"What is that, *Perry Mason?*"

"I'm not joking, Addy, you need to trust God on this one."

"Freiberger, no scripture, please."

"What *scripture?* The holy spirit is whispering in your ear. Always. Listen for holy instructions."

"I love ya, dog," I said, unable to mask exasperation, "but *nothing* seems holy right now. Even before this I was already wondering how everything got so ugly. It's like I wasn't paying attention and I backed my life into a dark corner."

Fry leaned on the cockpit and tied off the blue tarp. "Addy, I can see you're hurting, you're in over your head. But what feels like a *corner* could be a *portal*. And there is a whisper to guide you through. Call it whatever you want, but what's the spirit in your ear telling you *right now?* Be honest."

I held the rail on the gangplank and looked past the rows of boats wobbling in their docks, past the pennants whipped by breeze, out into the dark horizon.

I said, "It's telling me someone hurt her—and I owe her— for giving me hope when I had zero. And I'm pissed. 'Cause if I don't find out who—" I sighed. "If I don't find out who, maybe nobody will."

Fry hopped onto the dock and pulled the camera bag

around his shoulder. "Your honor, I rest my case. Noodge around, *talk* to some people, see what comes up."

Our eyes met. Mine must have telegraphed Big Worry.

Fry smiled. "Just don't lose your cool, daddy-o."

Evening passed watching Fry shoot pretty young starlets I'd never heard of. Sitting on the hood, I tried to picture playing detective, the actuality of it. There *was* a whispering in my ear but it was Annie's voice, not God's.

"*Adam—you promised to help.*"

She gave me the assignment—handed me destiny. Took my hand in hers, chaste and restrained, but it bonded us.

"*Adam, I would never ask you to do this if I didn't trust you.*"

Seemed like only days before, she'd asked to hear my demo. After that, how could I not accept her mission? We were a team—and I was on the path to do something good, finally. I would be the hero, the guy that got Annie Linden, *the* Annie Linden out of a jam—and she would love me for it.

And save me back.

"*Find my people, close my circles.*"

She was gone now, but it wasn't over. I had one last shot at dignity—to investigate her murder, uncover her secrets. Like Double Fry said—*the code of the detective is to solve a case once it has begun.*

I dropped Fry off around 3:00 a.m. and rolled home leaning way back into the dawn. When I pulled up to the studio, Old Man Santiago was waiting with a fresh unlit cigarette. "I couldn't stop 'em."

"Stop who?"

"Two guys—they made me show them your place."

"Cops?"

"Plainclothes. But they showed badges." Santiago snickered. "They turned the joint upside-down, man."

"Jesus. Did they have a warrant?"

"I'm sorry, kiddo, what could I do? You know I got a record, and I can't be—"

I ran up the stairs to my unit, unlocked, hit the center of
the room, 360'd. The place was usually a mess, now it looked
half-organized—clothes, papers, trash can, cassettes, everything had been slightly rearranged as if for methodical review.

Old Man Santiago stood at the door. "Zantz—you in
some kinda trouble?"

9

WITH THE SCENT OF
DEATH WE FIND THAT WE
ARE NOT SO VERY AWED

Shaken, I barely caught half a night's sleep. I could've called the police, but you don't mess with the LAPD when they're messing with you. Anyway, they found nothing because there was nothing to find. I didn't even have a working electric razor let alone a murder weapon. I got into my ultra-anonymous driver uniform—jeans, fading black polo, black hoodie, and a pair of red Onitsuka Tiger sneaks beyond reproach—and worked the late morning shift in a state of high unrest, but by lunchtime I knew I had to take Fry's advice and at least noodge around. I drove down to Venice to see if I could find Haywood "Hay" Kronski, Annie's producer, one-time husband, and for a long time after, co-songwriter, commiserator in aging, daily yenta. I'd seen Kronski at the funeral but I'd put off this visit and the reason was simple—he didn't like me. Or, if he re-membered me at all, he probably would not like me. Our few times crossing paths at Annie's, he refused to look me in the eye or utter a word in my presence. Once, I pulled into the loop to pick her up just as he rolled up in his tricked-out midnight silver Tesla. Annie rushed out, barefoot in a bathrobe, leaned into my ride and said, "I think you better split."

Kronski was a *tummler*, a stirrer of pots and cracker of jokes, and he had slashed more than a few Annie sycophants to ribbons with just a few words. Bix he referred to as The Human Sofa—who knew what nickname he had for me? It was common knowledge that Kronski was not Mr. Nice Guy. A pioneer dope farmer in Humboldt County long before it became the thing, Kronski always seemed above, beyond, or maybe below the law. In '76 he was indicted for tampering with the Billboard Charts, in '81 there was some kind of a coke bust—nothing stuck. Also there were women, impossible slinky young beauties with waterfalls of blonde hair, and Kronski didn't think twice about parading them in public where Annie would surely find out. For nice Jewish boys like myself, so bedazzled by her, this flaunting was more than mere infidelity, it was indication of a man less afraid of her than we were. I mean, the guy actually *shacked up with Annie Linden during her prime*—and then dissed her! And who was he to do such a thing? Some middling keyboardist and a B-lister songsmith. His work with Annie was not her best. By the time she married him in the early eighties, her blue flame was out. And yet her dedication was unwavering. Once, when she was accepting some kind of lifetime achievement thing, she referred to him as "my beloved depressive Russian"—but what was so fucking beloved?

Supposedly, he was the reason she went full hermit. Supposedly, they still spoke every day, right up until the end, even though they'd been separated for twenty-five years. Supposedly, *she* was the caretaker—rare for a pop star.

Supposedly, Kronski was verbally abusive. Supposedly, she couldn't live without him. But maybe he missed her as bad as I did. And maybe he had answers.

Kronski lived in the ratty part of Venice in a little blue bungalow on Rialto. Now why would a man with twenty gold records to his name flop out in a musty-dusty part of town like that? Well, it was obvious: He worked it local—the beach bars, the coffee shops. Rumor was he could be found every afternoon on Abbot Kinney at Van Gogh's Ear, drinking coffee and journaling, chatting up the fresh arrivals. Because who wants to get into a car and bring your prey all the way back up to some palatial mansion when you can invite them over for a tussle a half-block away.

When I ducked into Van Gogh's, the shag-headed blonde at the cash register, hypnotized by her iPhone, didn't look up.

"What can I get you?"

"I'm looking for Hay."

"*Jusssst* missed him." Her eyes never left the screen.

I cut back onto Abbot Kinney and walked in the direction of Rialto. The sky was overcast, the narrow streets were empty, and I was annoyed to find myself so jumpy. These Venice residentials made a strange hodgepodge: A ramshackle mint-green shanty right next to an ultra-modernist tall box in bright crimson next to a house shaped like a boat and then a straight two-bedroom draped by a white picket fence with a tire swing hanging from the willow in the front yard. Streets and back alleys were too thin, virtually indistinguishable. But as soon as I turned the corner, there was Kronski, his back to me in a long black cashmere Commes des Garcons trench coat, opening the door to his little blue love shack, fumbling with the key.

I called his name. He spun around slow in jet-black

glasses, Alexander Graham Bell bushy beard, and that giant schnozz straight out of Nazi cartoonery. A devilish stoner's grin stretched across his face as he took me in.

"What is happening, man."

"I don't think you remember me, but—"

"Course I do. You're the *driver*, man." His grin hadn't disappeared but calcified so that it maybe no longer represented good will. "Saw you at the thing."

In an instant, it dawned on me that I'd made a boogie man out of the guy. Up close, there was tragicomedy about Hay Kronski, Yiddish pathos. In another life, he'd have made a dynamite extra in *Fiddler on the Roof*.

"I just, I was in the neighborhood," I said. "I wanted to tell you how sorry I am. I—"

"Yeah. It's. Well. What can one say, man. We're all freaking out." A gust of wind whipped the leaves at our feet, but I was easing, thrown by his affability.

"I guess," I said, "I'm still in shock."

He acknowledged with a tilt. "It's *unthinkable*. And Mr. Troy—that's a tragic trip too." He glanced over his shoulder at his house, the funky beach cottage with battered wainscoting that looked like a guesthouse to another house that didn't exist. Two little concrete steps led to the newish door, the only part of the place that hadn't been tortured by sea breeze. When it was clear that the Lyft driver wasn't going away, Kronski said, "Well, hell, come on in, man. It's gettin' cold out here."

The place was ascetic, a low rectangular coffee table alongside a beaten couch on which his drooling Labrador lay, not that psyched to see me or his master. The walls were dark like chocolate, but out the window that weeping willow with the hanging tire bent in reverence to the white sky. Hay Kronski took off his shades and lay them on the coffee table.

"Lightbulb's busted," he said. *"How many blondes does it take to screw in a lightbulb?"*

"I don't know."

"Two—one to hold the lightbulb and one to spin the ladder around."

I strained a smile and he smiled as he flicked on a giant workstation with six or seven screens stretching around like Cinemascope. They gave the room a fever glow.

"That's where I *jam*," he said with a snort. "My workstation. Sit down, man, she don't bite. Djuna—make some space for our guest, you colicky ol' bitch."

"Annie's dog?" I said.

"Yeah, but she always liked me better." He nudged and the dog rolled off the couch, circled to his feet.

"I'm really sorry to bother you. I'm just rolling around with so many unanswered—"

"No, no, I get why you're here, my man. *Loss.* Serious, I get it. She . . . was *our leader*, man. Hey, I lost my leader, too." Now, without the sunglasses, his smile was tangled in vulnerable eyes. He pulled a tin box out of his pocket, started to piece together a joint, all the while looking right at me, like he didn't need to know what his hands were doing. "Annie was emblematic. *Is* emblematic, man. Always will be. All *kinds* of people are losing their cool, coming to me for answers. 'Cause she represented something that's happening to the consciousness of man, like, on a spiritual plane. Am I making sense, man?"

I nodded, under the curious pressure of our age difference. He was the old man and I was the young dude, yet he was more like a teenager somehow, more oblivious to the rules. I said, "Are *you* okay?"

"Better than some, man. 'Cause to me she was no emblem.

To me, she was just a woman." Now he licked the joint in one hand and dug for a lighter in the cashmere with another. He dragged—the size of his take was enormous, a sea-going freighter revving its engine. He held the hit and in a pinched voice he said, "Absolutely a woman." Then he blew like the ship's smokestack, a giant cloud of grays, dark and swirling. Even the dog looked up, agitated. Kronski tried to hand me the joint, but I waved him off. He said, "*You* at least are a real songwriter, so for you it's gotta be a bigger thing."

"Me?" I blushed, refused.

"Yes sir. She told me all about you, man. Straight up. She had a old lady crush on you. Oh, yeah, they get 'em all the time, those broads." He took another super-drag. "Don't kid yourself, it *is* erotic. *How many Freudians does it take to screw in a lightbulb?*"

"Tell me."

"Two—one to hold the ladder, and one to screw my mother, I mean the lightbulb."

Now I laughed. His tough guy shtick was melting away before my eyes.

I said, "We never went that way."

"That's cooool," Kronski said. "I'm not gonna say I wouldn't have cared, but she *was* a free agent." Once again he tried to hand me the spliff. This time I took. Kronski stared down his dog. "What I was saying is—what was I saying? Oh yeah. When was the last time you gave her a ride, man?"

"I was supposed to pick her up the night she went missing." I took an extra toke on the joint to buy a hesitation. Telling him about Annie's little search felt like a betrayal somehow. All I could get out was, "She sent me a text, to pick her up at eight."

"She mentioned to *me* she was planning on visiting Eva," he said with complete confidence. "Up in Morro Bay, out by

San Luis Obispo. Evil Eva the Superbitch. Eva Silber-Alvarez."
He smoked again and then I did too.

"Is that the one she called her mentor?"

"Mentor, my ass. They were *lovers*, a long time ago. You
could even say I stole Annie from Eva if you'd like to get techni-
cal about it." His tired eyes went heavy-lidded, nostrils flared.
He passed me the joint again, a third or fourth round—I was
losing track.

"But were they still close? I never took her up there."

Kronski licked his teeth. "They were gettin' close again.
They had a *unnatural attachment*, those two. Fighting cats
and dogs and then ten years of silence and then all twisted
up again. Annie mentioned they were speakin' again last
Christmastime. I said I don't wanna hear about it."

"Evil Eva," I said. "Sounds like you adore her."

"Oh, Eva's alright, Queen of the *Feministas*, respected at
universities worldwide. *Now—how many feminists does it
take to screw in a lightbulb?*"

"*That's not funny*," I said deadpan.

"Ahhh, you already heard that one. Look—Eva—she was
just a rival is all. At my age, you learn to cherish 'em. They let
you know what's worth fighting for."

"Meaning Annie?"

"Annie had something me and Eva both wanted, man. The
kind of thing that ain't that easy to forget, or to live without
once you've had a taste. Look at me, man!" He raised an up-
turned hand to his chest, like he was catching his own heart.
"I mean, look at me. I *dumped* Annie, man. For sure it was *me*
that dumped *her*. And yet, and yet, I could not let her go! For
like, more than twenty years!" His eyes were pleading now,
gray amazement. "Twenty years."

I was not a midday weed smoker and this sad face and
the bad jokes and the blue light and the big laconic dog at

Kronski's feet were adding to my sense of the unreal, but the stuff must have been strong, too, because I found myself swimming and flailing mentally, lost and drowning in his elegiac monologue. "Who do you think *did* this?"

His expression flattened. "Bix? Maybe? I never did like the guy, but I really don't know, man. And maybe she didn't want me to know. 'Cause I *would* know. And I hate to say it but . . . it coulda been her, she coulda done it herself."

"Like, drown herself?"

He shrugged. I found this hard to believe, especially considering Annie knew an innocent person could be punished for her death. But I zipped it.

Kronski said, "Look, I don't know about the security guy, but it's not like Annie was Mrs. Hope for the Future." Without announcement, Djuna the lab stretched and headed for the kitchen. Although I hadn't exactly loved her presence, the room felt more lonely now, and this seemed to wake Kronski from our shared stupor. "Uh listen, man, I gotta go meet some ladies over at Hal's. They're celebrating my birthday early and, uhm, I really should spiffy up an' all that."

I thanked him for the hang, he said fall by anytime, and then he gave me a gentle pat on the back, an awkward attempt at the fatherly. But when I stepped out, down the two stairs to the narrow street, I was disoriented, couldn't remember where I had parked, and the sky was very heavy now. I needed time to process, not the different things he said so much as the broken way he said them, this old jokester who had seen it all and done it all and was still mourning for a love that he somehow hadn't, couldn't ever really have. I held off more driving, found a bench and watched the bicyclists and joggers along the path that curves the dirty beach, waiting for the buzz to die. Finally, as the sun set on the horizon, I stopped dancing around it: he didn't seem shocked that she was gone.

10

TAKE ME DOWN TO THE SANDY SHORE

Eva Silber-Alvarez was listed. She lived along the foothills of Los Osos, about three hours up the coast near San Luis Obispo. Next morning, I took Highway 1 and made it before noon. She was on her knees in the front yard of her woodsy cottage, yanking weeds with impunity—a few years older than Annie maybe, but it had to be her. As I pulled up, she stood and pulled her gloves, ran a hand through her square head of short gray hair, lodged her fists at her sides, and gave me the stink eye. In her red-and-purple plaid shirt tucked into jeans folded up at the ankles, she was part elderly woman, part lumberjack. But the buzzcut yelled death camp prisoner.

Then, just as I got out of the car, she reached behind a hedge and pulled out a rifle so big and long it looked like a movie prop musket. She aimed it right at me.

"State your business, little man." Her accent was Polish or Russian.

I raised hands. "I'm Annie Linden's driver—I was, I mean."

"And."

"And I—I'd like to ask you a few questions."

"I got no obligation to talk to you."

"Annie asked me to see you. She . . . hired me. To look into some stuff for her."

"Stuff?" Her lip curled. "What kind of stuff?"

"That's what I'm trying to figure out."

Eva snorted, the rifle pointed toward the dirt.

"Inside—for gin." It was early for gin, but this was a test. I followed her in.

For the Queen of the Feministas, Eva Silber-Alvarez had an awful lot of masculine stuff in her home—a pair of African muscleman statues, a big, framed reproduction of "Napoleon Crossing the Alps," the angry white marble head of Beethoven staring down from her black baby grand. The cowhide rugs were clean, the couches brown leather. Then there were the magazines on the glass oval table, all from NYC—*New Yorker, New York Review of Books, NY Times, NY Law Review.* She was like someone from a foreign land who had not yet accepted the fact that she was an expat, but that country wasn't her original birthplace of Warsaw, it was Greenwich Village 1952.

Over the fireplace mantel, one sign of the contemporary: a framed photo—Eva in a white suit standing by her somewhat younger red hot Latina bride on their wedding day.

She brought a bottle of Bombay to the glass oval. Outside the sliding glass doors that led to the backyard, a ravine ran down to a creek where egrets darted around in shallow water.

"They do not bother me," she said, pouring from the blue bottle. "And I do not bother them."

"Are you very shaken by the news?"

"I am not shaken by anything. My father escaped Treblinka. He shook me enough. Now what is this so-called stuff you are in need of."

I explained Annie's request, the gist of it. "Do you have any idea what she might have been looking for? She said she wanted me to find an old cassette, some papers—"

Eva scrunched with disgust. "She was looking for *a self*, of course. And using you, her primary mode."

"I don't understand."

"Forgive me but Annie Linden lived moment to moment. As an animal does. With no care for who she worries. Whatever she *thought* she was looking for was some insane whim that she would have forgotten about the next day."

"Maybe, but—"

"Not maybe. Please. I looked at the obituary, I could hardly hold my laughter. This was not the Annie I knew, the user. Oh yes, she was a user in every sense of the word. For years, she used me like a mother figure—" She gestured across her plaid chest. "And anybody can see *I ain't the mother-figure type*." Her faux American joke accent was a goofy mix of Eastern Europe and East Jersey.

"You were together."

"Only later, when she got tired of me."

"I don't understand."

"Annie wanted a Santa Maria to watch over her. When I refused, she tried to get sexual. I was hot stuff then. But . . . I don't go that way."

"Okay." I tried not to blush.

"What I mean is, I am a romantic girl underneath. A June Allyson type. I need to be seduced. Oh yes, I am not casual." She jutted out a prideful chin. "And truth be told, I loved her too much to just . . . *potchke* around."

"Annie told me once you were her spiritual mentor."

"That's cute. Spiritual mentor. But if that is what I was, it looks like I failed."

"She didn't see it that way."

Eva leaned back into memory. For one quick flash, her leathery brow softened to reveal wistful girl eyes, carbonated by ideals. "I had a *mission*, a political mission. And for a minute there, a long time ago, I imagined Annie was with me on this mission. But she wasn't. She was a dabbler. In everything. She could not commit to banana pancakes for breakfast. She could not commit to *anything*."

"Except her music."

"You think so. With her gifts, with her access to the unconscious, she could have been a giant, a *thought leader*. Not some fancy little songbird."

Eva poured more gin—I was getting blasted in daylight for the second time. Maybe it was a long-held tradition for Annie's people to decimate visitors with booze and drugs. After Eva slid me the refreshed glass, I said, "On the night she went missing . . . do you think she planned to come here?"

"This is doubtful. I hadn't seen her in years."

"But she talked as if you guys were still close."

"Young fellow." She looked me over—just how naïve could I be? "We all tell ourselves fairy tales. To make believe we have not done the damage we have done. What Annie did to the movement—was not forgivable."

"Which movement is that?"

Eva laughed. "The *feminist* movement, naturally."

"But wasn't Annie considered some kind of feminist icon?"

"Icon, sure. *For her own ends, don'cha know.* She grabbed our ideas in a manner that was so baldly ambitious, most of my colleagues found her embarrassing. The diehards . . .

cringed. *Yes.* Because she wanted to have her cake and eat it too. Not just with men and women, not just with glamour and so forth. At the end of the day, Annie Linden wanted the revolution to be about Annie Linden. And everybody else could go to hell."

"Aren't you being a little rough on an old lady that just drowned?"

"Old lady? Give me a break. She's seventeen forever in the hearts and minds of the whole world. While I will most likely be remembered as that bull dyke Annie Linden toted around for a few seasons. All my work, all my intellectual inquiries, I cashed them all in for *what*? This canary? This little cowgirl with the blues." Eva cracked her knuckles. "Who the fuck did she think she was, strutting around in her little boots and spurs like Annie Oakley. Another male fantasy. For masturbation purposes only."

"But you loved her, you just said so yourself."

"*So what if I did?* Okay, the songs, I concede, were great. *Seemed* great. Now I look back, I don't believe a fucking word. Poetry? There was no poetry. It was Hollywood, the hippie model. Shortest skirts and loosey-loosey blouses. Art? Try *pornography*. You want me to hitch my cart to this horse and I cannot. Sorry, I ain't your *butch bitch*. Running around like a sparkly-time princess—even this need for a driver, please! *Drive your own damn car, lady!*"

"Well, anyway," I said, trying to cool her rant. "She loved *you*. She told me so. She said you were the only person who ever made her feel safe."

The remark was meant to soothe, but it was like I couldn't have offended her more. A kind of slow terror came over Eva's face, like someone catching the first whiff of a deadly chemical smell. She went ashen-faced and killed her gin, wouldn't look me in the eye. The sunlit room grew quiet, with little finches chirping in the far off. To the floor, she mumbled, *"Annie"* and something else, it sounded almost like *"my poor baby"* but it could have been Yiddish or Polish or I don't know what. Then she lifted her head slowly—excruciatingly—and shot me a funny look, half stern, half pleading. We both knew it was time to go.

"Young fellow," she said at the door, "forgive me but— forget about the dead. Your own meter is running."

I took Highway 1 heading back to Los Angeles, shadowboxing Eva's vision of Annie. I dug Eva, this brassy, ballsy broad with her gin and her straight talk—she didn't seem capable of lying. But wasn't Annie more than the ambitious, childish songbird of her memories? Annie was sun-kissed, free, barefoot, but she was also cool, discerning—there were two sides. At least. I hated to admit she was as selfish as Eva said, but maybe she was. And yet Annie was also crazy generous—for someone at her level to try and help me was way not Hollywood. Yes, she threw tantrums when she didn't get her way—practically a daily thing—but they didn't last long. She was unpredictable, got panicked over tiny surprises. A missing guitar pick could send her into shrieking hysteria. Then she'd find the stupid purple pick and get depressed, apologetic, self-mocking even. She was this and she was that, she was *all of it*—and through the gaps I fell.

> *She was the undertow*
> *Strong and pure*
> *She was the hurt*
> *And she was the cure*
> *Your long-lost lover*

You tried to run
But you didn't get far
Wishing upon your secret star
Your long-lost—

From San Luis to Pismo Beach, I tried to write a bridge but the song went nowhere and finally the booze wore off and I went mindful at the wheel, breathing long and hopeless. Because I knew I was done playing detective. Whatever Annie had wanted from me, whatever she was looking for, it was just too damn late. Promise or no promise, I was not equipped or not crazy enough to go prying into her private affairs, poking around the dark corners of her life. I was a Lyft driver, for fuck's sake.

Enough—she was gone.

And I had to let her go.

Adrift in this poignant daze, it must have taken me a few minutes to notice the cop car behind me, one of those new hatchback black-and-whites that look more like a family wagon than the long arm of the law. In fact, I didn't really see it until the siren went on.

11

EAST RIVER TRUCKERS ARE CHURNING WITH TRASH

Take my word for it: From the back of a cop car, leaning on cuffed wrists, the mountains of Malibu are not your friend. Who knew lush jacaranda could look so cruel? Up Agoura Road, the destination came into view: Malibu–Lost Hills Sheriff Station, cozy as a new suburban library, with mint pyramid roof and newly painted parking stripes. And on their low concrete banner-wall, the golden Sheriff's star, six-pointed.

The CHP schmucks that breathalyzed and cuffed me didn't seem to know their way around. After walking me up the hall, then down, they found their way to the desk of Lieutenant David Bottrell. Soft-faced and blue-eyed, Bottrell looked less like an authority figure, more like a middle-aged enjoyer of milk 'n' cookies. He greeted with boisterous cheer—then froze when he saw me. "Take his cuffs off, for crying out loud, he's not a fugitive. I want to *talk* to him—in 2A."

"He was driving under the influence," the CHP cop protested. "Point oh-eight-two—we BAC'd him."

"I don't care about that," Bottrell said. "Mr. Zantz, I'm sorry about all this—I'll catch up with you in a few minutes."

The chastised arresting officers popped my cuffs off in silence and led me to a little pastel olive room that also didn't exactly scream tough justice. Three felt-back chairs—I got comfy, massaged my sore wrists and waited.

About fifteen minutes later, Bottrell came in with a woman.

"Sorry about the wait. This is Officer Linda Nguyen."

They both smiled. If Bottrell was Sir Laid Back, Nguyen was Lady Compassion. Maybe a child of Vietnam, maybe not, but she spoke gently, without accent.

"So you were Annie Linden's driver?"

"Adam Zantz." I fished for a card, placing it on the table. "Am I under arrest or something?"

She smiled, flirty. "I don't know, should you be?"

"He's *fine*," Bottrell said. "Chief Bernhardt just asked us to get a statement. He'd like some help with known associates of Bix Gelden."

"You didn't have to cuff me for that," I said.

"Yeah, the DUI thing really isn't important." Bottrell picked up my card and handed it to Nguyen. "You were *kinda* right on the line. Let's talk about your relationship with Bix a little—we'll see about clearing that up."

I breathed deep, took in the bargain. "I'm happy to cooperate anyway I can."

Thumbing at Nguyen, Bottrell said, "This one didn't even know who Annie Linden was before yesterday."

"I'm more a Beyoncé gal myself," she said. Then, to Bottrell: "How do *you* know so much about the vic?"

"*Me?*" Bottrell said. "I idolized her."

"I didn't know you were a music guy," she said.

"Actually, I play a little *gee-tar* myself."

"You do?" Nguyen seemed genuinely surprised, but their repartee came off vaudeville.

"Believe it or not," he said, "I was in a band before Academy."

"No way, what were you called?"

"Oh, you never heard of us. We were *Chaparral*."

"Sounds like country," I chimed in.

"Country *rock*." Made eager, he fished out his phone and placed it on the table, started scrolling around. "Got an old YouTube of us live at the Palomino." He found it and pressed play, tilted to widen the screen. There he was, younger, clean-shaven, strumming and singing in a pearl satin cowboy shirt, leading a clunky bar band through "Lying Eyes."

I swayed a little, feigned interest. It was the most awkward half-minute of my entire life.

"Dan!" Nguyen shook her head in wonder. "That's *terrific*."

"Just don't tell Chief," he said. Then he swiped the video off the screen mid-song and put his phone away. "Jammin' with your buds—nothing better."

"So," Nguyen said to me, "you heard about Bix, I take it."

I nodded.

"You know him?"

"I do, yeah, we're sort of pals. I mean, it's crazy."

"What's crazy?"

"Well." I raised palms. "I just don't think Bix hurt anybody."

Nguyen nodded thoughtfully as she glossed my card. "And you were employed not by Ms. Linden but by Lyft."

I nodded, shifted in my seat.

"But you were her exclusive driver?"

"I guess so."

"Wow, is that—do they allow that?"

"Technically no, but you know, she's older and . . . I guess I thought it was a worthy exception. So we, we went off-app."

"I understand. But how long ago was that?"

"Our first ride? It'll be three years in August."

"And . . . you knew her strictly as her driver?"

"Well—yeah. But she had me over for a few dinners. Social stuff but—"

"Nice." Bottrell said. "Dining with the rock star."

Nguyen said, "Is that unusual?"

"Is what unusual."

"Hanging out socially with your riders?"

"No. Well, yeah, in general. But with Annie—"

"Did she say *why* she had you over for dinner?"

"I guess because we . . . we hit it off. She liked me?"

They exchange lightweight glances, like approving parents. No good cop, bad cop—they were both nice. Maybe.

"Adam," Bottrell said, "who were some of her other employees, did you know them?"

"Yeah, yeah, a bit."

"So, who else worked for Ms. Linden that you associated with?"

"I mean, it's not like I *associated*-associated. But, uh, she had a private chef, Nikki, a woman, three or four nights a week. Also, Lucero comes to clean on Tuesdays. Came. Troy, of course. And once in a while there were landscapers, I don't know their names. But I can find their numbers if—"

"That's great," Nguyen said. "This is really terrific."

"Not as terrific as the Lieutenant singing Eagles," I said and they both laughed.

"Now about Bix," she said. "On site, you mentioned to Lieutenant Guiterez that he usually stayed in the main house."

"He did. But Bix . . . Bix's been fired a few times."

"How many times is a few?"

"I didn't keep track."

"We heard Linden could be hard to work for." Bottrell spoke warm and easy, buddy to buddy. "Any idea *why* Bix kept gettin' fired?"

"No, but they had a *lonnng* relationship. Like, from his childhood. I don't really know the details." I pursed lips, held his eyes.

"Our records show that Bix had a drug problem." Nguyen tilted with the weight of the concerned citizen. "What kind of drugs?"

"That I don't know."

"Mr. Zantz. *Adam.* According to the Chief's notes, Ms. Linden texted you for an 8:00 p.m. pickup at approximately 7:00 p.m.—*off-app*, as you say. Do you still have that text?"

I nodded, scrolled my phone, and slid it across the table to her. First Nguyen hand-wrote the message on a pad and double-checked that she got it down right, then she took her own phone and took a shot of mine. Phone-on-phone photography, probably held up in court.

Watching her, Bottrell raised a jokey eyebrow—all this techie stuff. He'd rather be strummin' *gee-tar.* "Guiterez told *me* you said Linden didn't usually give such short notice."

"I had mentioned that to him, yeah, that it was unusual. Unusually short."

"And, uh, *come to my arms*—that's a little romantic for a Lyft call, isn't it?"

I went hot in the face. "It's just—"

"Give it to us straight. You have an amorous relationship with this old dame?"

"*Nooooo,*" I said, "that was just her humor. She, she sent little lyrics in her texts. I could show you others."

Bottrell faked a baffled smile but not for long. "Where do you think she was *headed*, Mr. Zantz?"

"I have no idea. I mean, later, I found out she had, uh, an old friend named Eva in Morro Bay she might have been planning on seeing. But that's a wild guess, I never actually took her up there. And . . . Annie sometimes called for rides just to, like, ride."

"Okay. But . . . " Nguyen shifted, spun her pen—first sign of a budding impatience, "when she *did* stop somewhere, what were some places she stopped?"

"Like, besides errands and stuff?"

"Yeah. No. Like, *everywhere.*"

I studied their friendly, probing faces. I said, "Did you guys speak to Lyft at all? I truly want to help but I think I'm bound by confidentiality to—"

"Adam," Nguyen said, "we understand that you want to be a reliable employee, that's great. But with a double homicide and a suspect in custody, the DA can subpoena your ride records—*on-app, off-app,* all of it. We just didn't want to get you in trouble with your company."

I sat up in my seat, surprised to find my back itching from sweat. Despite good manners all around, I had a growing feeling I was getting soft-pedaled somewhere not nice.

I said, "Ya know, weird as it sounds, I mostly took her to hotels. She liked to hang out in hotel lobbies. Or restaurants around Malibu, Zuma. Once in a blue moon we went to her ex-husband's place in Venice. Kronski, I mean, Haywood Kronski."

Bottrell nodded. "We've spoken with Mr. Kronski. Anyone else?"

"Annie was kind of a loner. I can make a list of the two or three bars she went to—very rare. Some restaurants. She went out alone—like, for dinner. She also . . . she liked *staycations.*"

"*Staycations?*" The word made Bottrell squint like a lemon-biter.

Nguyen said, "It means checking into a local hotel for a quick getaway."

"Yeah, like," I said, "sometimes she'd spend a random night at The Surfrider. Also, the Topanga Motel."

"Alone?"

I shrugged. "As far as I know. She said it helped her write."

"I see." The thought of such creative vagrancy seemed to tickle Country Boy Bottrell.

"*But*," I said, a little overeager, "I can't imagine this was for a staycation."

"Why's that?"

"Well, she usually planned those for weeks."

"So—no other ideas?"

I shrugged. Other places, east, deep in Hollywood, I didn't mention, places I'd taken her only a few times, but I didn't want to get into it because I was pretty sure they were places she went to score. "I really want to help but—"

Nguyen cleared her throat. "Can you be sure Ms. Linden didn't employ other drivers?"

"Like I said, I don't know—but she wasn't very trusting. She wouldn't touch the app after our first ride. If she left the house at all, it was usually me that picked her up. She was kind of rigid that way, you might even say ritualistic—"

"Okay." Nguyen smiled but her eyes frowned. I was getting talkative in a way that bugged her—too much spontaneous psychoanalysis. "Was that *rigidity* what made Bix lash out at her?"

"I don't know that he did lash out at her."

The room went cold.

"Oh?" she said. "Are you sure he didn't?"

"I don't know." Queasy now, the ugly fluorescents cast

a death glow. "This has been a really bad time. Confusing. Annie was practically a friend."

Bottrell wasn't buying. "And Troy Banks—was he a friend?"

"No, not exactly. But I liked him."

"Any idea why somebody would want to kill *him*?"

"No. Not at all."

"Why is Bix nicknamed Spider?"

Another shrug—my heart sunk. "'Cause he drove one of those Miatas?"

Bottrell repeated *"Drove one of those Miatas"* like words from a foreign language. They danced a little two-cop eyebrow ballet—now I knew I was being played like a squeaky accordion. I couldn't tell who was good cop or bad cop.

Nguyen to Bottrell: "We may have to pull Adam's ride history, cross-ref with the timeline." And to me: "We'll c.c. you."

"The dispatch has all that," I said. "Could I get a glass of water?"

"*Absolutely.*" Nguyen gave me the forced maternal but didn't budge. "But we only have a few more questions. Now, Adam, you live in a recording studio, located at 8337 Venice Boulevard, and you were living there at the time of Ms. Linden's disappearance, is that correct?"

"Yes."

"But you use a P.O. for your mailing—"

"I stay in the studio. It belongs to my second cousin's husband. Jaime Santiago."

"Oh. Generous second cousin's husband. Lets you squat in the workspace."

"Sort of. I don't *live* there—it's temporary. A place to flop while I save for—"

Nguyen said, "We know how long you've lived there—"

"And don't give a rat's pajamas," Bottrell added.

He meant it to be funny, but an invisible curtain dropped on the Warm and Fuzzy Show once and for all.

Inside a breath, there were no good cops.

Bottrell tapped the table to excuse himself and suddenly I was one-on-one with the Wicked Witch of Malibu.

We had a staring contest. She won.

"Am I under arrest or something?" I said. "I told you *I'm happy to help any way I can.*"

She took me in anew, as if Bottrell's absence freed up the full spectrum of her sadism.

"Let's . . . worry about the arrest thing later and talk about Eva Silber. Our sources say you went to speak with her today. Showed up on her doorstep claiming that you were *close* to the late Ms. Linden."

"Did she complain about me or something? I really only just met her, I—"

"She didn't complain," Nguyen said. "But she is a powerful personage—bigtime political donor. And *our sources* claim you practically barged into her home uninvited."

"No, that's not true. I was just interested in meeting her. Annie might've been planning a visit to see her and—"

"But you just told us you had no idea where Annie Linden intended to go."

"At the time I got the text, I didn't."

"So you decided to just show up and—"

"*I wanted to share the loss.*" High nerves, going goofy.

"Just what is it you're looking for, Adam?"

"Looking for? I'm just—"

"We've got you tracked for thirty-two rides past the Linden estate in ten days."

"Maybe I just miss her?"

Bottrell returned with a cardboard file box and dropped into his lavender chair, which had shrunk into children's furniture under his large frame. His reappearance gear-shifted the mood to even worse—I had been badly mistaken when I read him breezy. Now, he radiated the seething *noblesse oblige* of the Burdened Frontiersman. With Nguyen at least, you knew where you stood: Indochinese testosterone and shit to prove. There was geopolitical turbulence in her snicker as she took the box from Bottrell and drew out some ancient forms from a folder—handwritten. *My* handwriting.

"We pulled your investigator's license, in order to cancel it. But it turns out it's been cold for almost a decade."

"Oh *that*? That was just something I tried, like, a million years ago. My sister's a lawyer, she got me a gig with a guy who sponsored the license. I wanted to help her, I . . . anyway, yeah, that's . . . that thing expired a long time ago."

"So now you're back in action," Bottrell said, "without a license, and you want to play private eye."

"Nobody's *playing* anything. I'm in shock, ya know? I knew Annie, I gave her rides. *More*. She was giving me . . . giving me songwriting lessons in a way."

"Oh," Nguyen said—it was her favorite word. "So you're a musician too?"

"Was. A wannabe. That's not a criminal offense, is it?"

They looked me over with a kind of mutual bemused disbelief. And just how did I appear in their eyes? Without a doubt, I was a scrappy little city mouse of the gig economy. I didn't need to qualify myself as a wannabe because my very existence was wannabe.

Bottrell sucked on his teeth, adjusted his chair.

"Let's put aside your musical aspirations for a second," he said. "Concentrate on the murder of an innocent woman."

"*Yes, let's*," I said, sounding shrill. I ached from the knees up. "I'm just . . . still trying to cope."

Nguyen chucked my ancient investigator's license into the box.

"A seventy-three-year-old woman," she said. "I ask you— what kind of sick maniac does that to a person who is *already* so fragile and so defenseless."

"I really cannot imagine."

"Someone *furious*," she said. "Someone who thinks an old lady owes them something."

I said, "How could anyone possibly think—"

But she wasn't listening. She reached back into the orange file, pulled up a short stack of photocopies. She pushed the stack toward me: Three or four photos to each sheet. The shadowy underbelly of the pier from different angles, slick with foam, garbage strewn in Xerox gray. A mound of wet dirt before the land slopes down to water. The dark pillars, the uneven water line, brush cutting spontaneous miniature streams—it all had the eerie feeling of pre-history or post-history. This was the kind of place they'd film a movie about the world after an atom bomb, starring a dinosaur-sized hissing cockroach coming up out of the sea to chase the last couple on earth, their clothes all torn from the blast. . . .

She flipped open the stack revealing a second photocopy: Annie on the rocks. More than mangled. Almost folded, bloated. Not like the funeral. Wedged into a muddy ditch. From one-two-three angles. Bruised everywhere, but old people bruise easily. She didn't look peaceful. No. A kinetic frustration was made statue by rigor mortis—*annie why?*

"Okay," I said, breathy, dry-mouthed.

"Adam, you see this black line, this tangle around her neck and wrist?"

I nodded.

"That's *cassette tape*. And we are fairly certain it's from a cassette tape owned by Mr. Gelden."

Wide-awake fade-out, face going hot to cold. The tape— *find my tape, silly songs.*

"Okay," I repeated, licking lips. "She was tangled in his cassette?"

They nodded.

"But you can't kill somebody that way," I mumbled.

No response.

"I didn't hear about that."

"No," Bottrell said. "No, you didn't. And what we are curious about is just what you think you're doing meddling in the investigation of a high-profile double-homicide when you don't have the legal right, you don't possess a fraction of the available evidence, and you clearly lack the good sense to keep out of people's way." He pointed at me, all cop now. "If you're not careful, you're gonna get yourself hurt."

There was nowhere to look away—the pictures splayed between us yanked me into seasick recklessness. "When you say *we*, who're you talking about? You two? Eva Silber? Who's so curious about me?"

"We can't share that." Bottrell reached into the box like it was a magician's top hat—out came a slim silver laptop. He handed it to Nguyen.

"*Why am I here?*" This time it came out like a moan.

Bottrell said, "Let's review one more time."

"Again? I still don't understand—*am I under arrest?*"

Bottrell said, "From the beginning."

"The beginning?"

"Annie Linden texts you this, uh, *lyrical text.* You arrive. You're alongside the force until about midnight."

"Right. *Helping them.* I've been through all this like ten times."

"And then you go home."

I sucked air. "And then I go home. Well, not at first. I cruised around awhile, then I went home."

"Cruised around?"

"I drove to Hollywood to do a shift. And *then* I went home."

They looked at me like parents again—but this time, disappointed.

Bottrell said, "Not exactly."

Nguyen cracked the laptop, scrolled for something and turned it to face me: a video, staticky blue-black surveillance cam, some random empty 7-Eleven parking lot. Dated: *5-31 7:06 a.m.* The morning after the night of Annie's disappearance. Even before I saw the Jetta pull up, I knew they had me.

She reached over to click full-screen: Bix in my passenger seat, gesticulating wildly. And there I was, looking concerned, depleted, also not hiding disgust very much.

"Yeah?" I said. "So?" I gave my head a single shake. "It was nothing, I just—he was in a rehab there and—it really wasn't some big deal."

Over the looping clip, Nguyen spoke. "The DA's already prepping a confession for Mr. Gelden. His possessions are on the vic at the murder site, and there's a long history of substance abuse there. *He's charged.* And this little clip shows us that you knew exactly where to find him the night Annie Linden and Troy Banks were killed, when you had *specifically* been asked to inform the PD should you learn of his whereabouts. That, my friend, is called accessory after the fact. Lieutenant Bottrell will read you your rights. And you're going to need a lawyer."

12

TIME IS AN OCEAN BUT IT
ENDS AT THE SHORE

I spent the rest of the day and all of the night in a cell with a babbling loon of a homeless man. Puffy and balding with thin long black hair and a stringy gray beard, he ranted, first in this accent, then in that—lots of "You did" and "No you are" and "So shut up" and "Leave me alone"—from a whisper to a terse admonition to a throaty wail. It was more sounds than words, but the longer it went on, the more it resembled a whole family arguing at a dinner table. Maybe he had a syndrome. In another life, he could have been an actor. Sitting on the hard plastic bench in tatters, his filthy hands on his thick lap, he was a one-man show, a connoisseur of heartbreak and recrimination. But then, mid-argument as it were, a new voice emerged, the mousy whimper of a beaten-down child. And I knew at that moment, the phantoms had left the room. That was the real him.

No sleep—at the break of dawn they gave me my call. My sister Maya came to get me around 7:45. Technically, she was my cousin—when my mother got institutionalized, my uncle adopted me, and Maya never forgave him or me for it. Now Maya was a partner with Schenkel Schreiber, a progressive law firm big on civil liberties, immigrant rights, and worker's comp. Walking me out to the Lost Hills parking lot, she was her usual uptight, perennially bothered self.

I said, "This is completely insane. I just—"

"I don't want to discuss it. And I am *not* going to represent you."

"Maya, you have a right to be mad, but—"

"Mad?" She stopped in her tracks. "I could fucking kill you. You haven't come to visit your niece in six months, I have no idea where you are or what you do—and then this?" But her voice was trembling, more hurt than pissed.

"Maya," I said, "*this* is not my fault. I just got—"

"Adam, you're an accessory after the fact. For a felony."

"How is that even possible?"

"It's possible. It means you assisted, relieved, or sheltered *a felon* after a crime has been committed."

"By giving Bix Gelden a ride to 7-Eleven?"

"It can be anything. It can be emotional support."

"He isn't a *convicted felon* yet."

Maya went edgy, all hard whispers. "Bix Gelden is being held at Wayside without bail for both murders."

"There's no way he did it."

"Adam," she said, "we aren't talking about this. Period. I don't want to hear something I can't unhear."

We trudged back to her military green Subaru in silence. Poor Maya—she got the brains and I got the looks, that was the cruel family joke. But the truth was worse: I was our uncle Herschel's favorite, and we both knew it. Uncle Hersch had been an amateur clarinetist in the big band days, but by the time I came around he worked for the DWP. Consumed with pity over my mom's craziness and later her suicide, he'd pinned his musical hopes on me. And despite my complete losing streak, despite my almost total lack of gratitude, despite even abandoning him the second I came of age, he adored me. On his deathbed, when he could barely speak, Hersch said, "I don't care who your pop was—you are *my* son." Maya, on the other hand, did *everything* right. She got degrees, got the super-*mensch* job helping the needy, got the highly presentable banker husband. She was one of those supermoms too, a blackbelt in social-emotional whatever, sewing up Halloween costumes for happy little Stephanie like the world revolved around her. Maya was the one to be proud of, but despite bending over backward to please Uncle Hersch—her actual father—she simply could not get that coveted First Place Love. My very existence galled her—but she loved me anyway.

Maya clicked the car lock and I rode shotgun. The back contained three file boxes of paperwork, all perfectly labeled and organized. Whereas it took every ounce of energy I had to keep my own vehicle free of used Starbucks cups. Maya got in—she herself looked like someone had reorganized her with unnatural precision. She was pretty in her way despite being a female version of my uncle. She had willed this change of face, softened herself up, but the anger vibing in her jaw made the journey incomplete. She came off imperious, hard to sympathize with, and she knew it. For juries, it had been a problem, but I didn't care—I loved her anyway.

A few blocks after the police station, I said, "C'mon, sis, let's go get some pancakes at Norm's on Pico, like the olden days—my treat."

"Norm's closed like two years ago. And I have to get to work."

We rode in silence on PCH. When she cut east at Venice, I said, "Where we going, cuz?"

"Your car is at Westside Tow on Granville. It'll cost you $275 to drive it off the lot."

"That I can handle," I said.

"I hope you didn't have anything important in the car because sometimes they strip 'em."

"I got nothing worth stealing."

"Yeah. That's too bad, Adam. Because I just had to post five thousand dollars in bail."

"And I will get a loan to pay you back in full. I'll talk to Fry."

"It's not the money, Adam. You seem to forget that I work for the criminal justice system. Half my colleagues will know I bailed you out by lunch today."

"They should applaud your compassion."

"Noooo, they'll be shocked at my poor judgment! You've built up this obsessive fantasy about a woman you barely knew and the rest of the world can go to hell—please! They have *evidence*, Adam. They have footage."

"Yeah, I know—of me giving a friend a ride to 7-Eleven, big deal. They've got nothing. They didn't even mention the angry letters he wrote her."

"He was *harassing* her?"

"Their whole case is made up."

"They have security cam footage of you talking to him *hours* after he murdered your client and that is *all* they need."

"She was more than a client, Maya. I've been her driver for almost three years. She knew all about me, our family, you, Aunt Aviva's cancer, everything."

Maya's eyelids lowered, pressed the wall of silence. She might have been world's greatest mom to Steph, but with me? She was the anti–Mary Poppins, *anything's impossible* was her motto. She gave me that look, familiar from earliest childhood. It was a look that said I had brought this on myself, by being flighty, offensively so. That I didn't understand the gravity of things. I'd seen that look a few times before—like when I borrowed money to make my second demo, or the time I asked for her really hot friend's phone number, or the month I slept on an air mattress in the kid's playroom. Since the deaths of Uncle Herschel and Aunt Aviva, the look had intensified, calcified. Now it carried a second message: *I am not taking over as your mommy.*

"Adam, we are talking about murder in the first degree."

"Look, Maya, I know today's been a huge pain in the ass. But I'm mixed up in this whether I like it or not. I was on the way to pick her up when—"

"Adam, I can get you someone but do not indemnify me with things I shouldn't hear."

"It's nothing like that—but, I was late, she had asked me to look into—"

"I swear you've got a hunger for this drama, *bro*. Get a new line of work. You've got higher education—which cost Uncle Herschel a fortune. Use it."

"I'm a songwriter, let's not get into this."

Her look softened and she turned her face away, pretend-studied the freeway.

"Adam, professional songwriters write and sell songs." Her voice cut to cruel softness. "I haven't heard anything from you in years."

"Maya, she was my friend. Can you hear that? I loved her. I played her my music. And she thought it was good. She believed in me."

She sighed. "Oh, Adam. She could *afford* to believe in you. You're pushing forty. This *bon enfant* act—it's getting a little heavy."

"Pardonnez-moi?"

"Like, for instance, instead of meddling in this fantasy that you were Annie Linden's best buddy, why don't you try being an *actual* uncle to Stephanie?"

"Well, for one, your husband doesn't like me."

"What's to like? You only visit if you need something. You *borrow* money from us every season." She hung a one-handed quote sign on the word *borrow*. "When you do bless us with your holy presence, you treat Marty like he's an un-cultured doofus—and you think he doesn't know how you see his vocation?"

"Vocation? He protects oil companies."

"Yeah. What does your car drive on? Apple juice?" She hit the offramp, checked her watch, and turned right onto a side street. A long fence ended at a dingy office—a prison for autos. "Out, get out of here. I have work to do."

"Maya—"

"Out."

I opened the door but I stayed seated. "Like I said, you got a right to be mad, Maya. Nobody wants to be woken at five-thirty to post bail. But there's one thing you don't understand. You may think of me as family but *I'm not like you*. I'm *not* family. I'm not loyal because life has not been loyal to me. I loved Uncle Hersch and Aunt Aviva and I love you too, but he was not my dad, she was not my mother, and you are *not really* my sister, you couldn't be even if you wanted to be, which I don't think you ever really have. I don't hate you, but *I am not like you*."

"What's that supposed to mean?"

"I didn't have a mother. Not for long. Mine got taken away and Annie Linden—somebody took her away too. So, yeah, I am going to find out who did this if it's the last thing I do. 'Cause I got nothing left to lose."

I got out and closed the door. She did a smooth three-point turn and drove away, out into the city of strangers. I paid up and drove home, slept away the day, washed up at 4:00 p.m., and waited for nightfall. Fighting with Maya always brought back the early days, before her dad adopted me, the hardest days. At seven, eight, nine, my kiddie daydreams were all about doing *something*, one magical thing that might help my mom and change our way of life. But nothing changed anything. We went from Section 8 housing in dingy stucco apartments to living in her orange Datsun, hiding from the police and social services, always moseying along, moseying along, in fake-casual panic. Maybe that's why I was more comfortable in cars than houses—they were my natural home.

At sundown I went back to work. Out on the job at 11:30 p.m., I found myself dangerously close to Annie's place. I rolled down the window, caught the shadow of her perfume on the jacaranda breeze. Cautious, winging it, I parked a block and a half up Pacific Coast Highway. I walked the coast with the ocean wind whipping my coat. An unusual night sky the color of sharkskin gray threatened more rain. How powerful ocean rain is, the harmony of it. The water of sky returning to its source. But it wasn't raining, not yet.

She wanted you to find something, she wanted—

The gravel loop came into view, so different on foot, the mint door, the potted plants, the salmon stucco—it all seemed to cry, "Turn back, idiot!" Without slowing down I spun around to look behind where I'd been walking: Nothing. No cars. Then I turned forward just as a Ford Explorer whizzed past. I entered the property, eyes 360. Moving fast, I knelt, held the ceramic pot, my hand fumbled and it fell, cracked—worry about that later. But the wind-up tin fire-breathing dragon was still there. I lifted him and fingered the silver key, right into my palm. I opened the side gate and angled past overgrown brush.

The back door to the water heater room took my key without protest, but at first the door wouldn't open and I was relieved, the whole idea had been a terrible mistake, there was time to go home and pretend none of this happened. But I pushed a little harder and she gave. That's when my heart started pounding the rhumba.

Have you ever been inside a famous person's house? You feel like you're trespassing even when you've been invited, which I wasn't.

13

SPILL THE WINE TAKE THAT PEARL

The lights were out save for the heater's single red blinker, which lit up a tiny path into the main kitchen. In darkness I punched the code and cut the alarm. I slipped around the corner and into the pitch-black sunken den, fumbled for a light switch. With a tiny tap the room lit up—not up-up, just a dim glow. Empty of people, the space was exactly like I remembered: lonely. I pictured her stretched across the couch with her Martin acoustic and her cigarettes and wine and not quite at work or play. She was alone in a way not everyone knows—monstrously alone. Keyed up as I was, I felt it descend on me. Outside the ocean roared into white sky.

I'd never been to the home office, so I worked random—bedroom to bathroom, guest room to studio, hallways, closets. It was all shellacked, all a page ripped from the Restoration Hardware or the Cisco Brothers catalogue—really rich people's homes are often like that. They go out of their way to conceal the owner's personality. She had a dozen art books stacked on the glass table but even these seemed mostly for show, flanked by the stocked bar of treated pine, original Warhols of her and others, Kienholz, Pollock, the two or three Ed Ruschas and the giant Baldessari.

I slipped through an adjacent sitting room and turned into what had to be it—the home office, Bix's workstation. Six black file cabinets, oak desk and aging Apple, empty wooden In and Out trays, all squeaky clean before the CinemaScope ocean view. You could go crazy trying to type emails in front of a view like that. On my knees, I scrambled through the files, flipping A to Z, but I sensed what was coming: Nothing. Not under B for Bix or PA or Office. The G section was too loose. *GASSET LECTURE, GATEFOLD, GEAR: BUDGET, GEAR: F.O.H., GEAR: STAGE MAP, GIG CALENDAR, GOOD BAD REVIEWS, GRAHAM, BILL, GUEST LIST, GUITAR SPONSORSHIPS, GRAMMY NOM.* No Gelden in sight.

I was late to the party.

I closed the cabinets, stood, and backed off, out the office and down the hall, and turned into a decent-sized screening room I hadn't remembered or was never invited to. She could have had a popcorn party for two dozen on these big cozy white loveseats, all stacked up a slope of wide stairs. But what movies? Annie loved *The Sandpiper* with Elizabeth Taylor and made me watch it with her on TCM in the beach house once. There were not two dozen people in the modern world who would sit through *The Sandpiper*. Other side of the screening room was yet another sitting room, this one with a fireplace, surrounded by plants that needed little or no water but had still withered. This gave me a chill because it meant practically no one had been in this room all these years. She was hiding elsewhere, biding her time. Her true space was inner space, where the melodies lived. Doubly depressing because it meant I was probably going to find nothing here. Each time I left a room I popped off the dim light. This time I didn't want to leave. I sat down in the dimness almost paralyzed. A bowl of potpourri stared back at me, scentless, and for a cringing second I knew what was at stake: the jukebox id spit out "Ruby Tuesday": *Lose your dreams and you will lose your mind.* The jukebox id was not an instrument that mollycoddled. It simply never failed.

I could hear the ocean now. My heartbeat thudded down to its usual state of dysregulated anxiety. I was not in the clear. For all I knew I was on camera despite what Bix said. But I had tried and this alone almost relaxed me. I would have to go soon. I wanted just a few moments of her presence. Corny as it sounds, I prayed for Annie's soul right then and there, for all souls, for the soul of my dead mother. It was hard to think of her without pain, my mom, but you had to at least pretend to come to terms in the face of death. I was in a mausoleum of wealth, cleanliness, and perfect furniture—death never had such a pretty face nor seemed so real.

Then a sound, a door clicked. Voices. A frustrated low male grunt.

An electric shock bristled through my body. I jumped up and cut the lights, froze in front of the Hockney, looked both ways in the pitch dark. Somewhere else a light went on, the sunken den. I groped for the hall, felt a doorknob and placed myself in a closet, caught the scent of mops, Pine-Sol—the cleaning lady's closet. My pulse was pounding.

More voices, a young man's guffaw. Kronski. And—a dude . . . *someone.*

"Aw fuck," Kronski said, "where's the light?"

"This place is fuckin' *huge!*"

"Don't I know it. They're gonna have to unload this crib and it's gonna be a major pain in the ass."

"I'm just like totally in awe."

"Yeah, 'cause it's *awesome*. Hey, don't touch that, don't touch nothin', it ain't mine—*yet*."

"You mean you're getting this place?"

"California law, baby."

"I thought you two were divorced."

"Nope."

My face went hot with rage. Kronski could take it all, her properties, her royalties, every last song.

"Me and the old hag didn't want to do all that paperwork shit for divorce. We just kind of, whatever. Go fetch that bottle of Kirschwasser."

"*Nice* bar."

"I *designed* that bar, man, I set this whole place up. Annie wasn't really into house and home. She had properties everywhere, man, and couldn't give a shit. Don't get me started about my old lady's South Bay real estate shenanigans."

Glasses clinked, booze was poured.

"Wait, I got one for ya." Kronski was winding up for a gag. *"How do you give a woman an orgasm?"*

"I dunno, how?"

"Who gives a shit?"

The young fool howled with cloying laughter. When he settled down, he said, "Man, I could live it up in a pad like this."

"Me too, and I *will*." Kronski let out a nefarious cackle, the kind bad guys did in old-time stage melodramas when they twirled their moustaches. "That's why I had to kill the bitch!"

They laughed again together big-time, but there was something in the yuks that telegraphed unseriousness. Kronski was joking, he had to be, the sick fuck.

"C'mon, let's find that shit," Kronski said, and then they moved to a far room and I could barely hear them, despite straining my ear against the door. All I got was the sound of puttering, tinkering, drawers opening and closing, then quiet.

Now I was stuck. I remembered my phone, put it on silent and let its light flash the closet. Nothing of note: a bucket, a red Dyson vacuum cleaner, one of those new detachable dusters. Some shelves. A drill and its bits. Screwdrivers. Hooks for wall-hanging. An old flip clock wrapped in its own cord. A Topanga, CA, coffee cup with assorted blue Bics. A ramekin half-filled with guitar picks and coins, some foreign. Those mothball discs on plastic hangers, still in shrink-wrap. And a combination padlock—I grabbed it, hyper-focused, trying to keep my breathing quiet in the glowing dark. The numbered knob had a Public Storage sticker, the other side had masking tape with a Sharpie scrawl—*AML Personal.*

Suddenly, Kronski howled from far-off with delight. "Voi-*la*!

The young man said, "That's why we came here? For a crate of old records?"

I rolled my eyes.

"These are *my* LPs," Kronski said. "Now let's get the fuck out of here."

The lights went out in the living room, the front door opened and closed, but I waited. And waited. After maybe a half-hour of dead silence, I busted a move.

I was halfway down the walkway, having locked myself out of the house with all its lights turned off and the key returned to its chipped pot under the little tin dragon, when I flashed on that padlock from the closet. A minute later, a few footsteps from my car—unarrested, uncaught by Kronski and his goon, walking PCH at three o'clock in the morning, a lunatic getting into his Jetta and heading back on the road under a light drizzle—I flashed on the padlock again, I couldn't shake it.

Driving home, I felt the throb of a new song coming on.

I got an extra lock
I keep it in the closet
Oh yeah, oh yeah

No, no, no. More upbeat, more like—sung to the tune of "Hot Line" by the Sylvers . . .

Padlock, padlock
Found myself a padlock
For your love for your love

Got myself some sweet inspiration
Now all I need's the right combination
The right destination with a

Padlock, padlock
Found myself a padlock—

I was still singing it out loud when I pulled up to my pad, still singing it up the stairs, practically ecstatic to find half a bottle of Trader Joe's cheapo Seraphin in the fridge when I got home. It didn't take too darn much to please a guy like me. My nerves had fried like bad sound cable, emitting white noise. I wasn't much of a driver, or a songwriter, but apparently I wasn't the world's worst detective. Because I myself had once had an extra Public Storage padlock—what happens is you lose the key to the original lock you brought and you have to pay to cut it, a royal pain. Then they sell you a new *pair* on the spot—since, hey, this guy'll probably lose his key again. Which you won't. Which means you're stuck with an extra lock for all time. Point being—Annie Linden had a secret storage space. And it was Personal.

14

THE WINDS OF
MARCH THAT MAKE MY
HEART A DANCER

Annie Linden never rented a Public Storage space in her own name, and her former business manager Lindsey Gatz had no record of one. Bix didn't remember one either and I certainly wasn't going to bug Kronski about it. Probably it was the handiwork of one of Annie's other personal assistants. She ran through them two or three a year, hired and fired without a moment's notice. California Fan Club prez Meghan McMahon would remember, since she always had to get the current PA to sign off on the chatty little Annie column she wrote for *Gatefold*, a Linden fanzine read almost exclusively by guys in sweaty underwear.

We exchanged emails and after a little prodding, Meghan remembered meeting me—the driver, way down the totem pole of hangers-on. Meghan lived in Ojai. If I could make the trip, she *might* be able to put together a list of names, *if* she thought about it hard enough. There had been so many PAs, so many drivers. Such is the nature of obsessional devotion—she was extremely reluctant to part with insider info, even if it was useless to her. I called her bluff and set the date.

Ojai is about an hour north of Malibu, a quick dash up the coast, then a swift right inland into an enclave of domineering redwoods. The little town is famous for its "pink moment"— a burst of cotton-candy-orange-blue sky at twilight. It's also known for moneyed hippies, redneck farmers, Gold Standard golfers on vacation, and equestrian freaks. I wondered if Meghan McMahon was any or all of the above.

The address was off the main drag, down the first dirt road, a large wood-fenced Victorian with a fresh coat of amber paint, surrounded by a sprawl of muddy, unused acreage. Meghan came off the porch to greet me in a long, Amish-style button-up flower-print dress and cardigan, chickens pecking around her moccasins, but I could tell in a glance she wasn't really rural. Around her pretty eyes was the strain not of farm work but of American wealth.

"Annie mentioned you," she said. "She liked you, so I'm figuring you're not a total con artist."

"I'm just trying to tie up a few loose ends for the estate," I lied.

"Well, I can't just hand over Annie's private information."

"Understood," I said. "But a long time ago, Annie told me she had a personal storage space—I thought I might find it, if I can figure out whoever signed for it."

"And what do you plan to do with the contents if you find it?"

"Send it to her archives? Or maybe I can turn it over to you to decide what to do with it."

She smiled, but I sensed skepticism. Up close her mouth was sensual, bold. Curly auburn hair fell around her long neck and on her chest was a black oval brooch, maybe an opal, set in a silver sunburst, a witchy amulet resting on her heart. She was living out a fantasy about country life. The dress, the shoes, even the house all served to make her look like a grown-up Holly Hobby or maybe Laura Ingalls. You could see where Annie had caught her imagination too. Annie offered modern women a return to the rustic, the mystic superstitious primordial power of female, pre-Hollywood, pre–Barbie Doll. Meghan was a few years older than me and I reckoned somewhere back there was a fake cowboy husband, too, a grizzly lawyer in expensive snakeskin boots who barely tolerated her little Annie obsession. Probably they met in Brentwood but settled in Ojai, last depot of Ye Olde West.

I said, "I'm grateful you took the time."

"You are lucky," she said. "I'm like the last remaining true Linden expert—and this month has *not* been easy. Have a seat. I'll bring us some lemonade. You want a kicker?"

"By all means." She sat me on a little ice cream chair at a round glass table on the side porch, overlooking the dirt fields inside her fence. A lazy dog ignored the chickens. It was all too perfect, a life-sized diorama based on a painting by Jasper Francis Cropsey.

Getting her to cough up the data was gonna take skills.

She came back with the drinks and I smiled. I said, "Annie said you knew more about her career than she herself did. That's a big reason why I wanted to meet you. It's a pleasure to talk to someone who really knew her and understood her."

Meghan sighed. I thought she might dab a tear. "Nobody really knew Annie and nobody will ever understand her because she was not a normal human being like you and me. She really *was* supernatural."

"How do you mean?"

"I *mean* she had the powers of a real priestess-witch. I wrote about that in my column—one of the last ones before she left us. And I'm pretty certain she read those columns. She took a certain interest in deeper interpretation."

"She did have a special energy," I said. "I mean, she was still touring in the late eighties when half her audience had fizzled out."

This made her scowl. "Annie Linden was not meant for *quotidian* life. Do you know what that means?"

"Not sure I do."

"*Day to day.* It didn't suit her. It was beneath her."

"But was she lonely? Did she have—"

"She was *so* lonely. She had *so* few people she trusted. Almost none—I was really one of the very few. And she confided in me, but it was stuff of a deeply confidential nature. Girl stuff. I'd love to share with you, but I can't." The strong drink was softening her up. Her eyes lit like they had extra battery power—they begged to be begged. There was something nutball about this woman. I couldn't quite put a finger on what. She was like someone who, having convinced themselves that unicorns exist, wants to put a hex on all doubters. She was high on the lie—which lie I wasn't sure.

"I understand you can't talk to me about the really deep stuff. It wouldn't be right. But . . . how did Annie, you know, how did she find help?"

"Help?"

"Like the assistants, you know, they came and went so fast. I mean, I just drove her, but even I got to see a few come and go."

"She must have fired one every season! Because they were all *total losers*. Look at Bix. That sick, sick man. I am usually a complete pacifist, but I'm sorry—that prick needs to hang."

"I don't really know him." My second lie. "I mean, I barely met him."

"That's strange. But don't you see, she kept everyone separate. She couldn't trust any of them, not just Bix."

"I guess she must have really trusted you."

Meghan pushed a short, exasperated breath through her open mouth, as if I just could never and would never grasp the complexity of it all. But I could also tell she kinda liked me. Talking Annie was her fave pastime after all. I poured the pitcher. After more lemonade from Hades, she stood and patted down her dress. "C'mon, you drove a ways. I think you've earned the right to see the shrine."

"The shrine?"

"Follow me."

The Victorian exterior was a front. Inside the living room, the Information Age clashed with the Gilded Age: deluxe PlayStation thumb sticks hooked to a giant widescreen in an antique armoire, a seven-hundred-dollar treadmill hid behind a carved ivory partition, and a bear skin rug was despoiled by a pile of Nordstrom bags and Johnny Was and Sundance catalogues. The bear looked startled by his feminine burden. Down a creaky, polished hall, she led me to the holy place—erected in the same room as her husband's pool table, another bizarre mismatch. But everywhere you looked was Annie: gold and platinum LPs, CDs, and 45s, Annie autographed snaps, original Annie watercolors, even a giant Chinese Annie fan splayed on the ceiling over the pool cue rack. There also stood a life-sized cardboard cutout of Annie from the *Capistrano* album, leaning on a closet door, and it jarred me to see her standing tall, young, and beautiful in two dimensions.

"Wow. What does your husband think of all this?"

"Oh, he can't stand her music. But he says she's okay to look at."

"So you listen on headphones?"

"At this point? I don't even need her music. I can hear her voice when I close my eyes."

There were picture discs and several old magazine covers over the bar and one framed cocktail napkin from BB King's Santa Barbara with a smudged marker signature that said TO MEGAN, ANNIE L. with a little four-leaf clover drawn by the signature. Not exactly intimacy but beggars can't be choosers. To my surprise, Meghan took my hand, her cheeks blossom red, her eyes wild with the hunger for exchange. She led me to the leather couch. She was ready to confess.

"You know, when I finally met Annie in person, I was so blown away that she even talked to me that I did . . . I did a foolish thing."

"Oh yeah?"

"I kind of went off my rocker and wrote her this very, very long letter. I mean, I told her *everything*. All about how I grew up in Phoenix with this total rageaholic alcoholic single mom who was basically—not a whore but she kind of *was*, you know? Very loose. Anyway, I like, poured my heart out to Annie in this crazy, crazy letter. Oh God, it was awful. All about how my mom would come home drunk and wasted and I'd dress up and perform Annie's greatest hits for her. Like I'd mime all the songs, with the phonograph player we got at Sears."

This was my in.

"Oh, come on now. You opened up to Annie out of . . . *true connection*. That doesn't sound so foolish to me."

"No, it was." She waved a teacherly finger at her former self. "Very foolish. My letter just went on and on. I mean, I told her about my abortion. Abortions. About how I understood her soul. How I had these physical feelings for her. Typical fan stuff but after that . . . " Meghan shook her head. "She backed off."

"I saw her cold moods, too," I said. "Here and there. She could be like that."

"Oh, this was worse than a mood. One of the zillion handlers actually gave me the brush. A guy named Ellis, little skinny black guy. He answers the phone and he goes, *I'm soooo sorry, Annie has told us to let you know that . . . she thinks you're great. Buuuuuut she thinks it would be better for you to focus on . . . other things right now.*' I mean—I'm her fan club president—how am I supposed to focus on other things?"

I laughed at her imitation of a gay fashionista, and her resilience. "Annie needed you, and she loved your column. She told me herself. That's one of the reasons I wanted to meet you."

"Really?"

I nodded, reinforced the lie, and she blushed deeper. Once again, she had exposed too much and vibed hunger for reassurance. On every wall, Annie stared us down. Through the lace-curtained window, Ojai was also blushing, having its pink moment—across the basin, fast and furious. Meghan pulled her cardigan tighter but also moved closer, bringing body heat. Our faces were close, expressions searching.

"It's so nice to meet a *man* who gets all this," she whispered. And then: "My husband will be home soon." It was a gentle request to leave. I nodded and got up, and we walked outside together, down the dirty path to the gate. The dog was out wandering, the chickens preoccupied. Under the last of the pink sky, Meghan's bony shoulders caught the light and I had an odd desire to hold her—to protect her from her own muted hysteria. Or maybe from mine.

Meghan smiled. "Will I see you at the Linden Hop?"

"The what?"

"It's a tribute—at the Glendale Civic. July nineteenth."

"Is it a concert?"

"Oh, it's more than that. It's a convention. Memorabilia, lectures, a museum display. It's a big deal. I'm on the board."

"I'll be there."

"I'm glad," she said. "Then I'll see you again."

The lines around her eyes were working overtime to keep some dream alive but it was a losing battle.

"You know," she said, "I still can't accept that Annie Linden is gone. I mean, I just really can't stomach it. And I'm not sure I'll ever be able to." Her eyes searched mine for comfort—I had no idea whether or not she found any. "She was kind of . . . the mother I always secretly wanted."

"Meghan, I do know what you mean. But we have to carry on."

As I gave her a polite hug goodbye, she kissed my cheek, reached into her sweater pocket and handed me a folded-up piece of paper. "It's all there," she said. "Dates and names."

I drove down Ojai's main drag, heading back to the city, stuck with a spooky, bristling sensation—like I'd just met myself in female form. I had to shake it off. At a red light, I unfolded the paper and held it over the steering wheel: A printed-out Excel spreadsheet. Thirty-two assistants since 1994—seven of them Bix. I was going to find that locker, bust it open, and uncover every last personal item in it, do or die. Annie's secrets were beckoning.

15

I WONDER WONDER WHO
BA-DOO WHO—

There are seventy-two Public Storage facilities in Southern California. That meant seventy-two phone calls, but I had a feeling she wouldn't go Valley or mid-city, and on lucky call number thirteen, I hit it: Public Storage San Fernando Boulevard. Former PA Abby Bledsoe had opened up a twenty-by-ten there during her twelve-week tenure as Annie's assistant in the spring of '89. San Fernando Boulevard—at the far east border of Burbank, no man's land. You couldn't get much farther from Malibu.

The gated facility required an entry code but just about anybody could slip in behind the trucks that are in and out of there every fifteen minutes. I parked down the street—it was getting to be a habit—and walked in behind a breadbox SUV like I was part of the caravan.

Once inside the gate, the building rose like a jail, one big slab of gray brick. I was headed for locker C22 on the third floor. I followed yellow stencil–painted signs to a service elevator. Just before the elevator closed, a wizened, hunched-over old man with long, stringy white hair and thick beard stepped in carrying two 99 Cent Store bags. His stale, untucked button-down and torn jeans were stained, his sneakers ripped, and he smelled of something awful—caked vomit meets burnt sewage. He was tiny, pushing ninety, bones strained by the groceries. I offered a hand and he gave me a wide near-toothless smile, shook his head. Only after the elevator opened and we went our separate ways, only after I took my first full breath did it occur to me that this man lived here. In a storage space. Not a storage space like mine, at least mine had windows. I looked up—the high ceilings were ventilated and a track of fluorescents kept the place lit, but this was no place for a human. What did he sleep on, how did he stay warm? And how many others like him—like us—were there in this labyrinth of the undead?

I watched him hobble down the long hall. He stopped and fished a key out of his shirt, tied around his neck by black shoelace. He opened the padlock like it was the door to any old regular apartment and went inside.

I turned away and walked on, past rows and rows of identical industrial doors, until I got to C22. I slipped off my backpack, zipped it open, and pulled out a hammer. I looked both ways down the endless hall: nobody. This time I was really *breaking* and entering. I eyeballed the lock to make the necessary hits short and sweet and started slamming, but of course it took more whacks than I'd hoped. I paused and started up again, with increased rage. The sound was brutal in this echo chamber. Somewhere an old geezer was trying to eat his ninety-nine-cent lunch. One last *thwack* and the lock popped. I inhaled and pulled open the door. Rat traps—little bags of poison feed—sat in the dark corners of the room like Dodger game peanut treats. The rest was boxes. I'm not sure what

I was expecting—exercise equipment? beanbags?—but the whole damn room was tall leaning towers of identical cardboard boxes. Only one way to find out what was in them—open every last one.

I took out my car key and slashed one open and found books—psych, anthro, hardcover, paperback. I was part-relieved—at least I knew now this was Annie's storage space for sure. I slashed another box: more books—biography, autobiography, memoir, fiction. Another box: more books. And another: books. I stepped back, already sweating, and guesstimated—maybe two hundred boxes. Four open, 196 to go.

Cardboard ripped with dread and confusion. What were all these books doing here? She had the space at home. What was this fortress built to obscure? I opened another box: Books and books and books. Old classics with the running man on the spine. Hundreds of little poetry chapbooks with random press names like New Athenaeum and Evanescence. One slim volume of poetry was called *Quotidian Queen*. There was a lot of psych in there too: Jung on Guilt, and Skinner on Separation, and Klein on Motherhood, and a whole boxed set of Freud letters with the spines peeling off. Old glue, sticky ideas. I had no idea Annie was so invested in that stuff but it wasn't exactly a surprise. Alfred Adler, Fritz Perls, R. D. Laing, names I maybe heard somewhere but maybe not. Finally, at the bottom of box number 73, a book that wasn't psych: the *Columbia Concise History of the World*, a single, big fat volume. That cracked me up.

For more than two hours, I tore open those babies and flipped through like a nut. Had she really read them all? Cover to cover? Was this behemoth the secret behind her lyrics? There were 175, 180 boxes, forty or fifty books a pop. In theory, you could read them all and still not be Annie Linden, still not bring the magic. But you had to marvel at a world, a time, a person who would gobble these up just . . . for the fuck of it. *Damn, woman*, I whispered to no one, *you sure did get your read on.*

Deep sweat had seeped into my shirt, all around my hair and neck. *Like a moron*, I had not brought water and had not eaten lunch, but I pressed on, past box number one hundred. The books—a lot of them, maybe most of them, were *serious*. No airport paperbacks here, no junk. This woman wanted to figure out life in the worst way.

As the day waned, about 70 percent of the boxes had been sliced, forming a staggered pyramid. I sat on a box and closed my eyes for a break. Conceivably, I could live here with the books—like the *Twilight Zone* episode. I'd need a few good rat traps. But the loneliness would be febrile, hallucinatory. Or maybe I'd befriend the old man.

I kept going, flipped titles—they formed a poem of their own. *The Lotus and the Robot. Must You Conform? Welcome, Stranger! The Lonely Crowd.* Then I came upon a lone tied-off shoebox, a hider. My pulse skipped. It was lodged between two of the largies, and it had been strangled shut with thin rope in tight knots, which had congealed over time into little bumps. I couldn't pull it open. I had no scissors. I got out nail clippers and snapped it. Inside were handwritten notebooks, some letters, and a rolled-up Xerox of a signed contract of some kind. I'd seen her handwriting and it could have been hers, I wasn't sure. I stuffed the whole shoebox into my backpack. There were still dozens of boxes to go.

About forty minutes and four hundred books later, I cracked open one other unusual box. Inside: just a Safeway Supermarket bag. And in the bag were a dozen or so porno mags, called *Hers & His*, all dated between '77 and '81. Pre-Kronski, just. Not mags exactly, not the usual glossy stuff, this was eighty-by-ten, two-tone, stapled newsprint: mostly classifieds, super cheapo, fifty cents. It was the kind of rag you'd see in a newspaper dispenser on Hollywood Boulevard a million years ago. I grabbed the issue on top—the stark nude black-and-white cover model had a cartoon talk bubble in blue ink that said *Eat My Saucy Furrito*. I cracked a smile: What the hell was Annie doing with these? I flipped random—*Reader's Tales of Adventure* and "Super 8s for Sale," Massage Parlor ads and a non-fold-out two-tone centerfold squeezing her large breasts with the Germanic Letraset caption *ANY TIME AT ALL IS THE TIME FOR MILK*. More classifieds, more nudies, more stories: *AUNT AGNES FROM IDAHO*. B&W amateur shots, bizarro suck-fest collages, *Taboo Confessions*. Still more classifieds: "My name is Colonel Thompson and I'll spank your ass raw." More ads: The World's First Auto-Suck Vagina—"Plugs into your car lighter!" And more Super 8s, $3.99 / 3 for $10: "Watch me shoot the goo!" And, of course, the mandatory *Life-Sized Inflatable Doll!*—but the photo looked like a real blonde in miniskirt and boots. "Made of soft, smooth, pliable vinyl, Judy looks and feels amazing—just add air and instantly you have a life-sized beauty. GUARANTEE: This is the ULTRA deluxe model. There is no other doll as Life-Like. With a human softness that will amaze you and your friends. $9.95 + .95 postage or $16.95 + .95 postage for Complete Package including bikini, pajamas, and wig."

In the middle of all these books . . . *this*. I flipped back to the masthead.

HERS & HIS, BIG BUCKZ ENTERPRISES
806 East Fourth Place, Los Angeles, CA 90013
Editor: Evita Alvarez.

Evita? Feminista Eva? This? Holy. Fuck. I stared at the dank room, the stacks of opened boxes with their books restuffed haphazard. I felt like the butt of a practical joke. Everywhere around me, the heavy volumes, the consciousness of humankind reaching for its apogee—and then . . . *this*?

I went back to slashing, determined to go complete. By late afternoon, I had popped them all open and Annie's secret storage space looked like a cyclone had hit it. It took a whole extra forty-five minutes just to put it back together. I shoved the towers back into place, grunt by grunt. I did not come across a long-lost magic cassette or another shoebox of private journals or another bag of porno or a signed confession of murder. Last minute, I threw some random paperbacks into my backpack: R. D. Laing's *The Divided Self* and a book called *The Company She Keeps* by McCarthy somebody. Why, I'm not sure—the covers grabbed me. Also maybe just to prove to myself that I'd actually been here, it was real, there was a Public Storage where old books and old men hid. Last minute, I pulled the Safeway bag too—that was coming with me. I backed out drenched in sweat and squeezed the door shut, let the broken lock hang, busted. Anyone could come in now and get themselves quite an education. Not that anybody would.

16

WHEN I'M ALONE
AT NIGHT WATCHING
THOSE RERUNS OF
DRAGNET

Back in my own storage pad, I sat up in bed reading every last page of every notebook, rapt, but really it was a lot of hooey, drafts and scribbles. Half-assed attempts at verses and choruses, not one of which I recognized. Maybe that's why it had been pulled from her larger collection of drafts and diaries, already catalogued and bequeathed to UC Berkeley on her seventieth. The notebooks were also undated, which drove me nuts, but I was sure this was the work of a younger artist, Annie noodling, groping for a voice. Her handwriting, her nervous scrawl, hadn't changed in half a century.

It's all gonna end in tears
the way this dream is built
you gotta see through me now

you gotta see through my vow
and it's all gonna end in tears
end in tears

The lyrics were confessional yet opaque in a way Annie Linden would learn not to be. They were personal all right, but somehow not *weird* enough to get the job done. She had yet to grab for the sparks of strange specificity. Also her "talking style" wasn't there yet, her naturalism. In blue ink, you could see the struggle to throw off the shackles of songwriterliness.

Apparently, she'd have to read ten thousand books to figure it out.

I'm calling out to you
like oceans to the rain
'cause you hold me,
you hold me
to the pain
of what is true—I'm calling out to you

Okay, the last line was cringey in the extreme. But that was the game—fake it till you make it. Reading by midnight bedside lamp, I heard her whisper, *"Keep pretending, reaching—don't ever stop"* and I got a chill. I flipped through the pages again and again, but it was like trying to divine the universe from a small, old, dry leaf.

Then I started reading one of the paperbacks I had stolen, *The Company She Keeps,* and about six pages in, a little photobooth strip slipped out, a long-forgotten bookmark. And there, like a jack-in-the-box of love, was her young, sweet, laughing face, next to a guy, a black guy with a conk. Teenagers. Rock 'n' rollers. She with the flat-ironed blonde hair. Him greased back, a jet black do, and, in his African

American way, trying to pull off a James Dean juvenile delinquent look. Three shots: First one all smiles. Then, one fake serious—teenyboppers putting on grownup grim airs like those early Rolling Stones album covers. And then the grand finale so typical of photobooth strips: tongues out, eyeballs rolling in goof-out ecstasy. I stopped reading the book and stared at these very alive photos for a long time. Who was he? The first boyfriend in her bio was a varsity letterman type, not a black guy in Brilliantine. I must've stared at that strip for more than an hour before getting ready for bed. I taped the picture onto my bathroom mirror, revisited it while brushing my teeth. It poked at me like a story, but not a story you could pin down. What was cool was how they both just knew to do the same face in each pic—they were sync'd up like the really close. I even envied the guy, because she was telegraphing a very relaxed, very center-of-the-heart kind of love in the pics. And the Annie I knew, if I knew her at all, had not felt that for a long time by the time I got to her, had not smiled unencumbered like that for maybe decades. Could this be what—or who—she wanted me to find?

The dirty newspapers quote-unquote were something else altogether. Time had rendered them more curious than sexy— all those posed collages and erotic tall tales and Super 8 ads. They were throwaway—so why on earth had Annie Linden *not* thrown them away?

On closer inspection, page after page revealed that this was less a moneymaking operation like the *Playboy/Hustler/Penthouse* stuff of its time, more of a tool of the Sexual Revolution. The "models" were not attractive in the usual wanton way. They were amateurs. Ungraceful. Barely posing. Often, their eyes were concealed by a single black bar. Also, no nudie shots of Annie, Eva/Evita, or any other known as-

sociates. I was mostly relieved about that. But the classifieds
went on and on. Call girls, orgies, wife swaps, the works. Each
entry was a crazy portal into the secret life of a lonely city, its
wretched huddled masses yearning to get off.

We are an adventurous couple seeking other adventurous couples for relaxed and stimulating exploration. Call
us—The Kirschbaums.

I am a 5'9" busty Latino she-male named Dolores and
I am providing for you the Total Love Experience.'

Rendezvous at the A-Frame, City of San Pedro. All
swingers welcome. NO rough stuff.

You sleep with my gorgeous ladyfriend. I observe and
take Polaroids for private use only. Sound like a bargain?

To place an ad, you apparently had to call it in. That alone was
funny. I imagined the typesetter pounding out these haikus
with the phone tucked under her ear, dictation-style. And each
ad ended in a phone number—213, 714, 818—all landlines,
natch.

Technically, these were "some old newspapers, some classifieds." But was this paydirt? I read and read, read until my
eyes fritzed. But I didn't see what any of this had to do with
Annie Linden. The opposite. Annie was world famous in these
years, '79–'81, and these were people in hiding, the obscure.
Plus, if she wanted sneaky kinky stuff, she didn't need to go
through a fifty-cent newspaper. And what was a paid aca-
demic like Eva doing on the masthead?

I kept reading, issue after issue, classified after classified,
garish, shy, cocky, guilty, intrepid. I don't know how many

I had scoured when I first noticed that I had seen the name Dr. Milt or Dr. Milton addressed at least three, maybe four times. One persistent customer. Always a specific time and place to meet but each time signed with a different name. I flipped back, reviewed, caught the pattern, broke into a cold sweat.

> Dr. Milt waiting for you Sat. Feb. 18 May Co South Bay Center 11 a.m. Bringing surprise XOX AM Madrone.
> Eager to see both of you Dr. Milton Sat. March 6 Eucalyptus Park, truly—AM Sequoia
> Dr. Milt of Redondo Connect please call the Editors re meeting/ha urgent, AM Willow.

Something about the street names bugged me. I took the AM for morning, then checked street names: *Wrong.* Sequoia was the tip-off. I googled Sequoia Blvd, Lane, Avenue, Street—no such place in Southern California. *AM Madrone, AM Elm, AM Sequoia, Willow, Oak, Aspen* . . . every tree but Linden as in Anne Marie. I got up, paced the room, stifled an animal scream, sat down, shaky hands on the laptop keyboard.

A surprising number of Dr. Miltons in SoCal—first and last name, four alone in the South Bay—Miltons Smith, Sampler, Weisner, and Sandra Milton, all living, all too young to see action in '79, the very tail of the comet known as the Sexual Revolution.

Then an obit, from year before last: "Dr. Milton Goldfischer, beloved husband, father, and grandfather, known affectionately to his friends, colleagues, and patients as Dr. Milt, died this Thursday, November 22, at the age of 89."

I went trance-heavy, pressed my temples. Hello, late Dr. Milt, urologist, Hermosa Beach, California. Who the fuck are you—and what're you doing meeting Annie Linden in secret, 1979, '80, '81?

Frantic surfing coughed up damn little. Dr. Milton Goldfischer belonged to that generation whose identity existed above, outside of, or beyond the internet. But cross-hatching the obits, Truthfinder, Healthgrades, and a few old online newspaper articles, I gleaned what there was to glean. I wasn't sure yet why it mattered, or if it mattered, but the internet is like that: it's the ultimate auto-suck.

He was a grad of Brooklyn College and NYU, had done a stint as acting director of urology for St. Vincent's before heading west, where he opened his own clinic in the South Bay. Married to Nannette Goldfischer, PhD, house still in her name. Three children, Thomas, Patricia, Ron, and *they* were of the age of digital disclosure: Thomas was a Jacuzzi dealer with a showroom on Hermosa Ave. Ron lived in Idyllwild and had a website for his services as some kind of a yoga instructor. Patricia was an employee at Fox Casting, a mother of three with a lot of Facebook posts about being a devout Catholic. Nowhere did I see any pictures of Pops. Nothing about Dad's hobbies or interests. And nothing about his predilection for writing classifieds to a rockstar in a fifty-cent porno paper.

If, in fact, this was *the* Dr. Milt.

But an old PDF of a half-column in the back of the South Bay's *Daily Breeze*, which had been miraculously preserved online, did cough this up: Dr. Milton Goldfischer and his clinic had made a name in the wonderful world of prostate surgery for helping to perfect a device called an internal penile pump, an implant to help correct erectile dysfunction. This curious operation was apparently the hot ticket in the very years Dr. Milt was setting up secret meetings with

Annie the Tree Lady. I read the article, doing my best to hold back the wince.

> The three-piece implants Dr. Goldfischer has designed consist of a fluid-filled reservoir in the abdomen, a pump with a release valve in the scrotum, and two inflatable cylinders in the penis. Patients simply squeeze the pump, transferring fluid from the reservoir into the cylinders, causing an instant erection.

Pre-Viagra—a major commitment. Sounded like the inside of a souped-up Camaro. Which maybe was the point. But did the desperados need to find him through some secret channel, bounced by Annie via Eva "Evita"? And why? And how could any of that have anything to do with a dead woman found under the boardwalk almost half a century later? Blow-up dolls and blow-up dongs—I was out of my league.

I called Eva for answers but her wife picked up the line and immediately got terse. "She doesn't want to talk to you." Defeated, I tossed the mags back in their Safeway paper bag, rolled up the top and slipped it under the bed, the whole screeching horny almost-liberated triple-X black-and-white newsprint underworld still moaning in my ear.

Sleep evaded. There were still two days until the Linden Hop, the Annie convention in Glendale, and I was restless as hell. Up before dawn, I threw on some khakis, my one dress shirt of blue gingham cotton under a charcoal sweater, and the corduroy sportscoat I nicked from Uncle Herschel. The Professor Look—minus the wisdom. But I didn't want to look like a hobo. I was headed for the home of Nan Goldfischer, PhD, widow of the late Dr. Milton, to see what I could see. Pulling out of Starbucks on the way, I felt the shrapnel of a song swirling around me like space junk, one of those psyche-delic Halloweeny folk rock jams, Rickenbacker twelve-string with the reverb on ten.

Doctor Goldfischer
What's your plan?
Doctor Goldfischer
Where you headed, man?

You're talking with the Lady of the Trees
Whispering secrets on the breeze
All I wanna know pretty pretty please is—

Not exactly Top 40 material—what do you want for 6:15 a.m.?

17

I CRAWL LIKE A VIPER THROUGH THESE SUBURBAN STREETS

The Goldfischer home, just over the Hermosa foothills, was an art deco mini-palace sitting on a steep field of grass shrouded by gentle morning mist. All bone-white Depression Modern chic and sloping, groomed green lawn—too steep for little boys and girls to play on. Great curved beveled windows wound around the place—a big one for the living room and a smaller one for the kitchenette. Probably built late, when California was out of the Gold Rush and into the Movie Rush. California was always stirring up a hot rush of one kind or another.

It was about 7:00 a.m.

I got out of the car and crossed the foggy street. I told myself I was only going around the house to the garbage alley for a closer look but soon found a narrow path into the Goldfischer backyard and was peeking into the back windows of downstairs rooms. Behind me, an enormous field of green, surrounded by ivy walls. Through the kitchen I could see a massive chandelier hanging in the open vestibule, reflected in the beveled glass, surrounded by a spiral staircase leading up to one of those railed balconies, maybe to bedrooms—a long sweeper of a staircase. I went up close, peered into the breakfast nook. Not much: A glass case with Hummels, a little boy pushing a little girl on ceramic swings, a glass vagabond clown, a little dancing girl with a poofy yellow, lime, and baby blue umbrella over her shoulder. The world was big into these scenes of sentiment—once.

I backed off, turned and looked down into a half-staircase leading to a sunken den—the TV room, with a full bar. Three framed posters stood majestic on the big wall: one schmaltzy Toulouse Lautrec, one close-up of the backside of two nudie toddlers standing side by side, the boy pinching the girl's tush, and one cartoony two-tone graphic of an empty-pocketed, loose-tied unshaven hitchhiker standing next to a bright red sign that said WELCOME TO LOST WAGES, NEVADA. I was getting hypnotized by this insanely tacky triptych when I heard the sound of someone opening the front door. I panicked, slipped behind a tree.

An old lady called out: "Patricia, is that you?" Was this the voice of Mrs. Goldfischer, wife of the penis doctor? Before me, the great lawn, the ferns, the old wooden jungle gym shimmered in morning dew. The American dream—a fenced and empty backyard. I crouched, cursing in silence because now I'd probably be stuck for a while.

"Hi, Momma." A younger woman's voice, sing-songy. "You're up early this morning!"

The time to leave was now. I didn't budge. Their voices carried, a sorrowful theater of the aged and the burdened.

"What a long day it will be. I don't like the summer."

"But we've got the floor man today, Momma."

"I don't want to give that idiot my money, what for? Find a different floor man."

"He's the best one. Tommy recommended him."

"Tommy? Tommy didn't tell *me* that. Tommy doesn't visit—nobody visits!"

"Mom—I took half the day off to be with you. That's not visiting?"

"I haven't seen your brother Thomas since January. My back is killing me."

"Why don't you have Ronnie come over and give you a treatment?"

"Don't be ridiculous. The last thing on earth I need is one of his so-called treatments."

"He's been doing really well lately, he says—"

"Pseudo-psychology for imbeciles."

"Ronnie *so* wants you to be proud of him, Momma—he's got, like, over a dozen regular clients."

"Whoop-dee-doo."

A sigh. "You need breakfast. I shouldn't even talk to you until you eat your Cheerios."

"I don't want Cheerios. I want something *good*. Something I *like*."

"I'll make you an omelet. You have mushrooms?"

"No."

"Then I'll whip up your favorite—huevos rancheros."

Silence. Then: "No."

Another silence. And then the sound of weeping, a sudden hysterical wail, jarring at this hour.

"Don't cry, Momma. Everybody *loves* you. I love you, all of us do. Tom is . . . just busy. With the shop. Ronnie's working hard. And I'm going crazy carting around the kids."

"Not carting them here you aren't."

"But I brought them for lunch only last, only last—" She was trying to remember.

"That was just after Easter! That was *months*, you nitwit!"

Another sigh. Silence. Then: "I don't like to see you cry, Momma."

But the old lady didn't stop for a long time. I waited, my only movement breathing foggy air, until the weeping sound was gone.

"Let me help you down the stairs, I'll cook you some awesome rancheros—*come on*, you know you'll love it. We'll go to the park, after the floor man. Get you some sunshine today. You and me. We'll get you a beautiful tan."

Behind the jungle gym, up a short flight of outdoor stairs, was a kind of unmowed greasy mound topped with a pagoda—I hadn't noticed it before. And inside the pagoda was a hot tub surrounded by ivy in long, reaching arms, growing right up the concrete walls. Here you could picture kids playing hide and seek.

Now I caught the sound of the older woman and the younger woman on the stairs. I stayed low, moved close to the walls, made a fast turn past the window of an office of sorts, a room I had passed too quickly before—it stopped me in my tracks. It seemed to have been unused for a long time, this room—the good doctor's home office, maybe he made house calls. A late model electric typewriter sat alongside an early model answering machine. On the pine desk stood a one-piece leather mat and pen holder, matching the faded brown leather swivel chair. On an end table, next to a brown leather couch that had seen better days, was a small sepia photo in a gold frame. Disneyland—the whole family in Civil War duds. The two boys, close in age, with identical muskets, the sturdy boy and the sloucher, flanking their parents—a seated cue-ball headed, jolly-looking Dr. Milton and standing next to him, his wife, Nannette, voluptuous, once possibly very sexy, but in the pic, long-suffering and stern. Also the girl—a little younger than the boys, cautious, and, unlike anybody else, freckled.

It was time to split.

I was making my way across the lawn as swiftly as possible when the front door opened.

"Wait, wait!" the young woman said. "I didn't hear the doorbell ring!" I froze in my tracks, turned around. A stunning strawberry-blonde in her mid-thirties beckoned at the door, dressed in an open dark-gray lululemon hoodie and matching joggers. Across her black tank top, a plain silver cross guarded her cleavage.

"Come in, come in," she said, frantic. "We're waiting for you."

I entered the vestibule with great caution. Nan Goldfischer was in a wheelchair in her faded pink terrycloth bathrobe, clutching a rolled crossword puzzle mag in her bony fist. Her pale eyes on me were curious and controlled.

"You aren't the floor man. I've *met* the floor man."

"No, ma'am. No, I'm not."

"Well, then, who are you and what are you doing on my lawn?"

"My name is Adam Zantz. I worked for the late Annie Linden."

She gave me a startled glare. "The singer? That just passed?"

"Yes ma'am. I—" I raised my hands like they had a gun on me. "This might sound crazy. But I have reason to believe she may have known your late husband."

"My Milton? How curious. What on earth makes you think so?"

"They—had a correspondence of sorts. A few exchanged notes."

The younger woman was on high alert, as if she was considering calling the cops. But Nan herself was neither surprised nor angry to see me; she had the heavy-lidded amphibian-like serenity of the almost senile yet knowing. She rolled away from the couch and raised a hand to give me a seat.

"Please don't trouble yourself, Mrs. Goldfischer."

"At my age, a little company is hardly what I would call trouble. Patricia—please fix us both breakfast. Huevos rancheros, orange juice, coffee for the gentleman, not too much half-and-half in mine. Please sit."

In one stroke she had gone from weeping child to Duchess of the Colonies, with the measured command of high elegance pressing through her frail voice. I remained standing.

"What did you do for Ms. Linden?"

"I was her driver."

She considered the meaning of this and let it go.

"It's unspeakable," she said. "I saw it on CNN. I felt as if someone had bonked me on the head."

"Ma'am, we're all . . . all shocked."

"Shocked? Young man, in my day people killed soldiers. Or gangsters. Not old ladies. I happen to be one."

While she spoke, I took in the living room in my peripheral from this new angle, the inside. The antique bar, the framed photos of Dr. Milton and the kids, the opaque maroon and blue modernist glass ashtrays—it was more sophisticated than first glance.

"Please sit down. You can't eat breakfast standing up."

This time I did as she said.

"Milton certainly never mentioned Annie Linden—I'm an old fogey but I would've remembered *that*. But he *may* have known her. He had a very large clientele. His office was just down the street."

"I see."

A little bell rang—Patricia worked fast. Nan Goldfischer said, "Mr. Zantz, please push me to the kitchenette. My daughter is a fine cook, we won't be disappointed."

There we were, seated with the Hummel brigade watching over our sumptuous feast, with Patricia standing at attention, pouring coffee out of a ceramic teapot.

Nan said, "Do you drive a limousine, young man?"

"No—I'm a Lyft driver."

Nan gave me a puzzled look. Patricia's suspicion seemed to jack up with this information—she looked down upon me with the grave judgment one reserves for gig-jobbers. Then she said, "It's an app, Mom, you order a ride on your cell phone," which didn't exactly wipe Nan's puzzled look away.

"I see," she said. "You must be in a terrible state of grief about your client."

"I am. I also have my doubts about the man they think killed her. He was her personal assistant—a little unstable. But—"

She gazed upon me in that soft gray zone that is neither pity nor sympathy nor understanding yet somehow all of the above. "He was your friend?"

"Not really. But I don't think he was capable of hurting Annie."

"It is not wise to be convinced of what somebody is capable of."

"Maybe not. Mrs. Goldfischer—I hate to stir up trouble— but can you think of why your husband would have had to keep his contact with Annie a secret?"

She forked her eggs and considered the plate. "Certainly. She may have had a friend who needed his services. He was a men's doctor. He was bound by strict confidentiality to all his patients. You can talk to his partner Elliot—he still runs the office here in town."

"I'll do that. But—can you think of any reason why your husband might have communicated with her through unusual channels."

A weight of concern rippled her brow—I felt guilty for it. She said, "What do you mean?"

"Well, it's just that I—" They stared me down, the silence was deafening. I wasn't about to bring up the stack of pornos. "She may have contacted him through some old newspaper classifieds."

Mother and daughter exchanged a glance.

"I believe my husband may have advertised that way on occasion." We kept eating but some invisible something had changed, I could feel it under my nerves. Then Nan said, "Mr. Zantz, are you investigating your client's death in a formal capacity?"

"No, no, I'm just . . . trying to make sense of things."

She put down her napkin and studied me again—the sympathy had evacuated from her eyes. "Well. That's understandable. Mourning is a complicated process. I'm sorry I couldn't be of more help. Patricia, what time is the floor man coming?"

"He's due any minute."

Nan rolled herself from the table with finality. "I better get out of this bathrobe. Good luck to you, young man. I'm very sorry for your loss." And then she wheeled herself out of the kitchenette.

Daughter Patricia walked me to the door and gave me a quarter-smile that said *this bizarre interruption is over.*

Three blocks inland from the pier, the offices of the Hermosa Center for Urology sat halfway down another short foothill, the last of the fading blue deco office bungalows—probably super-chic in its day, now just short of crumbling antiquity.

Seaside places got beaten down faster by wind and salty air. I would've assumed the place was out of business had Nan not sent me there. A plaque on the door still advertised Dr. Milton Goldfischer, Dr. Elliot Fleiss, and Dr. Marshall R. Fleiss.

Just as I opened the door, a patient was leaving, a stout white man in Brooks Brothers. The nurse/receptionist told me they were already running behind schedule, but when I told her I wasn't a patient, she took down my name and disappeared behind a blue curtain. The man who came out to greet me introduced himself as Dr. Elliot Fleiss. He was a lean, gray man with great creases along his mouth and under his tired brown eyes, but like the building, he looked as though he might have cut a handsome figure in his prime.

"Thanks for seeing me, Doctor. My name is Adam Zantz. Nan Goldfischer thought I might want to talk to you. I'm a private investigator looking into the late Dr. Goldfischer."

"Milton? What on earth for?"

"He's loosely connected to a homicide that took place in Malibu early this month."

The doctor was pinched with curiosity. "Ten minutes in my office," he said, half to me and half to the receptionist. In his small consultation room, he sat in an ancient wooden chair, escutcheoned with the crest for Stanford Medical School. "I find it hard to imagine you're talking about my old friend Milt."

"I understand that Dr. Goldfischer passed away only a few years ago. Were you still business partners at the time?"

"We were. Milt and I worked side by side for almost forty years. Now what is this case you're examining exactly? Did you say homicide?"

"Yes, a client of mine. Last month. An older woman."

"Is this about that singer who they found under the pier?"

"It is. In the late 1970s, Dr. Goldfischer was having secret meetings with her."

"The 1970s?" The phrase seemed to zing like a lemon drop in his mouth.

"I don't know the reason for their meeting in secret—but I want to find out everything I can about those meetings."

"This is all nonsense. If Milt was having an affair, I would have known about it. And in the 1970s, he was too busy running this office for shenanigans. Where the hell are you getting your information?"

"I discovered a series of messages passed back and forth between them."

"Where?"

I paused. "In the classifieds of a pornographic newspaper."

He looked at me like I was a crazy person—who wouldn't?

"Mr. Zantz, just what do you expect to find out from me here today?"

"Well, I'd like to know what kind of man the late doctor was, for one. It may not help my case but it'll certainly help me understand my client."

"Milt?" Dr. Fleiss blanched, shuffled memories the way older people sometimes will, as if flipping through a big imaginary phone book. "Milton Goldfischer was *goodhearted*. In every sense of the word."

I repeated the word without emphasis. This annoyed Fleiss.

"Yes, that's right," he said. "Goodhearted. I guess that phrase has already gone out of fashion and that's a damnable pity. He was decent, considerate. He put others before himself."

"Did you know much about his family life?"

"I *knew* the man since we were both second-year med students." He paused. "Before and after he met Nan."

"You make it sound like there was a big change."

"No, not really." Dr. Fleiss licked the inside of his teeth. "But Milty Goldfischer always had an innocent quality about him, even after school. He was just a good egg, he couldn't help it. Nannette appreciated that quality in him. And as many will do, she sometimes took advantage of it."

"How do you mean?"

"Milt was a giver. He had to work extra hard to please Nan, and she seemed to need even more from him when the family grew. It isn't abnormal, any decent husband would give more under those circumstances. He worked like a dog to provide for his children—to the great benefit of this office."

I glanced around the room as if for the first time. Much of the equipment looked like it hadn't been touched in years.

"You guys had a pretty robust business in the seventies."

"We've done well. We subspecialize in impotence, but the money wasn't important to us. We wanted to help men who were suffering. Give them a second chance to enjoy love."

"Do you think Dr. Goldfischer might've used the porn magazine to solicit new patients?"

"Of course not. What a ridiculous question."

"Did Dr. Milt suffer himself?"

The doctor smirked with paternal impatience. "Do you know how many people thought they were being humorous or candid asking me or Milt that question? *'Did you have the operation yourself?'* Neither of us needed it, but I can tell you we both agreed that it wouldn't have been beneath us. When a man loses his power to love, the problem is pathophysiological but the toll is emotional, psychological. You wouldn't make jokes if he'd lost the power to eat or to breathe. Milton Goldfischer personally felt the frustration of every one of his patients, and he wanted to end their pain."

The doctor stood—our interview was over. As he opened the door, he said, "The poor man died of pancreatic cancer eighteen months ago. If that doesn't exonerate him, I can't see what would."

The morning mist was long gone as I got into the Silver Lemon and tore away down the hill, trying to outdrive the black Jell-o in my heart. I felt the puzzle pieces of a kooky song coming together, all twanging Peter Gunn–theme new wave guitars and big brass.

Lyft driver! Lyft driver!

You're not sleeping
You look like hell
All that weeping scares the clientele
The queen is dead
And you can't revive her
—Lyft driver!

The pounding melody chased me all the way home. That crumbling clinic, the home of Nan Goldfischer, the whole neighborhood had left me with a great empty and wobbly feeling—of being stuck in time, back there in the past, without poetry to save you. A neighborhood can be like a species that can't evolve and is condemned to watch the world from its cage.

Just before ramping off the freeway, this orgy of despair was broken by the thought of that hokey gold-framed Disneyland pic, the one in the home office. Good Lord, it was corny. The boys were maybe fifteen and sixteen in the photo, the girl maybe eleven. The photo dogged me the whole ride home.

They were a conservative family. Stricter than California average, for sure.

The father drank and liked the occasional trip to Vegas—not a real ladies' man. But *Hers & His* maybe didn't make him blush, either.

The boys looked a little displaced in those itchy Civil War duds—like chumps who'd been talked into a bad prank. Whereas Nan looked truly unhappy, driven to correct the moment. Okay—obvious. Go deeper, all the way into that odd, falsely stern and not very believable analytical expression of hers. A child psychologist who didn't practice, a doctor's wife—that was something. Status and title. Delusions of respectability. A certain aloneness.

And again: The little nerd who grew up to be a good-looking dame. But in the pic, she was the smart one. Skeptical, rejecting the mandatory fake-smile. She alone wanted something *else*—unlike the boys, she wasn't trying and failing to live up to the posed moment. One photo, five people in costume.

The Goldfischers of Hermosa. They worked overtime to keep the past in place. I burst out laughing but when the yuks faded, it sat like a crab on my heart.

Back to work, driving for dollars in the all-night rain. Wet passengers came and went, each with their own private mystery to solve. Mine was a tangle of crisscrossing traffic lights, a dead weenie doctor, some porno rags, a photo strip with an unidentified somebody, a long-lost tape I'd probably never find. I felt like a man on the verge of a nervous breakdown trying to draw connections at the wheel. On the cracked Samsung smart phone clamped to the dashboard, a little silver rectangle repping the Jetta made its digital way across an endless city matrix, jutting ninety-degree turns in a hiccup. But in the car on the slippery streets in the downpour night, I turned with care on the long slow fade to dawn, squinting from lamppost glare, groping like a child playing Marco Polo, and no app could possibly know how lost I really was.

It wouldn't let me go.

Then, walking out of Denny's at 6:00 a.m., the sight of my silver Jetta gave me a start. The front windshield shimmied like a great spreading spider web smashed at the center. I ran to it like an idiot, looked up, sideways, circled her—she was tilting, capsizing in the gutter puddles—three of four tires slashed. I scoped Jefferson Ave a full 360, keys cutting my grip. Nothing, no one. Inside, on the driver's seat—a wet, empty Capital One envelope. Across it in blurry black Sharpie scrawl: *WARNING #1.*

18

THEN OFFER ME THE
SAME THING IN
A DIFFERENT GUISE

"But what did the warning *say* exactly?"

"That's it, just . . . *warning number one*."

I was talking in hushed tones to Fry on the cell, seated in the waiting room at VW of Santa Monica. On the wall, dough-faced Dr. Phil ranted on the soundless TV screen. It was a little like being at the hospital while a dear relative undergoes risky surgery. In whispers, I got Fry up to date about Kronski and Eva, my arrest, the storage space, the classifieds and the photo strip, Mrs. Goldfischer and the broken windshield.

"What a fucking *violation*, man," Fry said, "Like, whoever it is—why hurt the car?"

"Right?"

"Steal my wallet, crack my skull, but leave the wheels alone, *schmuck*. This is LA, not Coulterville."

I didn't laugh exactly, but his wisecracks took the edge off my nerves. "Freiberger, I'm getting scared."

"Who wouldn't be?"

"Like—what am I even being warned *about*?"

"I don't know, man. My gut is—somebody wants Gelden to take a fall, and *somehow* they get that you're trying to prove otherwise."

"I mean, it could be anybody. Plus . . . "

"What?"

I cupped the phone, dropped to an even lower whisper. "I've been lying to cops, breaking into people's homes, fronting that I was asked to manage her estate—I don't know what's come over me lately."

"*Welllll*, you do have a habit of, uhm, being a little bit, uh, *fanatic*?"

"That's great coming from an orthodox Jew—so what are you saying? This is, like, the moment where a sane person would back off?"

"You feelin' sane?"

I thought about it. "Nope."

"Look, whoever savaged your ride—is obviously a dangerous nut. So you *do* have to be careful. But you can't completely go into hiding. Just, you know, be stealth. Poke around here and there."

"It's the Linden Hop today, the convention thing over in Glendale. You think I'd be safe there?"

"Oh yeah, there's gonna be a zillion people there. In fact, maybe you can try to find out about the guy in the photo strip. You've got a good enough excuse to track him down."

I exhaled. "They do look like they were close."

"Well, that's something. If he knew her way back when, he *might* have a line into her past."

They called my name on the intercom so I signed off. And $1,316 on a Best Buy credit card later, my baby was like new, but I was still shattered. I drove home, ripped the ancient black-and-white photo strip off my bathroom mirror, stuck it in an envelope, slipped it into my inside coat pocket, and headed for Glendale. Fry was right. Somebody at an Annie Linden convention had to know who the guy in the photo was, and maybe even why he was hiding in Annie's secret stacks.

I took side streets through whiter than Wonder Bread pre-war suburbs, now one of the thriving Armenian centers of the States. But the Hop took place at the Glendale Convention Center because of what the town used to be: a hotspot for hobbyists, toy train collectors, plastic model builders, *Dungeons and Dragons* players, baseball card mavens, and super fanboys of all kinds. Revell and Testors paint held their annual soap box competitions in Glendale since the early sixties. The town is close enough to LA to gather fringies from all corners but not so close that they stop traffic. A vigil for a thousand-plus Annie Linden fans in mourning was certainly no geekier than the *Magic the Gathering* Magicfest that preceded it.

But you wondered, pulling up to these things—just what is culture? Shared fantasies? Shared desires? For here in the Convention Center's corporate dome, lit by a fluorescence that drains the human pulse, the most diehard fanatics were converging to revere a woman who would never have set foot in a place like this. I parked and waited in line with some Renaissance-clad young girls, aging leather rockers, cautious thrill seekers, and quasi-professional YouTube influencers filming themselves waiting. I bought my hall pass for $24.50, not sure what I'd see—but I had a feeling it would look a lot like Meghan's poolroom to the nth degree.

By noon, a river of bodies flowed in, crowding the booths, chatting up vendors, hugging, weeping. It was ten times more passionate than her funeral. An Annie cover band called The Tunnel Diggers piped in through the loudspeakers—they were playing live on a stage in the east wing of the hall. Only a few walk-weary stragglers actually sat down to watch The

Tunnel Diggers but part of the problem was the singer. She looked just enough like Annie to make you double-take, but not enough like Annie to make it stick. She cupped the mic with long black fingernailed hands and leaned in, shaking out her frizzy golden hair like a crazed sorceress—but singing "Soul Sorceress" with a backing band, so which Annie era was she trying to catch exactly? The band behind her also seemed a little confounded—they stood too far back, like they didn't want to be associated with a bad imitation of a woman who had just been murdered and tossed in the drink.

I made rounds, walked the aisles, flipped through familiar back issues of *Rolling Stone*, *Creem*, *Bomp*. I browsed endless tour posters and publicity stills. It didn't take long before I spotted Meghan holding down the fan club registry booth, at the center of a flock of awkward, excited gypsy ladies. She wore an all-white neck-high Victorian dress and a black armband—the whole gang wore them. I gave a hand signal. She was charged up, happy to see me, her color high. This was her pink moment.

"You made it!"

"Big day," I said. "What a crowd."

"All these people *loved* her." She raised a fist to her heart. "This is going to be a tough one."

"I saw on the program you're speaking later. I'm looking forward to it."

"Oh, it's nothing, just a lot of thank yous and stuff. I'm on the board."

Her gang dissipated and I leaned in. "Meghan, listen. I have a picture I'd like to show you. A really old one, Annie and a guy. I'm wondering if you can tell me who he is."

"Please!"

I shushed her, pulled the envelope from inside my pocket

and removed the strip with great care. She went slack-jawed with delight: Annie and the black dude with the conk.

"Is that real?"

Our eyes met.

"Adam, I've never seen that. Can I take a picture of it?"

"Not until I know who the guy is."

"I wish I knew! Please let me take a picture. Or something—she's so young and beautiful. I'll send out a group email, we'll—"

"Not yet." I slipped the envelope back in my pocket. "When I know who it is, maybe I'll just give it to you."

"You're a big tease." She frowned. "But someone here has *got* to know." We gazed out at the throngs. She was more convinced than me.

A chubby girl with glasses yelled her name and Meghan opened her arms—they went into a tight hug of mourning-faced joy. I patted my jacket pocket, winked, and strolled off down the aisle to circulate. Enthusiasm on the floor was rising, as if enough of it might resurrect the heroine. Most of the booths were doing busy commerce, plenty of T-shirts for sale—at least one new one said ANNIE LINDEN 1947–2019, and there were vintage concert tees, and imitation vintage tees, and capes, and hats, and buttons and jewelry and wristbands. You could wear nothing but Annie Linden every day for the rest of your life. There were Annie lava lamps, Annie Christmas ornaments, Annie cups, diaries, skateboards. There were framed ticket stubs and laminated backstage passes and broken wristbands. I ducked and moved through the crowd, looking to hide in endless trivia.

Toward the far end of the hall, a couple of old-timer collector types were gathered around a table bobbing their gray heads to a time-worn ghetto blaster that was competing with the piped-in band. As I got closer, I saw they were surrounding an elder bespeckled Ashkenazi in a tie-dye shirt and army jacket hocking a giant case of bootleg concert cassettes, each one hand-decorated in silver ink: LINCOLN CENTER 12/23/'96. CAL JAM II FESTIVAL ONTARIO 3/18/'78, VENTURA FAIRGROUNDS 6/26/'86.

The crowd opened up and I moved in for a better listen. The clean-shaven Ashkenazi, face tugged bright by a long, gray tied-off ponytail, straightened his horn-rim glasses, drummed his fingers on the cassettes, and said, "Ten bucks a pop—I bought these puppies at auction and they're priced to move." He gave me a wink.

"Some kind of end-of-the-era special?"

"Yeah, well," he sighed, "they're cassettes. Not everybody has a player. And I don't have the time or energy to convert 'em all. 'Cause I just can't see CDs as legit *bootlegs*, you dig?"

"I think I do."

"Digital is the devil," an aficionado chimed in.

The seller said, "Don't get me started."

I ran my finger along the giant wooden case—so many concerts, so many towns, so many nights. I pulled WINTERLAND 10/13/'78. A set list had been meticulously handwritten in purple calligraphy on the cassette flap. "I'll take her."

"Sold—to the man in black." He pulled a little gift bag and tossed it to me. "Good gig."

I peeled off a ten and handed it to him. "Are you an expert in all things Annie?"

"Expert? Let's just say I know an incredible amount of information about a ridiculous amount of useless shit."

I read the name on his convention pass. "Jeff the Vet," I said, "can I ask you something?"

"Sure thing, Mr. Adam Zantz of Los Angeles."

"I have a picture, a photograph, of Annie and a friend. A real old one. I can't talk to you about where I got it or anything like that. I'm just looking for someone who can tell me who the guy is."

He grinned that goofy hippie grin, his curiosity flared. "Try me."

I got behind the booth and we turned our backs to the crowd, huddled over the photo booth strip. He fogged his glasses and put them back on, reached for the envelope, but I wouldn't let him touch. He raised palms like I was The Man busting him for walking barefoot. Together, we leaned and gazed, long and hard. But after a while, he looked at me, sagging with disappointment in himself.

"Sorry—I'm stumped."

"That's cool."

"Is that . . . an original?"

"Pretty sure."

"How in the world did you get your hands on that thing?"

"Told you I won't discuss that. But . . . I worked for her."

"Right. You know, man, I could probably get you at least a couple of grand for that. We could date it—there are photo pros out there who can approximate the month, even the week it was taken."

"I'm not really looking to sell."

"Understood," he said. "But you might want to cash out while Annie's still news."

I thanked him again, slipped the envelope and bootleg cassette into my coat and took his card. "Thanks again, Jeff."

"We tried, brother."

Head down, I wandered through the ever-growing legion—a whole army of devotees. But these people didn't really know Annie. All they knew were Xeroxes of Xeroxes of

Xeroxes of something she tried to project. It was like asking a Civil War buff about what it was like to fight Gettysburg. I turned around and made for the food court, past the rows and rows of old LPs, frayed at the edges. I got myself an unwanted veggie burger and a Coke and looked for a place to sit, somewhere incognito. Fry had warned me about being overeager, getting sloppy—I had to be careful.

Meghan broke my reverie. "I've been looking everywhere for you! How's the burger?"

"You know, it's not bad for a fake."

"Adam, come with me, there's someone I want you to meet."

Meghan dragged me to a large, professional square booth draped with a row of Martin guitars, Annie's signature acoustic models. I knew about them because she had told me the story: Inside each one, the words LACK OF PASSION IS FATAL had been markered in tiny print on the wood. Why? Because Annie herself had written that inside a broken guitar after she smashed it onstage at the Troubadour. A clean-cut gray-haired man about Annie's age came out from the booth's private meeting room to greet us. In his company polo and faded denim, he could have been a mortgage broker on casual Friday.

"This is Adam, Annie's driver and friend. This is Bill Cranston, the *true* Annie Linden expert. He writes for *Guitar World* and he's been working on a three-volume biography. For how long, Bill?"

"Oh gosh, forever. Almost a decade already."

I said, "Well, lack of passion is fatal."

"Ha—sounds like you know a few secrets yourself."

"It's so noisy out here," Meghan said. "Can we talk in the meeting room? Adam has something *incredible* to show you."

We went inside the booth and closed the door—it cut the din about twenty percent. "Let's see whatcha got."

We sat at a round table—I placed the photo in the middle between the three of us.

Cranston trembled, almost welled up. "That . . . is . . . something."

"True. But who's the guy?"

He and Meghan exchanged glances.

"Tell us!" she demanded.

"I won't testify in a court of law. But I'm guessing this is the guitar teacher."

"No!" Meghan said. "The first one? What was his name?"

"Nobody—and I mean *nobody*—knows his name." Bill pushed air through his nostrils and shook his head. "And the problem is I've never seen a *picture* of him before. But I just don't know who else it could be. One thing I can say is she's sixteen, seventeen max in this picture."

I said, "How can you be so exact?"

"Because that's the striped top she wore in every darn high school photo. And he's black, the guitar teacher was black. Plus, he's got the groovy hair so he's *got* to be a music guy."

"This is Arizona?" I said.

"No, no. Her family had already relocated to Santa Monica just before her fourteenth."

"Wow," I said, "I thought she came over later, as a free agent. She talked about her small-town upbringing and stuff."

"Santa Monica *was* a small town then, very sleepy. Dad was a banker for Wells Fargo, and a real heavy alcoholic. Mom was a housewife. They relocated in 1959 for his work." He sighed deep and shook his head. "Yeah, this has got to be the first guitar teacher."

"Isn't it weird, though?" I said. "She never mentioned the

guy, this incredible story? I mean—look at him. If that was my guitar teacher, I'd be telling the whole damn world."

"Something happened there and I haven't been able to figure out what. I tried to speak with her about him and she absolutely refused, her sister too. I think they may have parted on bad terms."

"Have either of you ever heard of a Dr. Milton connected to Annie?"

They both shook their heads. Bill said, "Her main doctor was Griner over at Cedar's."

"What about . . . porno magazines?"

Bill cracked a smile. "What about 'em?"

"Did Annie have anything to do with them?"

"Actually, believe it or not, her mentor, Eva Silber, oversaw a feminist hippie porno newspaper back in the seventies while she was with Annie. Extremely rare. I got my hands on a copy or two but there wasn't anything about Annie in there. She was already a star at the time."

"See?" Meghan said. "Is Bill the totally amazing real deal? Whatever there is to know about Annie Linden, this guy knows."

"Maybe," Bill said, "but I've never seen this shot before today."

For a long time, we sat there in that convention booth meeting room, under the bars of too-bright fluorescence, surrounded by the thud and whir of noise and music and chatter outside, our hands on the table, our eyes staring at the photo strip as people in a séance might gaze into a crystal ball. I hated to break the hypnosis, but I didn't want to deal with the end-of-day car line. I got up and thanked them both.

"Now. Adam. Do I get my copy of this pic or what? I swear I will blow this thing up, poster-sized, and hang it in my shrine."

"Wait a minute," Bill said, "I was just going to ask him if I could use it in the book."

"Don't fight, kids, there's enough Annie to go around. But until I get a name, I'm hanging onto this baby." I slipped the pic back in my pocket and made my way out through the crowd. I was just turning for the big doors when I spotted the almost-teenage couple from the funeral—the greasy dude and the skinny girl with the fuchsia hair—they were leaving too. And I still couldn't place them. I watched them go out into the parking lot, light cigarettes, and get into a yellow dented Nissan hooptie. They were different now in their groovy street clothes but as I got in the Jetta and turned on the ignition it all came back to me: I had thought they were some kind of dealers. Annie hooked up with them one night, I assumed she was just slumming it—they lived around Playboy Liquor near Cahuenga. But who the hell were they *to her*?

I tailed them from Verdugo down to Los Feliz to Western to Franklin to Playboy Liquor, as twilight began to bathe the city in darkness. The world it seemed—Hollywood especially—sent its children out into the night.

Just before the boulevard, they tried to lose me.

19

CAN'T YOU SEE THAT IT'S LOVE YOU REALLY NEED?

The mystery teenyboppers swerved up a curving residential and slammed on the gas. They pulled into a tight alley behind a motel apartment with a central pool drowning in banana plants and I cut around the other side of the street and blocked them at the opening. In a flurry they ditched their hooptie and I ditched mine. They ran fast for spindly dorks—in a flash they were down the street and into Playboy Liquor. I ran in there too but they were already gone—I didn't know the tiny place had two entrances. The Korean owner scowled at the sight of me, wary and pissed. Either he knew them or was sick of people chasing other people through his shop. I exited out onto the street and grabbed my knees, out of breath—looked around. I thought I lost them. But then I caught the last flash of the girl entering the Wilcox Arms.

I yelled, "Hey—wait up!"

That didn't stop them.

I broke for it.

Into the old building and down the poorly lit chocolate halls I chased them, time-worn carpet thudding under our feet. They wanted to get away from me in the worst way, this skinny dude and his slinky companion, the chick with the stringy, fuchsia hair, maybe his girlfriend, maybe I don't know what. Bass thumped, someone behind some door screamed in Armenian.

I got a notion, cut outside around the back of the building, and blazed a trail to the hallway's back exit—unlocked. I cut in and up the stairs and caught them at the door but they kept moving, dodging.

I said, "Stop—Jesus—" But he scrambled away and I grabbed at him, he resisted, swung, and now we were tussling. I tried to get the words out: *"I was Annie Linden's driver"*— but he was in a blind panic, clawing at me and not listening. I yelled, "Wait!" and he swung again. I ducked and pushed his jaw, shocked by the effectiveness of my own hand. Then girlfriend grabbed my elbows from behind and I shook her off hard, punched him once good in the belly and he lunged for me.

Now I am not a fighter by any stretch. I was kicked out of weight training class in high school for skinniness and low participation. But this young fellow was just a little bit wimpier. I held him off me as we did an unhappy foxtrot down the hall. He kept coming, I kept pushing.

But even as we wrangled, I got a dèjá vu and wondered what I'd wondered before: Why would Annie Linden who could get the finest coke delivered to her Malibu door in fifteen minutes, cross town to the shittiest back alley mini-mall parking lot on earth to score weed at a phoneless payphone from this skinny punk? Was Annie slumming, hanging with the tatterdemalions? I got sick of waltzing and legged him at the ankles, and he slammed hard into the garbage chute door.

He stood up, sneered the false smile, a greasy strand of hair collapsing into his eye.

"What can I do for you, officer?"

"Not here." I looked around, gasping. "How 'bout in there." I pointed toward his door, which instantly put him on guard—I knew where he lived. With a defiant shrug, he fished out the key.

Fuchsia-girl scowled. "You *are* a cop, right?"

"Do I really look like a cop?" I was still catching my breath. "I'm not here for chemicals. I got questions."

"About *what*."

I pulled cash, splayed the bills like a short stack of cards. She fought going wide-eyed. He froze at the sight of the pretty greenness, looked both ways.

"Enter."

I followed them into the smallest apartment I'd ever seen— a perfect box of a room with one dirty window looking out over the Playboy Liquor parking lot. In twenty years of driving by, I had never noticed that the Y in the neon sign was a martini. The too-skinny girlfriend dropped cross-legged to a sheetless mattress and eyeballed me with a mix of trepidation and curiosity. The guy closed the door soft but it creaked loud.

They had scotch-taped a torn-out magazine picture of Justin Bieber or some other pop kiddo on the back of the door, the sole aesthetic choice in the room. I couldn't tell if it was irony or idol worship.

"Okay, listen. I don't need your dope and I *know* Annie Linden didn't either. But you can have the bread if you tell me what the hell your business with her was. That's all I want to know. And do not lie to me because I brought her here myself at least two times."

The girl looked up, pale and slack-jawed.

The guy snickered. "The singer? You fucking kidding me? Babe, didn't she come up the other day on Spotify?"

I sighed, rolled my eyes. "Aw, come on, man, you don't wanna tangle ass again." I looked around the stark room: An IKEA box was their only table—with a ghetto blaster, an e-pipe, a box of Swisher Sweets, a lighter, and some nail polish bottles for worldly possessions. "I'm Adam."

"I'm Runions, this is Minnie." He shoved his greasy hair back into the hat. "And *we don't know anything about Annie Linden*, besides what anybody knows. I never met her."

"I wish I *had*," Minnie suddenly blurted—the worst actress in Hollywood, which is saying something.

"*Please*," I said. "I saw you at the damn funeral—*and* the convention."

"Look, I don't know who you are but—"

"I'm her *driver*. Was. And I've got mental images of the three of you standing right outside this building, practically playing ring-around-the-rosy."

"Yeah? So?"

"So I don't want to get police involved and tell them I saw you with Annie weeks before she was murdered—but I will if I have to. Now why did she come here? To score? I'm not a narc and I don't care. I just want to know."

This time they exchanged a different look: scolded children. They loved each other in that youthful symbiotic way where everybody's got to check every move with the other one. Runions now backed up and leaned on the mini fridge, pulled a smoke from his shirt pocket. His commie rockabilly cap, chained wallet, and black bowling shirt draped over a too-bony body gave him the look of a junior hooligan, but now that the only lightbulb in the room dangled near his face I saw he was older, the seventeen forever type, the hidden jerk on the Camel pack, always thrusting out into the world without a plan. Minnie was droll with her purple bangs and her striped Salvation Army pullover dress, maybe more mature than him, maybe smarter than him, but deeply sorrowful about some hidden something. They were both stuck in the youth game, the aging high school dropouts that just kind of stay there. I didn't dislike them. Like me, and Fry, and so many others, they'd been abandoned, then they abandoned themselves.

"Talk to me," I said more gently. "If you cared about her, just talk to me."

All along the girl had been winding herself up, tightening, her Indian sitting position growing more and more fidgety—she was practically vibrating now.

"Just tell him!" she said.

"Okay, fine," Runions said. "But first *you* tell *us*. What's it to you, driver?"

"Bix Gelden is in jail. The cops think I helped him. But neither of us would've hurt a hair on that woman's body."

They got the gist, like they'd expected it. Runions lit his cigarette and shrugged. "I dunno how to explain it, man. Annie was just a cool old lady. She didn't visit us that many times. She was a trip. I was as surprised to see her down here as anybody. She rolled up one time to Playboy—like a ways back, in a limo. And we're all, like—"

"I'm all like, maybe it's Lady Gaga . . . or . . . someone old, like Elton John," Minnie said with a kind of laughing rock on her skinny legs. "And then the door opens and it's really Annie Linden. We're all like—what the *fuck*."

"And you—you knew her music?"

Minnie's eyelids lowered. "I worshipped her. My mom used to lullaby me to sleep with those songs. When I saw Annie Linden step out of that limo—"

"Minnie goes, 'I'm gonna get her autograph' and I'm all

'Don't bug her.' But we kind of followed her into the liquor store—somehow she just started talking to *us*. Like we didn't even approach her. And she didn't try to score. She asked if *we* wanted to get high. So . . . we invited her back to the pad."

"Here?"

"It ain't much but she was happy as a clam, man. She said she was sick of the ocean and all the fake-ass rich people that lived there. Then she was like, 'Minnie needs a massage.' He let out a short breathy laugh through his teeth. "I'm thinking maybe she wants to like, get busy with her or with us or whatever. But . . . "

Minnie shrugged, half-smiled. "She just wanted to be our friend."

I nodded. This sounded like Annie. My Annie.

I said, "You got any idea who did this?"

Minnie closed her eyes, shook her head violently. "It's beyond heinous. It's beyond . . . "

Runions looked down, inspected his shoes. It was the first time I noticed them, his brothel creepers, with thick clear jelly-like pink soles, pink suede and a fancy green stitch. I chided myself for being the world's least observant investigator.

"You know what?" he said. "She told us about you. She said once her only friends were us, her driver, her ex, and this dude who taught her to play the guitar."

Hands shaking, I said, "What?"

He shrugged. I fumbled in my pocket for the strip. Minnie got on her knees to look. She looked to her boyfriend for the green light.

He said, "That's him. Her guitar teacher. That's Manny."

"You *met* him?"

"Just once, man. Old black dude, Emmanuel. He has a machine shop off Jefferson, on West. We brought him an envelope, a message from Annie."

"A message? What kind of message?"

"We didn't open it," Minnie said. "I refused."

"Did he say something about this message?"

A pallor set over them, they looked harassed by their own naiveté.

Minnie said, "He read it and shoved it in his pocket. He thanked us and asked if we needed money for our trouble. We said no and he kind of motioned for us to split. That was it."

"Who's Dr. Milton?"

They went blank.

"Did she ever mention porno mags?"

Nothing.

"Eva? Did she mention an Eva?"

Nada.

"What—what else did she say about the teacher? Did she say anything?"

Zip.

My back hit the wall and I slid to the floor. "Well, I guess you two didn't kill her."

"*Kill* her?" Minnie blurted. "We loved her."

"She was like our goddess or something."

"She was totally our guardian angel."

I believed them. I saw it.

I said, "Three or four months ago, before . . . before all this shit, I dropped her off, she was in here a long time, longer than usual. She practically spent the night."

They nodded in unison like bobble-head dolls.

"What was she doing in here that whole time?"

"Not much," Runions said. "Hanging out. She did complain about this dude Kronski."

"That's her ex," Minnie said.

"What'd she say about him?"

"She said even though he dumped her she couldn't, like, get rid of him."

We exchanged helpless glances. I exhaled, big-time. I got up and placed my card and the two fifties and four twenties on the towel at Minnie's feet—the last cash in my wallet. "All right, you guys, I'm around. Call if you remember anything at all. Call if there's an emergency or even if you need a free ride. Okay?"

They nodded but there was no trust in their eyes.

Then I was out the door and down the thumping hall with its shouts from foreign lands, and I got a chill because they *lived* here, these two, Annie's last true pals, they weren't slumming hipsters on a temporary vacation, this box of hell was their place in the world, visited by a funny kind of so-called guardian angel in the flesh, who maybe wanted to save them but didn't get around to it and now was no more. What was Annie doing with these two innocent street rats, why would she deploy them like pawns? They insisted they were all best buds, but whatever went down . . . was less than maternal.

And it was night in that vestibule round the clock.

20

MERRILY MERRILY
MERRILY MERRILY LIFE
IS BUT A DREAM

Manuel "Combs" Bullock-Rutledge wasn't that hard to find. There was only one machine shop on West off Jefferson—he owned the lot. There was one other record for property ownership also in his name, way up in Turlock, California, a residential he co-owned with Clarissa Bullock, ninety-four. Maybe his mother. There were identical listings for Manuel Bullock with an "e" and Manual Combs Rutledge with an "a"—maybe a mistake. No listings for Manny or Emmanuel Bullock or Rutledge, but it didn't make me Sherlock Holmes that I had figured out Combs was maybe a nickname. I drove down to West.

It was a mixed-up neighborhood, the last semi-industrial section of West Adams that had not yet totally gentrified. Black and Mexican families made a life in these little bungalow cubes right there alongside tony modernist furniture workshops and digital design firms. The industrial and technological worlds, the haves and have-nots, they were all staging a showdown right there on Jefferson, the border of black and white LA. A half-block north on a service alley, Manuel's place was neither-nor, a dingy yellow house with a large lot hidden by a big black steel gate. The dented silver Shleppa fit right in here.

I parked on the residential side and walked past the handpainted sign chained to the alley fence: COMBS TOOLS N HARDWARE CHEAP RENTALS with a phone number underneath. I tried the front door—no answer—so I walked around back to the high metal gate and peeked through the place where the gate doors were chained. Nothing but used construction machinery, very used. Either Manuel had been there a long time or he collected vintage stuff, because the machines behind the gate looked outmoded, rusty—but it wasn't Sanford & Son, the whole thing was organized like a nursery in alternating rows of metal and dirt. I dialed the number on my cell—straight to voicemail. I called out his name a few times—nada.

About to give up, I banged and rattled the gate loud as I could and soon an old, stooped man idled out of a side door of the house.

"Yeah?"

"I'm really sorry to disturb you. I was Annie Linden's driver."

"Who?"

"Annie Linden."

"I don't know no goddamn Andy Linder."

I said, "No, no—Annie Linden. The singer."

He gave me a long, suspicious glare. Up close, his face had the intensity of permanent confrontation. He'd been burned and never would be again. But it was definitely him, the guy in the photo strip—time hadn't erased his high school heartthrob eyes.

He said, "Wait there, I'll open the gate" and disappeared into the yellow bungalow. It was only after he left that I caught the afterglow of strong liquor vapors—he had done something to mask it, maybe Listerine or cologne. His organized yard, his bony shoulders and lazy hands and gold LCD watch, all gave the impression of a calm, clear mind, a sober tinkerer. But really he was buzzed on booze and propane and voltage—and he was hiding permanently in this metal pile-up. Hiding, just like the old man in Public Storage. How many of these hiders did any American city contain? I'm guessing tens of thousands. Including me.

I took another peek through the crack in the gate: old machines. A Powermatic 66 table saw sat solitary, aqua blue with orange on the cranks and a plug-in hi-speed circular blade that still resembled a swirl of rolling thunder despite rust and warp. The cord lay unraveled in the dirt—it led to one of those old school rounded sockets like the kind you'd find on an LAUSD phonograph.

The gates clanged open. Combs was standing there with a small taped-up Beretta pointed in the direction of my forehead.

"Whoa—" My hands went up without request.

"What you doin' here, boy? And don't give me no bullshit about power tools."

"No, no, my name is Adam Zantz, I just wanted to talk, I—"

"Do I look stupid to you? You some kind of chauffeur, I know who you work for. Or I should say *worked* for. I already saw you out my window circulating the neighborhood like some kinda junior Adam-12—now tell me what you want before I shoot you the fuck off this property."

"Okay, okay. Put down that thing, I'm begging you."

"What you want." His gun didn't budge.

"I used to drive Annie."

"That part you already told me." But a ripple seemed to crease his face each time I said her name, a muscle memory begging to be released.

"I found a photo. A very old one. You're in it."

"And?" His gun didn't lower.

"And—I thought you might want to see the pic. A man writing her biography thinks it's important. Thinks you're important. To her story."

He didn't relax exactly, but he did downshift to his comfort-zone paranoia. By instinct, his gun hand lowered to his side. "Show me the picture."

I came into the yard and reached into my coat pocket ultra-slow. "I wasn't sure if Annie was a sore subject or—"

He grabbed the photo strip and smirked, then smiled. "You some kind of male groupie?"

"No, no. I was just her driver, her last driver."

"Yeah, well, you can't drive her anyplace now."

"To say the least."

"Alright." He absent-mindedly placed the little gun on a table crowded with hand tools. "I don't want to be in anybody's bio. But come in and drink something, I'm thirsty."

I followed him through the yard—it would have made a terrific miniature golf course. From the back door, we entered a ragged yellow kitchenette where a scruffy orange cat was nudging his empty green plastic bowl across the floor.

"They're trying to convict her assistant," I said.

"Yeah, I know all about it."

"Then you know he's innocent."

The old man gave me a curious look, straight-up animal fight or flight. "And you saw some old photo and you think I did it?"

"Not at all. But maybe you know stuff."

He shook his head in amazement. "You're a freak, man. I need a drink." Out came the sweet vermouth and a pair of small, clear yellow plastic glasses, the kind pancake houses use for orange juice. He poured and slid one to me and sat. "Who *you* think did the dirty deed?"

I shook my head, solemn.

Combs waved a toothpick while he spoke, but never brought it to his mouth. "More than a few people might have done that to Annie. I'm not saying I'm not surprised. Nobody should go like that. But a woman like Annie could not help but make enemies."

"Yeah? You're not the first person to say that to me."

"Oh yeah. She was a user in every way, man. And a real snob. I don't mean racially. Annie was a snob about beauty. She could not stand anything average. And she could be nasty if she didn't like you. She liked me, because she could use what I had, plain and simple."

It was hard for me to see Annie that way—but not impossible. And it was getting easier with every burn victim I met.

"Man," he said, marveling at the photo, relaxing into it. "Different world. It was like a different planet."

"It looks like you two were close."

"We were more than close. I taught her how to write a song."

"Which one?"

"I mean *any* song."

"For real?"

"Yup. I was a delivery boy to a record store called Wallich's on Sunset and Vine—center of the world. She rode the bus to that store every day after school. Had a crush on me—'cause musically I knew what was what. But she made me nervous."

"Why's that?" The sweet vermouth was killer strong—earth meets vapor of seaweed.

"In those days an underaged white girl could get you killed, man. Even if you were underaged too. So I told her, 'You got to have a reason for hanging 'round me. Otherwise— *arrivederci*, baby.' And she says, 'I heard you can play guitar. Teach me.' She did not know one thing. I mean nothing. First question was 'What's a chord?' "Not 'Help me play a chord' but 'What is it?'" He drank and refilled in one swift arc. "I gave her the skills she needed and I transformed her. As a person, and as an artist. I taught her how to listen to herself." He downed the second glass and raised an eyebrow, a challenge of belief.

And there was something disarming about listening to this wiry little drunk bragging about shaping a world icon here in this lightless, yellow-tiled kitchenette overlooking a backyard of broken metal in the forgotten part of a dying city with a desperate orange cat trying to get one last taste off its bowl at my feet. It was a trip. But that didn't mean Manuel wasn't telling the truth.

"Tell me what you showed her."

"Huh?"

"I mean—your techniques, your guitar stuff."

"You're a funny motherfucker. Drive around the neighborhood like Joe Friday and now you want me to jam for you?"

I refilled both of us, that pleased him. "I've been known to write a song or two myself," I said. "Annie liked them."

"People don't even know what a song *is* nowadays. You got so much dressing on it, all this complex BS, *electronic noise*. But a song don't need bells and whistles. A song has to stand alone."

"You mean like be an original progression?"

"No, no, no." Combs electrified himself with the desire to make me understand.

"So, what do you mean?"

"A song is something a child can remember, otherwise it ain't a real record."

He got up and disappeared into his small, dark living room and fumbled behind a couch, then came back with a handsome purple sunburst Telecaster. It was as frayed and faded as every other machine on the lot. Unplugged, no amp, he tuned with the pick in his teeth and he started playing a looping groove. And it was almost silence, this glassy strum of notes falling like raindrops into a river. His eyes closed and he burrowed deeper, gentler into the changes—this old man who minutes before had pulled a gun on me.

He stopped, opened his eyes.

I said, "Pretty."

"Maybe—but that ain't a song. *This* is a song." And then he started to pluck out the melody for "Row, Row, Row Your Boat." But he did it in a steady, controlled way that brought more feeling, more power than you ever thought it could possess—each note popped like a little firecracker, bursting right on time and not a fraction of a millisecond early or late.

I said, "That one I think I've heard before."

"Not like this you haven't."

"You got me there."

He grunted. "You see, I taught your lady friend what music *is*. Not how to play it. How to live it. How to bypass what has to be bypassed and *be* it. And well, she just naturally got attached to me."

"Was she, like, your chick?"

"Hell no." He hesitated. "I was more like a father figure, even though I was sixteen and she was fourteen."

"But don't tell me you didn't think about it."

"She had a boyfriend at school, man, white dude named Lawrence. Real square John, football quarterback and everything. He wasn't crazy about me."

I said, "Where is he now, the football star?"

"That idiot is dead and buried out on Veteran Avenue. They sent him to Saigon in sixty-five and shipped him home in a bag."

"So they didn't stay together?"

"When he died, she was racked with guilt." Combs shot me the blue steel stare but he was too sauced to pull it off. He said, "I didn't like the man. Yeah, he was a war hero but so the fuck what. Any dumb motherfucker can escape into that mess and go kill some brown people on the other side of the planet. If he had lived, he probably would have come back a junkie, a homeless, or a racist cop."

He paused, measured the past for relevance. Finding the mess of it, he drank another slug and played some more. I drank too, but the music was another wall, another gate I wanted to push past.

A few bars in, I said, "One thing I don't get. Why didn't she give you credit or—"

"Credit?"

"Yeah, c'mon. Like, in interviews and stuff. She never mentioned you. And I had a hard time finding out who you were, it doesn't seem *right*."

Combs didn't flinch. "That's on me. 'Cause I told her, when she started to get famous, I said, 'Lady, I don't want nothing to do with your legacy, and I really mean it.'"

"But why not? She burned you, man."

"She burn me? I told her to walk on."

"Yeah but—"

"Ain't nobody want to admit what that bitch was really about." He stopped playing.

"What was she about?"

"I don't talk trash about the dead. But that woman's whole thing was *fuckin' with a man*, with *all* men." Combs pointed a pinched guitar pick at me. "I believe her father must have been a terrible badass motherfucker of a man. I only saw him once, from afar, but that was enough. I skipped on home fast as I could. Most white men—"

He stopped himself, cracked another eye at me, askance. It served to ask: Was I ally or enemy?

Well, which?

He slugged his drink and blurted, "Most white men have no souls."

"Aw, come on now."

"No—*you* come on. I don't mean music. I don't mean they had no soul. I mean they had no *souls*."

I smiled. "You mean they were zombies?"

"Well—they did not really love anyone or any *thing*. Not their women, not their children. They was robots."

I blanched, poured us again, reached for the words. "It couldn't be easy being—"

"Naw, naw. Don't get it bent around. It ain't got nothing to do with what I am or am not. You aren't really listening and I'm trying to inform and educate—because I can see you're alright. You're a driver, I did that job for twelve years. 1981 to 1993. Calves like steel from putting in twenty-hour days."

"So educate me."

"Ann Marie Linden came from a place and time where the fathers were cruel beyond belief and the mothers weren't all there neither. Yeah, man, you might call it a zombie game."

I laughed, he laughed too—two drunkies hashing out racial discomfort late in the day. But when the yuks died down, he said, "See, when she was hanging around me, Annie fronted like she had a mission. She wanted to *destroy*, like, *on behalf of black people everywhere*. And I told her, 'Ann Marie—I don't want no part of that. It's unholy.' She went on about, 'You and I have a common enemy—the pigs, the hog-people.' I said 'I ain't got no enemies, hogs or pigs or ducks or otherwise. But I do have to let you know that I'm not gonna be no foot soldier for a crazy-ass white girl and her crazy-ass agenda.'" Combs got thoughtful, then: "Zantz—that's a Jew name. You *are* a Jew, right?"

I nodded.

"Well see, there it is. I respect the Jewish Lord. I may not always like every Jew—but that's *the source*."

"If you say so. But what's that got to do with Annie? She wasn't Jewish."

He flopped back into the chair and did not pick up the guitar. His long, bony hands gently did the explaining. "Some shit went down. In the early days. I tried to intervene. She handed me my dog papers for all my trouble. After that—" He shrugged.

"What kinda shit?"

"You don't need to know."

"C'mon. Driver to driver."

Combs inhaled long and deep. The room vibrated with alcohol and hesitation. The orange cat perched on the living room couch waited on the verdict.

I said, "If you loved her, you'll tell me."

"There was a pregnancy. She was never gonna have it. In fact, the parents were hot to get rid of it, practically gleeful. I had a problem with that. My dumb Sunday-go-to-meeting ass."

"How did you know about it? Was it yours?"

"No, no, nope. Not at all. The boyfriend, the asshole, *Lawrence*, he sure as hell didn't want it. The parents didn't even know about him, let alone me."

"You—you said you tried to intervene."

"She asked me to take her to the thing. She needed a ride. I said, 'Don't even think about it—a Negro at one of those kindsa hospitals?' Picture me showing up with a pregnant white girl."

He breathed in the long chain of years and paused like he was stopping time. "I told her . . . she could go off and nobody would ever know. I told her someone could raise the baby even if she couldn't. I told her it was *wrong*. And you know, back in the day, Roe v. Wade wasn't happenin'—you just showed up and prayed you didn't get killed in the scrape."

"I see."

He nodded, grim. "Anyway, she went away. And then she came back. And she was different. I even said to myself—she reminds me of the fathers now, the white fathers, all the men. She . . . *it's like she became a man.*"

"Meaning what?"

He went deadpan, the world's greatest yarn spinner.

"I mean *she went cold* like only a man can. A cruel man. With no soul. She got bossy, for one. With me. And I said, 'Who the fuck you think you're talking to, little girl? I taught you how to strap on that guitar.' So we couldn't even do the lessons anymore, it wasn't working. She went from respect to . . . I dunno what. Bam!" He smacked his palms. "Like that. The rest I watched from a distance."

Now he placed those aged hands on the table, his eyes sorrowful, depleted. He shook his head. And it blew my mind how many people from Annie's world stayed wary of her, felt betrayed in some permanent way—but also stayed tethered to her, twisting in the wind. This punched me in the gut. I got up, propelled by sorrow, but I was too drunk. DUI City. Just one could put a driver out of biz for life.

"Where does Minnie fit in?" I blurted. "And Runions."

"Who's that?"

"Some young people. They brought you an envelope."

"You know them?" He was pissed. "You drunk, sit back down."

I did as I was told. "Tell me about the message. I can take it."

"Why would I tell you *shit*? I told you enough already."

"'Cause I'm a fellow driver?"

"You really do think you're Adam-12!" He burst into a cackle.

"No. Just a friend. You lose someone, you want to know what they were about."

He considered this and shrugged. "Look. An arrangement was made to keep silent about this baby, its . . . *situation*. Annie started to become a celebrity and all that and—"

"Wait—this baby? She *had* it?"

"Ain't you listening? I told you, I set it up. Years later, when the father died—*boom*—Annie calls on me. Like all those decades didn't pass."

"Father—you mean the boyfriend, Larry?"

"No—the one who raised the baby—you need to open your ears up, man. I'm not surprised you didn't sell any songs."

"The baby," I repeated. "She had it."

"The baby became a man because that's what they do. His name was Thomas. And Annie wanted to meet him. Technically, to *re*-meet him. She was desperate—and I wasn't surprised. 'Cause I knew she'd been pining about that shit the whole time."

"And you contacted this Thomas and—"

"Not exactly. I tracked him down. Dude's got a Jacuzzi store. Annie sent the kids down there to, like, broach a hang.

She was damn nervous about it too. But I told them where to go. Now you get it?"

"Down where?"

"Hermosa, Redondo."

"What's his last name?"

"Goldfischer. Thomas Goldfischer."

I went ashen. Manuel Combs picked up the guitar but didn't play.

"Man, it don't matter now. They didn't click—it was nothing."

"I'm, I'm not so sure about that."

"Well, I am. It was nothing. And you just keep me out of it. Or else."

Without looking, he started strumming, running scales, skipping notes, playing nothing in particular. When a guitarist canoodles and meanders like that, cascading toward melody in search of a song but not finding one, and you close your drunken eyes to follow him nowhere, the effect is hypnotic, mystical. You drop into a waking dream.

But that's always what a song is supposed to do, isn't it?

For what *is* a song if not an invitation to dream?

It's a mystery thing, a little chant, a chariot, a flying vibration that springs from nowhere and doesn't exactly take you somewhere, doesn't drive the car, and yet it does. A song is not a house, but it's a home. The person is singing something. In your head. Are they singing to you? Or do you imagine that you are the singer, sending your imaginary listeners into a trance? *What is a song?*

Once upon a time, long ago, even before Emmanuel Combs met Annie Linden, before recordings, a popular song was a few sheets of paper, and the singer was . . . anybody, irrelevant. Wax changed all that—suddenly people seemed to believe the song birthed directly from the singer's mouth, spontaneously, for all time. Whoever wrote the song didn't matter so much anymore. It was "Sinatra's song" or it was "Billie's song." But most of the time, back then, someone else did write that song and they could've been a *shlub* in an office building or an amateur humming to themselves on the street like a schizo. Arlen wrote "Over the Rainbow" in the back of a hardware store. You could picture it. A lonesome man sitting there among little boxes of nails like the kind on Combs's big tool table, scribbling about lemon drops and chimney tops.

Combs played and I dreamed—the best deal at bargain prices. I dreamt awake of Annie Linden and her long-lost child, and I was filled with feeling. A song, a good one, had a curious power, wherever it came from. It could tell you where you were, even who you were. Schmucks, illiterates, insensate blockheads, and other assholes who would not admit to a single human emotion might accidentally burst into song. And *mean* it. Good mothers and bad mothers sang to their babies. And Combs was right about kids remembering melodies, they needed songs to live. Then you grew up and all you had to guide you was the jukebox id poking at your soul.

The music stopped. When I opened my eyes, Combs gave me a funny smile.

I got up again, sobered now by the gravity of abandoned babies. I thanked him for the drinks and let myself out the screen door and down the small staircase. Everywhere I looked was broken metal shining in the waning sun.

He called after me from the screen door, "You shouldn't worry about her, man. Her work is done."

I drove home and slept like a man whose case was breaking, as in not much.

In the morning, I made coffee and called Fry, told him everything in a hazy, hungover flurry.

"You think I should call this Goldfischer guy?"

He thought it over. "No. Don't prep him, just show up—shop for a Jacuzzi. But if the dude seems violent? You blaze on out of there."

21

STRANGE AND
MOURNFUL DAY

If Thom Goldfischer resembled Annie Linden at all, it was in
the faraway glow of his pale blue eyes. Otherwise, I didn't see
it. Sitting there in a large white showroom of empty Jacuzzis,
leaning back in a swivel chair with his stretched-out feet dangling flip-flops, thumbing *Sports Illustrated*, he was tall where
his mother was slight, lumbering where Annie was light, a
cool customer, which she wasn't.

Still, you never knew how the DNA traveled.

I arrived unannounced, wandered the tiled floor, marveled
at the large jet stream spouts, the placards reading *Seats 4–5,
Seats 6–7, Seats 10*. They were expensive as used cars, too,
these big round baths. From the corner of my eye, I watched
him as he watched me. He was good-looking but there was
something self-tasting, willfully complacent about his chiseled
handsomeness. Too tanned, too satisfied. Well, he worked in
the hot tub biz, after all. Getting mellow was his calling.

"How'd they get the name?"

"Jacuzzi?" He smiled, put down the magazine, locked into his sandals and stood. "It's a family name. Italian brothers. They tried their hand at airplane propellers. Then they made water pumps for the orange groves upstate. One of the brothers had chronic back pain, so they used their knowledge of irrigation on the human body."

"Nice," I said.

"People associate that name with . . . the seventies, the party lifestyle. But they really come in handy these days."

"How's that?"

Approaching, he was at least six-foot-two and solid, in a white polo shirt with company label and unfaded jeans. "Besides the health benefits, Jacuzzi time is family time. You have a family?"

I told him I didn't.

"Well, either way, friends or family, you put away the cell phone, the iPad. You turn off the TV. Whoever you're with, you face each other. You talk to each other. Sometimes it's the only real together time in the day."

"I'm Adam Zantz." We shook. "I'm actually not in the market for a hot tub. I was Annie Linden's driver."

He got tight around the neck and jaw. "The singer who just died?"

"Yeah, the singer who just died. Listen—I know some of the history."

He bristled, lost his smile. "And you want me to pay you to keep from—"

"Nothing like that. I'm not here to harass you or waste your time. But I'm a former licensed investigator and I'm trying to figure out what other secrets Annie might have had."

He looked around the empty store. The farawayness in his eyes was tallying something now, losing glow. "Okay. Well. Come sit down, let's talk."

I joined him at the big oak table. He was all calm control. I sat on the plastic seat and fidgeted like the runt Jacuzzi brother.

"Listen," I said, "I'm sorry to disrupt your day. And I'm even more sorry about the news."

"I figured it was a matter of time before someone from her camp came around. Did Minnie Olivera tell you about me?"

"Not exactly, but I do know her. I did ask your mother about Annie Linden—"

"Yeah?" He sat up, tightened up.

"She pretended to know nothing about Annie."

"My mother is contractually obligated to do just that. What is it I can help you with?"

"I'm trying to put together a timeline of Annie's last days."

He leaned back. "You'd have to talk to the police about that. They arrested someone, didn't they?"

"Right. And he may be guilty. But I have reason to believe there's more to it."

"I see. I don't have much to offer you. It certainly was a strange episode in my life. It's like I just met her and now she's gone."

"How long ago did you first . . . hear from her?"

"She contacted me a little over a year ago. Sometime in March."

"That's funny. I was already her driver then, but she never had me drive to see you."

"Well, we only met a few times, maybe four times total. She tracked me down when my father passed away."

"That's what I understood—but isn't that illegal too?"

"It's not the done thing, but whatever. I don't hold it against her. I knew I had been adopted, of course. I never really felt all that compelled to find out the details. Is all this interesting to you?"

"Very. I was just her driver, but we were close in a way."

"Did she tell you about me?"

"Not in so many words. She said there were some people from her past, she wanted to close some circles—" I stopped myself. "Did you grow up here in Hermosa?"

"Yup, just up the hill. Terrific place to be a kid."

"Do you know how your parents got you and all that? I couldn't find any records."

"I do know, actually. Annie had a guitar teacher whose mother was my mom's cleaning lady. My folks couldn't have kids so the whole thing just kind of worked out."

"How old were you when you found out?"

"That I was adopted? I want to say five or six. I don't re-member but I do remember my parents having that conversa-tion with my brother and sister. You know, they sit you down, it's a big deal, you cry, you protest. You walk away in a daze but later, when you think about it, it doesn't mean that much."

"Yeah?"

"Well, your parents are your parents, you know what I mean?"

"I guess I do. I was raised by my uncle, but I did think of him as my dad."

"So you get it."

"What was *your* dad like? I heard he was a doctor." There was just no way to bring up the porno mags and the secret meetings, not yet.

"Look at this." He pulled up the sleeve of his white polo and bared his shoulder, exposing a giant tattoo of cursive cal-ligraphy: *DR. MILT.*

"Wow. That's commitment."

"I got this the week he died. I was practically suicidal."

"You loved him."

"Oh, my dad was just the most wonderful, the most caring

man ever to walk the earth. I still get teary-eyed talking about him. His old office is just up the hill, I pass it every day on the way to work. You see this?" From under his desk, he pulled up the most random object, a blue chrome metal detector—the old, long stick with the worn white plastic disk at the bottom. "I keep this baby by my side at all times to remind me. I'm not even sure it works anymore."

"You were coin hunters?"

"Weekday afternoons, he'd take me down to the beach and we'd go scouring for loose change."

"Did you score?"

"Not too much!" He smiled and sighed. "My dad, he just put us *first*, you know what I mean?"

It was just dawning on me how quickly we had gotten away from the subject of Annie Linden when a customer came in, a nervous-looking curly-haired blond surf rat in shorts and flip-flops. The dude stayed near the door, reluctant to shop, maybe stoned. How somebody that young could afford a Jacuzzi was part of the uneasy reality of SoCal economics. Thom shot me a knowing smile, tapped the desk and strode over to the guy, went into his smooth talk.

"That one's okay for old people with back problems," I overheard him say, "but if you're looking to get really mellow and party, come check out the X-243." The moneyed beach bum laughed, blushed, played along, hustled into the prospect of big pleasure. While they circulated the machines, with Thom in happy-go-lucky monologue, the kid started to lighten up, and for a rare moment, I saw the beauty in sales, the art of it, the way it was about sharing fantasies, painting pictures. A pitch wasn't that different from a song in its way, and Thom Goldfischer didn't come off like a pocket picker, more a natural enthusiast. He wanted to get you into a Jacuzzi 'cause it was his way to end human suffering.

When the surfer left, Thom came back and flopped into his seat, swigged the soda. "Now, what were we talking about?"

"Your father—hunting for coins?"

"Yeah well. Anyway. I still miss him. A couple months after he passed, Minnie Olivera visited and told me about Annie Linden. Came right in here just like you and told me Annie wanted to see me."

"Had your folks already told you about her?"

A blank expression took hold of Thom's face. "Not exactly, not in detail. Anyway, imagine this teenage girl with purple hair—she walks in through that door and says, 'You may want to close up the shop for this. I have some life-altering news.'"

"Wow. And then you met Annie and—"

"Yeahhhhh. And then I met Annie. Man." Now Thom crinkled, warding off a complex feeling. There was a hardness within him, scar tissue. *That* reminded me of Annie. "You know," he said, "being a corndog, I offered to give her a new Jacuzzi, second or third time we met. I told her I'd install the very best model out there on her deck up in Malibu. For free, obviously."

"And did you?"

"No. She kept putting off the job. I was kind of surprised she never had one, didn't even like them."

"Were you disappointed?"

"I think I may have disappointed *her*, to tell you the truth."

"I doubt that. She probably just wanted to—"

"No, it's okay. I'm glad . . . I'm glad she had me. And I'm glad she found me. But I know I let her down."

"Why would that be?"

"We didn't have *too* much to talk about, you know what I mean? She asked a lot of questions, about my work, my girlfriends. She asked if I remembered meeting her as a little boy. Which I didn't."

I wanted to press it, but his force field was up, and all at once I saw what he really shared with Annie—the off button, that cold readiness to shut out the world. I said, "Well, it's cool that you got to connect."

"*Did we connect?*" His fast reaction surprised him and he recoiled from himself. "No, seriously, I guess you're right, it was cool. We hung a few times, it happened. But . . . truth is . . . it was forced." He shrugged and smiled, his graying stubble curling around his mouth like the ebb of a low wave. For an instant, I wondered if he thought he was letting *me* down. How could he? But there was something decidedly reluctant about this guy, not just about his birth mother, about everything. He just did not want to make a big deal about anything, ever. This ability to be a major minimizer was certainly a trait Annie Linden did not enjoy. And I wasn't sure I bought it—not from him or anybody else. Because at some hidden locus, mellow is rarely true mellow. Too much hakuna matata is a hot signal that someone is deploying a violent shutdown of operations. This guy, he had that, that heavy-lidded ability to draw curtains on the outside world. It was something a lot of good-looking tall guys seemed to share, this No Big Deal-ism. Maybe the ease with which they got laid made the normal life pursuits seem like so much wasted effort. Why sweat it? Crack a beer and take a dip in the ja-*cooz*, bro.

He left me no choice but to crank up the jets.

"C'mon, man," I said. "Tell me you didn't flip out when you learned that an icon was your *mother*."

He shrugged slowly, his smile disappearing. "I wasn't floored by the news. Not at first. I was never that into rock music or even music in general. I barely knew who she was."

"Really. But she was a celebrity when you were a kid, right? That must have freaked you out."

"Well, yeah, it was weird. Like suddenly finding out you're a member of some club you didn't even know about. I looked her up, of course. I downloaded a greatest hits. My brother told me which songs were the good ones. I even ordered a biography on Amazon, but it kind of bugged me to read it."

"Because you weren't in it?"

"Maybe. But also—it was one of these tell-alls. A lot of dirt about who she slept with and all that. And they were talking about my . . . my birth mother. It didn't feel right."

"How about the morning she drowned?"

"What about it?"

"And it happened right here in Hermosa."

"Awful."

"How did you hear?"

"I didn't hear. I saw it on that electronic ticker tape at the bottom of the TV. I was watching NFL reruns—it was a Saturday. Patriots were losing. I had a babe over and she was making me a grilled cheese."

"How'd it make you feel?"

"How do you think it made me feel? It made me feel bad. Listen, I got a busy—"

"I understand. But what about Annie's estate? Wouldn't you be an official heir?"

"Is that why you're here? You got me figured for a suspect?"

"I never said that."

"Annie Linden was still married, man. And in California that means there *is* no estate, it all goes to the spouse unless she said otherwise. Which far as I know, she didn't."

"But she hasn't lived with that guy for a long, long time— does that bum you out? You could take it to court and—"

"You're not getting it, man." Thom Goldfischer was all

business now. The salesman's joie de vivre had burned off like the morning fog. He rubbed his light moustache with his thumb, stared me down like a target. "I was happy with my lot in life before I met her and I'm happy now. She was a fine old lady—you probably knew her better than me. Also—" Some thought-motor worked harder to come to terms. He held out two gripping hands like a water-skier. "Also—I've *got* a mom." He dropped the hands. "A *real* mom, you understand? The one that changed every diaper, packed our lunches, walked us to school every damn day of our childhoods. And it was a great childhood, right here on the beach. Because of her. My *real* mom. You follow me?"

"I think so," I said carefully, but his outburst overheated the space between us and he quickly tried to regulate the temperature with a softer tone.

"Look, my mom, my real mom, isn't doing all that well. And I care about her too much to bother with all this business."

"Yes, but—"

"Remember, I didn't go looking for Annie Linden. She came looking for me. I didn't need a second mom. But . . . she wanted to get over her guilt and stuff, and I understood that. No point suffering. So I went along, played along kind of. I'm relieved, too."

"That you got to meet?"

"That *she didn't raise me.*" The very last remaining remnant of casualness had evacuated his face. "Who knows what kind of people a woman like that ran with. Especially back then. How they would have raised me. Or not raised me."

"You've got a point. Annie might not have made a good mother."

"Nope. She might have made the worst. I could see plain as day, normal life was obviously not good enough for that woman—I was *obviously* not good enough for her."

"Thom, I knew Annie, and I know she must have loved you. But in those days—"

"I didn't love her. I didn't hate her. I didn't care about her. I didn't know her. And she sure as shit didn't know me."

He smirked and gave a comic mocking tilt of the head—another side came through. He wasn't just Annie's son, he was the product of a teenage quickie with some random jock. I wanted to ask about his birth father but Thom Goldfischer got up and shook himself out. The DR. MILT tattoo disappeared under his white polo—my cue to exit.

As I got up to leave, a skinny man in loose-fitting linen slacks and a KCRW T-shirt entered. "You ready for lunch?"

Thom introduced: "My brother Ronnie. This guy was Annie Linden's driver."

"Oh wow, so sorry." Ronnie actually had compassion in his eyes. "What an awful thing."

"Yeah, man, I'm sorry, too," Thom said, showing me the door. "About *your* loss. But I do hope that whatever you're looking for, you'll leave me out of it. 'Cause the truth is, I didn't know Annie all that well, and I'd honestly just as soon put the whole weird deal behind me."

I walked to the car in the late morning sea breeze and drove the beach back into the city, in a hazy daze, still reeling from the whole weird Annie deal and the whole weird Annie's son deal. The sky was vast and overcast, a blanket of white, and it was time to get back to work. Bix's trial date was approaching and I was going broke playing private eye.

But I didn't like this laconic dealer of hot water, didn't like him much at all. Probably Thom Goldfischer *did* bore Annie, just as he suspected. And then she turned down the free hot tub—that cracked me up. But what did I have on him, really?

So she had a secret son, so what?

22

A LITTLE DREAM CASTLE
WITH EVERY DREAM GONE

A twelve-hour shift with an eight-hour break was the Lyft legal limit. Bachelorette parties, airport runs, geriatric pharmacy pick-ups, movie drop-offs, Starbucks drive-thrus—the carousel of strangers came and went. I kept moving and postponed, for the second time in a month, my Lyft car check-up, but I was in grind mode where you don't want to stop because once you do, you're finished. All the while, my loneliness hung in the air like the homely vapors of a scented tree on the rearview. Annie wanted me to find someone but it wasn't her son—she'd already found him. What was she trying to piece together? At twilight I took a carload of tourists to the Pantages to see *Hamilton* and was veering toward the end of my shift when I got a call from Runions.

"Can you meet me at the pool hall?" He sounded frantic.

"Sure—I'm like, blocks away."

Three left turns later, the *Playboy Liquor* neon glared like cartoon sin. I parked and entered the grim pub next door— six crimson pool tables, no players. The jukebox—the real one, in the corner—played "Karma Chameleon." A bartender with the standard hipster longbeard eyeballed me incuriously. Runions sat in the way back, the sole customer, hiding in the dark in that same faded purple and white bowling shirt, even a shade more sickly than before. He watched me approach with the sting of impatience on his face.

"You said to call."

"I'm glad you did." I pulled up a chair. "Where's your girl?"

"She left town."

"Huh?" I couldn't picture her anywhere but this sorrowful pocket of the universe.

"Fayetteville. She took the bus back this morning."

"As in . . . Arkansas?"

"*Home sweet home.*" He vibed nausea, shakes.

"Lover's quarrel?"

"Someone beat her up."

"What? Who?"

"Some random dude." He hugged himself, folding like a human potato bug. "*I couldn't stop it* and then . . . then she split."

"Oh my God. I am so sorry, dude."

Through his teeth, he mumbled the most unconvincing "*Whatever*" ever spoken.

A preppy-looking Armenian couple, a little older than me, came in and ordered beers, racked up at the other end of the pool hall. The man dropped quarters in the jukebox and "Church of the Poisoned Mind" started up.

"What," I said, "what'd this *random dude* look like?"

"White guy. Not too tall, five-ten like me. But bulkier. Short hair. I didn't get to look at him for long."

"Why not?"

"He, like, bagged himself."

"What?"

Runions watched to make sure the couple weren't listening. Boy George sang: *who am I to say that's crazy? Love will make you blind in the church of the—*

"With his beanie. We were at the all-night falafel place on Hollywood, super late. This dude was at the only other table in there, sitting behind us. He seemed friendly enough at first. He leans in and he's all, like, 'You guys looking for some chalk?'"

"Chalk?"

"Crystal. Anyways, Minnie got all psyched and—" The ripple of a scowl started to test the strength of Runions's lip. "—and he goes, '*Not here—in the bathroom.*' They got up to walk back there and after a split-second I followed. I had a sudden feeling about this guy, but he like, moved us both in there fast, this cramped nasty-ass bathroom and he locked the door. Suddenly he pulls his ski mask down over his face and he pulls a gun and he goes, '*Don't you fucking look at me*' and he rams the gun right up to Minnie's throat."

"No—"

"She started to say *please please* and he goes, '*You shut it, Minnie Mouse.*'"

"Runions—"

Our eyes met in the land of gravity.

"He didn't rape her. I thought he was going to. But. He made Minnie like—" Runions went clear pale now, stone-faced in the shadows, a pleading minus words.

"What?"

"He made her, like, suck the gun. She was gagging, crying . . . then—"

"No."

"—he like, pulled back the gun and smacked her hard with his other hand and grabbed her by the throat. I flipped out, I tried to pull him off her but he elbowed me hard. And I. *I just crumpled up.*"

His tears were streaming fresh, he covered his face. I tried to catch his eyes, like that would help.

Runions shot me the intimidated glare. "He just like, pressed her against the wall. He. He called her a cunt. He said all kindsa sick shit. He said it was time for *her* to—to learn to *please.* To me, he said something like, '*You* better swallow the red pill, *Runions.*' He knew our names, he—" Runions dropped his hands from his face, but his eyes were still elsewhere. "Then . . . he just kind of . . . he dropped her, let go of her. He shoved the pistol back in his jacket and . . . he left us there, all shivering and crying in this fucked-up toilet. Minnie just, she started throwing up. And I . . . I . . . "

"Nightmare." I either said it or thought it, I don't know which.

His tears had stopped. But he was too silent. An agonized stretch passed to the sound of clacking pool balls. The couple at the far table played a measured game and did not speak. "Miss Me Blind" kicked in on the jukebox—we were in greatest hits mode.

"How . . . how did he know your names?"

"I don't know."

"Runions." I leaned in. "I wanna help you, both of you. But you gotta let me know what you're mixed up in."

"I don't *know* what we're mixed up in. And I didn't lie to you. Annie was just our friend, that's what we thought."

"That's not the whole story," I said, trying to stay gentle. "I went and visited Manny Combs. And Thom Goldfischer. You guys helped orchestrate some visits."

"Yeah, but that has nothing to do with this."

"You completely sure?"

No answer.

"Why don't you just tell me what really happened with Annie."

Across the dusty tile of this hope-free room, Runions seemed to measure and then spot just how little he had to lose.

"A while back." He looked me in the eye. "A while back, Annie read that the Goldfischer dad died. Maybe Christmas before last, online. She saw his obit. And she *freaked*. That's when she asked us to track down Emmanuel Combs."

"Did she say why?"

"Not at the time, no. But Minnie found him. She just went down to West Adams and started asking around—crazy brave. She got to Combs and told him about the doctor dude and he knew what to do without her saying anything."

"So you lied about the message."

"Yeah, sort of. I mean, we knew what was in the envelope. Couple weeks later, Combs came up here with Goldfischer's address—for his Jacuzzi shop."

"And?"

"And then Minnie went down there and she just kind of brokered these secret meetings for Annie. There were only maybe four times they got together, Annie and Thom. Far as I know, anyway."

"The big reunion."

"Kinda. Except Annie didn't want anybody to know. I rented an SUV and took her."

"So this was all, like, last year? Behind my back?"

Runions gave me a funny look. "Was it any of your business?"

"I guess not. But I *was* her driver—why the secrecy?"

"She thought paparazzi might have followed your car around once or twice. She didn't want publicity. She didn't want to mess with their family."

"Yet she *did* want to disturb him?"

"It was, like, an experiment at first." Runions wiped his dirty face with the back of his wrist—a weird tic that made me wonder if he was still using. "I barely even saw the guy. Me and Minnie would wait in the car."

I said, "Where'd they meet?"

"Down in Hawthorne, Eucalyptus Park. There's a playground. But it would be super-early in the morning and empty. You know, like, incognito."

"And that's all? Did anything change meeting to meeting?"

"Oh, totally. The first time she was in pretty good cheer after. I think he even made some crack about musicians or something, but she didn't care. Going home, she was all, giggling, like, '*What a trip—my son . . . Thom.*'"

"And then?"

"Well, we didn't see what happened. But the next two times, on the way back, Annie was in really bad shape, crying and getting all spun out. She'd be, all, like, '*I don't know him, something's not right, he's changed—he's a total stranger to me.*' It was brutal."

"Anything else you remember?"

"She . . . I guess she asked him a lot of questions. Oh, and he, uh, she said he casually mentioned he wanted to give her a free Jacuzzi."

"How about the last time?"

"Super cold. She just got in the car after, like, '*Let's get outta here.*' Minnie asked how it went and Annie said, '*He talked about his mother the whole time, he kept checking his watch.*' She didn't say one more word the whole way home. Then, when we pulled up to her place, she goes, '*Well, that'll probably never happen again.*' Kind of like, trying to joke— but it was majorly awkward."

"And that was that?"

"Nope. 'Cause then she called him, like, ten days later. The Jacuzzi was her big excuse. They made the date for the install and then . . . " Runions shrugged.

"What."

"He flaked."

"What do you mean?"

"Well, first he postponed. Then they made another date and he was a no-show. And then she invited him *again* and he actually passed."

"And she told you all this?"

He shook his head. "That's just what I heard from Minnie."

"And now . . . Minnie's gone home?"

He nodded, his lip curled. I tensed, felt the strain of our age difference. I was only thirty-seven—maybe too young to play father figure to this kid. But he needed one. I was searching for the right words when he whispered, "There's something else."

The man across the room leaned over the pool table to take a concentrated shot, pumping his cue backward. His lady watched him with a skeptical smile.

Runions lifted his skinny face to me—the potato bug unravelling. His wet gray eyes met mine.

"The guy . . . that jumped us. He said another thing. Right before he left."

Through gritted teeth: "What."

"He said tell the Lyft driver I'm watching his every fucking move."

23

YOUR SHOES GET SO
HOT YOU WISH YOUR TIRED
FEET WERE FIREPROOF

Marble halls, 100 percent gravity, Clara Shortridge Foltz Criminal Justice Center downtown. The courtroom was packed, claustrophobic. As we squeezed down a bench into the only empty seats, Double Fry eyeballed the crowd, he wanted a who's who. Mostly I had no idea. Troy's widow, Lauren, sat up front—she looked sedated. Barbara Linden snuggled beside Kronski near the far-right wall, which was odd. On the other side of us, Eva Silber-Alvarez held down a far corner in a charcoal linen suit, her hard jaw trembling. Judge Moyer, on the other hand, had a soft face—Droopy Dog could've been modeled after him. He was a straight-up Boomer with the Lennon mustache 'n' glasses combo and you just knew he had an Annie Linden LP somewhere in his crates. The jurors uniformly looked like they'd never heard of her. Face by face, I scanned them for the compassion Bix needed now.

Then Bix appeared, dazed and half-asleep in a dark blue

Men's Wearhouse suit. They led him to his seat. The guy repping Bix was Charles "Chuck" Moscowitz, a beaky shuffler of papers with an uneven haircut and a belly like third trimester pregnancy. At the other table, District Attorney Andrew R. Edler beamed civic vigor, hot to make opening statements. He stood swift and lean and approached judge and jury, opening his long arms as if to conduct between two invisible poles.

"Your honor, citizens of Los Angeles. Baxter Gelden didn't just *lose control* one night and kill his boss. That would've been bad enough, but no. This thirty-nine-year-old on-again off-again *personal assistant* had a *life-long* obsessive and destructive relationship with the late Annie Linden. And a sexual relationship with her security guard that he went out of his way to hide, even to his closest cohorts."

My pulse raced—the closest cohort had to be me—but Edler was playing for the room. He was a kind of folksinger himself, a young Leonard Cohen delivering the heavy.

"After being *hired* and *fired* a total of . . . *seven times*, this *forty-something adolescent*, unable to find work, and carrying the baggage of a *long* history of narcotics abuse, came to a *decision*. To finally exact his revenge once and for all. First, on the boyfriend who wouldn't . . . *tear apart* his marriage for him. And then on the boss—the fragile, aging, female boss—who had given him *another last chance* one too many times."

Edler made a big production of picking up and waving a stack of letters at the jury. Bix went slack-jawed at the sight of them. Edler read: "*'Annie, you've given me another last chance just one too many times.'* Mr. Gelden's own words, right here in his very own *screed of desperation*."

The jury were like kids mesmerized by a scary puppet show. Outshined in every conceivable way, Moscowitz hammered his client with whispers like an annoying schoolmate.

Bix turned away in disgust and our eyes met in the line of fire. His peepers widened and dilated—a beg, but what could I do?

The pressure popped me. Up and out I went, sliding around the knees with whispered apologies, out into the hall with the AC hitting like a fever chill.

Fry followed, let the court doors shut behind him. "Where the heck you going?"

"I can't," I said. "I cannot be in there."

"Okay, deep breaths. It's not you on trial."

"It's not?"

"Of course not, bro. Have they got an affidavit out of you yet?"

"No. But I think they videoed my interview."

"Okay—*calm. Down.* First of all, you were under duress. And if the state's case against Bix is based on a few letters, it's far from open and shut. They don't have a weapon, they don't have a witness. You'll be fine." Fry steadied me with a smile. "His lawyer is kind of a *shlemiel* though, right? Where the hell did Bix find *that* loser?"

"Yelp?"

"I was thinking bus bench ad."

"What happens next?"

"Early depositions."

I watched Lauren Yvette leave the courtroom and disappear down the glossy hall. I felt dizzy.

"Addy," Fry said, "look me in the eyes. Accessory after the fact is a *wobbler.* Prosecutors will likely file as a misdemeanor. You have no record, they have no evidence."

"Stop bullshitting me. What happens if Bix is convicted? And don't butter it up."

He adjusted his Grateful Dead yarmulke and glanced up at

the heavens, calling on holy powers to help deliver bad news. "Up to a year in county if it's misdemeanor, sixteen months in state prison for felony."

I said, "Wonderful."

"Is that Linden's ex-husband sitting in the courtroom?"

"Yeah, practically holding hands with her sister. Him I don't trust at all."

"Well, he's got an airtight alibi. Cleared a hundred percent."

"How do you know all this?"

Fry grinned. "I met a girl on J-Date who works in the DA's office. She told me Kronski turned over some records. He was on a binge."

"What kind of binge has records?"

"He was webbin', man. With Russian girls, cam-babes."

"Like—the whole time?"

"Days."

"I don't buy it. A guy like Kronski has no trouble getting real women in real life."

"Maybe he wasn't looking for real life. A pile of Bolivian pixie dust, good wireless, he's fixin' to party. I couldn't believe it myself when she told me about the summary—he had six screens going for almost seventy-two hours—laptops, tablets, phones, everything."

"Seventy-two hours?"

Fry nodded slowly, transmitting comical subterranean knowingness.

I said, "So good it's suspicious."

"Fixing an alibi?" Fry shrugged. "C'mon Addy, let's go back in. We're missing the fun. You can handle it."

Back in the court, we slid into our seats. Now a slim, forbidding-looking Persian woman in her early thirties was recounting on the stand. She had been jogging along Redondo Beach toward Hermosa when she saw what she thought was a sleeping homeless woman. She approached the old lady, got scared when she didn't respond, backed off in a panic. The old lady's eyes were open.

"She looked affronted," the young woman said. "And contrary to some reports, I didn't recognize who she was."

The audience tittered, Edler got stern. "Then what happened."

"The paramedics came, but they wouldn't get out of the van. They waited for the cops. Then the police came and I screamed at them."

Edler said, "What did you say?"

"I said, 'Her neck is black and blue.'"

"Thank you, Ms. Mizraki, that will be all."

She stepped down. Judge and jury broke for lunch and the citizens filed out. Fry had to split, but I stayed put, paralyzed sick in the almost empty courtroom.

The jogger's story made it all cut again. The look on Annie's face—*affronted*—the shock of the never-fooled. But she *had* been fooled.

By someone she couldn't mesmerize.

Glamor—from the Scottish word for *grammar*—a fancy way of describing a witch's incantation.

And just this one time, Annie's didn't work.

Eva Silber approached and slumped down in the row in front, threw a shoulder over the bench to face me.

She said, "I'm not going to stay."

I said, "Me neither."

"Are you still a jitney jockey? I need a lift back up north to Los Osos."

24

YOU SAID THE DEVIL TOLD YOU THAT ANOTHER MOUNTAIN WOULD APPEAR EVERY TIME SOMEBODY BROKE YOUR HEART

Out in the parking lot, I opened the passenger door for the feminist icon. Eva lowered herself into the seat with a familiar look—the reluctant and aggravated self-admission of age and exhaustion mixed with a drop of gratitude. I came around to the driver's side and started the ignition.

She said, "I am happy to pay your top rate, I just couldn't stand another minute in there."

"It's ugly to watch."

"What's the point? I cannot stand the sight of that pig Haywood, and this *mishigas* isn't going to bring Annie back." She turned silent till the 101 spit us out onto the 10—we jettisoned west across the basin like a pinball set free. "I haven't been so nice to you, I certainly hope you did not take umbrage."

"Other than pulling a rifle on me, lying to me, siccing

the cops on me, and not returning my phone calls, you've been wonderful."

"I certainly did not call the police!"

"They called you a *personage*."

"Ha. Maybe I am. But I'm not the mean ole bull dyke you make me out to be."

"I don't make you out one way or another. But you did keep me in the dark about things. Important things."

"A girl's gotta protect her friends." She sized me up. "So, what've you figured out?"

"Not enough. In the mid-sixties, Annie had a kid. She gave the baby to a family in Hermosa called the Goldfischers, through her guitar teacher. The teacher's name is Combs. For some purpose I have yet to figure out, the adopting dad, a urologist named Milton Goldfischer, was meeting Annie in secret. They sent each other ads in *your* porno rag—or at least your name was on the masthead. Which blows my mind. When Dr. Milt died, Annie reached out to her long-lost son for the first time in almost fifty years. That doesn't quite sit right either—but that's what I got."

Somber: "*Mazal tov.* You've done good legwork."

"The Malibu PD don't think so."

"The police are petty bureaucrats with guns. From Warsaw to Zuma." She shook out a Camel unfiltered, lit it, and rolled down the window without a word of permission, more pure Annie. She didn't have Annie's lithe grace or introspective tenderness but they did share something deep, a rare electric crackling something.

I said, "*Hers & His*—what on earth was a nice girl like you doing with a magazine like that?"

"The truth?" She pressed a frown. "On one condition. My wife can't hear about that stuff—it would deeply offend her."

"Deal," I said, "but this time tell me the whole story—or else."

"Or else what?"

"I'll publish every single issue online and hashtag you six ways from Sunday. It'll be the first thing that comes up when somebody googles your name."

"To do that, you'd have to have the magazines, my dear, and I assure you, they are not so easy to get ahold of."

"The fifteen issues I've got are in mint condition."

She didn't laugh. "What can I tell you? Those were different times. Much more radical than today if you can believe. We were *vilde chayas*—wild animals." Recollection transformed her into the stern *Yiddishe momme* she probably ran from. "Hard for your generation to understand but we really aimed to turn the whole thing *upside-down*. And not just this namby-pamby identity politics shit. I mean, we aimed to tear the edifice *down*."

"What edifice is that?"

"*The discontents of civilization.* All of it. But at the center was s-e-x, of course. Sex was going to be *free*—free of rules, and I mean *all* rules. Sinless. Don't give me that look, watch the road. The magazines were Kronski's idea—he wanted Annie to do it—a dirty poetry journal. She laughed him out of the room. She was already too famous to attach her name, but I took the dare."

"That's a crazy dare."

"Well, at first it was a joke, and a challenge—if a man can do smut, why not me? Control the conversation. Also, I thought I could make it . . . healthier. But once the ads came in, forget it."

"And the classifieds?"

"We provided a service, did we not?"

"Yeah, but for Annie?"

"The last place on earth the good Dr. Goldfischer's wife would look was some ratty thirty-five-cent nudie magazine. It was a stroke of genius, no pun intended. Mr. Combs dropped off a plain-wrap copy at the doctor's office, and the lady of the house was none the wiser."

I tried to picture him flipping through *Hers & His* in his office. "Were Annie and the doctor having some kind of an affair?"

"Oh God, no."

"So why were they meeting?"

"For the kid, obviously. Once she got over the first bump or two of being famous, that first thrust, all of a sudden she decided she wants to play mother. It was selfish. It was wrong. And I told her so."

"But you helped her."

"I was in love. Have you ever been in love?"

"I'm afraid so."

"Didn't go too great for me either, buster. She hated me for pointing out this young boy already had a mother, already had formed a bond. He didn't need her to confuse him with secret visits to the pony rides and all that shit. But it's very hard to tell famous people they're wrong. That's one of the reasons we started fighting. I'd just . . . had it with her moral equivocating."

"So the meetings stopped?"

"That's right, I wore her down. But I lost her in the process."

We blazed up the coast now in silence, turned up the highway at Point Mugu. A thousand sprinklers on a lettuce farm set off a field of tiny arching rainbows.

"*Ms. Silber*," I said, "first you pretend there's no kid, then you tell me they didn't know each other, now you say they were *meeting*, in secret, when he was a little boy? You're still hiding something. And I'm just trying to help a woman we both happened to love."

Another unfiltered cigarette. Her nature, her core compassion, was taking up arms, parrying and thrusting its way past the shell and the shame. She spit a little tobacco onto her finger, got it out of the way. "He came to me, years later, the Goldfischer boy. Already, he wasn't a boy anymore. He was in college or—*that age*. It was 1987, the year after the last year I saw Annie face to face."

"What did he want with you?"

"He wanted to see his mother, naturally. He had gone through the usual channels and he didn't get far. What Annie thought, I don't know. I only know Haywood blocked him, even threatened him. The young man told me so. He was desperate, so he came to me. He remembered me from . . . the times when he was small, a few of our get-togethers. Me, he could get to."

"Wow. Not what I heard. What did you tell him?"

"What could I tell him? That the woman who gave birth to him left me for a psychopath? I tried to *ameliorate*—that's what foolish women do when they're stuck. But I was absolutely furious at Annie and Haywood for this mess. And furious at myself more. Because in some way, it was really my fault."

"How's that?"

"I told you, I was the one who thought those meetings were not a good idea in the first place. Little boys become *attached*. More than their faces show. I told Annie she was playing a dangerous game, *making this child love her*. The two hours she saw him twice a month were going to foul his psyche—you didn't have to be Sigmund Freud to see that. He already had a mother and he needed to—" She cut herself off, flipped open the ashtray and smashed out the cigarette prematurely.

I said, "What?"

"Nothing, just—what did it matter what I thought? By law and by contract, Mrs. Goldfischer was the boy's mother." Eva sighed. "And that, young man, is why Annie left me."

I took it in.

"*Nowadays it's different,*" Eva blurted. "People even have what you call open adoptions—*come by any time, see what you left behind!* But back then, everything was *how will it look, how will it look.* How will it look if this kid ends up loving his real mother more than the one who took on the burden of raising him? Mind you, Annie wasn't ready to *take him back*, wasn't ready to *adopt* him herself. She wanted to play auntie, to play at love. No. To me, it was not right."

"So twenty years pass and he comes around trying to connect with his mom? And now she says no?"

"Something like that."

"And then he turns to you in a last ditch—"

"Yes, that's what happened, a last-ditch attempt. It broke my heart."

"Then what? He just . . . gave up? I went down to speak with Goldfischer—he didn't say a word about any of this."

"He didn't *give up*, not exactly. Believe it or not, I followed up and called him, about three months after he came to visit. I was wracked with guilt. Well, he had met someone, a girl his age, and he was happy. You can't imagine the relief I felt. He said if Annie wasn't interested in him, she could go fuck herself. I told him this was the right way to think. Absolutely right."

Traffic gummed up on the 101 like it always does around Santa Barbara—we still had a ways to go. I was fighting an image of Annie I'd never seen before or refused to consider—ugly entanglements and real enemies, turning her own son away, being too self-involved to even know he came looking for her.

In the crawl, I said, "One thing bugs me. If I understand correctly, as far as *you* know, Annie never even knew he came around. Kronski could have blocked him or sent him away all by himself, is that right?"

"Yes. I myself couldn't even get to her. First of all, she was on tour most of the year and in those days, you had to track a person down. I got pushed from one lackey to another. I was *enraged*. Then I spoke with Kronski and it didn't take long before we disintegrated into our usual shouting match. According to the cocksucker, she didn't want to speak to me *or* her son." She raised her trembling garden-weathered hands, without cigarette for the first time all morning, palms out in jittery self-arrest. "My Annie, my princess. What a *fucking* mess." Her chest heaved up, her voice went commanding. "Now you make me cry and I'm not the kind that's good with that. You have tissue?"

I popped the glove—she had to pull out a little brown bag to get to the Kleenex.

I said, "Look inside."

She pulled out the cassette from the Linden Hop. "What's this?"

"Annie at Winterland—it's a bootleg. I haven't played it yet 'cause I don't have a cassette player."

Eva said, "I'll give you my boombox. I haven't used it in years."

"Let's listen together."

"Absolutely not—I don't need to hear her sing ever again for as long as I live. I already have her playing in my head enough."

I dropped Eva off at her sunny cottage. She opened the garage to get me her boombox—one of those clunky one-speaker mono jobs that only people born before 1955 ever seem to have.

I thanked her. She said, "It needs batteries. Good luck, boychick."

As I drove away, I caught Eva in the rearview, still standing in front of the open garage, watching me with a grave look on her face.

25

TEMPERATURE'S RISIN' THE JUKEBOX'S BLOWIN' A FUSE

On the way back down, I stopped at San Luis Obispo Best Buy to score some C batteries. In line, my confusion was coming on in jolts, like a bad acid trip. Thom said he never knew Annie before *she* showed up, yet there he was, allegedly knocking on her door when he was a pimply-faced college kid.

And Annie allegedly *wasn't* there to receive him—or didn't or wouldn't or couldn't?

It didn't add up.

After some fumbling in the parking lot, I popped my boot-leg cassette in the sodden old gray or formerly silver monstrosity and lay it across the passenger seat and pressed play, cruising onto the highway, waiting on Annie.

10/13/'78. The crowd was one shrill scream overwhelming whatever tiny hidden microphone was poking out of some-one's jean jacket. An announcer rumbled stentorian—*"Ladies and Gentlemen...Winterland Ballroom is proud to present... Annie...Linden."* And the screams throttled worse—you could picture the spinning lights, the giant noise wave as she took center stage. The band kicked into some rolling bassy groove, with Annie's halting voice overheating her own mic, and it was low-fi all around—one rumbling, rolling mush. But you could make out the songs. She ran a medley of her greatest hits like she was trying to get it over with. It wasn't great, but I missed her in this moment more than before, an aching of belly and wrists, the guilty ecstasy of mourning, the selfishness of it, sure that she would be enraged by all this pity for the way she went. *This isn't what I want to say,* I could almost hear her scream. Also: I felt her position onstage, before that faceless crowd—her aloneness, disconnection, even boredom. You start out in a tiny café on a tabletop-sized stage practically whispering in someone's ear but then you get famous and it ends like *this*: the tidal wave of screeching humanity crashes down on you, merciless.

The last chords of "Midnight's Desire" dipped into a fuzzy silence. She was going to speak. Lugheads in the crowd shouted for the obvious tunes that hadn't been played yet. One drunky yelled, "I've loved you since 1965!" This got a rollicking cheer. But she waited, hushed them by her silence.

"Hey," she finally said, "I don't know if you people can dig this—but love is war." The downer bummerism of this statement, delivered mid-party by the party leader, absolutely stupefied the crowd into silence. *"That's right, man,"* she insisted, pressing on. "It's the war you win by losing. *Better believe it.*" She strummed right into "Next Stop, Goodbye" and the crowd went apeshit—they sang along with every word. No silly songs here.

It went on like this, my ultra-lo-fi bootleg from the salad days of bootlegging, probably copped off a slim handheld Panasonic, now playing on the world's least sensitive boombox with a tape head that hadn't been cleaned since the day it was created. At minute thirty, mid-song, the Emerson went *ka-chunk* and for a split-second I thought it had swallowed the tape, but it was merely flipping to Side Two automatic—hot feature back in ye olden days. At first there was silence and I was sure I'd been ripped off—ten bucks for half a concert. But then I heard a man's voice.

"Because, just as a child cannot fathom the responsibilities of adulthood —"

The acoustics were totally different, a smaller room and a more modern P.A. He was a public speaker of some kind—like a professor at a seminar, or a motivational guru. Someone taped some bullshit over my bootleg! I sat up in my driver's seat—his words caught my ear.

"So a woman cannot understand the *accountability* of being a man. Their limbic system simply won't allow for rational accounting."

I leaned over, pressed rewind—a smooth, measured voice, a seasoned pundit delivering a spiel he had down pat.

"*Natural alphas*—actually there are none. Every man receives training vis-à-vis womankind. Some just get it early, this . . . this training. But natural alphas, what we call natural alphas, never learn the *distortions of compromise*. Write down that phrase, the distortions of compromise."

For all his radio DJ conviction, the speaker had a youthful, pleading quality to his voice. Like he himself was a new convert or zealot. Somewhere back in his past, he had been wounded. Now he saw the light.

I heard a click—the whir of a projector. He had an Excel spreadsheet or a PowerPoint.

"The distortions of compromise. Alphas don't learn it.

They never get programmed by the quote *vag-o-sphere* un-quote. You can write that one down too."

There was a smattering of quiet laughter.

"Betas on the other hand, suffer—they aren't *to blame* but they do suffer *so* much because their belief system, or their BS, as I like to call it—" Now a slightly louder chuckle passed through the room—I couldn't tell from the sound if it was packed or what. "Betas—their BS is what they've been force-fed. Often, by unhappy moms. '*Go out there and be a white knight, save my soul.*' Well, I don't have to tell you, getting guidance like that, it's tantamount to castration. Yeah. Castration. Literally. I mean, these moms are so sick, so depraved that they *don't want their own offspring to reproduce.* You think about that a minute."

He let another silence fall on the listeners.

"And so, the average Joe, good intentions and all, comes to our group and says, 'Hand me the red pill. *I'm ready.*'" Long pause. "But are they?"

Back in the apartment, I turned my desk inside-out looking for the hippie guy's business card, the old geezer from the Linden Hop that sold me the tape, but of course I had put it in the smart place, the cassette case.

I shook it out and dialed, paced my studio waiting for him to pick up.

"Yallo."

"Hey, uh, Jeff—we met at the Linden Hop. I showed you a photograph, you sold me a tape."

"Yeah."

"So you remember me?"

"'Course I do."

"Good. Uhh, listen—did you *make* the tape I bought."

"Doubt it. What was the gig?"

"Annie at Winterland, 1978?"

He laughed. "In 1978 I was trying to be an avocado farmer, man."

"No but—the tape. Did you tape the tape?"

"The one you bought? No."

"You wouldn't happen to know who *did* make the tape?"

"Hey—I never divulge a source—bootlegs being illegal and all."

"Okay. But this probably wasn't the original bootlegger."

"I'm joking, man, I'm joking. I could check my records. Pretty sure it was an eBay dealer. The set came together. Like, about thirty tapes."

"Have you *listened* to any of them?"

"Oh sure. I listen to the first minute or so of each, just to make sure it's legit."

"Yeah, but have you listened to any of them all the way through?"

"No. What's this all about? You get a dud?"

"Mine—mine was weird. It had a lecture on the other side."

"A lecture?"

"Yeah, like a . . . someone speaking at a seminar."

"Well, you know, some people don't take the time to erase whatever they're taping over."

"No—this was halfway through the concert."

He said, "Bummer."

I repeated the word just to hear how it sounded on my tongue. It was an old word but it still worked.

"Look, if it's a refund you want—"

"Not at all. I'm just wondering if you could check some of the other tapes, see if they're all like that. And also, if you let me know who you bought them from, I promise you I won't tell them you told me."

"Half a gig, I'm really sorry about that."

"I'll live."

"I'm prepping for a swap meet. I'll get back to you as soon as I can figure it out."

I thanked him and popped open the boombox, pulled the cassette, held it like a weapon. A song invaded my brain in the silence, a spinning organ grinder nightmare of a song—

Tape the tape
Rape the tape
If you wanna be a man
You gotta go ape

I had to turn on the radio just to make it stop.

There comes a point in the writing of any song that you might call "the ride"—where the songwriter knows a hook is coming, zooming through the clouds like a crop duster—but not yet. In the twenty-odd years I hacked away at the piano, I never wrote a single great song, maybe I never wrote a good one. But I wrote hundreds of them, verse and chorus, intro, bridge, and fade, tempo shift and key change, melody, counterpoint, and prosody—that devil-dog, nipping at my heels. I wrote songs in the shower and in my sleep, in line at CVS and waiting for my number at the DMV. I grabbed at a fragment of lyric fainter than a retinal floater and if I caught it I held it, turned it, flipped it upside-down and placed it on the altar of the muse, praying for a ride.

Any songwriter good or bad will tell you—either you take flight or spiral in flames, and never on schedule either way. If a silly little melody wakes you at 4:00 a.m., you better reach for the tape recorder and sing it in your PJs 'cause she flies when she flies and you *will* forget. The very best songwriters, the Irving Berlins and Stevie Wonders and Lennon-McCartneys and all your favorites, they were not great pilots, they were gliders, inhumanly expert at letting the breeze take over. When the ride came, they climbed aboard.

In my search for Annie Linden's end, I had stumbled into the crosswinds of confusion where a person has to get on and glide.

The cassette rattled in my grip.

I was on the ride.

26

BUT WISE MEN NEVER FALL IN LOVE SO HOW ARE THEY TO KNOW

Double Fry mopped the deck of the *Shechinah* with the care of a teenager smitten with his first Camaro. When he saw the boombox he said, "Dance party!"

"Not on your life," I said. "I need your ear."

"That you get for free."

He mumbled a fast *bracha* as he poured wine into metal cups—a blessing on the fruit of the earth. I ran down the chain of events since I'd seen him last, Eva's story, and the tape.

He said, "I've read that Silber woman. *The Masculine Conspiracy.*"

"You're into women's studies now?"

"I'm against all forms of ignorance. *Tikkun Olam*—heal the world."

"Well, the guy talking on this tape doesn't seem all that eager to heal shit."

We played the bootleg tape lecture—fifteen minutes of

Alpha blah-blah. Fry took it in with quiet bemusement. Super-mensch Fry knew just when to counter to my heightened state. On his iPad, we googled *red pill male power* and the internet spit forth a tundra of chaotic contradictions. It was a move-ment or a perspective or a philosophy or a burgeoning theory, all about this amorphous thing called "men's rights." *Business Insider* had an article from a few months back describing a whole subculture of guys whose main life objective was learn-ing how to macho up.

I said, "Seems like a lot of this shit is about picking up women. Casual sex, learning *game*. It's confidence school for horny losers."

"Right," Fry said. "But intertwined you get the angry fringe hooked on something else, something darker. It's like any idea. You've got the pragmatists and the pervs."

We chased the links to a weird, verbose manifesto called "The Misandry Bubble" all about the so-called four horse-men of the Male Apocalypse: *Easy contraception, No fault divorce, Female economic freedom*, and *Female-Centric so-cial engineering*, whatever the hell that meant. It was hard to find the through-line, but in a nutshell the writer—who called himself Imran Khan of all things—ranted that feminism had gone too far. He was drowning in his own vehemence, but he wasn't alone—a whole little cult of disgruntled dudes was out there heating up the talkbacks. Like everything on the Godforsaken internet, half the info was specious—*Center for Disease Control Finds Women Commit Half of Domestic Violence.* And the other half wasn't even claiming to be fact-based—*12 Reasons Why You Should Never Say I Love You First.* But nevertheless, there they were, these wronged party animals, prodding each other on.

Fry said, "You gotta wonder, did one of these dipshits accidentally record over some random Annie Linden bootleg? Or did he *purposefully* record the lecture on top of her? Or what? Who's he trying to educate?"

Sitting in beach chairs on deck, we browsed together, passing the tablet back and forth, drinking and reading out loud.

"Oh Jesus, look at this," Fry said, "listen to this. This is from *Return of Titans dot com*—very low budget. The graphics are cheaper than the anti-Semite blogs. Nothing but stock shots of chicks in their undies, listen to this. 'Diary of a White Man Who Woke Up,' listen. Good Lord."

Fry stood, cleared his throat, and read like a stiff-necked high school biology teacher. "Today the modern *whore* is everywoman, spreading her legs for the world. So corrupt is her *Pussy Power Credo* that she will accept nothing but . . . ahem . . . nothing but *brown-skinned primates and money-grubbing hook-nosed Jew rats* for her bedmates. She has soyled—S-O-Y-L-E-D—the concept of white motherhood for all time."

I fought a nervous smile. Fry standing there reading his tablet with his shirt half-untucked, yarmulke dangling, made it nut-on-nut theater. "Will you stop joking?" I said. "There's some psycho out there smashing windows and tracking me like a hawk."

He raised a hand to silence me. "She has spread her legs like the ocean, an *open harbor* letting in every black cock and, uh, Kash man cock—that's Kash with a capital K—every Kash man cock she can find. In *all of history*, there has never been a female more hungry for multiple cocks than this *average modern woman*—but does it liberate her? *No, reader.* It makes her a modern day *witch*. The witch of cunt. The witch of clit. She has one dream. For the whole of planet earth to enter her like a giant supersized monster cock. One in her mouth, at least two, three, four elsewhere, and most of all a big one up her ass." Fry broke character with a burst of laughter. "Jesus, this guy's good."

"Go on, please."

"In the name of *pleasure*. In the name of *destruction*. In the name of *hate*. The Queen Bee of All Whores, she has one goal: to get a bigger and more manly dick inside her. It simply cannot be big enough. She wants to be impaled. Even the gorillas she cavorts with are *not big enough*. She requires elephants or *larger. Godzilla himself will not be big enough.*" Now Fry was wet in the eyes from holding back chuckles. "This guy's a poet!"

"Can you just keep going?"

"Okay, okay. *However.* Her mind is *split.* She is *torn up inside.* No sooner does she get the cock she has hungered for, does she want to ABORT—all caps, A-B-O-R-T—all life. She wants to turn life into garbage. *Oi vey, here we go.*"

Fry got quiet. I knew his marriage had fallen apart after his wife had an abortion. Now he sat on the rail of the deck and read the rest without the vocal shtick, straight and grim, kayaking down the river of hate. ". . . and so do NOT expect forgiveness from the L-R-D."

"What the hell is L-R-D?"

"He doesn't spell out Lord—it's L-dash-R-D."

"Oh. Duh."

Fry sighed. "Dude, it just goes on and on. *The L-R-D, more dick, more ass, cunt is a soul-eater.* You get the gist."

He dropped back into his beach chair and we sat in silence, night water sloshing the docks. Fry threw his head back to take in the starlight. I copied the gesture, but what comfort were the stars? Annie's Janus-face laughed and cried behind the night haze. Had somebody found in her the perfect object of hate?

And could that someone . . . even be her own son?

Fry broke the silence. "What's your gut?"

"I dunno. This Alpha stuff is just some garden-variety Nazi bullshit. Crazy as it sounds, I keep circling back to Thom Goldfischer."

"Really. So you're fairly certain he's the one Annie wanted to reconnect with."

"I know that just doesn't make sense—she'd already reconnected. But . . . something's wrong there, too *opaque*." I started counting fingers. "First he agrees to see her—as a grown man, offers her a jacuzzi even. Then he starts to back off, for no apparent reason. Then? He drops her like a hot potato, won't even return her calls."

"Yeah but—"

"Suppose he *had* been to see her as a young man. And suppose he got turned away and—"

"Addy, even then I'm still not sold. I mean—she was his birth mother, okay? With a few unfortunate exceptions, people don't tend to haul off and kill their moms."

"Yeah, I *know* that," I said, feeling chastised. "But there's something off with that guy. He's like a stray puzzle piece from some other puzzle."

27

BLACKMAILED EMOTIONS
CONFUSE THE
DEMON AND DEVOTEE

I slept on the deck. Early next morning the clouds of gray promised a free car wash—good for business. In the Marina parking lot, I dust-busted the Jetta, intending to work a full shift, but my mind was swimming, I had Goldfischers on the brain. I turned on the Lyft app and drove south, headed for Hermosa, Redondo, the great South Bay with its karate chop coastline. Something was drawing me back to them, something I couldn't fight or put my finger on.

A light sprinkle hit as I coasted past Nan Goldfischer's deco mini-palace. This time the curtains were drawn, the kitchenette light was out. That's when I remembered the daughter, the redheaded beauty. Handling her brittle mom, she seemed saner, more open. If her brother was into this manly man stuff—and he certainly came off like a steel-girded shed filled with explosives—maybe she'd know it, and maybe she wouldn't be so sticky about covering for the tribe.

I put it in park and googled: Patricia Goldfischer had married and changed her last name to Huber. She worked at Fox in Feature Casting. Her FB profile pic had her in the arms of a leading-man-type hubby—he dipped her backward for a movie-style kiss. A little more poking around taught me that his name was Alan and that he was a chiropractor with a clinic of his own on Sawtelle. There were also three handsome strawberry-blond grade-school kids on the Facebook wall. The Hubers were vocally Catholic, too, big church donors—weird 'cause the Goldfischers had been raised Jewish. But besides that, it was Nan and Dr. Milt all over again—the three children, the doctor husband, the play for Big Stability. They lived on Cheviot Drive in Cheviot Hills—the ritzy stretch. Inside twenty minutes, I was there.

I pulled up caddy-corner and idled at a turn in the road where they couldn't really see me but I could spy their front door. The Hubers lived in one of those three-story LA Tudors that looked like it escaped a Welsh village. Probably had a suit of armor in the vestibule. I watched and waited in the morning gloom. It was early yet.

Around 8:07 two of the kids split for school—one caught a ride from a friend, one went skateboarding toward Motor Ave weighed down by a droopy denim backpack. At 8:26 the hubby pulled out of the ye olde knotty alder garage in his burgundy Ford Expedition with the youngest in tow—a seven- or eight-year-old girl with bright orange pigtails.

They drove off, I stayed, eyeballed the windows, the stone staircase leading up to the front door. No action. Maybe a half hour passed in the steady morning drizzle. The jukebox id was silent.

And then, something in the way of a minor miracle happened. My app lit up.

P. Huber of Cheviot Dr. was calling for a Lyft driver.

I said, "Oh shit," sat up, swung a wide U and drove right

up to the steps, clicked the car doors unlocked. Four minutes later, out she came in big round black shades, aqua pashmina, and high-end peasant dress, holding her laptop bag over her head to block the drizzle. She got in the backseat, said, "That was fast" like we were old friends, tossed her bag next to her, and immediately buried her face in her iPhone.

I said, "Admin Buildings on the Fox lot?"

"Same as always," she said, not looking up.

Glued to her cell like that for the first quick minute, she didn't recognize me as we started off on the world's shortest commute—Cheviot Hills to Fox Studios. I had no time to waste, but I'd read her wrong when I vibed openness. Up close, her softness was like a shellac this time, held in place to obscure what it could. Under the doll face seethed the finality of those who do not wish to be bothered.

We drove in silence onto Motor headed for Pico. FOX STUDIOS came into view. No longer *20th Century* Fox but beggars can't be choosers. Just as we pulled into the arches of the giant empire, I blurted, "Do you remember me, ma'am?"

She lifted her shades up onto her red hair and looked at me in the rearview as high agitation washed over her face. "You visited my mother."

"That's right. Adam Zantz."

She nodded. "And you just happen to be my Lyft driver?"

"Crazy, right?"

But she didn't believe me, and her jaw stiffened as we stopped at the gate booth. For a second I thought she might jump out of the car.

"Good morning, Jorge," she told the armed booth guard.

Jorge slapped a sticker pass on my hood and was about to wave us past the honey-wagons when he noticed the icy anger in her eyes.

"Everything okay, Mrs. Huber?"

Her eyes met mine in the rearview, then she turned back to him. "All good—have a nice day, Jorge."

Now she kept her gaze fixed on me as we drove a winding road through fake Olde Time Brooklyn, past a little corporate park of aluminum trailers. A movie studio was a curious thing on a rainy day—fakery interrupted. Just as we approached the giant soundstages, she looked around and when the last lone grip disappeared behind some big doors, she hurriedly unzipped her laptop bag, fumbled in it, and pulled out a serrated karambit knife.

"You see this?"

I nodded.

"Turn into the alley," she said, "and stop the car."

I did as told, twisted to face her.

"Keep your hands where I can see them."

I showed her my palms.

"Now *tell me what you want*," she said slow and methodical, "or I'm going to slash your face, scream for security, and *hashtag me too.*"

Rain was gushing now, tapdancing on the car roof, transforming the windows into falling smeary blurs. I breathed deep. When a serrated karambit knife is pointed at your throat, practicing mindfulness is the move.

"Ms. Huber, do you know why I called on your mom?"

"I know who my brother's birth mother was, if that's what you mean."

"Okay. But your mother pretended she didn't."

"So?"

"So she lied to me."

"Yeah, well, that's her specialty. *What do you want?*" The blade trembled in her jeweled hand.

"I just . . . thought . . . you might know why all of this is such an extra-big secret."

"All of what?"

"Annie Linden's secret son."

"Thom and I don't speak."

"Why is that?"

"None of your business."

"But you still see your mother."

"I'm not crazy about her either, but she's my mother. What do you want, *dude*?"

"Okay," I said. "Let's try this one. Annie Linden had secret meetings with your father, years after Thom was adopted."

"So?"

"Why?"

"Paying him to keep his mouth shut? What difference does it—"

"You think your father might've had an affair with Annie Linden?"

She cracked a grimace. "Uh no. My father let his wife control his every breath—may Jesus bless his soul."

"I thought you guys were raised Jewish."

"Barely. What are you hoping to get from me?"

"Were all three of you adopted?"

She didn't answer. I pulled for eye contact.

"I was adopted," I said. "By my uncle."

"Okay."

"He was all right."

"Lucky you."

"Were Nan and Dr. Milt all right?"

No answer, but I could feel her gears turning.

I said, "Is your brother . . . *all right*?"

"My brother—" She eyeballed me with a casting director's discretion, but for what role? "Look," she said, "*you* seem all right. And I *get it,* you lost someone you cared about, in a horrible way. But you're barking up the wrong tree."

"What tree is that?"

"My brother's an asshole, but I highly doubt he's a murderer."

"Unlike his sister." I went bug-eyed at the knife and she almost smiled.

"You're gonna get yourself killed harassing random strangers."

"Yeah? Maybe."

The rain intensified. She calculated her stuckness. "What do you want?" This time, she said it more softly.

"Thom was super-defensive about your mom. Like, he gave me the impression she was saintly."

"She's a saint alright. She's the patron saint of cruelty."

"Wow," I said. "Pretty un-self-aware for a child psychologist."

"Yeah well—she wanted the title, the better to torture us."

"You make that little old lady sound like a tyrant."

"Maybe your friend was a rock star, but in our home? Nan was *the* star. And Thom—" She stopped herself again.

"What?"

"He was her little teddy bear. She literally called him *my dum-dum teddy bear.*"

"What was her name for you?"

"*Bimbo.* And Ronnie was *shorty.*"

"Awful. But if all that's true, then why would Thom treat Annie Linden's reappearance in his life like such an unwanted interruption?"

"It's called identifying with the aggressor."

I nodded.

She said, "Psych 101," to punctuate.

"Where was your dad in all this?"

"Oh, Daddy got it, too. Constantly. She made him sleep in his own room. Then she'd come up with some line about why she couldn't divorce him. Usually *we* were the reason."

"Did he force her to adopt?"

"Quite the opposite, *she* forced *him*. He would have been happy spending his weekends fishing in Lake Arrowhead."

"Huh."

"You getting the picture? It's not that complicated. My mother is a *bitch*. The fact that Ms. Linden gave Thom to her is just . . . some bad luck." Despite the assault weapon in her grip, I had the overwhelming desire to give sympathy, but I couldn't find the words. Patricia stared through the windows, the whitewashed memories. "But at least I don't *lie to myself* anymore. Nan isn't just careless or outspoken or whatever. Something in her actually kind of hates us. My brothers couldn't own it, they *still* can't. Especially Thom because she hates him the most."

"But why don't *you* speak to him?"

No answer.

"Did he do something to you?"

She gritted her teeth, didn't answer. In the still air, her eyes held firm. The sky would have to cry for her.

I said, "You talk to the other brother?"

"Yeah. A little."

"Youngest?"

"No, I'm the youngest by three years. But Ronnie's the sweet one."

"Maybe 'cause he had Thom as a buffer."

She shrugged. "Ronnie's a healer. At the Natura Spa. We don't hang out too much anymore."

"How come?"

"That's what happens with people who make it through hell together. They can't stand the sight of each other." Patricia considered the knife in her hand now, like she might take a stab at her own history. Then she reluctantly shoved it back in her laptop bag. "She was *just loco*. With her fucking chandelier collection."

"Was she a hoarder?"

"She hoarded us, that's for sure."

"Was she getting subsidized or something?"

"Oh, it wasn't about money, our dad was a successful doctor. She just *was who she was*. And you know what the punchline is? After Daddy died, she moved into his room. Cried herself to sleep every night hugging one of his sweaters or something." Patricia checked her watch. "May I go to work now?"

One last try: "Why don't you speak to Thom anymore?"

After a cold stare, she shook her head a little, pulled her sunglasses down over her eyes.

"Enough—drive me to the Admin Building."

When we pulled up, she got out with her bag and shut the door. She was about to walk away when she turned and leaned into my window, dropped to a low whisper.

"He's mommy's little favorite, okay. And I can't stand the sight of him. Get it?"

I still had the curious half-fragile, half-tough lilt of her voice in my ear as I worked the rest of the morning shift. Around 2:30 in the afternoon, I pulled the Lyft light off my dash and shoved it in the glove—the opposite of the old cop cars. *Adam Zantz, Private Eye*—I was back on the case, headed for Hot Tub Emporium.

Across the street I waited and watched the door until Thom locked up shop from the inside, a little after 3:40. He drove out the back in a baby blue Porsche which, like the movie studio, didn't quite look like it belonged to the world on a rainy day, and when he turned south, I cruised behind, did my best to hang back a half-block, but it wasn't easy on the up-again down-again hills of the South Bay, which have been constructed to resemble a rolling wave. Just past Herondo, Thom looped the block and parked.

Rinky-dink shops lined the street—Wrapsody Cards & Stationery, South Bay Vacuum and Janitorial, and a gift store called Great Lengths with handmade puppets, spinning crystals, and baseball-sized mirrored disco balls hanging in the window. Thom went into the vacuum cleaner place and was gone a long time—almost an hour. I wondered if he owned it as a second biz.

At 4:43 he left the vacuum store, went back to his car, and headed straight back to the jacuzzi store, reopened at 5:00 on the dot. Customers were in and out of there for another hour. The jukebox id played "Tired of Waiting" by the Kinks.

At just after 6:00 p.m., a blonde in her late twenties went into his store and together, she and Thom closed the place up, grates down, locks on. Soon, they were in the Porsche cruising 190th into Torrance. I followed. They pulled into a parking lot. I slowed down—if I'd been a real detective, I would have popped the glove and yanked a pair of binoculars. Instead, I circled the block and cruised past it—

TURNER'S OUTDOORSMAN: HUNTING & FISHING

I said, "Firearms . . . lovely" to nobody but myself.

I circled the block maybe four more times before Thom

Goldfischer and his NRA date came out and got back into
his car. If they bought something I didn't see it, but in a flash
they were up the on-ramp, 405 South, where I followed and
quickly lost them.

I cursed myself. Adam Zantz Private Eye couldn't even
tail a baby blue Porsche in rush hour. I literally didn't have a
fucking clue.

28

ISN'T IT A LOVELY DAY TO
BE CAUGHT IN THE RAIN?

The Wi Natura Center was nestled in the basement of a boxy twenty story along the heart of the Miracle Mile. Once a destination for white men in gray suits, now it was Korean and casual, but it had always been down market and half-abandoned. There was no heyday, some buildings are just born that way. In the lobby, used laptop kiosks, watch repair, and perfume knock-offs all stayed barely alive by way of cheap rent. I took the golden elevator down to Natura, paid my twelve bucks to an unwelcoming pair of women, and made my way past the men's lockers looking for Ron Goldfischer. Down the tiled hall, naked men, mostly older Koreans but also some Russians, were wading in the large sunken Jacuzzis, coming in and out of doors that belched puffs of great white steam. In the air-conditioned Relaxation Lounge, Ronnie stretched out on a long leather chair in his Billabong T-shirt, Bermudas, and flip-flops, watching a Korean bloopers program on the widescreen with no sound.

He didn't look like his brother or sister, but I recognized him from the shop.

"Yo man, hey. You made it. Tricia told me you'd buzz."

"Sisterly warning?"

"Not at all—she said you were a standup guy. Come have a seat."

"This is quite a place."

"I know, right? It's cheaper than a motel and cleaner too."

"You stay here?"

"I spend the night when I come to the city to work—I run a clinic here every other Tuesday."

"And they let you sleep here?"

"So far nobody's thrown me out." He had a wide, jolly face, not quite the leading man type his brother was, but his tan was rich and, like Thom, his beachside attitude was ingrained. His ponytailed long hair was graying faster than his sibling's, but exercise had kept his forearms and calves strong.

I said, "Patricia mentioned you practiced . . . the Rosen Method?"

"It's pronounced *ro-zen.*"

"What is it, like a yoga thing?"

"It's one-on-one. Body work plus spiritual consultation, simultaneously."

"Like a massage with therapy?"

"In a sense. But integrated. Mind and body are one, Westerners forget that. You can't wish away the heart's pain—the body rebels."

"So a person lies on a table and—"

"Right. And together we tune inward, explore the body. People carry a lot of suffering, memories, cramps—they actually *carry* it in the muscles. Trauma changes the way you breathe, the way you stand and sit. It reshapes your body. The way a constant wind will reshape a tree."

"Wow."

"Yeah, it's intense. You make a habit of sorrow and then it's like, you're permanently crinkled up. Well, not permanently. That's where we come in."

"Does Thom do the Rosen thing with you?"

"My brother? He's not the flexible type. He's just a year older than me but he slouches like a senior—I can't get with the way he stands, the way he sits at all. I'm always trying to correct him. I tell him those Jacuzzis are ruining him. It's kind of a bone of contention."

"Not that easy to change a brother," I said. I was thinking of my sister, Maya.

A Korean man in his early sixties came in wearing a bronze bathrobe. He took a seat in the nearby easy chair and picked up a Korean newspaper. He seemed to pay us no mind but something about his presence made us both sit up a little.

Ronnie said, "You could probably use the treatment yourself, driving around all day. Happy to give you a free trial— but that's not why you're here."

"Right. I guess I've been harassing the whole family."

"It's okay—you've had a pretty brutal loss. And you must have tripped out to learn she had a son."

"How long have you known about Thom and Annie?"

"Oh gosh, probably when she started coming around. Six months, a year? Thom didn't tell us right away."

"Why not?"

"Typical foster home shit. It's kind of an unspoken rule among adopted sibs, like, keep mellow about where you're from. Especially if it's positive, which it rarely is. But this was a hard secret for Thom to keep. Who can blame him, right?"

"Yeah." I measured him for the ability to stomach random weirdness—he seemed ready. "I recently uncovered some strange notes. I *think* even after the adoption, Annie might have had some kind of ongoing connection to your dad. Neither Thom nor Patricia seems to know anything about that."

"The hell they don't."

"Really?"

"They completely know. But it's not a pretty story." On the television, a Korean teenage boy balanced an egg on his forehead—it forced him into an unstable squat. Ronnie gave me a hapless smile. "I hate to badmouth your old boss."

"I can take it."

"In a nutshell? My parents were milking Annie for every penny they could."

"How's that?"

Now he sat up fully. "This is just the way I heard it. Nan wouldn't tell us the whole trip. When Thom was born, Annie couldn't wait to unload him—and she never looked back. That is, until she got famous. She went into a panic. She sent people around to make sure Mom and Dad didn't go spilling the beans. You know, it doesn't look nice, you're this big glamorous star and you've ditched your kid."

"Right."

"But the joke is my parents never would have gone public in a million years. They had too much pride as parents. Annie insisted on making a formal deal. Hush money, nondisclosure contracts and everything."

Now the boy on the television had dropped the egg, it lay cracked at his feet. The mini-skirted gameshow host tried to console him.

I said, "Fair enough. But why would Annie wait until your dad passed away to seek Thom out?"

He shrugged. "Guilt maybe? My dad was just a regular guy. A sweet guy, really. Total cornball. He collected plates—you know, like *Gone with the Wind*, *Annie*, the Broadway show—commemorative plates. My dad was no threat to a woman like Annie Linden."

The line struck me funny and I took an uncomfortable second to digest it. "So she waited to seek out Thom because—"

"Like maybe her conscience just finally got to her. She was getting up there in years herself, right? Your priorities change. She wanted to know her son, see his face. I totally get that. And then . . . this unspeakable tragedy went down."

"You think it's a coincidence?"

He shrugged in earnest. "I should hope so. What about the guy on trial? Do you know him?"

"I do. And I don't think he did it."

"Okay—but . . . somebody did."

"That's why I've got to ask you. Did Thom ever express any resentment toward Annie? For what she'd done, for ditching him? Was he angry?"

"Well—" His jaw bristled. "My brother doesn't do angry. He never said much of anything to me about any of it." Uneasy silence. "One time he did mention they'd set up a meeting, one of the last ones."

"And?"

"He seemed a little strained by it all, like it was getting to be a burden."

"When I spoke to him, he seemed to want to protect your mother's feelings most of all."

Another ripple of tension—right through the jaw. For a guy whose bread and butter was muscle memory, he didn't have too much control over his own. Probably nobody did.

"That's more bull, *protecting my mom's feelings.* My mom is not that easy to hurt. And Thom and her aren't that close. He just likes to act like he's the new man of the house and stuff."

"Did you ever go looking for your own parents?"

"I did, and Milt and Nan were totally casual about it."
Ron stretched his long arms out and pulled the rubber band
off his long gray and auburn hair. He was no kid anymore, but
there was something of the Eternal Little Brother about him,
complete with a dimpled smile. "Look—I figured you were
wondering about all this. I admit our story is a weird one, but
not any weirder than most adoptions. Our parents were simple
people, regular people. Dad was kind of a sap and Mom was
kind of a toughie, but they did their best. They were winging
it and trying to follow the rules, and all of a sudden they got
swept up in this big trip, ya know? The *sixties*—what did they
know from that stuff? They didn't want Annie's money but
they didn't want to shake up the family even more."

"Do you think your brother could have killed Annie
Linden?"

"Thom?" He smiled with beatific jokeyness. "Thom's an
asshole, definitely. But a murderer? Doubtful."

"Yeah—that's what your sister said too."

We looked at the Korean man in his leather loveseat, now
fast asleep, the newspaper with its indecipherable headlines
stretched across his belly.

"I'm serious about the free treatment," Ron said, hand-
ing me a little one-sheet with his info above some yoga poses.
"No offense but anybody can see you're holding on to some
serious stress."

29

FOOTBALL SEASON'S OVER NOW SO YOU'RE COMING BACK TO ME

Taco Sabbath at sister Maya's. After dinner, she and I did dishes in uneasy sibling tandem—I soaped, she rinsed. In the adjacent den, her husband, Marty, watched New England face off Tampa. My eight-year-old niece Stephanie dragged a plastic princess comb over his bald head while he yelled at the TV.

"Maya," I finally said, "do I have to guess why you asked me here?"

"I got a call from an old professor of mine. Sam Teitel."

"Yeah?"

"He saw you milling around at Bix Gelden's trial."

"Okay."

"It just so happens the DA was also one of Professor Teitel's students."

"Edler?" I said. "Gnarly."

She put her plate down. "No. Going to your friend's trial

when you've been booked as accessory after the fact is *not gnarly*. It's idiotic."

"Is that what Professor Teitel said?"

She sighed. "He said this case is open and shut."

"Now that's what's idiotic."

She shot me one of those murderous skeptical looks of hers and in my typical baby brother fashion, I said, *"What?"* And when she didn't answer I went on a defensive rant, recapping all my secret exploits. Annie's anxious request and Kronski after hours at her place, Dr. Milt and the porno rags and the Goldfischers and the long-lost son, Combs and the teenyboppers and the assault and the bootleg and the vacuum store. In despair, she cut me off.

"Adam, I don't know what you think you're doing, but this stuff is just random junk any crazed, overeager fan would find digging into some famous person's past. And you're going to get yourself arrested again, *or worse*."

"Somebody slashed my tires, Maya."

"People have family secrets—it doesn't make them murderers."

"Maya, I need your help."

"*I know, goddammit*. My favorite professor called me to tell me to look out for you. How do you think that makes me feel?"

"What else did he say?"

"Nothing."

"Come on now."

"*Nothing*. He told me they've received dozens of bogus confessions."

"From who?"

"Nobody, psychos. Half weren't even in California the day it happened, the other half were chronic confessors."

"Why would somebody get their jollies confessing to murder?"

She rolled her eyes. "Probably dreaming of an Oscar—best affidavit by a psycho. Isn't that what you're dreaming of? *Ladies and gentlemen, the man who saved the famous lady, what a guy!*"

"I can't *save* her, she's already dead." I thrust a glass bowl at her and turned away in disgust. In the next room, Marty howled—on the TV screen, a dreadlocked black Hercules strutted into position and knelt with cool force, his fist jamming the green stadium grass. I cut to a whisper. "Maya, if I can just get into Kronski's accounts—"

"Huh?"

"Don't forget, I used to be semi-pro. I still have my former boss's old license. Maybe I can use it."

"Adam, you need psychiatric meds. I'm serious. And the next time you end up in jail? Don't call me."

"If I can just—"

"No, you always do this. It's completely chronic."

"Do what?"

"Court *disaster* and drag everyone along for the ride. You know what I think? This is your little revenge on all of us. For not being your mother."

I stepped back, hands up. "Where is this coming from?"

"In music, with your girlfriends, everywhere. Your ex was right—she said you wouldn't know what to do with success if you had it."

"Yeah, well, glad you both have me figured out. But somebody I loved got murdered. And I need to—"

"What do you mean *loved*? You wanted her to make you famous."

"*Bullshit.* This has nothing to do with that. I just, I—"

But she snuffed me out with an icy, droll glare. "Focus on yourself, Adam. Look at *yourself*. You've got enough on your plate with that particular project. You live in a closet. You're broke. You're alone. You've pretty much isolated yourself from anybody that could turn your life around. And you're pushing forty. This—this isn't what my dad wanted."

She was fighting tears as she turned off the faucet. Before we turned around, Marty was in the kitchen. Little Steph had discovered the yoga instruction sheet, which had fallen out of my coat pocket, and was already trying a stretch on the kitchen tiles.

Marty grabbed the sheet. "Which one is that?"

"*Richie's positer*," she said, twisting and bending like an eight-year-old human origami.

"Huh?"

"Richie's pose."

"You're doing it wrong," Marty said.

"No, I'm not!"

"You're doing it *great*, honey," Maya said, "don't listen to him."

"Sorry pumpkin, it says right here—twist your torso so that one arm reaches toward the opposite ankle to discover deeper spiritual knowledge." He burst out laughing. "Jesus, Adam, you into this crap now?"

"Give me that," I said and grabbed it. At the bottom of the sheet it said, *Your body is your child.* I refolded it and shoved it back into my coat pocket.

"Heard about your customer." Marty angled around his contorting daughter and cracked the fridge to yank another beer. "Bad luck for you, bud. Oh shit, look at this." He pulled his iPhone from his back pocket and scrolled. "Here—thought of you, of course."

It was a YouTube somebody made of a naked Ken doll attacking a naked Barbie on the sand with Annie's "Travel Light" for a soundtrack.

"Martin, don't play him that!" Maya yanked the phone from his hand. "He cared for this woman—Jesus."

30

I CAN SEE CLEARLY FROM
MY DIAMOND EYES

Next day was crazy hot out. Too hot to move, too hot to think. I got behind the wheel, cranked the AC to four, and worked the River Styx—the business loop to and from LAX and the Hilton, the Hyatt, the Residence Inn. I put on the stoic driver face but inside I was wounded, wildly restless. My sister was wrong about me. I wasn't just some *overeager fanboy* trying to make a name for myself. But as usual, in her wrongness she wasn't *all* wrong—so far, I knew nothing an overeager fan couldn't have figured out. Eleven grim customers, then I hit the drive-thru at Carl's, parked on the spot, and killed a burger. Watching a jumbo jet tear off into the blue, I decided to phone Eva Silber. This time she took my call.

She was unsurprised to hear from me.

"I find myself *worrying* for you," she said. "I believe you have gotten the bug."

"What bug is that?"

"The Annie bug. And I know how it goes. She's a vampire. She ignites people in a way that makes them give their blood."

"That's funny, my sister just told me *I* was the vampire."

"How can I help you, kiddo? The radio is working?"

"Too well," I said. "I was just . . . I was wondering. The visits, way back when. Where did they take place?"

"With the little boy?"

"Yeah, was it, like—at Eucalyptus Park in Hawthorne? Or did he come up or—"

"It *was* in Hawthorne, but not in the park. She kept an apartment, not far from the Goldfischers. A wretched little one bedroom."

"Did you see the place?"

"Did I ever. A few years after the visits, she asked me to go there to pick up some dresses she left behind."

"So she kept the apartment?"

"That's right, she refused to get rid of it. I was trying to win her back—like an idiot. I drove all the way down there. All so the Princess could have her gowns for the ball."

"But down where exactly?"

"Hawthorne, *boychick*, somewhere in Hawthorne."

"Yeah but—*where* in Hawthorne?"

"You think I remember? Some godawful apartment building. Near a hardware store. You wouldn't believe it if you saw it. Dis-*gusting*. She left and never went back, and nobody else did either. The dust was so thick I had to go back to my car and tie a T-shirt around my face."

I tried to picture it. "Did you get her dresses?"

"I did. I took them straight to the dry cleaners. A lot of good it did me. Not even a thank you. I told her, '*Why don't you get rid of this little hellhole?*' She was still paying rent, like a *schlemiel*. She grabbed the dresses and shut the door in my face."

My stomach tangled like ship rope. "Eva. *Where is that apartment?*"

But she didn't answer, she was lost in memory, mumbling. "Candy wrappers they left. Awful."

"Eva, do you remember what the *building* looked like? The street it was on?"

"Looked like? It looked like a wretched apartment building in the godforsaken middle of nowhere. *Let it go*, boychick. Before the vampire drains you dry."

I thanked her for the call and signed off, already pulling out of the gas station headed for Hawthorne—I was blocks away anyway. But when I got there, the long, humid, sun-beaten malevolence of El Segundo Boulevard stretched before and behind me like a video game where the same mini-malls and Toyotas keep appearing on loop. Lost in the sprawl, gawking for a hardware store, I dialed Fry for help. Within minutes, he was clicking away at a laptop.

"Lotta hardware stores in Hawthorne it turns out," he said. "I'm counting fourteen."

"Yeah, but are they all near apartment buildings?"

"Well, *yeah*," he said, almost chuckling. "Pretty much."

"Right," I said. "And all those apartment buildings are more or less *in the godforsaken middle of nowhere.*"

"I could try to hack into Annie's financials," Fry said, "look for regular rent checks."

"Please do," I said. "But it's hard to believe she paid rent on a place she never went to *for forty years.*"

"Not if she was secretly dreaming of a reunion all along."

I turned toward Eucalyptus Park, circled the block. "Eva Silber told me Annie would meet Thom Goldfischer when he was a little child. But Thom acted like he never laid eyes on her before a year ago—why would he lie about that? Or maybe *she's* lying—or they both are."

Fry said, "If Annie stopped seeing Thom before he turned four, it's likely he wouldn't have remembered. Actually, there's a peculiar scientific phenomenon called childhood amnesia. Most of us *do* remember the early years—but only until about seven. Then it all starts to fade. Maybe he remembered then forgot."

"Could be," I said. "But why the reunion at the park?"

"Maybe she wanted to jog his memory."

Exasperated, I pulled over, stared at the empty playground. "I don't remember too much childhood. The bad parts stick like crazy, but I can't *see* them. At this point, they're just stories I've told myself."

"Addy, that's how it is. We remember what serves us, for better or worse. Time picks and chooses the stories. You know that kid's book, *Are You My Mother?*"

"I don't think so."

"This little baby bird goes looking for his mommy. It isn't a hen, it isn't a cow, it isn't a dog. So he starts to wonder—is mommy an airplane? A tractor? A forklift?"

"I can relate."

"Pretty sure everyone can. Lemme get back to you with that banking stuff."

"Thanks, amigo."

It was 3:35—I still had six and a half hours left on the shift. Instead, I headed back to Hot Tub Emporium.

Once again, Thom Goldfischer closed up shop at 4:00 p.m. This time he drove the Porsche to a homey little liquor store called Dawn to Dusk—he came out chewing gum and smacking a pack of yellow American Spirits against his forearm.

Then he got in his ride and drove right back to the vacuum cleaner place he'd been at the day before. He slowed down; I cut around the block and when I returned, he hadn't parked, he hadn't entered, he was gone. I parked a block up and ducked under the awnings, hoping to get a better look at the place—I didn't want to be seen so I moved quick. But I was determined to find out why Thom Goldfischer went shopping for a vacuum cleaner so damn often.

On a quick pass, the place was as advertised. Brand models stood in the window like mute jurors—Hoover, Dyson, GE. But the place had a dusty, forbidding feeling and when I peered in and didn't see anyone, I didn't go inside. Instead, I played customer outside Great Lengths Gift Shop, watched the mini disco balls dangle, waiting to see if Goldfischer would return. Up the street and down the street, no dice, I'd lost him. I drove back to the Jacuzzi store—it was open for business. Something changed his mind.

This time no girlfriend came and he closed up shop at 8:00. From my slim vantage, he locked up in a state of agitation. His brow furrowed with determination as he got into his car. He started for Pacific, but he was playing games with acceleration and it wasn't long before he blazed a right and disappeared, I'd lost him again. With a jolt, he reappeared on my left lane, rolling down his passenger window.

"You," he shouted. "Pull the fuck over. Now."

I turned up a sloping suburban street and parked, veins in my head and wrists pulsing, braced for a brawl. With a man a head taller than me. Who might've killed his own mother. And who might be packing fresh heat. He screeched to a halt behind me—the Porsche handled speed stops like a bully. I got out and he got out, stood before me, gripping his keys like brass knuckles.

"I'm getting tired of seeing you in my rearview."

"I don't know what you're talking about."

"Don't play dumb with me, ya fucktard. Doc Fleiss tells me you're grilling him about my family's history, then I find out you're harassing my mother, my sister, my brother, and

God knows who else. You're lucky I don't beat your ass down right here and now."

"I'm not *harassing* anyone. I'm just asking some pretty obvious questions. And they remain unanswered."

"Yeah? Like what?"

I looked up and down the empty street. These LA residentials are kryptonite to pedestrians.

"Like why was Annie so eager to know you just as soon as your dad was out of the way? After paying for his silence for years and years? That doesn't compute. Did you know her as a kid?"

"Huh? Of course not."

"When you reunited, did it matter?"

"Did what matter?"

"Whether or not you told the press?"

He snorted, shook his head. "I already told you, *brah*. I barely knew the lady. And my father had nothing to do with her. If he met with her, and I don't say he did, that was because *she* was hassling *him*. Let the man rest in peace."

"Who do you think did this?"

He was prepared for the question, maybe too prepared. "The man in jail? But it coulda been *anybody*. She was famous. Famous people have fans, and fans are locos." He took a step toward me, backing me into the Jetta, making me strain to keep eye contact. Close up, his face shone redder, snakier, more absent. "Coulda been you."

"Then why haven't you gone to the police?" I was surprised to find myself still talking—a recess of courage from God-knows-where. "Why not put your story on the table?"

He went still. "If you don't stop poking your big nose into my life, I just might. Or else I might go vigilante on your ass, and *you don't want that*."

With a swift single thrust of rage, he slammed me into my

own car and raised his fist, savored the moment—he showed me his teeth but didn't punch. He backed off a half-step, threw his arms out, *then* he punched—one to the jaw, one to the belly, and I doubled over, clutched my falling out gut exploding with nausea, out of oxygen, vibrating with shock as he turned and stomped off, got into the baby blue Porsche and blazed over the hill with a roar. The Jacuzzi man was mellow no more.

" . . . and the Grammy for Best Song Written for Visual Media goes to . . . "

By TV light, I sporked canned corn straight out of the can while trying to avoid a bloody lip. The camera fixed on their close-ups: my ex and her beau seated side by side.

"Kerrylynn Robbins and Jason Phillips, *'The Reckoning'*! *'Love You UP!*— "

They first registered shock, then ecstasy, then they kissed while the crowd cheered. Somehow, I managed to groan, say "Ow!" and spill half a can of corn at the exact same time—a feat I did not previously think possible—as the semi-unshaven schmuckface rose and pulled the cuffs from under his crushed matching velvet purple tux and took her hand, leading the way up the red TV staircase, her cork-slab heels wobbling on super-tilt.

And since when did my ex get so *movie star hot*, decked to the nines in a flowy hippie dress, curly hair all up, makeup, jewels, her green eyes hiding behind zillion-dollar Nerd Girl glasses? Since when did her shrugging gait and tilted smile detach from the Human Realm and go floating into Celebrity World?

The phone rang—irritation and relief. I hit mute.

"Hello," I grunted.

"This Adam Zantz?" Jeff the Vet, the tape man.

"I thought I'd never hear from you."

"Yeah well, I'm not the world's most organized person." His voice was panicky. "This is too weird, man."

"Every tape?"

"Every one. I been gypped. You been gypped. I can't believe it, man. I'm gonna smack the living shit out of that dealer."

"Jeff, do me a favor. Don't do anything. Don't even talk about this with anyone. Give me his details and I'll buy the whole set."

"I can't charge you for these."

"Please do. But I need every single record you've got of the transaction you had, any emails, anything."

"You think the guy who sold me these tapes killed Annie Linden?"

"I don't know. But I don't think he was her biggest fan."

I drove down to Jeff's place in Sherman Oaks—he lived in a guesthouse over a parking garage on a handsome suburban street just around the corner from Hamburger Hamlet. He was waiting for me, sitting on the stairs smoking a cigarette. Despite his balding head and long gray ponytail, he had the rosy kinetic face of an excitable teenager. Maybe everybody had that face if they were excited enough.

"I'm still freakin' from this, man, this is the creepiest thing that's ever happened to me. And here's the *really* creepy part— the fucker's already closed out his account."

He handed me a rolled-up printout of eBay sales. The seller's handle was victorimmature@yahoo.com, location Irvine, California. About fifty minutes south of the South Bay. One hundred percent positive feedback, only one written review:

Fast delivery, five stars. And then: *Based in United States, victorimmature has been an eBay member since May 27, 2011.*

Jeff got up and reached behind him, handed me a paper Trader Joe's bag. "They're all in there. Wait, this you gotta see." He pulled one cassette from the bunch and unfolded the little sleeve. In scratchy blue Bic were the words SMEAR LIST, a squiggly happy face, and five names: *Annie Linden, Meryl Streep, w Carly Simon, Beyonce.* We exchanged perplexed looks.

I said, "Let me at least give you what you paid for these."

"No way, brother. Not on my karma."

There were several Victor Immatures on the internet but no yahoo accounts and nothing that looked remotely related to Annie or Men's Rights—it was a gag handle for every witty schmuck who ever heard of Victor Mature. In frustration, I started poking around Irvine for red pill stuff. More nothing. Irvine—it was a money place, maybe a white flight haven. Plus, they had the university—that had to attract more than a few lonely, horny hombres. But far as I could see, Irvine had no Men's Movement, at least not out in the open. They had The Team, a fitness program specializing in afterburn training, and the Christian Businessmen's Connection, a benign organization focusing on personal and professional development as a Christian man: *Has God put in your heart a call to ministry, but you don't know what to do or where to start?* I said "Nope" out loud and kept searching. I entered *Pick Up Artist Irvine* and got Alpha Training Boot Camp. *I will train you how to successfully approach a girl on the street, hook her, attract her, get her number, <u>even get laid with her on the same day.</u> Moreover, I want you to learn amazing dance skills, witch* (sic) *you will use in night game.*

I called the number.

"Is this the boot camp?"

"You know it." He was in a rush to go get laid somewhere.

"Listen, man," I said, "I'm pretty much trained on the pickup stuff."

"If you say so."

"I was just wondering—is there, like, a good red pill meeting anywhere in the 'hood? Like—something more serious?"

Long pause. Then: "Take this down. It's a good exchange. The M.O.R.E." He gave me an address. My hands were trembling as pen hit paper: 11217 Catalina Way, Redondo Beach.

The vacuums. Thom's number one hang spot.

"And if they ask—tell 'em Master Mitch sent you."

31

JOIN A CHAIN OF MALES
OR BE THE MISSING LINK

By daylight, the old Hoovers in the dusty, purple-curtained window outside didn't look so spooky. But the vacuum cleaners inside, the ones that had been pushed to the wall like an audience of somber stick figures, those were plenty macabre. The place seemed preserved in invisible formaldehyde, like Nan's Hummel doll display. I was the fourth or fifth guy in the store—they sat under the fluorescents in a circle, support-group style, and I joined them with a kind of purse-lipped hardness. I was playacting a bitterness I probably actually had, but they didn't know that. A few gentle silent nods were exchanged—nobody spoke yet.

These were sporty types in their thirties and forties, probably not too big on public displays of vulnerability. Still, you could tell they were chomping at the bit to get started. I glanced back at the door, hoping and dreading Thom Goldfischer would show. My head was spinning with questions—what brought these men together? Who was the leader and what were they after exactly? And who among them harbored a secret hate for an aging folksinger?

A few more joined and then a suited mortgage broker type pulled up a chair and called the gang to attention.

"Welcome everyone, my name's Mike, and I'm a strong man."

"Welcome, Mike," they said in unison.

"The Men's Organization for Rights and Equality is not here to condemn or vilify women. We're here to venerate them and sanctify our relationships both *to* them and *with* them. We in the M-O-R-E believe the last century has seen a devolution in male/female communication and male/female life-building. *We are the living correction.* Is there someone who'd like to share some experience, strength, and hope?"

I blanched. No way was I going to speak, but just sitting there made me an object of suspicious curiosity. The biggest guy in the room raised an eager hand and introduced himself as Jonathan. He had the atrophied burliness of the out-of-work construction worker, but as soon as he spoke, the betrayed boy-child rocketed through all in an instant.

"I'm a strong man. And it's good to be here."

The guys greeted him back and he put his attention on me, the rapt newcomer. His story was a heartbreaker. He had been a typical "white knight" until just last year when he caught his girlfriend in bed with her boss. Like a crazy person, he tried to salvage the relationship, which, of course, didn't work.

"On the day she left, she called me, and I quote, '*a professional whiner whose mommy had pussy-whipped him into being ashamed of being male.*' She thought that was the most clever shit, it's like she was *dying* to get it off her chest. So fuck her. But also—thank God for her. 'Cause you know what? She was right. And she woke my ass up."

Jonathan gave a hefty nod and the group rumbled with thank yous, applause, gently shook fists.

Mike said, "We are the heroes, and we're turning the tides of history. Who else would like to speak today?"

It was a recovery group like any other—but I still wasn't 100 percent clear what they were recovering from, not yet. I kept my hands down and my lips zipped.

"I'm Kevin—and I'm a strong man. And it's good to be here." Kevin was on the shorter, chubbier side. "I love this meeting, love every one of my fellow soldiers, I really mean that. Before I found MORE, I had less. Seriously though, I had less than less, I had nothing. One domineering girlfriend after another. Serial masochism. See, I came from a house of a lot of sisters that didn't get me at all. I can still hear my mother say, 'Kev is *sensitive,* Kev is *sensitive.*' It was her way of pimp-slappin' me, 'cause I tell ya—*she* wasn't sensitive! She was a raging bitch! And my wimp-ass dad didn't say *boo.* He was just—she ran roughshod all over him, like old furniture." Kevin exhaled long. "You know, I wasn't really so sensitive underneath it all but I thought I had to be like *them* to survive. Now I know better. Now? I *know* a woman can *only* get wet for a domineering man. A man who can keep her where she wants to be—in her place. The female of the twenty-first century is spoiled to the point of her own insanity—and she's *miserable,* man." He went into a little smirky imitation. "*My career, my self, my ego, my whatever!*"

The guys laughed. Kevin smiled with pleasure, spoke to some invisible dame. "You're lost, baby. And I can't help you get found. Until you can learn to tame that inscrutable hungry pussy of yours? I. Don't. Need it."

Lots of nods. A close-cropped Brit said, "Thanks for sharing today, Kevin. Inspiring, man."

I felt the increasing pressure to raise my hand but my mouth was dry and my hands sweaty. I wouldn't have been more nervous if I'd been at a songwriter's competition with Dylan, Jagger, and McCartney on the judge's panel.

Now a black guy in a red Ralph Lauren polo raised his hand. "I'm Ellis, I'm down from Lakewood . . . Long Beach. And I am *trying* to stay strong. It's hard. I got a lot of resentments I'm trying to work through. Y'see, where I come from, you got to be a man at age *five*. Or else. It's a lot to live up to— and not all of us are built that way. You don't make the grade? *Boo-ya*, you get it in the neck. I didn't get too much guidance, either. The opposite. I got the *school for fools*. Lemme tell you something—we got *our* fools. Just like *any* community. Even got our Don Trumps." The room burst into convivial laughter—but laughter isn't always a good seismograph on who voted for who. "Yeah, we got our blowhard dads and we got our moms that are dazed and confused. We got all that. But . . . good fathers? Those are on short supply. And I for one intend to give my three-year-old what I didn't get: a real man to look *up* to." This got a robust round of thanks and applause.

Mike, who had been angling all along to make eye contact with me, said, with great delicacy, "We've got a newcomer today. No pressure, but if you want to jump in, we're here for ya."

The time was now—I got hot under the collar, made a single comical head bob. I was not that easy around dude-dudes and these guys were the very definition. But the faces in the room were patient. I went real. When you're lying, it's always better to tell the truth.

"I'm Adam. I just learned about the group. Seems like, uh, seems real helpful." I gave a nod toward Ellis. "No dad. I . . . was raised by a mentally ill woman. Very loving but very irresponsible. Not up to motherhood at all. When the state separated us, I went to live with my uncle. Then my mom died in the . . . the hospital. It seemed like the worst thing ever but actually my troubles had just begun. My new sister—technically my cousin—was very, very pushy. She *is* pushy, what am I saying?" The group laughed—a welcoming burst of approval. "Basically, she's always there to tell me how to fix my life, free advice nonstop. And I'm thirty-seven, you know? I shouldn't need her help."

I sounded nervous to myself. I licked my lips and scanned the room. Now, watching them listen to me, their attentive faces appeared under the fluorescents like bitter masks carved by the cruelest sculptor—disappointment in love.

"I got, uh, dumped a few years back. My ex and I were songwriting partners, we had a manager and everything. She left me for another songwriter and now I'm stuck listening to their stuff on the radio. And I *do* wonder sometimes, like— what is wrong with me, that I couldn't keep her, ya know? That could have been *our* song on the radio. But she . . . she gave up on us. On me. For someone with power."

Someone chimed in: "Modern women have *no* loyalty." It was a guy I hadn't really noticed. His eyes twinkled with slick conspiratorial brio. The group tensed at this interruption but I was grateful for the break, and I raised a hand to signal the finish.

Mike, the group leader, said, "That was great, Adam. Keep coming back. We can't make a man out of you . . . because a man is what you already are." The group applauded. Then Mike said, "Just a reminder that here at MORE we don't engage in crosstalk or advice-giving, that's not what we're about. We have nothing to preach. We are a support group, bringing masculine strength to the ones who deserve it most, our brothers in arms."

After the group was formally closed, I hung around to drink bad coffee in Styrofoam and see if there was anything I could pick up about Thom Goldfischer and/or a concert bootlegger with a score to settle with Annie Linden, but there was no way to raise the subject without coming off like an interloper. Anyway, the guys were too jovial right then for inquiry. They were relieved to be relieved. Also, I felt guilty for speaking on false pretenses, though I hadn't uttered a single fib. Was that what they called "White Knightdom"—this free-floating guilt?

Jonathan the gentle giant, the dumped man, came over to shake my hand and thank me for sharing. A guy like that could probably wrestle an alligator but he'd been KO'd by a pretty face, the poor sap. I was watching him leave when the jukebox id kicked in—*some people cry and some people die by the wicked ways of love*—and then the interrupter guy approached me with a bounce in his step. He was chiseled, gym-toned, with devilish blue eyes. If he'd been a few inches taller he could've been a male model.

"I'm Bart. You from the Oh See?"

"Naw," I said, "but I'm a Lyft driver so I spend a lot of time up and down the coast. My buddy Thom told me about the group."

He didn't blink. "Cool, glad you found us. It's a good exchange. There's a Wednesday thing too and they usually go out for dinner afterward."

I said, "What do you do for kicks on Mondays?"

32

I'M ON THE SHELF
JUST LIKE LAST YEAR'S
EASTER BONNET

The sign read HOUSE OF EDEN—the neon fizzed in gaudy glow-green handwriting, with GENTLEMAN'S CLUB in all-bold white at the bottom. You could search for the ironies, but who knew what a gentleman was nowadays? Standing in line behind Bart Bauer, I got the funny sensation once again that Annie was watching in the night air, floating along the unused telephone lines, down down to the sea. And I longed to see her face, just once more. Or for her to see mine.

Not tonight.

The bouncer took IDs and tilted them under a red flashlight. My DL looked tiny in the cup of his giant hand. He nodded and we entered—it was loud, hectic as a casino inside, to keep you alert—but not for the roulette wheel. Here they spun your lust. The Eden was lit like the belly of a luminescent spaceship, with great plastic palms and straw hula umbrellas and tiki heads blasted by the multicolored Malibu lights. It was tropical meets outer space—the superstitious past and the cold, plastic future.

I followed Bauer to a pair of soft brown cowboy-leather couches cordoned by a kind of faux white picket fence. Whoever did the interior décor for this place was either making do with scraps from B-movie sets or had a funny idea about sex as permanent Halloween. Then there were the girls, the dancer-waitresses, in heavy makeup, see-through tops, mini-miniskirts, glow-in-the-dark heels. The girls were a trip, gilding the lily of natural beauty to its hard, unnatural limit. But it was the colored lights—spinning, flashing, nonstop roving—that were especially sci-fi. You weren't just coming to the House of Eden for a warm body. You were here to get zorked and zoinked by a she-creature from Planet X.

Bauer ordered an old-fashioned and I got a Black Label on the rocks. He was hard to make out, this Machiavelli alongside me on the couch. He was neither hick nor aristocrat, yet he played at both. The drinks came and we drank. No talking, lots of watching, side by side like co-pilots. With choreographed disinterest, we studied the girls straddling other men, watched them perform their rituals of hotness. They grabbed, they twisted, bent, angled, wiggled, but for the most part they remained expressionless. Each one was elsewhere.

"Hi Big Bart-man."

"Janine, this is Adam. Don't mess with him 'cause he's a gangster."

"He doesn't look like a gangster. He looks sweet."

"You're making me blush," I said.

She leaned into Bart, icy blue eyes twinkling. "You or your friend want a private room you just let me know, baby-face."

Bauer was pleased as she walked away. He believed himself to be an insider in a room full of tourists. But all the guys

here saw themselves like that, played the part of the junior
Mafia Don, all of them. The construction worker dudes and
businessmen and college types and a few champion beer drink-
ers and the nerdsters—the whole gamut of male Americana.
It wasn't so strange that they each wanted a naked female
body up close. But it was strange that they wanted to share
the experience with so many members of their own sex, and
maybe that was the secret exchange. This place was a kind of
confessional, this loud frenzy of a place. You came to say you
needed. You needed a human touch and you needed it *bad*.
You said it without saying it.

A Russian waitress offered us a dance. In the throb of music and flickering lights, Bart shook his head. "Not yet, babe."
She nodded, official—a strange hardness of shoulder revealed
as she turned. Even here, a million miles from Odessa, she
had the all-business cool of a gulag warden. Now a burly man
entered through the foyer and idled in front of us. His stud-
ded belt buckle said JACK in wrought iron. After Jack sat
down and ordered a Coors, he locked eyes with the slightly
chunky stripper onstage. She did a special bend-over just for
Jack—perhaps they were old friends. On cue, Jack tucked a
fiver into her red undies with great pride and satisfaction. His
hard-earned money was well-spent.

Bart leaned to me with a wink. "Good ole Jack likes the
lady in red." And then: "But you know what? It's guys like
Jack that made America, man. Manifest Destiny, baby, all the
way." Bart sniffed and leaned back with a curious pride of his
own—he had figured out the world. It was a devilish world, to
the core, and he thrived on this crackling information, dug it
to his own core. We clinked drinks. It didn't seem like Bauer
could be pals with Goldfischer, and the odds of him having
a line in to whoever made the tape was low. Still, he was the
kind of man who knew things and kept score.

He said, "I'm glad you came out, amigo."

"Wouldn't want to miss this," I said.

"Me, I used to be intimidated by these joints—before the big switch-o change-o."

"Big transformation?"

"Oh fuck yeah—but in stages, man. I mean, my full first name is Bartholomew, right? I was just *destined* to be a beta dork. And like most guys in the MORE, I was dumped by the so-called dream girl. Actually, me and her were barely together except for in my deluded mind. I had a disease known as *one-itis*, and when she gave me my walking papers . . . I mean, I went suicidal. I started going to CODA meetings—Codependents Anonymous. Complete loser brigade. But I stuck with it, 'cause even though this chick treated me like a welcome mat, I was still fantasizing about winning her back. This Japanese dude at CODA, a *dentist*, smelled a fellow loser and pushed this book on me, *No More Mr. Nice Guy*. Dude handed me the bible and didn't even know it. I couldn't put it down. Everything described in there was *me*. The ass-kissing, the white knight BS. The *toxic shame* for my healthy male desires. Actually now I realize the book was too tame, but suddenly everything looked different. My ex, Miss Can't-Live-Without-Her, was just six, tops. But to salvage her ego, I had to act like she was hotter than Kate Upton or something. This book just opened my eyes. I stopped apologizing. I started workin' out. I started saving. I *stopped* jackin' off—that was key. I don't know how you're livin' on that one, but don't get offended when I say you cannot see male-female relations in a realistic light when you're worshippin' at the porno altar three out of every twenty-four hours. Oh yeah, dude. With every wank you're sending your brain a message: *I will never attain this*."

"Wow," I said. "I *think* I see what you mean."

"I just went cold turkey, bro. Cleaned up my act twenty ways from Sunday. I haven't had a gf since, haven't needed one, and haven't wanted one. I'm my own man—and it's thrilling."

The lady in red left the stage, replaced by a super-young-looking Hispanic girl, spinning like a tetherball around the pole. She was slinky, feline, very confident for someone her age. We ogled in tandem. I was just about to bring up the death of music icon Annie Linden when Bart went serious philosophical. "We're changing the narrative, man. You'll see. Feminism—the kind we know—is less than a hundred years old, bro. It won't be around in another fifty. Look at how ideas change. Look at psych."

I shook my head to indicate I didn't understand.

He said, "Freud is out, DNA is *in*."

"DNA?"

"Oh yeah, DNA is *all*, dude. Everything that pours out of some fat lesbian's mouth is not worth *the snailtrail of one strand of it*. DNA is the real boots-on-the-ground in this war. Period. The city is *full* of *yapping swipples* and hairy-assed fatties who think women should run the world, bro. And they need to be shut down—just like your muff, man, your ex. DNA is what really shuts 'em up good 'n' proper."

"It does?"

"DNA is tomorrow's reality today, Papa-san."

"I don't get it."

He leaned into me again with that conspiratorial twinkle in his eye—he was a scientist with raw data. "Did you know that the whole human species only comes down from something like twenty-five percent of all men? That's how many no-pussy jacking-off beta fucking losers there have been *through history. Seventy-five percent.* Let the trannies squawk. Let the homos squeal. Impregnation is the *only* future reality, and—"

His spiel was broken by a doe-eyed redhead who sidled up to me and me alone and said, "Hiya handsome. Buy me a drink?"

I said, "Not unless you tell me your name."

"It's Hope. And *don't* say I'm just what you need."

She seemed slightly exasperated with her own hot-babeness. I liked her.

Bauer got up and gave me a wink and a tap on the shoulder, then he headed for busty Janine. Arm in arm they disappeared behind a sparkling magenta curtain that led to some kind of a private cave. Hope flagged yet another "waitress" and I bought a round—she had ginger ale.

"This your first time here?"

"That obvious?"

She smiled and nodded.

I said, "My buddy's a regular."

"Yeah, him I've seen."

"How long you been working here?"

"Me?" She leaned back and sighed, her pale skin and baby blue bikini top shimmering in the Day-Glo. Her face was young but her body language was wise, even weathered. "I haven't been here a year yet. Almost. It's not so bad." She sipped her bubbly drink and surveyed the dancefloor like she was still in shock to find herself sitting in a place like this, let alone as an employee.

I said, "You OC?"

"Buellton. I got a son, a three-year-old up there. My momma's raising him, but I raise the funds."

"That's honorable," I said.

"A girl's gotta do what a girl's gotta do."

"What's your boy's name?"

"Patrick."

"You must love him very much. You visit often?"

"Visit?" She laughed. "I live up there. I commute."

"But isn't that like two and a half hours each way?"

"Hell yeah."

"I drive Lyft and you drive more than I do."

"I work hard, man. Some of the other girls do stuff, you know. For extra. Not me. I couldn't live with that."

"Right."

"I *will* give you the lap dance of your life, though. For forty."

I might have blushed a little—it'd been so long, and the men's meeting had me raw, way more exposed than the dancer next to me. I broke out my wallet, shook out the last of my cash. "If it helps pay your bills—why not?"

Hope tucked my twenties under her drink and straddled me in the pulsing disco glare, right then and there on the old Victorian couch behind the white picket fence under the spinning beams. It was only as she mounted me and pulled off her top that I noticed her bikini bottoms were an American flag. And she *was* a good American girl, this young woman named Hope. Industrious, earnest even. On the field of desire she met me, human to human, with total understanding. Of course, I felt my body ratchet up to the edge of mad hunger, but compounded by many layers of paradox—it was a transaction, forty bucks' worth, and yet she threw her personal best into it, onto me, like some piece of her genuinely wanted me to feel good. She caught the soul of customer service in her grind. All her focus, her oceanic God-given tenderness, her DNA fire was upon me.

And then, as she leaned closer, gyrated more, her breath hovered into the zone of my ear and the song switched up. Shante's "Love You Up"—lyrics by KL Robbins, melody by

Jason Phillips. I had never heard past the opening bars but now, under Hope's writhing embrace, there was nowhere to run. While she ground down on me, enveloped me in her powdery lightness, verse became chorus and powered up into a full-charged throb.

Electricity
Passes through me
When you're inside me
Inside me
All night long

My ex's words to her arrogant lover, her Svengali. It was a monster hook—cold and caroming, digital dominoes collapsing in rigid formation. You couldn't even call it music exactly. It was aural porno—it had the stim, the distance, the glossy undimensionality of a fast-paced Triple-X close-up—sonic wallpaper for a lap dance.

Hope picked up my static and tried to bury it with a Coca-Cola girl smile.

Next thing Bauer and I were out on the suburban streets of Fullerton, bar hopping like best buds. By the time we got to Public House, I was drunk but Bauer was drunker, pushing through the crowd, hollering for some expensive-sounding Scotch over the blaring guitar grunge. In the jostle, I leaned into him on the bar to raise certain questions, nice 'n' easy.

"Say man, you ever hear of a dude from the men's group named Thom Goldfischer?"

"Goldfish?"

"Thom . . . Thom Goldfischer. He's actually the guy who told me about it."

He shrugged—"Funny name!"—and waved impatiently at the bartender.

"You never heard of Goldfischer? I'm looking for this guy that made some tapes."

"Huh?"

"Some tapes, a thing, like a prank. With some bootlegs."

"Don't know what you mean, *broheimmer*. Like a cassette?"

"Yeah—you ever hear of Annie Linden, the singer?"

"From the seventies?"

"That's right, I got some tapes, some live shows. And they're recorded over on one side with these lectures—like, how to man up, stop getting taken by bitches, it's insane."

He burst out laughing. "That's genius. Where'd you get them?"

"This convention—you never heard of Goldfischer?"

He shook his head.

"The tapes?"

"Sorry, bro."

"You ever meet a guy that went by the handle Victor Immature?"

His eyes glazed as the drinks arrived and he ducked for a sip. "You got some friends with funny names, sport—cheers."

We clinked. I said, "Thom Goldfischer, Victor Immature? You know about a . . . a *smear list*?"

"Wait a minute. You aren't some kind of journalist or something, are you? We got those coming around—"

"Naw, me? Told you—I'm a Lyft driver." I raised a fist. *"And I am a strong man."*

He stared me down, almost suspicious—drunk to drunk. But then he tasted more single malt and soon he was waxing philosophical afresh.

"You know, the white man is really to blame for all this. 'Cause it's the white man that lost the plot. When a dog goes crazy and attacks a child, you don't blame the dog. And you don't blame the child. You blame the owner who forgot to strap on the fucking leash, bro. Now the dog is the black man. And the child is *unscrupulous female sexuality*, all of womankind, all the horny hos. And the white man has got no one to blame but himself." By the end of the next round, he was onto the thickness of skulls and statistical proof of racial hierarchy, which then led to a particularly annoying "pro-Israel/pro-Jewish/pro-Occupied Territories" rant that sounded a lot less *pro* anything than it purported to be. He was kissing my Jewish ass to hold back his not-latent anti-Semitism, the better to bond, and secretly I was grateful because his rawer and rawer lunacy kept me in check, peeled the edge off my buzz though I tried not to show it.

I said, "Check it out—we got some unscrupulous-looking babes right here tonight" eyeballing a table of beach-tanned junior real estate agent lady types.

"Good focus, amigo!" Bauer got drunk-earnest, threw a brotherly arm around me, and raised a flat hand to frame the scene. "Enough small talk. Time for lesson one."

"What do you mean?"

His whole life force hunkered down like a platoon commander on the cusp of battle. "What I *mean* is the time has come for you to walk the plank and jump into the deep waters of the female soul."

"Huh?"

"*I'll wing you.* You hit that table and call me over when it's time for reinforcements. You do not bail *sans phone number.* You're A-MOG—the Alpha Male of the Group."

"Oh, I can't—"

"No, no, no. You're a superdog, a pit bull, and don't you forget it, Chumley."

I froze, killed the drink. I'd been off-market with a broken heart for so long and these two OC Barbies were *not* going to be responsive to a dork in Target's finest.

Bauer, catching my nerves, said: "Make your move. *Now.*"

Two seconds later I was at their table, about to deliver the nice Jewish boy "Howdy" like Goober of the Year. But then, all those stories from the meeting kicked in—boiled my blood. I smirked.

"Wait," I said to the ladies, pointing—"you're her older sister, right?"

Stares—invisible shields.

I smiled. "'Cause I just placed a bet on which one of you is the bossy one."

A moment of hesitation and then, cracked smiles, glances exchanged, and to my secret shock they started laughing, arguing about it. A chaos of small talk ensued. Nobody was anybody's sister. They worked in pharmaceuticals, they grew up in Mission Viejo, they had just come from a steakhouse that had peanut shells all over the floor, they were drinking tropical and yes, I could call in another round of Maui Island Breeze. One's name was Lara and one's name was Larissa, but which was which? No matter—I pulled up a seat, talked them up in a kind of half-dickish half-interest, played them off each other, cracking half-jokes at their expense *but they laughed*, they dug it. In the corner of my eye, I could see Bauer's slow nod—Master approval. More small talk, Lara or Larissa could not believe what happened to Lara or Larissa on a heinous business trip to Phoenix, and I fake-yawned, waved Bauer over, another trip to Maui for all, more BS teasing, Bart was keeping the field open, I asked this one or that one for the phone number and now she was texting it to me with sweet drunken concentration as a new layer of heat fell upon the night.

Digits scored, I excused myself, flew into the bathroom and splashed water on my face, caught a reflection in the mirror.

For a split-second, I didn't recognize myself.

Cheetah eyes stared back—predator eyes—glowing like hazel fire.

I dried up, took a deep breath and broke out of the bathroom, heading back to the table with a bounce in my step, still high on my own vaporous pheromones of dangerous desirability, when the sight of Bauer sitting there alone snapped me out of my stupor and stopped me dead in my tracks—but pronto.

He didn't see me.

I don't know what he'd said to make the girls leave but they were already at the door, all business.

Caught by the discomfort of this moment, I stood transfixed in the bathroom hallway like that and watched Bauer for a frozen second. He stared suspended into the crowd, a small, aborted scowl at the end of his mouth, like someone remembering a bad joke. The powerful loathing in his eyes—for himself, the revelers, life itself—made him seem fragile, like a child among partying adults. He was the loneliest little boy I'd ever seen.

All in an instant, the night of frivolity fell off me, and I remembered I was on a mission.

Outside the bar now in the dead 2:00 a.m. Fullerton heat with Disneyland's Matterhorn in the not-so-far-off distance, I faked drunker than I was and slurred, "Fuck, I better call an Uber myself, man. No way am I driving my ride up the Indy 405 tonight, she's a fuckin' cop magnet."

Bauer's ruddy face exploded in conviviality. "Oh dude—

we're comrades. You crash on my couch. Just don't slip me a roofie and try to buttfuck me in my sleep."

I went white knuckles as he drunk-drove us in his orange Camaro to a condo townhouse all in dark slanted wood, a real 1970s Buena Park monstrosity. Pulling into his private garage, he said, "I'd call us a couple of escorts but Ol' Johnny Long Schlong would pass out before they showed, man."

With a flick of the switch his place lit up—pristine, spotless. A classic framed Nagel tilted against the wall unhung. A massive black leather sofa and a glass table cut into thick white shag, a bachelor fuckpad supreme. Chugging bottled water at the open kitchen, he said, "Blankies in the closet, I'll grab you an extra pillow. And that couch there is comfier than my bed."

"You're a true gent."

"Don't ever tell my bitches that." He tossed me the pillow and staggered up the stairs. For about an hour, I lay in darkness, making a mental map of the place, letting the booze dissipate. I was keyed up from the night of frolic, seriously wondering about the meaning of the word Man, but even in the pitch black I had not lost my recaptured sense of purpose. I vowed that I would pocket any cassette I found, any shred of evidence, and if there was a weapon, I'd grab that too and beat it the hell out of there. I sat up. In the distance, the low light of a computer screen floated from some workroom somewhere or maybe it was a bathroom nightlight. When his snores got louder, I made my move.

The downstairs had nothing, not even a fridge magnet. His one desk near the door was organized to the point of madness—inside the top drawer, Wite-Out and paper clips and ballpoint pens and watch batteries had been separated into their own trays. The walk-in closet wasn't messier—I started rummaging to the rumbles of his apnea. Everywhere the faint smell of potpourri—to chase moths. Behind cashmere winter coats was a box—I slid it out and opened it. Four years of H&R Block tax returns in perfect folders. This gave me stomach acids as I considered my own mess—I hadn't reported in two consecutive years. Then another box: old Club Magazines, at least a year's worth. It didn't mean he lied about his abstinence but maybe he did lie. A third box was three-ring binders, some kind of invoices for his appraisal gig. I made a mental note to see if the Linden estate had been appraised in recent years. But besides that, the closet was a bust—no cassettes, no Linden, no Goldfischer, no Immature, no eBay anything, nada. I knew damn well I had to go upstairs.

Like Jack up the beanstalk, I made my way past the sleeping giant on socked feet, thanking the Lord for carpeting, my boozy ears trembling. If confronted, I would say I was looking for a john. The condo had an odd shape—no room was a perfect square, and the second bedroom was like a broken Ritz cracker. His private home office—just what the doctor ordered. I used my cell phone to light the way. For a so-called radical thinker who wanted to be Mr. Masculine, he sure was tidy. Either he had the world's best housekeeper or he went out of his way to self-present generic.

Like Thom.

I slid open every drawer, popped the armoire, got on my knees and looked under the desk. Socks were rolled Bento-style, and all the books on the shelf were self-helpy: *Unlock the Power, The Book of Afformations, No More Mr. Nice Guy.* I stood in the middle of the room, hypnotized by the blandness. I was getting nowhere. Then I saw a filing cabinet that had been masked by a black silk bandana and a vase, and I made my way through it as fast as possible. Anthem Blue Cross,

Bank of America, South Bay Chevrolet, bills bills bills. I pulled
bank statements and scanned by phone light. Heart pounding:
If I got caught now I'd be completely fucking caught. Deposits
from all kinds of sources—he was one busy appraiser of
homes. Tustin, Anaheim, Azusa—the Orange sprawl.

Then: a landline rang *loud*, startled the fuck out of me. A
red landline, right there in the room on the floor. I watched
it, transfixed, buzzed, heart pounding. One ring, two rings,
three—down the hall, Bauer picked up another line.

I heard mumbling.

To eavesdrop, all I had to do was gently lift this red phone
right in front of me.

Heart ramming—did I have the balls?

C'mon, cheetah.

One quick motion—

Bauer: "*–almost* took home a stripper."

A man's voice, low, jokey: "Oh boy."

Bauer: "I know, right? Loser should've banged her."

The man: "*Incorrect.* Gotta be careful with a bitch like that."

Bauer: "Oh yeah—probably got cooties."

"*Cooties?!*" A chuckle—there was something familiar
about the man's voice, but in a vague way. Was he a celebrity
or someone I'd heard on the radio? "VD would be *the least*
of your problems. A few strategic fucks and that broad gets
knocked up, she's got you on the hook for an SUV, a three-
bedroom condo, and a lifetime supply of SnackWells."

Sleepy Bauer burst out laughing.

The man stayed serious, for comic effect: "Listen to me,
young man. You screw a toots like that, afterward you've
got to take your condom, go into the backyard, dig a ditch,
drop the condom in there, pour a liter bottle of sulfuric acid
over it, throw in some kindle sticks and kerosene and have

yourself a marshmallow roast. *That's* the kind of birth control I'm practicin'."

Bauer was in hysterics now, but it was driving me nuts,
the familiar cadence of the other guy's voice—*sulfuric acid,
marshmallow roast.* I had to steady my hands not to grunt.
Down the hall, I could hear Bauer sitting up, something was
clinking, glass on a night table. I pulsed in the dark, mouth
agape—I had to get out of there and fast.

But who was that voice? That man? *I knew that voice.*

No time to ruminate—they were still talking. I gently laid
down the open receiver, backed out slow on the rug, made my
way down the dark hall to the stairs, down quick, moving
swift, grabbed shoes and slipped out Bauer's front door under
the orange glow of OC streetlamps. I beat it to the edge of the
complex and called a Lyft, to drive me to my Lyft, drunken
mind swirling.

I knew that voice.

On the ride, I shaded my eyes, tried again to call it up, that
voice, that man, *get a face on it*—but all I saw was the flickering throb of streetlights down too-wide OC streets, blinking
past like spinning strip club strobes, with KL's sex song throbbing in my ear—

Electricity
  When you're inside me
              All
                    Night
                          Long

At a red light, it hit me in a rush of crazed confusion: That
voice—it belonged to Haywood Kronski.

33

THE BLUES OF DAYS GONE
BY WEIGH ME DOWN

I woke up in my car on some random Torrance residential, cursing the sun. I'd been too drunk to make it home, way too drunk to connect the dots. The tape, the vacuum cleaner place, Goldfischer, Bauer . . . and then *Kronski*?! *Annie's ex*? I threw the door and puked onto the street. There was a world of hate out there, a silent war—*hers and his*—and a war in my heart.

Head back, eyes pressed, gasping, temples slamming. Who was Annie Linden to me, anyway? Some old *passenger*? Some old lady yodeling over an acoustic guitar? Some old *dead* lady? Why did I have to want to save her so bad? Why did I have to be another sorry-ass White Knight? I hit the ignition.

Pulling into 7-Eleven for water, a text broke my dark reverie.

Ronnie G here, had a cancellation, free sesh at noon?

It sounded like the perfect antidote to a throbbing hangover.

Soon I was back down the golden elevator to Ronnie Goldfischer's private room in the Natura Spa basement—he dimmed the silver lamp and silently motioned toward the massage table. I kicked off my sneaks and lay down fully clothed, but he threw a white sheet over my body anyway. He moved my shoulders, my elbows and ankles and so forth, but it wasn't *massage*, exactly—the movements were barely noticeable, like someone arranging breakable dolls in a glass case. He told me to think of my body in halves—top and bottom, left and right—and to see if there were conflicts between the sections. I admitted with a closed-eyed frown that, when you thought of it that way, each part really did seem to have its own will, its own POV. Where my right yearned to root down, my left wanted to make a run for it.

I wanted to ask him about Thom, about red pills, about vacuum cleaners, about brothers-in-arms, but the room was too quiet and he spoke too soft for confrontation.

"Tell me if any part of your body expresses discomfort."

"You mean like—"

"The key is not to fix it but to just notice."

I felt flashes—left side of the belly, right nerve along the neck, a pocket of hurt down in the small of my back. I said, "Everywhere."

He said the body stored memory, especially trauma, embedded between the muscles. Not in the head, the brain, the mind. "Memory," he whispered, "is in the *body*. Only through discovering the body can we uncover the past, the grip it has on us." He placed calm hands under my shoulders.

"What do you see?" he asked. "Within."

I gulped. "I see . . . the last day with my mother."

Anguish rippled through me.

He said, "Tell me."

"Our last time together" was all I could get out. Tears were pressing through closed eyes, throat swelled. They took her away when I was seven or eight. The police had chased us through Griffith Park, cars kicking up dust as we raced through the night, past the Greek Theatre toward the Observatory, then down through the long, wild, winding sagebrush that ends at Fern Dell. We had been living in the Dodge, the two of us, surviving on Cheerios and Gatorade, hiding in parking garages and public parks. My mom was an aspiring actress. *Aspiring* meant you didn't act in movies, you acted in real life. She was an "unfit mother." I knew this before the judge explained it. But I didn't care. I didn't want to live with Uncle Herschel. *I wanted my mother—my crazy irresponsible batshit beautiful loving psycho mother.* My eyes were fully wet now, I lifted a hand to wipe them and that broke the spell.

"It's good to cry," he said softly. "The soul's hygiene."

"Do you—do you ever get memories like that on the table?"

"You kidding?" he said. "When I think of my father, I crinkle up like a Cheeto."

He shifted his focus to my feet, aligned them, gave them the gentlest shake, elongated me without pressure. I wasn't quite hypnotized but when the forty-five minutes were up and he turned on the light, I felt the curious cottony wonder of childhood.

I sat up and sighed and said, "That was hardcore."

With great focus and compassion, he said, "You cared deeply about this woman, Annie. Was she like a second mom?"

I nodded like a child. "And like my own mom, she disappeared."

"Probably she cared very deeply about you, too—otherwise you might not feel this way."

"I'll never know."

Now he sighed and shook his head. There was a moment as I lifted myself off the table, light and dazed, where I thought

I might ask him some questions—about Thom, Patricia, his parents—but my mood was too tender and I let it go. I thanked him and tried to pay him.

He said, "First session's free—like I told you."

"I may come back," I said. "I've needed to get centered for a long time."

"When you're ready."

For three days, I didn't go near the Goldfischer family or the Manosphere. I worked Larchmont Village, empty and obedient, like a Charlie McCarthy doll with a driver's license. I thought of calling Lara or Larissa or whatever her name was but by the light of day it seemed crazy. The sky broke and the city went down in sheets of rain. Into the night I kept driving, avoiding the case—seventeen customers in six-and-a-half rainy hours. Stoplights and turn signals glowed in the city torrent. I ignored my riders and they ignored me—the new standard in human relations. But in the running streams down my windshield ran sketches of the disgruntled faces of everyone Annie ditched without notice: Bix and Kronski and Eva and the Goldfischers, her sister, her fan club president, and now all the weeping fans with their molten expressions, each face slashed away by the steady windshield wipers.

Suddenly without a customer and alone behind the wheel, I tried to dream a song about that feeling on the Natura table, that floating feeling, all space and sunburst light, losing Annie, my ex, my mother—*the light of loss.*

At Wilton crossing Second, where the road bends for no apparent reason, a melody came on me in a fever rush, lyrics falling from nowhere—the jukebox id was spinning an original number.

I followed you down to the shore
into the unforeseen
across the rocks and pools of blue and green

I thought if I could make you love me
somehow I'd be free
like the diamonds shining on the
  sea-eeeeeeeee-eeee-eeeee

I held the last note long as I could, a placeholder. But just as I pulled over to sing the thing into my phone, it rang. No Caller ID—I cursed as the melody darted away like a vexed hummingbird.

"*Mis*-ter Zantz. How ya doin', dude." *Thom Goldfischer,* sounding buzzed.

"I'm . . . okay."

"Right on, right on. Listen, man. You and me—I been thinking. I *do* believe we got off on the wrong foot."

Pause. "That's one way of putting it."

"You . . . you really cared about my mom, my birth mom, and that's a beautiful thing."

"Uhm, okay."

"No, listen, man, listen. I got the wrong impression about you, and I'm sorry for *rasslin'* you. That was wrong."

"Gee whiz, thanks for saying so."

"No, come on, man. Serious. Some of my buds down at the men's group said you fell by. Said you were one of us."

Gooseflesh. *Bauer, Kronski.* "I thought that place was supposed to be anonymous."

"Course it is, I ain't blowin' your cover."

"What do you want?"

"I just thought we could rap. And, uh, I could tell you how it really went down, you know, my reunion with the old gal."

I shook my head in disbelief. "Any fucking time."

"Well how 'bout now, bro? Come over here and hang."

"How do I know you won't slug me again? Or shoot me with that pistol you just bought?"

"Pistol?"

"Over at Turner's."

He burst out laughing. "I'm not a—my girlfriend wants a quiver for her paintbrushes. I seem like a *gun guy* to you?"

I said nothing.

He softened. "Serious, dude, I can't do this over the phone. Come on over. I swear, no more aggro. Fall by, we'll talk, take a dip if you like. Fire up a little peace pipe."

Speechless—almost. "What's your address?"

"I'm, uh, over in Palos Verdes, Villa Coronel. 1373. Just before Clovercliff Park."

"Alright. On my way."

The line went dead and the app lit up—another customer. I hit DECLINE and fired the engine, tore down Hollywood, 101 to the 110, down, down, down to Palos Verdes. Thom Goldfischer lived on the curve of a hill, like the couple that adopted him, but his place was one of those A-frames designed to look like a post-mod log cabin. Giant solar panels on one side gave the place a comical tilt but the slanted beams of '70s wood were washed out—modern was no longer modern.

I parked and cut the radio—it was almost midnight and the rain had stopped.

34

AND THE WATER'S TURNED TO BLOOD AND IF YOU DON'T THINK SO GO TURN ON YOUR TUB

Okay, I told myself. *Zantz in exotica. Be friendly, get the whole picture, and stay cool.*

I sauntered across the street with studied bravado, knocked, rang the doorbell, waited. Nothing. Had the schmuck fallen asleep? I redialed on the cell—no answer. I knocked again. The night sea breeze blew strong and steady. Nerves going jumpy—in a burst of semi-decision, I cut around the long parking lane that reached into his backyard. Surrounding hedges were prickly—nature's barbed wire, stopping no one. I caught a glimpse into the lit-up yellow and baby blue kitchen. Too late to yell his name. Around the corner past the double garage, the backyard opened up to a longish staircase leading up to a high wooden deck. The closer I got, the louder the sound of jet streams. Of course, Thom Goldfischer would be sitting in the world's most tricked out hot tub, duh. He lived for it.

I said, "Goldfischer?"

No answer.

"You up there?"

No answer.

I was about to bound up the stairs when I hesitated—for all I knew he was up there *in flagrante* with a foam-covered beach babe, or maybe conducting group meditation, chanting "Namu Myoho Renge Kyo." Just as I wavered, the jet streams cut off. The stillness was abrupt—too loud in its quiet. The overhanging ferns did not budge—no breeze now. Silence. But someone was up there.

I said a quaky, "Thom?"

Nothing.

"Thom—it's Zantz, is that you?"

Nada.

I squinted with displeasure and made my way slowly up the wooden stairs. There Thom sat, alone in his super-Jacuzzi—a twelve-seater even the store didn't sell—but he was alone. His eyes were open, his expression relaxed, even pleased, despite the milky lake of red that had bunched up around his graying chest. Color had fled from his face for all time. I turned my back to him, almost gagged but my heart was still pounding, lower, like it descended into my gut. I spun 360 in the too-bright too-dark light—no prowlers but me. Then the jets came on with a swoosh and a shot cracked through the air, blasting the deck—I flew ten feet, right off the deck, slammed into wet ivy, rolled and ran—never scrambled so fast in my life. Another shot, I only heard it, but *loud* as I raced for the Jetta, choking on throbbing throat, clicked, got in, jammed the key and tore down the hill, screeching onto Golden Meadow. As I burned the corner, I caught a black Audi Q5 in my rearview, all tinted windows and night glare. I slammed on the gas,

Verdes Drive to the 213, jamming the long curving on-ramp, not breathing, 213 to the 1 to the 110.

Thom—shot down—by who—and why? Thoughts crashed into each other like a six-car pile-up. Freeway zoomed in flying metal—trying not to look back but the Q5 was never more than a hundred yards behind.

Panic decision: I exited for Inglewood residential, cut frantic down bumpy alleys and flew back up onto the 405.

I was sure I'd lost 'em.

One exhale. I pressed 405 north. The Jetta, *my baby*, handled pretty good for a $212 a month piece of crap. Haywire blood returned to heart and head in jagged little increments. More cars everywhere—a rare comfort.

I passed the airport, turned east on the 10.

From nowhere, the Q5, same one, closing in.

Speed limit bye-bye. I gunned it, off at Arlington, down into West Adams residential, north, norther. *Uncle Hersch's shortcut*—you lie at Park La Brea security, say you're picking someone up, take the maze that spits you out on Third.

You get lost in Park La Brea, you're toast.

I drove unsteady over the speed bumps and out onto the boulevards, north and more north. This time I knew I'd ditched them—for now.

Late night, second rain. Playboy Liquor's neon martini drew moths to the flame. *Two entrances—score a burner, report the body, chuck it in the gutter, lay low at Runions's place.* I parked in the glaring lot and was about to slip into entrance number one, when I saw the Audi two blocks down. I panicked, ducked inside, hovered low behind the shelves of mini-donuts and phone chargers, snuck low out the other door, cut through the dark, rainy alley—I don't think the clerk even saw me. I was just turning the corner softly on fast sneakers when pain detonated from behind my right ear and I dropped fast into a jet-black dream—

A synthesizer cracked and popped, the melody was still playing when I came to. *Nausea.* AC. Under me the ribbed curvature of backseat. I reached a slow hand in the dark to touch my concussing head—it was still there. The melody was car radio. Bumpy highway. The pain in my head rippled out now like concentric lightning bolts off a radio tower. Someone was talking low—over the synth. The passenger.

"I got one for ya."

Kronski.

Then the driver. "Tell me."

Bauer.

"*How many bitches does it take to screw in a lightbulb?*"

"Tell me."

"Just one. Since, ya know, the world revolves around her."

35

WHEN I ROLLED RUBBER TIRES IN THE DRIVEWAY

Bauer's laugh was pasted-on.

"This guy," Kronski said, sounding slightly disappointed. "Starting to become a major pain in the keister."

"Who? The driver?"

"Yeah the driver."

"He's a goof. He drove her around or some shit," Bauer said, trying to sound tough. "Now he thinks he can play investigator."

"That much I know," Kronski said, "but he ain't *playin'*. One thing I don't get and I never *did* get."

"What's that?"

"Why was he her driver?"

"Whatta you mean, why? He's works for Lyft. That's his job."

"Yeah, I *know* that. But why's a guy like that workin' Lyft? Aren't they usually Iranians or educated beaners or something?"

"Not anymore, man."

"So some smart-aleck that could talk poetry with my ex is driving for a living? Shouldn't he be a tax attorney or a marriage counselor or whatever?"

Through a reflection in the roof window, I saw the top of Bauer as he laughed, the vibrating curve of his slick head, a modernist yellow bronze upside-down flying saucer.

"Lover boy told *me* he was a songwriter."

"Okay so he's a wannabe. How come he knows all this shit he ain't supposed to know?"

"Sticky fingers—he knows. This fuckwad's been doing some serious digging. He pretty much talked to all of Annie's people. You, the Goldfischers, their neighbors. He even went to the dad's clinic."

"Jesus—why didn't you pick up the phone and tell me all this?"

"I was trying to figure out his moves."

There was a pause—nothing but the low buzz of car radio and the hum of engine—*there's people out there turning music into gold*—but it felt like silence. Then: "You went a *little* overboard tonight, cowboy."

Bauer half-grunted. "You said Thom was a goner, you couldn't let that asshole cockblock your inheritance. You said—"

"I said send a *message*, not plug the guy."

Another half-grunt, the grunt of the disapproved of.

"So now," Kronski went on, "it is imperative that you keep *this* guy off my ass."

In the upside-down reflection, Kronski lay a patronizing Vulcan grip on Bauer's robust college boy shoulder. Driving Bauer glanced at the old man's hand with a wince.

"You understand?" Kronski said.

"You want me to waste him?"

My belly tightened, fists bunched.

Long pause. "No. Throw him out, send him . . . anywhere. But get him out of my life."

"Best I can do is just waste him."

I felt my knees lock up. My body yearned to make a move. The throbbing head on my neck commanded stillness.

Kronski groaned. "*Look.* What happened back there was . . . less than ideal. But it's over. Last thing I need is you cracking up on me now."

"I don't feel bad, chief. I could just shoot this fucking dweeb in the head and be done with it."

Without sitting up, I groped for the door handle. I found it—but the stupidness of the notion held me back.

"This peon?" Kronski talked while lighting a cigarette— the car lighter's reflection made a trailing orange circle. "Not worth it. Slow down, play the long con. Maybe we pin tonight's bullshit on him. The key is move slow—I been in this since Annie went to *Rolling Stone* in eighty-one. Can you dig that? Nineteen. Eighty. *One.* Cut to now—I've moved into her place, the whole fuckin' empire's mine, man. So learn some patience. This loser can't stop what's goin' down—and believe me, it's going wayyyy down. Just . . . cut him loose."

The car screeched to a halt. Time to play dead.

Hands grabbed me—I let myself flop like a crash test dummy. I hit gravel with a thud—shoulder pain not worse than my head. I was hoisted and dragged for what felt like fifteen feet, then dropped. A smell worse than dead dog almost made me gag but I held it back. Gravity sucked at me—I couldn't be sure if I was blacking out again or what—until a hard shoe heel pressed down on my face.

Bauer, whiny, faux gangsta: "Go write a ballad, ya pussy-whipped faggot."

One kick to my belly for good measure and I heard but did not feel spit—then footsteps, the car, and they were off.

A weakness washed over me and I was out again. When I came to, my body was so sore it only raised itself to an ape-crouch. I was one fucked-up ape. In a torn corduroy sportscoat. On a quiet cul-de-sac. At the end of a residential. In a neighborhood hillier than the basin. Stairs reached up to another street somewhere. I could be anywhere—*anywhere*. Los Angeles was like that. Wherever you were, you were equidistant to the middle of nowhere. I tried to approximate the act of walking with an agonizing herky-jerky limp. The ape crawled up a staircase.

The upper street was just as quiet and twice as dark. I patted myself: they didn't take my cellphone, but it was dead. *Fuck*. Before the end of the block, I turned down into an alley, and staggered, alley to alley to alley to alley, a maze of darkness and flashing sensor-lights. No sound of cars and I was running out of steam. I curled behind a sparkly blue Ford F-250 in a dingbat parking garage. I had to wait out the pain. I leaned back on prickly stucco and breathed my way, long and slow, out of the pitch-black void. Sleep came and went. I let time pass, maybe hours.

And it's a funny thing about pain. It brings startling, vivid clarity, everything goes hyper-real. The stillness of alley night, the warmth of blue truck, its omniscient thick tires, made my thoughts louder than sound. *Thom frozen in hot water, his open eyes seeing nothing.* I closed mine, heart thumping, blood coursing through aching nerves. Behind lids, streaking white and red headlights crisscrossed in a fever-dream grid: Annie to Combs to Thom to Nan to Dr. Milt to Dr. Fleiss to Eva to Annie to Thom to Bauer to Kronski to Bauer to Runions to Minnie and back to Combs to Annie to Meghan to Bix to

Troy to Catelo and back to Kronski, always Kronski, flying by in fireball red. An ugly melody—flatted fifths convulsing over sharp nine chords.

> *Kron-ski, Kron-ski*
> *King of the hater's frontier!*
> *Kron-ski, Kron—*

Not now, not here.

I got up and limped off, exited the alley, through the cul-de-sac, made my way down another flight of city stairs, then down a winding hill of mid-century homes, a nicer street. I was east somewhere, inner Silverlake or the eastern border of Los Feliz, and it was way past anyone sane's bedtime. Everything hurt, but I staggered my way down to Sunset like a moth flapping for light. The buses run all night on Sunset, but only once an hour from midnight till dawn. I had just enough pocket change to take a near-empty 2 to Western, where I transferred to the 207 straight down to Jefferson, to visit the world's most hidden guitar teacher.

36

LOOK WHAT FEAR'S DONE
TO MY BODY

The hour of night didn't mean a thing to a man like Combs. He opened the gate in his tan terrycloth bathrobe with a patient sense of destiny as strong as the knowing in his eyes.

"Figured you'd be back," he said. "I just didn't know it'd be so damn soon. You don't give a motherfucker ten minutes to collect his thoughts."

"I don't have ten minutes."

He made a reluctant hand gesture for me to enter. As I did, he said, "You look like shit, by the way. Who gave you that shiner?"

"Some jackass who works for Kronski."

He grunted.

"They came after me," I said. "They want to keep me from something. And I think . . . "

"What."

"I think this guy wasted Annie's son."

Combs took this in with grim foreboding.

I said, "Should I call the cops?"

"Don't be crazy." He got up to lock the door. Inside, the bungalow was not smoky but still dank from a lifetime of cigarettes. Combs dug under the sink for a secret bottle of cognac hidden behind the Dawn and the Drano. The old one-piece turntable with detachable wooden speakers played "Mam'selle," breezy and melancholy, low enough to not disturb the neighbors. The record jacket leaned on a speaker, ancient and browned around the edges. *Harmonicats*—three old white guys that looked like the Pep Boys with extra Brilliantine, their disembodied grinning faces sitting atop three harmonicas stacked from longest to smallest.

Combs caught me looking at the LP and said, "Sit down, boy, this ain't a religious ceremony."

I took my place at the same dilapidated kitchenette. The same scruffy cat splayed on the checkerboard tiles, playing dead.

Combs poured shots into the orange juice glasses. "What you find out down there in Hermosa?"

I told him what I could remember—about Thom, about Bauer, about Kronski saying he'd pin it on me, all of it.

Combs was unshockable, but a ripple of sorrow long presaged rolled through him. He mumbled a shaky "Rest in peace." Then: "What you want from me?"

"I don't know. I'm not safe. I didn't want to go home."

"Well, you can hide out here if you want. But eventually you've got to face the music."

"You know Annie was meeting the doctor down in Hawthorne," I said, "with the kid. In secret. Like, many times."

"Yeah, I know." He placed a hand over his glass as if to keep from drinking it.

"Her girlfriend finally talked her out of it."

"Nobody can talk anybody out of anything, least of all being a mother."

"So why did she stop?"

"It wasn't . . . it wasn't quite the motherhood experience Annie was lookin' for."

"What does that even mean?"

He didn't answer. My lip was still throbbing.

I said, "Combs, why don't you tell me the fucking truth already, before I get my head cracked open."

Before he could answer, the record came to an end and without a blink Combs got up and lifted the arm and placed it right back at the beginning, as if he too were part of the machine. I got the feeling he had been listening to the same side all day and night in a lonesome stupor, snagged in a loop of the past like the needle in the dusty grooves.

Then he turned to me with unsteady hands.

"I told you the dad was a zombie."

I nodded.

"I told you he wanted her to get rid of the child, right? And . . . and she couldn't do it." There was a tremble in his voice.

"Yeah."

"But there was some shit I didn't tell you."

He assessed me. I was not an ace interrogator by any stretch, but I was learning when to shut up—life's single greatest lesson. He sat down, pushed his drink away, plunging deeper into the looping past.

"It's funny how these things happen. Her sister Barb tried to *persuade* me, man. To make a move. I knew she had a boyfriend, I didn't know if they were tight or what. We played Ouija together in the basement. Can you imagine what Old Man Linden would've done if he had found a nigro in his basement playing Ouija? Little Barbie said, *'Oh great oracle, is my sister in love with Manny Combs Rutledge Bullock?*'—she was that snotty kind of twelve-year-old brat—and then she slid the triangle to YES."

"And?"

He didn't respond.

"So you were together."

"Just one time. She . . . cheated. On her boyfriend."

"And she thought the baby might be yours. That's why she wanted to have it."

His gray eyes did a ripple, the closest a hard old man can get to tears.

"But it wasn't," I said.

"No. No, it wasn't."

He got up, stretched high, and walked off, as if disgusted with all this indulgent human sentimentality. We listened to the music together in a stuck trance.

Finally, Combs said, "Better turn that Haywood shit around."

"Yeah? How do you mean?"

Now the languorous sound of harmonicas not quite in harmony, which had been playing so sweetly in the near distance, faded to a crackly stop. Combs turned to move the needle again but this time came back with the gun, slid it to me across the kitchenette table.

"Put this motherfucker in his face."

37

A-LO AND BEHOLD
SOMEONE'S FUNKING WITH
THE MOOD CONTROL

Kronski's Tesla glowed in the Malibu lights on Linden Estate gravel. I parked behind the hedges, popped the glove compartment and slipped the Beretta into my coat pocket, weighed it with a queasy rush.

The wind-up dinosaur was waiting. Underneath, the silver key. I slipped in the side door and punched the code fast, crouched up the carpeted stairs. A television played—"Hear My Train A-Comin'." Jimi at Woodstock.

The old man couldn't see me but I could see him, reflected in long black sliding glass doors that vibrated in the hard ocean breeze. Kronski scratched his salt-and-pepper beard and splayed out in lime-green terrycloth robe—it hung loose around his taut shoulders and muscular throat. He looked strong for an old hippie joker, hardened by time. He sucked at a fancy water bottle, dosing electrolytes. Then he got up, out to the kitchen and back with a fresh pack of cigarettes— Dunhill Reds. He packed the red box against his palm in time with Jimi and slid open the giant glass pane and stepped out onto the balcony. Ocean air gusted right through the living room. His back was to me now, with no place to run. I slipped a finger through the Beretta, leapt the stairs and made my move. Before he could light up, I was out on the balcony with him, dark gusts whipping around us.

I said, "Get your fucking hands in the air—quick."

He lifted them slow, the unlit cigarette still dangling on his right.

"Now turn around, face me." He did.

Without dropping a stitch, he smiled. "*Driver man,* nice Beretta! What can I do for you?"

"Move," I said, "inside." I backed into the living room, directed him to the couch. "Now sit."

"Whatever you say, buddy." He flopped to the couch, supremely relaxed. I took a nearby seat, a little too close, but kept the gun on my knee front and center.

"Now," I said, "I need the whole story."

"What story is that, Sherlock?"

"Annie wanted me to find something for her," I said, "a person, a tape."

A look of recognition spread across Kronski's face. He fell into a broad grin under the dim flying saucer lamp—the old *heimish* village peddler, in negotiation.

"*Guy,*" he said pleadingly, "what do you care what that old broad wanted?"

"I care—plenty."

"Don't you see she was *using* you?"

I tried to snuff the wince. "Using me?"

"Wellll—"

"Last time you told me she said I was a real songwriter."

"Exactly. As in, a mark, a putz. The little gentleman driver with the corny love songs."

It was annoying to hold a gun on someone so unafraid. I thrust it like a reminder.

"Never mind all that—you sent the kid away."

Kronski processed this, a little thrown. "I wouldn't put it that way. I just didn't want him around—obviously."

"Why not?"

"I wanted her to have *my* kid—*obviously*, man."

"And she wouldn't?"

"She didn't *get around to it*," he said. "Too busy playing around down at the arms—buddy, you gonna shoot me or tell me what you're after or what?"

"Why haven't you told the police about Goldfischer?"

"'Cause it's a *non-issue*, man."

"Did he kill her?"

"No. Thom Goldfischer didn't do shit to her."

"Did you kill her?"

"Of course not."

"Troy?"

"No, never."

"*Thom?*"

Kronski shook a scowl. Thom's death displeased him— that confused me. He reached slow for the cigarette lighter and fired up. "You're way off, dude." Kronski leaned back. The gun meant zero—he knew damn well I wasn't gonna shoot. "I didn't *send him away*. Far from it. I took him under my wing. Twenty years after she ditches him, the kid shows up, right? UCLA guy, I went to meet him at the damn yogurt 'n' jelly-beans place over in Westwood. Told him he was wasting his time, she wasn't gonna pay any more hush money than she'd already coughed up."

"And it was money he wanted?"

"I don't know what he wanted, I'm not sure he did either. But he was in a hell of a state. Stammering, blotches all over his pimply face. He had some cockeyed dream that they were *deeply close* and all that shit. It was fantasy, man, pure delusion. I told him Annie was no mother, tried to wake his ass up. But he persisted—so I set him on the path to happiness."

"What path is that?"

Kronski looked me over the way a poker player might take in a new hand. "Let's just say he was a *shy* lad. I took him out."

"As in clubbing?"

"As in *whoring*. Few times. Gave him his first tussle of hashish, too."

"How . . . admirable."

"Hell, it was practically my civic duty. I put my arm around that boy and showed him the way to manhood. I said, *'Son, it is time for you to walk the plank and dive into the deep, dark waters of the female soul.'*"

I said, "Right." I'd heard that line before.

"This is decades ago, ancient history." Kronski reached for a little ceramic ashtray, a Roaring Twenties chorus girl in a bathtub. He smashed out the half-cigarette in her belly.

"So you stayed in contact."

"Barely. I got him out of the picture, that's what counts. And when I franchised the men's thing, I let him know all about it. He was downright tickled to hear from me."

I tried to picture it. Something wasn't gelling. "What's with this men's exchange bullshit?"

"I fund it."

"There's no way you believe all that Alpha Beta manly-man shit."

Kronski laughed, leaned in. "You better believe I believe. How do you suppose a person gets like me? *I was the worst case of nice Jewish boy there ever was.* Nineteen before I got laid and that was to a complete dog, an old drunk lady who gave me a quick pity-fuck in the dust up by Bronson Canyon. My mother's drinking buddy no less."

"Give me a break. I've seen pictures of you with Barbara Bouchet, Dawn Wells—"

"Yeah. *After I saw the light.* I'm doing good service, bringing hope to the millions of guys like me hiding in the shadows. And the great joke is—I'm doing it on Annie's dime."

Kronski tightened his green terrycloth, made a move to stand and I jabbed the pistol.

I said, "Stay down. We aren't done."

"Okay, okay," he said, wagging up hands like a cocky prisoner. "I don't know what you're so uptight about, man. I like you. I thought we could be buds. For real. You got *the motor.*"

"What motor is that?"

"You know—the fun thing. But you're too caught up in trying to save a dead lady. She can't be saved. Hey man, I got a songwriter joke for ya. *How many chick singers does it take to sing 'My Funny Valentine'?*"

I didn't answer.

"Apparently all of them."

I rolled my eyes, he made a frowny-face.

"Okay, how about this. *What are three words you never hear in Hollywood?*"

It was like a nightmare game of Make Me Laugh.

"The accordion player's Ferrari."

"You aren't funny, Kronski."

"Well, give me a minute, wait. I haven't deployed my A material yet. Okay. *Why do Jewish guys like to watch porno movies backward?*"

"Why."

"To see the prostitute give the guy his money back."

At his own joke, he let out a wheezing cackle that exposed his uneven teeth and for a flashing moment he looked almost female, a French revolutionary hag from Dickens. I didn't laugh exactly but involuntarily lowered my arm and he caught me off guard, lurched back on the couch and swung a lucky kick that sent the gun right out of my hand—it flew halfway across the living room. I lunged for it, he grabbed me at the legs, yanked me down and threw a punch, then I kicked him and we rolled, he pinned me, smacked me hard, then one fist to the belly, my legs thrashing, I tried to stand and he rose faster, ground his bare heel into my hand, one more fast foot to the face and I clawed out of his way backward like a crab, but the gun was already in his hand, pointed right at my temple. He wagged the barrel right in my face, put on the whiny voice. *"Sorry, officer, this crazy idiot broke into my house."* Then he stepped back to catch his own breath. "Fuckin' little creep. You just *cannot fathom* that I actually hated that woman's guts."

Blood was coursing through me as I scrambled up. "I don't believe you." I spoke softly, didn't want to hair-trigger him. "You called her every day. She was your world. *My* world."

"No," Kronski said, "don't get us mixed up. I'm not a fanboy like you. *You* loved. I hated. In fact, *I hated her too much to kill her*—that's a fact, ya moron. I didn't want her to *die*. I wanted her to suffer. Get old. Lose her voice, her legs, everything."

Even gun in hand, Kronski had an imploring twist in his eyes, as if he was confessing to a stranger, his ex-wife's Lyft driver no less. This was the Los Angeles version of intimacy.

"Get it?" he said. "It wasn't her *life* I wanted to destroy. It was her legacy."

"I don't understand. You want to destroy Annie Linden's legacy?"

"I'm heir to the publishing. Every last tune, man. And I can tangle up her shit in crappy TV commercials and cop shows for seven generations. In fact—" He started to chuckle to himself again. "—the licensing deals I already got on the table would send your mind *reeling*. Last week I signed a contract to use 'Her Fateful Inheritance' in a Wellness Dog Food ad. Can you picture that?! *Woof woof woof—wa-woof woof woof!*" He barked to the tune of Annie's masterpiece.

"But . . . why? What's that do for you?"

"*For me?*" Kronski ogled me like I was the stupidest, most naïve dork on the planet. "Fifty fucking *years* I stood in that lady's shadow. Fifty years a sidekick, and a sidekick is a *slave*. Oh yeah. Checking into hotels, getting called 'Mr. Linden' by the bellboy. Finding out half the hos sleeping with me just wanted a way to get closer to her. Random assholes stopping me on the street—'*How's Annie doin', how's Annie doin', how's Annie doin'?*' I'll tell you how Annie's doin'. She's fuckin' *dead*, that's how she's doin'—motherfucker. Oh yeah, man," Kronski went on in dreamy soliloquy, "I was her slave. And you know what? She *loved* me for it, too—my indentured servitude. Her gratitude was the worst fuckin' part, dude!" All at once, waving the gun around, he started howling like a maniac. "Fucking cunt—!" He jerked, threw another Tae Kwon Do kick that sent the low coffee table toppling over, the chorus girl ashtray spinning along the rug. "I *should* have killed her, driver man—sorry I didn't."

He showed predator teeth but the prey was himself—he was a real-life extra, the purse holder, the genius's ex-husband, the red carpet back-stepper, stuck with the pasted-on grin of someone who knows he isn't born to greatness, only born to stand alongside it.

It's a rare moment in life that someone holds a gun on you but you want to offer them comfort. For me this was it, cognitive dissonance to the max. Pity and dread slammed into each other like a high-speed car crash. "The magazine," he grunted. "Pick it up."

I looked to the floor—there was a toppled stack I hadn't noticed, copies of the same issue of *Entertainment Weekly*—for the following month, Annie on the cover, *A Songstress Murdered*.

Kronski said, "My interview, page 26."

I flipped glossy pages, my heart jabbing. Full-on spread— *The Wind Beneath Her Wings: An exclusive interview with legendary record producer Haywood Kronski*.

His turn to jab the gun. "Read it."

I scanned the pages, trembling.

. . . exclusive interview, Haywood Kronski claims that the public has badly misread . . .

. . . "My wife was not a moral woman" . . .

. . . a kid at nineteen and got rid of him as quick as she could . . .

. . . when the boy came looking for her, she refused to see him and . . .

. . . Haywood confesses that he had a long-standing affair with Annie's sister . . .

. . . Barbara, a professional psychotherapist, has diagnosed Annie as a narcissist with psychopathic tendencies . . .

"She turned her back on everyone who loved her."

Kronski said, "Read the end, man. The closer is *it*."

I flipped the page, scrolled to the bottom.

" . . . and I pray for a speedy trial so justice can be served. Most of all, for her security guard Troy."

"Were you close to Troy?" asks journalist Dalton Sandiver.

"Not close, no. But here's this war hero, a black street

kid who served in Iraq. Then he comes home and gets killed trying to save the most entitled white lady who ever lived."

Kronski beamed delight, pistol in hand. "Guy, that line is gonna be quoted and requoted, cut and pasted and forwarded across a thousand wires, blogs, *everywhere.*"

His eyes widened with the mirage of it. Even here, at gunpoint, though, I could see it was a curious immolation. Because, in dragging Annie down, he was blowing his own legacy to smithereens.

I said, "So you really want to be known as the whiny husband that squawked to the press."

Kronski burst out laughing. "That's what the fanboys'll think. The *men* will know where I'm coming from, 'cause *game recognizes game.* And you ain't got none."

He popped out the clip and flipped the gun to me like a frisbee. I caught it with both hands as it smacked my chest.

"Now take your little toy and get the hell off my property."

38

THERE IS NO ANSWER TO THE QUESTION WE ARE IN MUTUAL POSSESSION THIS IS THE CIRCLE THAT WE LIVE IN THESE ARE THE PEOPLE THAT WE'VE BEEN

Night winds ripped over the black ocean. I yanked my coat closed and beat a breathless path to the car, got in and turned it on and blazed onto PCH in a shaken fury.

Annie don't go—

Traffic rushed by—streaks of flying light. I was throat-sore, eyes wet from wind and rage.

—don't slip away—

Past Geoffrey's with the somber valets in their black vinyl windbreakers, past the lonesome palms, bent in prayer to the ocean. And in the rearview, changing lanes at 65 mph, the blank spot where she once sat, her frail arms folded and warding off the world, protecting her heart, her silver hair and open mouth, high voltage eyes fearful, disappointed.

No one there.

—do you know how bad I wanted to save you? When you were alive and so lonely you befriended your Lyft driver—

A woman on the run. From cascading mistakes. Who slept with the high school jock, then fell in love with another boy. Had the baby. Gave him away. Ran for her life. Natural mistakes. But mistakes, like people, also give birth. To other mistakes. And soon Annie had to know the child, couldn't live without him. Until she could.

And I can't let you go.

I cut the window, exposing the sharp salt air. So running away from love was the secret source of all that blazing inquiry into the human heart—the desperate yearning, for a *free heart*, and never finding or having one. She played along and played at love and promised the moon to him and me and anyone else who crossed her path but I didn't care, I would have done anything to save her, even now—long after it was way too late to save her soul.

Not yet.

A gray Forester sounded its admonishing horn as I took the long curve at Topanga Beach too fast and too wide. The surferless bay was a quilt of black, the sky above hung white with the glossy sheen of newly Windexed glass. I ran over her list *again*, the final text *again*, like someone with OCD in the throes of a minutiae freakout. *Come to my arms*—where did she want to go? Not Eva Silber's. Maybe it was code for something else. Maybe it was code for *come to my history, drown in it, drown with me.*

And it was at this moment speeding PCH and wanting to

die that a song came upon me, a terrible sailor's song from the Sea Shanty Inside:

Songs of envy—songs of hate
Songs at the gas station while you wait
Stuck in your head
But you can't sing along
Nobody can find the missing love song

And I'm down at the arms
Down at the arms
Down down down down down at the arms

"*Down at the arms.*"

Huh? Say what?

Kronski's words had hijacked my melody and now they were stuck in me like a skipping record. *Down at the arms, come to my arms.*

"*Too busy playing around down at the arms.*"

Down at the arms.

It was a strange shard of broken poetry. *Down how? Whose arms?*

In my fuzzyheaded rage, I tried to recapture the stormy tune I'd lost but the song was already going somewhere else.

Down at the arms, come to my—

Whose arms?

Or maybe it wasn't a who.

Maybe it was a what. As in armor?

Or a why—like why be armed? Be disarmed.

Or a where.

As in—The Arms.

I pulled up to Sonic Labs, ran up the stairs past Mr. Santiago

in session, yanked open my door and pulled the bag from under
the bed, shook the dirty newspapers out onto the floor.

Arms, the Arms.

I started flipping the classifieds again, more frantic
now—a handheld, black-rimmed square magnifying glass
gave new eyes. I was just like Sherlock Holmes, if Sherlock
Holmes had been a Lyft-driving crappy songwriter studying a fifty-cent porno rag. I hovered slow, looking for the
secret meets—Annie and Dr. Milt—threaded through the
endless lists.

> Bored Housewife, when my hubby's away . . .

> Dr. M, sundays find me at the ha . . .

> Honeypot massage, I'll BLOW your mind . . .

> The Tree Lass is so glad you came . . .

> Lusty ladies of Torrance are hurtin' for a squirtin'

> Good Doctor, meet me at the arms to feed the fisch . . .

Breath going jagged—I grabbed a Bic and, in the margins, as-
terisked lines Annie/Thom/Milt related. I circled, underlined,
crossed out what wasn't code—then I wrote an exclamation
mark for nobody's benefit but my own 'cause they had not
gone so very far to hide.

Google Earth spit up the view:

Hawthorne Arms—a fourplex on 135th, spitting distance
from True Value Hardware.

Halfway down the 405, I wondered if I'd locked the studio

on the way out. Ten minutes later, GPS lady chimed *"Use the right lane to turn right onto Hawthorne Boulevard"* and the glib sign came into view:

hawthorne HARDWARE . . , has it!

Has *what?* The banner rises up out of the endless stream of storefronts and says *here and nowhere else.* Then the big color hexagon starbursts call out the wares:

PLUMBING ELECTRIC PAINT TOOL TRANSMITTER.

I was warm getting warmer. I was red hot.

Right on 135th and the dirty stucco Hawthorne Arms shimmied before me by nightlamp—decrepit and uninviting. I parked, cased on foot. Through one window a little boy watched a Spanish-speaking cartoon pig on a giant widescreen. In another, I couldn't see anyone, but the lights were on and I heard water, clanging, talk radio: Someone scrubbing dishes. That left two apartments. Without getting to the second, I knew it was unit 3 from the rot around the doorknob. No landlord, no neighbor had bothered to turn that knob for God knows how long. I twisted it. As old as it was, it kept the place shut.

I kicked open the door. The light switch didn't work—at least Annie wasn't paying for that. I hit the cellphone flashlight: dusky air, thick sheet of dust. Before I could itemize, a surge of sadness washed through me—abandoned rooms, like abandoned children, give off a silent cry of despair. Windows filthy, wallpaper peeling. But otherwise the place was just as it had been left. Inanimate objects don't do a jig when we leave them behind. There was a low rectangular coffee table, a moth-eaten couch. The moths themselves had taken off ages ago. There were toys—some in an aluminum trunk that I think was once dark green, now black, other toys strewn on the rug, a fire engine and a wooden puzzle of musical instruments—most of the pieces were in place. And candy wrappers, strewn and mangled.

I cut through the living room, pushed open another door with my foot. One lonesome bedroom and a bed with rainbow sheets, all bathed in dust and time. The bathroom—no less or more dirty than the rest of her place—ancient plastics of long-ago toothbrushes in mauve and topaz, colors that either faded weird or don't get made anymore. I crossed to the kitchen, mostly untouched—Annie's hideaway alright. One cupboard door had collapsed from exhaustion, revealing a yellow pot. I didn't have the heart to open the door further. My eyes were tearing up, turning red from filth, but also there wasn't much to see. The ghosts of *them*, Goldfischer and his birth mother, were nowhere. A *People* magazine sat on the coffee table, February '75, *Olivia Newton-John: Hottest new pipes in pop*—a fitting end for Annie Linden. An empty onyx marble ashtray, and a cheap one-piece phonograph player—Sears. One 45 with the plastic, yellow spider, Pablo Cruise, and a short stack of random 8-tracks—Lynn Anderson, *Dueling Banjos*, Beatles greatest '67–'69, the blue one. A small bookshelf, but for a woman with ten thousand volumes she didn't do much heavy reading here. There was *Hawaii* by Michener and a warped fat paperback Scrabble Dictionary and a few other useless titles, Jane Fonda, fitness BS. Then: an old Panasonic Slim Line cassette player, black and silver. I flipped it—batteries corroded. A cassette case—it trembled in my hand. Track list in old ballpoint:

1. cucumber soup
2. I nose you
3. body remembory
4. a serious case of the sleepies
5. big stretch / little stretch
6. sea turtle is the one I love
7. lulla-bye-bye

I tapped Stop/Eject on the player. Inside—Scotch Magnetic 272, ninety minutes, hand-scrawled *silly songs*.

Heart pulsed, this tape, *the* tape. But the little white reels were empty, someone had yanked it. Eyeballs darted to the rug at the foot of the couch—I knelt, reached for it: a little handful of black plastic spaghetti. Useless.

This tape—unplayable—she wanted me to find it.

Here. *Why?*

Someone beat me to it.

Holding out my phone like a cross warding off the devil, I moved 360, scanned, re-surveyed, called on Higher Powers, mystical forces, bright and dark spirits. But the room still felt lonely as hell. Decades she paid the rent—even after death. And whoever passed through here didn't stay long. Without even knowing it, I had cupped one hand over my nose and mouth but it did no good—the smell was something decomposing, a moldy oak beyond stale.

Dust flowered all around, bright with a terror of living death. I wanted to cry, I wanted to run, I wanted to hold a one-man séance in the dark. De-threaded orange and yellow macramé dangled from the ceiling holding a cracked ceramic pot, plants long gone. A kitchenette table leaned slanted, one leg down. A moth-eaten lamp sat pridefully atop shelves caked in soot—the top shelf held a lopsided stack of LPs.

My heart jumped to my throat.

I pushed the coffee table out of the way then pulled the records off the shelf, all of them. One by one, I lay the jackets across a patch of dusty peeling carpet—what color the rug had originally been was the real unsolvable mystery. They made a curious collage, these records, a nightmare Tarot deck that could only predict the past. Kiddie stuff: *Mary Poppins* and *Free to Be . . . You and Me,* the "soundtrack" to the *It's a Small World* ride and *Boom Boom Ain't it Great to be Crazy: Songs that Tickle Your Funny Bone.* These were mixed in with faded grown-up clunkers, early Chuck Mangione and *The Folkways of Theodore Bikel,* Les Baxter's *Jewels of the Sea* and *Cantor Moishe Oysher Sings Kol Nidre for Yom Kippur Services*—that had to be Dr. Milt's.

One mustard LP dust jacket had faded almost beyond recognition but when I flipped it, I saw it was *Yoga for Life: Second Exercise Album*—a newish concept for some back then, complete with a moldy booklet of positions in the gatefold: Breath Standing, Roll Twist, Hip Bend, Rishi's Posture, Lie Down Sit Up—

I lay it down gently among the others and breathed into the feeling.

A stack of records . . . an identity card.

This stack crosshatched three lives: Annie, Dr. Milt, and somebody that did *not* grow up to be Thom Goldfischer.

Not. Thom. Goldfischer.

Rishi's posture: Niece on the kitchen tiles—*Richie's positer, Richie's pose.*

The jukebox id kicked in. A silly hopped-up dance song, I couldn't even remember who recorded it—a girl's persistent voice: *My body, your body, everybody work your body.*

Really? Disco? Here? Now?

And it was in this negative throb of chanting disco—*everybody work your body*—reaching out to touch the dirty yoga dust jacket that my belly wrenched and my eyes fritzed and I went gooseflesh.

And solved my case.

I had my killer.

Down at the Arms—your body is your child—come to my arms.

The memory of his words hit me like low and sudden thunder.

"*You can't wish away the heart's pain. The body rebels.*"

I scrambled to my feet and headed out of there, jittery but closing the door with great care. As far as I was concerned, this sorrowful room could sit undisturbed for all time.

39

PITCHING GLASS AT THE
CORNFIELD CROWS

Three hours east from Malibu, then up, up the winding two-lane highway, into the forest, white knuckles on the steering wheel. Worse at night, these trembling pines guarding the rustic village way high atop the San Jacinto Mountains with Palm Springs lolling at the foot of it all. California's that way: forest, desert, beach, fields all stuck together like stray pieces from different jigsaw puzzles. I pulled up just before dawn. He lived on Pine Crest in an A-frame of Tasmanian oak, dropped into the middle of a mini-patch of green woodland straight outta Hans Christian Andersen. Hand-painted cobblestones led the way to the murderer's front door. Yellow sunbeams blazed through the trees, increasing my blinking jitters tenfold. When the breakfast hour came, I made my move.

A woman answered, a pretty one, maybe mid-thirties. On her breast, she clutched a two-year-old girl guarding a yogurt squeezy. Mommy hadn't quite woken up yet, or already looked exhausted. Blonde hair was tied off in a lopsided bun on her head and splayed out like she had taken electro-shock. Behind them, two slightly older boys in PJs built a Lego fortress.

"If you're from Anthem, I already told the *very* rude woman on the phone that our payment plan—"

"No, ma'am, I'm an investigator. I'd like to speak with Mr. Goldfischer." I peered over her shoulder. The big kids clutched colored pieces and pretended to play but kept their big ears on us.

"Yeah, well, Mr. Goldfischer isn't here."

I said, "Are you Tiffany?"

"I am."

"Do you know where your husband is?"

She tried to shrug with the baby in her arms, but she was tightening up. "Ron is just—out at the moment."

I lowered my voice. "This is urgent, I wouldn't have disturbed you so early in the—"

"So call the police." She tried to close the door with her foot. I jammed mine in, stopped it hard. I wedged in, got a better look, pulse high. Behind her, out the sliding glass windows, a hot tub sat lonely in the fuzzy morning green.

"I *could* call the cops, but I thought better of it." I nodded toward the boys. "For their sake. They'll turn this place upside-down."

She dropped to a whisper herself. "Ronald is not here, and he hasn't *been* here for a long time already."

"What do you mean?"

"We're separated more than a year now. Far as I know, he doesn't stay on the mountain. What the fuck do you want from me?"

"Where *does* he stay?"

"Why don't you check his brother's place?"

"I checked, he isn't there." I said it flat as possible, but she sensed the starkness.

"*Has Ronnie done something wrong?*"

"You could say that. A great deal has been done to him as well. And I think he may be in a very bad way."

"Right." She put her daughter down—the little girl toddled eagerly right through the Lego wall, eliciting groans of protest from the boys. Tiffany Goldfischer turned back to face me with heightened conspiratorial energy. "*That's why I kicked him out,*" she whispered. "He's *always* in a bad way."

"He has a lot to be angry about."

"Yeah, well, Ronnie seethes and doesn't even know it. I knew it was a matter of time before he boiled over."

"You have a best guess where he might be? I need to catch him before he boils over again."

"He bunks at the Natura Spa—on Wilshire."

"He's not there—I called on the way up."

"Have you tried his mother's?"

"Same—she hasn't seen him."

She looked at me for an uncomfortable three seconds, turning something over in her mind. Her jaw flexed. "She's probably lying."

"You think she's hiding him?"

"He hides out there himself sometimes. She may not even know he's there."

"What do you mean?"

"There's a rec room, a wine cellar—" A lower fathom of worry set into her tired eyes. "—his little shelter. You aren't going to hurt him, are you?"

"Not if I can help it. You know your mother-in-law's house?"

"Unfortunately."

"I've been there. If I went looking for this rec room, where might I find it?"

She looked over her shoulder to watch her children squabble but her mind was on me, my character. And her husband's.

She said, "There's a door, behind the bar."

40

LIKE A CHILD SO YOUNG AND CAREFREE MY EYES SEE WHAT THEY WANT TO SEE

Down the Idyllwild hill was rougher—rush hour headlights and taillights seemed to fritz in a winding waltz. By the time I got to Hermosa, it was almost noon. Layered clouds blanketed the oceanside—a great shield from the universe but no comfort to me. I popped the glove. The Beretta was empty but I took it anyway. I parked once again at the curious deco House of Goldfischer and cut across the street, rang and rang until Patricia opened the door. She tried to ward me off but I raised palms and she backed off—I crossed the empty vestibule, under the heavy glistening chandelier, into the sunken living room.

"Where is he?"

Patricia shook her head.

"Don't stall me out, Patricia, where's Ronnie?"

She closed her eyes as if she could make me or herself disappear by sheer mindpower. That's when I spotted the door behind the bar—closed and forbidding. She noticed me notice and scurried to block. She shouted *"Adam, wait—"* in a kind of halting yelp and it broke my heart, her broken spirit and unbroken loyalty. I kept the gun in my pocket, I didn't want her to yank another blade.

I said, "I think you better step out of the way."

"Or what?"

I stepped forward and she backed off, teeth baring a childlike head-shaking laugh that masks terror. The door back there was locked but it didn't take much to kick it open—a half-flight led to somewhere dark, probably what was once a suburban wine cellar, neo plus ultra of bourgie must-haves, the Jacuzzi of its day, très SoCal. But soon as the door popped, Patricia stepped out of the way and her mother appeared in a wheelchair rolling to the edge of the stairs.

"Stop at once!" Nan Goldfischer said. "You have no business in my house."

I ignored both of them, turned and went in.

Patricia said, "Adam—*please don't.*"

The short flight led to a hexagon-shaped space, a little soda cracker of a windowless room. I don't know what I was expecting to find—a psychotic version of Meghan McMahon's Annie shrine, maybe. But this room was a bunker. No cardboard cutouts, no autographs. Just the low tilt of a slanted stucco ceiling and one framed poster leaning against the wall—Matisse, the famous goldfish.

Ron lay on an inflatable bed in his khaki pants and pastel short-sleeved plaid shirt, barefoot, eyes closed. His hands rested on his ears—he was wearing big headphones, old school Panasonic egg-shaped cans. I followed the cord sprouting from his ear to a component stereo, topped by an older-model Technics turntable. A record spun round and round but the needle rested in the run-out groove, gently stuck on a revolving whir of vinyl black, end of Side Two. I knew the eggshell blue label—*Midnight Desire*. I pulled off his headphones and whisper-yelled his name like a taut curse. *"Ron. Ron—it's time to wake up."* His heavy lids opened and caught me without surprise—he stayed listless, a little dopey, like he was medicated or something. I almost let go, let him slip back into his awful repose—in that moment he reminded me a little of Annie Linden, the dead Annie Linden. But he wasn't dead.

I yanked the headphones aside and shook him, pulled him up by the shirt and smacked him two ways. So much for letting sleeping dogs lie. A frown scrambled onto his drowsy face. In one move of hazy shock, he took me in for real and made a sudden grab from under the sheets, pointed a Glock 45 at my chest. Behind me in the doorway now, Patricia screamed his name like a moan, but I held still. Ronnie was woozy and one false move would tripwire oblivion.

"Put the gun down, Ron," I said gently.

"Put it down, Ronnie!" Patricia said.

He bared teeth to his sister. "You shut the fuck up, Trish."

She wailed and turned her head. I stayed ultra-still, upright savasana, the corpse pose. I said, "Killing one more person would be a serious shame."

He recoiled, like a scolded kid about to tantrum. "What do you know about shame?"

"Maybe more than you guess."

"Naw. Naw. I'm the fuckin' blackbelt."

"Ronnie—I've seen where you've been."

He staggered up. He was nervous. Real nervous. And it's contagious.

"So what. You know what you haven't seen? *Time.* Oceans of time."

"Maybe not. But—"

"*Oceans* I carried the dream. Alone. Every day."

"I understand but—"

"Someday I was going to tell the world—she was *my* mother. The beautiful . . . queen—was *my* blood, *my* home." His eyes were hot with pain—through them blazed a new brutal and cataclysmic vision of Annie I'd never before allowed myself to see direct. Her blue flame lit up the night, burned everyone that touched her.

He wagged his gun-arm forward, in a bad tremble, and I stepped back. He meant business. "So don't fucking talk to me about shame. To be what I was, what I *thought* I was, and now—*this*? It's worse than shame." I made a kind of pleading with my eyes but he chagrined at the request for mercy. He said, "I'm already dead, man—walking fuckin' dead. Dreaming my mother was Annie, *even if she threw me away*— instead of that witch, that fucking bitch—"

He moved his gun up and I looked over my shoulder. Just outside the rec room door in her wheelchair, Nan tilted her head as if receiving a blow, but she didn't resist—either she had heard this speech before or thought it herself for many, many years.

"—that un-*real* fucking witch. Who never loved anything. Least of all me." He growled with spittle. "To dream of Annie but get *that* instead—that's some fucking shame *you* couldn't stomach, you . . . you . . . *chauffeur.*"

The insult was crazy but my fear was real.

"Fucking white knight pussy," he said. "Don't educate me."

His face was tear-streaked. I stepped back—he could have started firing in that moment, he had it in him. But instead, he made a curious move: He looked at his couch-bed, where he had been lying, at the unmade quilt and the big black headphones. Then he turned back to me, with a knowing look, *knowing* death, ready for it. Embracing it, with gluttonous pleasure. And he smiled.

"Thom came around here," Ronnie said. "My so-called *brother.*"

The gun stayed on me, my hands were up. We danced a semi-circle.

"Bragging that this *rock 'n' roll skank* was his real mom. Bragging about how she was chasing him and he *didn't give a shit.* And he ditched her. Oh yeah, he was stoked to bail. *'I'm done with that old hag, who needs it.'* Well . . . I needed it."

"Ronnie. Thom can't hurt you now."

At the door, Nan let out a crackly sob. Patricia wept, shaking her head. I wondered what they knew. Ronnie went wide-eyed, looked to Nan then me. He stopped, trembled, and I stopped—his gun was on me and he was ready for finality. That's when I did something a quote-unquote *real man* can probably do better than any wimpy fanboy on Earth: I bluffed confidence from zero. I transformed the fact of down into the lie of up. In one cocky sweep, I scoffed and stepped to him and grabbed the pistol right out of his sick, shaking hand.

I said, "Get your hands up and get on the couch, Ron."

But he jerked into a crazy-man fighter stance—Patricia screamed "Don't!" and in the distraction, he leapt like a cat, flung himself at me, claws all up in my face, and we hit the floor, tangled, rolled, jabbed in double-time. I yanked at hair, a fist crossed my jaw and bent my wrist and the gun flew off my hand, we scrambled—too fast it was in his again, I strained to wrest it, shake him off me, no way in a single stretch. Still pinned to the carpet, I fumbled in my pocket for my gun and in one defiant thrust he turned his to his own chest and off it went, sending him ricocheting off me, crashing into the record player—he slumped to the floor, eyes open, fake thoughtful, out for good.

Freaked, I hoisted up and staggered backward, to the foot of the half-stairs, clambered up into the living room behind the bar. I turned—like magnetic Scottie dogs, Nan and Patricia backed off me, the face of family horror in double. A silent panic descended on the room—the gunshot was ringing in my ears as I watched them and they watched me. Patricia broke the freeze with a hoarse wail—"*Please don't hurt us!*"

I scowled and looked at the empty gun in my shaking hands and said, "It isn't loaded, shut the damn cellar door," and she did.

Nan glared. "*Patricia, call Thomas at once!*"

Patricia got frantic with her cell phone. Our eyes met—she picked up the bad vibes. "*Nobody's answering—where is he?*"

I shook my head. "I'll let the cops tell you all about it." Then I pulled my own cell and called Maya. "It's your brother—please don't hang up. I'm okay. I'm texting you an address. Yes—*and send police.*"

Nan white-knuckled the arms of her wheelchair like she was about to race, but where? A fully sorrowful Patricia moved behind and rocked the wheelchair back and forth with great maternal noblesse oblige. Together, though, they looked like children in way over their heads.

"How long has Ronnie been hiding out here?" I demanded.

"What difference could that possibly make now?" Nan was croaky, defiant for someone in her tan terrycloth bathrobe, ten yards from a corpse. But I had to agree. The answer was not worth much. Then she blurted, "*Stupid boy.*"

I shook my head, breathed in her madness. The gunshot ringing in my ear was taking such a long time to die.

I said the world's most useless word—"Why."

"Why what?"

"Why'd you switch them?"

Breaking from Patricia, Nan turned her wheelchair slow like a turret. Her eyes on me split two energies right down the middle: *Does he deserve the truth?* And—*What does he already know?* Her upper lip trembled.

"I made a *terrible mistake*, Mr. Zantz. I don't know if you can fathom, a man of your young age, what a *real* mistake looks like. It changes the shape of your life, only you don't really know it for years, decades. Half-centuries. Then you face the end and you *see*. You see *exactly* what you've done. And no amount of good behavior will ameliorate."

"Thom was Annie's son. Only your late husband . . . told her it was Ron."

She held her breath with a haughtiness that came from a whole other era. And then the part of her that knew it was an outmoded gesture sighed. "That's right."

"Why . . . why would he do that?"

"Because I told him to, Mr. Zantz."

"Okay. I guessed that. But why did you tell him to?"

From the couch, Patricia let out a fresh sob. "Leave it alone!"

I kept my glare on Nan.

"They were *babies*," she said. "Not . . . newborns, but close enough. And that horrible young woman came back into our lives, dressed like a gypsy from a little . . . *megalomaniacal dreamworld* all her own—with her money and her lawyers and her contracts. She wanted visits, wanted silence, she wanted . . . all manner of *exceptional demands*. She threatened to go public—and she *could*, she had made quite a name for herself among the immoral throngs. She could have taken our Thom away. *My* Thom away. She could have fouled our nest just as she had fouled her own. I told Milton, right here in this room, I said, 'Fine. Make her a deal. But bring Ronnie instead. She only wants a *fantasy* anyway—'"

"She wanted to connect with her son."

"Oh really? *Her* son? I believe I proved beyond a shadow of a doubt she couldn't tell her son from a stranger. I told little Ronnie to visit the nice lady and call himself Tommy and *she didn't blink*. She called him *angel face*. He told me so. *Angel face*. That idiot hippie didn't even care what his name was."

"Jesus."

"Jesus nothing—what made Thom and Ronnie so different to her anyway?" Now she pointed—right at me, aging hand jiggling. "I don't expect you to understand this, Mr. Zantz, but Thomas *was*. *My*. *First*. *Born*. Not hers. Every drop of milk that entered his mouth came from a bottle in this hand."

"And Ron?"

"Ronald was not an exceptional boy. But he was a good boy when he chose to be."

"Was he your boy?"

"He was. A painful birth that ruined me physically and emotionally. Worse since I had already just bonded to another child."

"Why did you adopt if—"

"Nobody would put Vegas odds on me getting pregnant—that's what my late husband joked. But it happened."

"This much I figured. And your husband had his visits with Annie, with Ron. Secret to you?"

"He thought they were. The real secret was that I knew."

"So why did they stop?"

Now she pushed the wheels just a little, rolled toward me, crackling vehement. "Aha! But of *course that's the part* you don't get, since you don't want to see your lady friend for who she really was. The visits *stopped* because she stopped giving a rat's tail. The child wasn't entertaining enough, didn't flatter her ego enough—"

"Or somewhere she sensed he wasn't really hers."

"So *what?* So. What. If she was a real mother, she would have *mothered*. She would have found a way to connect. She couldn't be bothered. He didn't *serve her*. And so she stopped coming around. Milton was heartbroken for the boy. He couldn't even set up a goodbye meeting. She actually had her *road manager* do the dirty work. '*Oh, so sorry, such and such, Ms. Linden doesn't want to disrupt his development.*' It was a lot of *phooey*. She got *bored*. And she gave up."

"And Ronnie?"

"Ronnie was inconsolable, deeply confused—what child wouldn't be?"

"But eventually Dr. Goldfischer explained?"

"Explained?" She cackled in a bad actress way. "That's a fine way to put it. Just before Milton's last breaths, when he knew he wouldn't have to deal with the consequences, he told Thom who his mother was. His big revenge on me. I positively *begged* Milton to take it with him to his grave. *He* alone set this madness in motion, he alone thought the truth would set everybody free. Well *look*."

She convulsed with disgust. But she did not cry.

"And look at *you*," she blurted.

"What about me?"

She tilted her gray head as a dark grin spread across her face.

"Savior to the beautiful," she said, "protector of the celebrated—how *weak*. Why, you aren't so very different from my son Ronald at all, are you? You've been cheated by a fantasy—a sick, infantile fantasy about a selfish woman, and now you expect the world to drown in pity as they cheer you over the moon. Well, keep dreaming—you both wanted what was never yours to begin with. You've been had."

I turned from her, stared at the dungeon door, mesmerized by her hate.

A series of flashes—

Little Ronnie—*angel face*—with Annie at the Hawthorne Arms—*PBS & Time Life Presents YOGA for Beginners* on the phonograph. *Devotional warrior pose*—

Then: eighteen and pimply faced—he's been visiting the apartment alone.

He escapes the South Bay for Malibu and Kronski intercepts, nudges him like a checker piece to a darker dark and—

Then Milton dies and—

Minnie shows up at the Jacuzzi shop and—

The visits—*one, two, three, four and*—

Thom bragging, fierce indifference and—

Ronnie, torn to pieces, gasping for air.

He goes to his former almost-mother looking for some explanation and—

This time there's no Kronski to get in the way and—

Annie, willing, maybe even wanting to explain, but finally understanding and—

Ronnie's rage flared and—

Back to the old apartment and—*did she even remember where it was?*—and—

Maybe she wants to soothe, to heal, but . . . no.

Way too late.

A chill ripped through me and I came back to the room before me, the woman in the wheelchair. And I knew all at once she was right.

I was just another version of him—the body in the family dungeon. The dream he clutched was mine. The dream of the perfect mother—a dangerous hallucination. It weakened you as you cursed the world for not delivering on a mirage. And I lived blinded by that dream, casting crazy demands on every woman I ever placed on a pedestal . . . not just Annie but my sister, my ex, my own mom with her fragile, loving glances as she drove us through the night.

Now: sirens in the distance.

41

DEDICATE YOUR SORROW
HERE AND NOW TO
THE SOUL OF THE SEA

Double Fry in his hokey swim trunks hollered when he saw me. "Sherlock Holmes! Miss Marple! Phillip Marlowe!"

I laughed in a blush. "More like Clouseau. I bumped my way."

"The *Shechinah* never lies, dog."

Over some cheapo cabernet, I told him the rest of the story—most he had already half-guessed. Then he said, "Dr. Milt could not have baked a bigger fuck-you-and-goodbye cake for his wife."

"You think that's what he wanted?"

"Maybe not consciously—but the whole family couldn't bear the secret. They unraveled."

"Yup. It takes a whole family to go insane."

"But, Addy, how the hell did you figure out Nan switched the babies?"

"At the hideaway in Hawthorne, there was this yoga record. It had a gatefold booklet with all these poses. I don't know—it stuck out. In his clinic, Ronnie was all about the stillness of the body, listening to the body. I knew he had to learn it somewhere."

"Wow—nice work, dog."

"Yeah, nice isn't really the word for it. Annie hired me to do a job. I guess I just got there too late."

"So, Ronnie had to be the person she wanted you to find."

"Without a doubt. She'd already met her blood son, but she knew something wasn't right, he wasn't the kid she had played with. For the first time, she began to understand that she'd been tricked. She was asking me to figure out just *how*."

"But before you even got there, this guy shows up on her doorstep."

"Right. With a half-century grudge. I mean, just by showing up, he had painted himself into a corner. She must have sensed something was off right away. So she called for Troy."

Fry said, "Then all hell broke loose."

For a moment, we marveled silently at the ugliness of it.

"I still wonder how much the sister knew," I said. "Maybe she could've stopped him."

"Zantz—on some level? They all knew. And nobody could've stopped him. Ronnie was *already* envious of his brother. Then, picture him on the day he learns Thom is Annie's real child. They're hanging out, right? The older brother makes the brag—but casual. He's taken everything Ronnie ever wanted, and now he's also taken his escape fantasy."

"The phantom mommy—the perfect one."

"But . . . did Ronnie kill Thom too?"

"No," I said gravely. "That nasty piece of work was taken care of by Bauer, the shmuck from the men's club."

"But why?"

"At first I thought Kronski put him up to it, but now I'm guessing it was more like . . . Bauer wanted to prove . . . "

Fry shook his head in disgust. "Prove to the alpha dog that he could . . . *do the manly man thing.*"

"Exactly."

"Was he the one who smashed up the Jetta?"

"I can't prove it—but that's my guess."

"But what about the tapes?"

I shrugged. "*No* idea. Apparently, there's a lot of haters out there. Anyway, I told my story to Lieutenant Bottrell over at Malibu. Pretty sure they brought Bauer in by now."

"Good. Now maybe he can test his manliness with the big boys in lockup."

I faked a smile but didn't relax.

"C'mon, Addy, you *did it.* Justice served."

"Yeah. I guess so."

Fry, true friend, picked up the wavy tension. "Enough with these *ferkakte* people. What is *really* going on?" He pointed. "With *you?*"

I shook my head. "I don't know. Annie just . . . she wasn't who I thought."

"Yeah?"

"She wasn't really who anybody thought. It's like she was like a mirage, everybody used her, projected their own little escape hatch onto her—even me. You know, to her fan club prez she was a totem. To her lover she was . . . some kind of wild 'n' crazy feminist deserter. Even to her ex-husband she was more a symbol than an actual woman. Combs had her number maybe—but even to him, she'd become the shadow of regret."

"And to you?"

"She *was* my savior, or so I thought—it's like Annie had

a sixth sense for who was needy. And she made awestruck devotees out of us with just, like, a word or a touch."

"Almost sounds religious," Fry said. "To have the golden one turn her countenance on you was like . . . *you* became the star, the anointed."

"Exactly," I said, "But then she seemed to almost get a charge out of cutting loose on people. Even the ones who loved her."

Fry said, "Maybe especially the ones who loved her."

"That's right. And if she'd lived?" I said with a self-effacing little laugh. "Probably I'd be next."

"Wow. It's like she transformed from the beyond."

"Totally. When Annie was actually my rider, I really and truly thought she was this . . . soulful angel. Then after she died, when I first started to unravel the web around her, she seemed shut off, like, almost to the point of heartlessness. But the deeper I got, the more I understood . . . other people consumed her. Like they literally ate her spirit alive."

"And now?"

I sighed. "I'll never know exactly what she was made of. Only that I loved her."

"That's good," he said. "That's always where it should land. By the way, I did get ahold of Annie's will for you."

I stared at him, dumbfounded. "You're kidding."

"That's why they call me Fonzie."

A real smile crept across my face. "Okay, *Fonz*—any surprises?"

"She wanted her ashes scattered at sea."

"No surprise there."

"Well—I can't condone it."

"What do you mean?"

"Cremation is strictly forbidden by Jewish law. Body is temple of the soul and all that. Then there's belief in the resurrection of the dead."

"Seriously?"

"It's not just some side thing, Addy. Maimonides put it in the Thirteen Principles of the Faith."

"Come on, man—"

"Look, as Jews, we believe there is purpose to life, purpose to this world, purpose to the act of Creation. We're *about* purpose, even in death. And also—" He pursed his lips.

"What?"

"Well, ya know, six million of us were cremated without our consent. Which was not nice."

I went silent.

"God said man is as dust," Fry said with a wistful shrug. "And that means he's supposed to return, like dust, to the land."

"So the sea part is no good either?"

"Not for me."

"But she wasn't Jewish, dude. And anyway, she's already cremated."

"I know," he said, "that's why I called Forest Lawn on your behalf."

"You *what*?"

"She's ready for pickup." He handed me a printed-out email. "It's not legal in Southern California to dump ashes into the Pacific. So let's pretend, first that I didn't do this for you, second that I have no idea where you're going to do it."

Maya helped me get cleared at Malibu–Lost Hills and for the rest of the week I slept downstairs in her rec room. If I was a little spooked by rec rooms that was okay, since this one had only one poster, my niece's *My Pretty Pony* with a great swishing mane of pink, purple, and glittering hair.

In the morning before work, Maya came down to check

on me. She was surprised to find me up and groomed, ready for the world.

"You can stay, you know."

"I think your husband would get sick of me after about another day."

"He isn't the decider. By the way, that Bix guy called, I don't know how he got our landline."

"Well, I'm ducking him."

"I told him not to call here ever again."

"Good. You did the right thing. I'm glad he's free, but I've run out of shining armor. The guy is just bad news."

"*The guy* is one lucky duck. My baby brother saved his behind."

"Maya . . . I have a favor to ask—but it's legit."

"Tell me."

"I discovered something about myself. I like snooping on people. And I want to re-up my license."

"Investigator's license?"

"Crazy, right?"

"Were you just put on this planet to make me worry?"

"I do my best."

"But . . . what about your songwriting?"

I shrugged.

"Your songs are good, Adam."

"Maybe. Either way, it's not like I can stop—they just . . . come to me."

Her eyes softened. "They're really a part of you."

"You know what's crazy, sis—when I was on the hunt? I got that same feeling. Like, when a melody's coming on."

Back in the silver Jetta, I put Annie's very first single on the Bluetooth and made my way to Forest Lawn. The sparkling melody bubbled up from somewhere true and it was like she was singing in my car all over again. Annie's World— we made a kind of estranged family, the whole lot of us. I didn't think I'd ever see Eva Silber or Haywood Kronski again, but win or lose, the drama of their lives was mostly done. My guess was that freedom would not be that kind to Bix Gelden—he was probably headed right back to Topanga Beach to sit on the parking lot bench, high and delirious, waiting on nothing. Runions told me he wanted a life make-over and I Venmo'd him the Greyhound fare to go visit Minnie. Manny Combs had laughed at me when I returned his gun and said, "I prayed for you, Mister—don't you forget that." Of course, I never would and I told him so. He considered the pistol, then slipped it into his coat pocket and said, "Ya know, she gave me the catalogue."

"What do you mean?"

"The songs, man, rights and royalties." He pulled off his mirrored shades, folded and clutched them in his aging hand. "Annie gave me her songs."

"Combs! That's the best news—*ever*."

He exhaled tender, shook his head a little. "Probate dude called me last night, told me I was in her will. Like, the whole time."

"Wow."

"Couldn't believe it myself, I . . . all those years." He looked away across the yard, his dark eyes reflecting junk-metal sunlight. "I guess she really did carry me around inside her after all."

When I got to Forest Lawn, the mortician said the same thing Fry had: "What you're about to do ain't legal in the county of Los Angeles, and the Coast Guard does hit you with a hefty fine if they catch you." He was a jovial guy for an avatar of death. He could have been talking about digging for sand crabs. I told him I understood and he led me to a holding station and handed me the box.

"Thanks for the warning," I said and walked off with my awkward package. I would have to stave off missing her bad now, driving along with this plain cardboard box beside me— but I wasn't even sure about the shape of what I was missing exactly. The person? Her spirit? Not this box.

It's a long drive from Forest Lawn to the sea. Up over the horse trails I drove, through the Hollywood Hills with the box on the passenger seat, past the Spanish and Tudor palaces surrounded by these dilapidated plants shimmering in the yellow of day. The bright green palm fronds were asking us to suspend our disbelief about eternal life. Which isn't easy to do. I felt mesmerized and lost, the way a person does when they've woken from a too-deep nap. In my mind, the ghosts of Hollywood's golden age floated by, embalmed in death for all time. But I was Annie's driver in the post-golden time.

I pulled onto Sunset and headed west right out onto PCH. Just before Point Dume, I parked behind a seaside Italian restaurant. I got the box out—it was both too light and not light enough for Annie, my Annie. By the time I arrived at the sand it was just past dusk.

I looked around—nobody watching. I opened up the package. Inside, the ashes were in a clear plastic bag sealed with a silver ring. I tucked the bag under my arm and took off shoes and socks, climbed down some rocks. I stood in an eddy and poured her out into the mint-tea ocean over the rush and retreat of foam, the call-and-response sea with its diamonds and riptides. For a brief moment, her ashes turned to a rainbow of sparkles across the ripples that cascaded between the eddies and then they were gone. Foam spread across the sand and rocks, making a fizzy, rumbling music that should have been terrifying, but it came out gentle.

It was a funny song the ocean sang, insistent on some mysterious thing. It was the first song any living creature out here ever heard, and it would probably be the last. I listened to it play for a while, searching for Annie's lost melody, and then I got back into my car and headed down the coast back into the city, rolling with a free heart.

PLAYLIST

1. "Here Comes the Night"—Them with Van Morrison (Words and Music by Bert Berns)
2. "Bargain"—The Who (Words and Music by Pete Townshend)
3. "Blackout"—David Bowie (Words and Music by David Bowie)
4. "I Cover the Waterfront"—The Ink Spots (Words and Music by Johnny Green and Edward Heyman)
5. "I Try"—Angela Bofill (Words and Music by Angela Bofill)
6. "Don't Fear the Reaper"—Blue Oyster Cult (Words and Music by Donald Roeser)
7. "Inside-Looking Out"—The Animals (Words and Music by Eric Burdon, Chas Chandler, Alan Lomax, and John A. Lomax)
8. "Elevate"—St. Lucia (Words and Music by Ross Clark and Jean-Phillip Grobler)
9. "Land of Treason"—The Germs (Words and Music by Darby Crash and Pat Smear)
10. "My Summer Love"—Ruby and the Romantics (Words and Music by Mort Garson and Bob Hillard)
11. "When the Whip Comes Down"—The Rolling Stones (Words and Music by Mick Jagger and Keith Richards)

12. "Oh, Sister"—Bob Dylan (Words and Music by Bob Dylan and Jacques Levy)
13. "Spill the Wine"—Eric Burdon and War (Words and Music by Papa Dee Allen, Thomas Sylverster ALlen, Harold Brown, B.B. Dickerson, Leroy Jordan, Lonnie Jordan, Charles Miller, Lee Oscar, and Howard Scott)
14. "These Foolish Things"—Benny Goodman (Words and Music by Hort Marvell and Jack Strachey)
15. "The Book of Love"—The Monotones (Words and Music by Warren Davis, George Malone, and Charles Patrick)
16. "Alone at Night"—Michael Franks (Words and Music by Michael Franks)
17. "Deacon Blues"—Steely Dan (Words and Music by Walter Becker and Donald Fagen)
18. "Each and Every One"—Everything but the Girl (Words and Music by Ben Watt and Tracey Thorn)
19. "Mama Can't Buy You Love"—Elton John (Words and Music by Leroy Bell and Casey James)
20. "Row Row Row Your Boat" (Traditional)
21. "Mother and Child Reunion"—Paul Simon (Words and Music by Paul Simon)
22. "Cottage for Sale"—Billy Eckstine (Words and Music by Willard Robison and Larry Conley)
23. "Under the Boardwalk"—The Drifters (Words and Music by Kenny Young and Arthur Resnick)
24. "Mountains"—Prince (Words and Music by Lisa Coleman, Wendy Melvoin, and Prince)
25. "Roll Over Beethoven"—Chuck Berry (Words and Music by Chuck Berry)
26. "Fools Rush In" (Where Angels Fear to Tread)—Bow Wow Wow (Words and Music by Johnny Mercer and Rube Bloom)

27. "Up the Neck"—The Pretenders (Words and Music by Chrissie Hynde)
28. "Isn't This a Lovely Day"—Fred Astaire with Johnny Green & His Orchestra (Words and Music by Irving Berlin)
29. "Football Season's Over"—Shelley Fabares (Words and Music by David Gates)
30. "Fire Spirit"—The Gun Club (Words and Music by Jeffrey Lea Pierce)
31. "Goon Squad"—Elvis Costello & the Attractions (Words and Music by Elvis Costello)
32. "Spring Can Really Hang You Up the Most"—Mark Murphy (Words and Music by Fran Landesman and Tommy Wolf)
33. "Wheels of Life"—Gino Vanelli (Words and Music by Gino Vanelli)
34. "A House is Not a Motel"—Love (Words and Music by Arthur Lee)
35. "Good Times"—Willie Nelson (Words and Music by Willie Nelson)
36. "Because You're Frightened"—Magazine (Words and Music by Barry Adamson, Howard Devoto, John Doyle, Dave Formula, and John McGeoch)
37. "Funkentelechy"—Parliament (Words and Music by George Clinton and Bootsy Collins)
38. "To Know You"—Wild Nothing (Words and Music by John Alexander Tatum)
39. "Resurrection Fern"—Iron & Wine (Words and Music by Sam Beam)
40. "Sounds of Laughter"—T.S.O.L. (Words and Music by Jack Grisham, Ron Emory, Mike Roche, and Todd Barnes)
41. "Soul of the Sea"—Heart (Words and Music by Ann and Nancy Wilson)

ACKNOWLEDGMENTS

I want to express deep gratitude to my brilliant agents, Janet Oshiro and David Halpern at the Robbins Office, for their care, wisdom, creativity, and supernatural patience; and to Carl Bromley at Melville House, the editor every writer dreams of, the one that knows what you're up to better than you yourself do. These three took my story way beyond where I imagined it could go and I am so thankful.

I also want to express my sincere gratitude to the truly outstanding team at Melville House—Maya Bradford, Michael Barson, Janet Joy Wilson, Ariel Palmer-Collins, Molly Donovan, as well as Beste M. Doğan for the exquisite cover art. So proud to be in such distinguished company.

In addition, I owe a massive thanks to the following: Kathy Robbins for assembling such a thoughtful, dedicated team; the supremely sagacious Lucinda Halpern—so delighted to be in your extended book family!; 10x mavens Rishon Blumberg and Michael Solomon; daredevil photographer Steve Appleford; Chuck Kelley, for the insider's Hawthorne, CA history lesson; and the early readers who helped shape this book—Francesca Lia Block, Renni Browne, Ross Browne, Diane Stockwell, Katharine Sands, H. W. Taeusch, Shannon Smith, Doug Magnuson, Barbara White, Mia Trachinger, Zoe

Mclaughlin, June Mclaughlin, and my mother Rama who de-vours books faster than most people eat potato chips.

I also want to share my lasting gratitude for these literary mentors and guides: Harvey Kubernik, who gave me a green light with no speed limit before I even had a license; Al and Hud from Flipside; the late great Craig Lee; Gene Sculatti aka Vic Tripp and Ronn Spencer aka Art Fraud; Daniel Shulman and Josh Schreiber; Jack Skelley; Steve Abee; Robin Carr; Amy White; Scott Sampler; Erik Himmelsbach-Weinstein; Lisa Rojany and late greats Larry Sloan and Leonard Stern; Rhonda Lieberman; Laura Nolan; Joan Leegant, Risa Miller, Allen Hoffman, and the whole mishpoicheh at Shaindy Rudoff Creative Writing Program and Ilanot Review; Jill Schary Robinson and the Wimpole Street Writers; Ari Haddad, Jon Shapiro, Pablo Capra, Troy Lambert, and Kenneth Kubernik.

Thank you Shalom Weizmann, Moshe Weizmann, Ethel Rudbarg, Morris Rudbarg, Dave "Id" Hahn, Aviva Blumberg, Raina Nichelson, Bill Morrison, Natalie Werbner, Davin Seay, Alan Grannell, Rita Davis, and Lenorah Hahn—memories of you are my beacons in the dark.

Most of all, my gratitude goes to my wife Clover and son Max—you keep the songs playing in my heart.